Everyman, I will go with thee,
and be thy guide

THE EVERYMAN
LIBRARY

*The Everyman Library was founded by J. M. Dent
in 1906. He chose the name Everyman because he wanted
to make available the best books ever written in every
field to the greatest number of people at the cheapest possible
price. He began with Boswell's 'Life of Johnson';
his one-thousandth title was Aristotle's 'Metaphysics',
by which time sales exceeded forty million.*

*Today Everyman paperbacks remain true to
J. M. Dent's aims and high standards, with a wide range
of titles at affordable prices in editions which address
the needs of today's readers. Each new text is reset to give
a clear, elegant page and to incorporate the latest thinking
and scholarship. Each book carries the pilgrim logo,
the character in 'Everyman', a medieval morality play,
a proud link between Everyman
past and present.*

Heliodorus

ETHIOPIAN STORY

Translated by
SIR WALTER LAMB

Edited by
J. R. MORGAN
University of Wales, Swansea

EVERYMAN
J. M. DENT · LONDON
CHARLES E. TUTTLE
VERMONT

Introduction and other critical material © J. M. Dent 1997

This translation first published in Everyman in 1961
This edition first published in Everyman Paperbacks in 1997

J. M. Dent
Orion Publishing Group
Orion House, 5 Upper St Martin's Lane,
London WC2H 9EA
and
Charles E. Tuttle Co., Inc.
28 South Main Street,
Rutland, Vermont 05701, USA

Printed in Great Britain by
The Guernsey Press Co. Ltd, Guernsey, C. I.

British Library Cataloguing-in-Publication Data
is available upon request.

ISBN 0 460 87640 6

CONTENTS

Note on the Author and Editor   vii
Chronology of Heliodorus' Life and Times   viii
Introduction   xvii

ETHIOPIAN STORY

Book One   3
Book Two   33
Book Three   65
Book Four   82
Book Five   104
Book Six   135
Book Seven   152
Book Eight   184
Book Nine   207
Book Ten   231

Notes   265
Heliodorus and the Critics   286
Suggestions For Further Reading   306
Text Summary   308
Acknowledgements   311

NOTE ON THE AUTHOR AND EDITOR

HELIODORUS signs off his novel as a native of the Syrian city of Emesa. Nothing else is known of him for certain. He lived in the third or fourth century, and has been variously identified with 'Heliodorus the Arab', a sophist who died in Rome around AD 240, and with a Christian bishop in Thessaly who enforced celibacy on his clergy.

J. R. MORGAN is Senior Lecturer in Classics at the University of Wales, Swansea. He has written extensively on the ancient Greek novel, especially Heliodorus.

NB. Since so little is known of Heliodorus, his biography is almost entirely speculative. Alternative datings are designated (1), (2) and (3).

Year   *Life*

AD 210–20   (1) Composition of *Ethiopian Story* if author identified with Heliodorus the Arab (?)

c.215   (1) Heliodorus the Arab representing his people among the Celtic tribes; speaks before the Emperor Caracalla, who elevates him to the Equestrian Order. Rises to office of *Advocatus Fisci*
Joins circle of Julia Domna (?)

217   (1) On death of Caracalla Heliodorus exiled. Recalled to Rome for trial on charge of murder. Proven innocent and released from exile.

CHRONOLOGY OF HIS TIMES

Year	Artistic Context	Historical Events
c.50 (?)	Earliest known Greek novel, the *Ninus romance*	
c.65	Petronius, *Satyricon*	
c.100 (?)	Chariton, *Chaereas and Callirhoe*	
c.125 (?)	Xenophon of Ephesus, *Ephesian Story*	
155–70	Apuleius, *Metamorphoses (The Golden Ass)*	
c.175	Achilles Tatius, *Leucippe and Clitophon*; Iamblichus, *Babylonian Story*	
c.200 (?)	Longus, *Daphnis and Chloe*	
201–17	Julia Domna's patronage of literature	
212–17		Caracalla (son of Septimius Severus and Julia Domna) emperor; *Constitutio Antoniniana* grants citizenship to all inhabitants of Empire; assassination of Caracalla; suicide of Julia Domna

Year   *Life*

c.235   (1) Heliodorus the Arab living in Rome, 'neither greatly admired nor altogether neglected' (Philostratus)

c.240   (1) Death of Heliodorus the Arab (?)

270–5   (2) A possible date for composition of *Ethiopian Story*, if by an otherwise unknown Heliodorus

Year	Artistic Context	Historical Events
218		Elagabalus proclaimed emperor at Emesa
219		Elagabalus introduces Emesan sun-cult to Rome
222		Assassination of Elagabalus; Alexander Severus becomes emperor
c.225–35	Philostratus, *Life of Apollonius of Tyana* Clement of Alexandria, *Lives of the Sophists*	
238–75		Roman Empire in crisis; emperors overthrown in rapid succession; German and Gothic invasions from north and war in east; growth of power of Palmyra under Zenobia, who conquers Syria, Mesopotamia and Egypt
c.240	Herodian, *Histories* Cassius Dio, *Histories*	
244–70	Plotinus (neoplatonic philosopher)	
248	Origen, *Against Celsus*	
263		Goths sack Ephesus and destroy temple of Artemis
267		Goths sack Athens, Sparta and other Greek cities
c.270–300	Porphyry (neoplatonic philosopher)	Aurelian proclaimed emperor; stability restored
272		Aurelian defeats Zenobia at Emesa

Year   *Life*

Year	Artistic Context	Historical Events
273		Aurelian destroys Palmyra
274		Aurelian makes Sol Invictus chief deity of Roman Empire
275		Aurelian assassinated; beginnings of Egyptian monasticism when St Antony retires into the desert
284		Diocletian becomes emperor; reorganisation of Empire; conservative religious policy
c.290–325	Iamblichus (neoplatonic philosopher)	
303		Diocletian's first edict against Christians inaugurates persecution
304	Diocletian's palace at Split	
305		Diocletian abdicates
307	Lactantius, *Divine Institutions*	
312		Constantine victorious at Milvian Bridge; converts to Christianity
313		Christianity given legal status by Edict of Milan
315	Building of Arch of Constantine in Rome	
321		Arian heresy propounded; opposed by St Athanasius
324		Constantine becomes sole emperor; foundation of Constantinople as new capital of Empire

Year   *Life*

350–60   (3) Most likely dating for composition of *Ethiopian Story*

*c.*400 (?)   (3) Heliodorus bishop of Tricca in Thessaly enforces celibacy
             on clergy; identified with novelist by church historian
             Socrates. Later story (probably invented) that Heliodorus
             chooses to resign rather than disown his novel

Year	Artistic Context	Historical Events
325–6	Eusebius, *Ecclesiastical History*	Council of Nicaea
337		Death of Constantine; empire divided between his sons
341		Pagan sacrifices prohibited; first Frankish invasion of Gaul
c.350–60	Julian, various works including mystic *Hymn to the Sun*, and panegyrics of Constantius	Third siege of Nisibis
c.350–90	Libanius (pagan rhetorician) Ammianus Marcellinus (Latin historian)	
361		Julian becomes emperor; restoration of pagan religion
363		Death of Julian; pagan revival collapses
c.370	Ausonius, *Mosella* St Basil and St Gregory of Nazianzus (Christian sophists)	
379		Theodosius the Great becomes emperor
c.380–400	Prudentius, Christian poetry (Latin)	
c.390	St Jerome's Latin Bible	
c. 395–430	St Augustine, *City of God*, *Confessions* etc.	
c.400	Hypatia, woman philosopher in Alexandria	

INTRODUCTION

At the end of his novel Heliodorus describes himself as 'a Phoenician of Emesa, of the line of the descendants of Helios (the Sun), namely Heliodorus, son of Theodosius'. There is no reason to doubt the authenticity of this sentence. The Syrian town of Emesa (modern Homs) was the centre of a major cult of the Sun (Baal), imported to Rome by the emperor Elagabalus, himself a native of Emesa, in AD 218. Clearly our novelist, whose name (presumably a Greek version of a Syrian name) means 'Gift of the Sun', was connected in some way with his local cult. This is virtually all we can say of him with certainty. Estimates of his date have ranged from the reign of the emperor Hadrian (AD 117–38) to shortly after AD 350. Many scholars have argued for a date in the third century, which would coincide with the zenith of the Emesan cult, perhaps in the reign of Aurelian (270–5) who adopted a less orgiastic version of it as the official religion of the Roman Empire. A tempting option is to identify the novelist with the sophist Heliodorus the Arab, who was living in retirement in Rome in the late 230s. This would allow for the possibility that the novel was written in the coterie of the Emesan born empress Julia Domna (died 217), a woman with philosophical and religious as well as literary interests.[1]

My own view, however, is that the novel was written in the fourth century. The argument revolves around striking similarities between the siege of Syene described in Book 9 of the novel and the third siege of Nisibis by the Parthians in AD 350, as recounted in two panegyrics of the emperor Constantius written by the future emperor Julian the Apostate. The question as to which of the two authors is recycling the other is complicated, technical and contested, but my belief is that Julian presents an essentially accurate version of what happened in 350 and that, since the chances that history was anticipated in such close detail by fiction are infinitesimal, Heliodorus must have written his novel after the siege of Nisibis, but before public interest in it had faded.

There is a tradition that Heliodorus was a Christian bishop. This is first found in the ecclesiastical historian Socrates,[2] writing in the first quarter of the fifth century. In discussing variations between the practices of local churches, he mentions a custom in Thessaly that a married man who was ordained priest had to stop sleeping with his wife, on pain of excommunication: 'the originator of this practice in Thessaly was Heliodorus, on becoming Bishop of Tricca there, who was the author, it is said, of an erotic book, which he wrote in his youth and entitled *Aithiopika* (*Ethiopian Story*)'. The accuracy of this identification of novelist and bishop has been hotly disputed. There is certainly no trace of Christianity to be found in the novel, but then Socrates does not say that Heliodorus was a Christian when he wrote it. At this period there is nothing intrinsically implausible in the idea of a pious pagan converting to Christianity and becoming a member of the Church hierarchy, and certainly the belief that its author was a Christian made the *Ethiopian Story* legitimate reading in the Byzantine period and so helped to guarantee its survival. Socrates' information is further elaborated by a fourteenth-century Byzantine historian, Nicephorus Callistus Xanthopulus, who records that the synod at Tricca, concerned at the danger their bishop's novel posed to the morals of young people, gave him the choice of renouncing it or resigning his see; of course he chose the latter.[3] However, it is difficult to see how Nicephorus could have got hold of accurate new information a thousand years after the event, and his story is probably an edifying invention.

We tend to think of the novel as a modern invention fostered by factors such as the spread of literacy and the invention of printing, or a new interest in the individual following in the wake of emergent capitalism or secular Protestantism in the seventeenth century. In fact, there are a number of extended fictional narratives in prose from the late classical period, which we may as well call 'novels' as anything else. The *Ethiopian Story* is one of five in ancient Greek to have survived more or less complete. The others, in roughly chronological order, are *Chaereas and Callirhoe* by Chariton of Aphrodisias; the *Ephesian Story* by Xenophon of Ephesus; *Daphnis and Chloe* by Longus; and *Clitophon and Leucippe* by Achilles Tatius. In addition we have summaries of two more (*The Wonders Beyond Thule* by Antonius Diogenes, and the *Babylonian Story* by Iamblichus) made by the ninth-century Byzantine patriarch Photius, and know of a number of other novels by title or from relatively recently discovered papyrus fragments.[4] These works and their authors are somewhat shadowy, since, for whatever reason, they generally failed to attract the attention of the ancient literary establishment. Our best estimate, largely based on internal evidence and guesswork, is that they were all produced in the period between the first century before and the second century after Christ. Rather better known are two comic novels in Latin: the *Satyricon* by Petronius (written in the reign of the emperor Nero) and the *Metamorphoses* (perhaps more familiar under its alternative title *The Golden Ass*) by Apuleius (mid second century); the latter is an expansion of a Greek short story speculatively attributed to Lucian of Samosata. A third Latin 'novel', *The History of Apollonius King of Tyre* (the source of Shakespeare's play *Pericles*) is probably a later Christian reworking of a pagan story originally composed in Greek.

Whereas the two Latin novels are comic and bawdy, and share a sort of low-life realism, the Greek texts can be grouped under the rubric of 'ideal romance'. The extant specimens at least constitute a tightly knit corpus with closely similar plots and recurrent incidents. Typically, two beautiful and noble young people fall in love at first sight, are somehow separated and travel around the world in search of one another, experiencing adventures which usually include shipwreck, bandits or pirates, the unwanted sexual attentions of third parties and apparent death, remaining true to each other through all their ordeals, until eventually they are reunited and implicitly live happily ever after. Within this schema, however, the individual novelist were capable of significant variation: in Chariton and Xenophon for instance, the hero and heroine are married before they are separated, whereas the three later novelists reserve marriage to form the climax of their plot. Chariton's heroine, for the best of reasons, is a bigamist, while Iamblichus' was apparently prone to fits of homicidal jealousy. Longus uniquely locates his story in a pastoral milieu and replaces physical travel with an inner journey towards erotic maturity, while Achilles treats the stereotypes of romantic love with a flippant cynicism verging on parody. Moreover, recent discoveries have made it

clear that the extant novels represent a relatively limited range
of the ancient Greek fictional spectrum: ideal love was obviously
more congenial to the scholars of Christian Byzantium, on
whom the transmission of classical texts depended, than the
pagan supernatural horror and semi-pornographic sensational-
ism exhibited by some of the fragments.

The origins of the Greek novel are a matter of unceasing
scholarly debate.[5] It is wrong to look for a single simple answer
to such a question, but, as with the emergence of the modern
novel, changes in social and political circumstances were
undoubtedly a contributing factor in the emergence of the new
form. Following the Macedonian and Roman conquests of
Greece, huge empires had replaced the classical city-state. The
themes and values of romantic fiction seem to answer to the
needs of an affluent and materially secure public whose
emotional focus has shifted from the civic and political to the
private and personal. Romantic love provided, as it were, a new
set of imaginative reference points against which to locate the
individual self;[6] although it is questionable whether the behaviour of the romantic heroes and heroines reflects anyone's
behaviour in the real world, the basic romance plot was clearly
a potent and enduringly successful fantasy. The classical model,
traced by Foucault, had been one of disparity between partners,
with an interior dialectic of mastery over potentially disruptive
passions; in the novels this is replaced by a fully symmetrical
and positively evaluated passion which provides a valid founda-
tion for lasting matrimony, without seeking to sublimate the
sexual into the spiritual. The period was also one of deep
spiritual uncertainty: while many sought for meaning in the new
salvation religions, including Christianity, for others fiction
apparently provided a key to an imaginary world where the
right ending was reassuringly guaranteed, despite the protagonists' powerlessness to control their own destinies.

It used to be widely maintained that the novels were a popular
and undemanding literature aimed at a new and uncritical mass
audience, including women, created by the spread of literacy in
the Hellenistic period. In retrospect we can see that such views
were in large part a way of objectifying prejudices about their
merit as literature. All books in the ancient world were hand-
copied and expensive. Papyrus remains suggest that the number
of copies of novels in circulation was not large in relation to

those of the canonical authors, nor were these books, as physical objects, down market of other types of literature. Moreover, even the earliest of the novels imply a reader with a wide reading experience, capable not just of recognizing tags from the great classics of Greek literature but of appreciating the resonances and associations of quite subtle allusions. The three later novels all announce themselves as works of some literary ambition; no one could take Heliodorus for an easy read. These works were produced in the climate of the intellectual movement of classical revivalism generally referred to as the Second Sophistic. This phenomenon centred on professional rhetoricians or sophists, who flourished in an environment halfway between university and theatre, dazzling audiences of connoisseurs with their displays of intellectual panache and oratorical virtuosity. The three sophistic novels are likewise texts of consummate subtlety at every level. The sophists also sought to produce a Greek renaissance, to recreate, by strict linguistic observance and controlled imagination, the golden age of the Greek past. Similarly the novels, for all that their authors (like many of the sophists, in fact) were often of non-Greek extraction, tend to be set in the glorious past and claim a classical pedigree for themselves by exploiting and absorbing the whole range of classical literature. The novel as a genre, then, is best regarded not as popular entertainment for a cerebrally challenged readership but as sophisticated relaxation, with a faint tang of the illicit, for the cultivated elite.[7]

The *Ethiopian Story* is the latest of the novels, by a large margin if the fourth-century dating is correct. It comes at the end of the tradition, and it is almost as if Heliodorus consciously set out to write the novel to end all novels. His is the longest and easily the most sophisticated and complex of the romances. His protagonists are even nobler and more physically and morally perfect than their predecessors, assimilated by a whole battery of allusions to the heroes of Homeric epic and Attic tragedy. In its substance, however, the work is something of a throwback, disregarding the psychological possibilities of character development opened up by Longus and Achilles. It retains all the conventional furniture of the genre – love at first sight, pirates, shipwrecks, apparent deaths – but presents the old story in a brilliantly innovative way, especially by not beginning at the beginning.

In the following paragraphs I discuss aspects of Heliodorus'
structure, narrative technique and content which have interested
classical scholars, but the discussion comes with a warning.
Much of the writer's innovation went into the production of
suspense and surprise, the creation of riddles and enigmas. Readers who want to experience the novel as it was intended to be
experienced may prefer to have not even a hint of the answers in
advance. They are advised to postpone the rest of this introduction until after they have enjoyed the novel in its own right.

The whole structure of the novel, starting in the middle of the
story and filling in the earlier portions by means of a retrospective narration which concludes about halfway through the
whole, is modelled on that of the *Odyssey*. Like that epic, this is
a story of a journey home ending in marriage and parental
recognition, rather than simply of separation, reunion and
resumption of interrupted happiness as if nothing had happened,
as in the stereotypical novel. Specific episodes, such as the
necromancy of Book 6, are intended to recall Odyssean counterparts, and Odysseus himself even puts in a guest appearance in
a cameo role at one point (5.22). Heliodorus' retrospective
narrator, however, is not one of his protagonists but the
Egyptian priest Calasiris, a character of Odysseus-like cunning
and ambiguity, to whom we shall return shortly. Apart from its
Homeric structure, the *Ethiopian Story* is also permeated by
references to the tragic theatre, sometimes in quite abstruse
technical detail. This is partly to underline the emotional and
tragic force of the narrative, partly to recast the reader as a
spectator of the events narrated, and partly to comment in
metaliterary fashion on the theatricality of the plot and presentation. There are, besides, allusions to specific dramatic works:
thus the story of a stepmother's infatuation for her husband's
son told by Cnemon in the first book resembles that of Hippolytus, the role of Phaedra being passed, as clear allusions
indicate, from Cnemon's stepmother Demaenete to the nympho-
maniac princess Arsace, whom the hero and heroine encounter
in Book 7. The duel between Calasiris' sons over the high-
priesthood at the beginning of Book 7 brings to mind both the
struggle between the sons of Oedipus for the throne of Thebes
and the confrontation between Achilles and Hector in the *Iliad*.
The final book plays around Euripides' two Iphigenia plays,
with the threat of human sacrifice in a distant land, and a king

confronting the possibility of having to slay his own daughter for the sake of his community.

The most important consequence of the novel's non-chronological structure is to redefine the relationship of the reader to the text. We must not only follow the story as it develops but reassemble it from scattered clues and make sense of it. In the opening scene of the whole novel, for example, we are confronted with a gruesome and graphic tableau of a massacre on a beach, but given no explanation as to its causes or significance. It is not until the end of Book 5 that the reader is in a position finally to understand what he reads at the beginning of Book 1. Among the dead bodies are a beautiful young man and young woman. Only slowly does it emerge that they are Theagenes and Chariclea, chaste lovers, and therefore presumably the hero and heroine of the story. Nevertheless a mystery remains as to who they really are, and this is only cleared as Calasiris relates how he had himself discovered the truth of the heroine's identity. In a sense, this section of the *Ethiopian Story* is the world's first detective story, and Calasiris the earliest literary ancestor of Sherlock Holmes.

This strategy of withholding information from the reader and explaining events retrospectively pervades the whole novel and translates down to the details of Heliodorus' narrative technique. It gives his novel a strikingly modern feeling in comparison with those of his predecessors. Whereas they tend to use the simple mechanism of an omniscient narrator/author who talks to the reader over the heads of the characters, as it were, and keeps him fully informed, Heliodorus has taken the step away from telling to showing. Often the reader is presented with a visually nuanced description of what an observer of the imaginary scene might have seen – one aspect of the work's implicit theatricality – sometimes (as in the opening tableau) through the eyes of fictional characters, but sometimes by a narrator who represents himself as having no surplus of information over the reader. When information is released, it is generally done so by one fictional character to another, so that the dramatic illusion is not broken by the intrusion of the author. The complexity of this technique is carried to remarkable extremes: at one point in the second book we are reading reported speech at three removes, as Cnemon hears from Calasiris what Charicles had told him he had heard from an Ethiopian ambassador.[8]

All this has the effect of drawing the reader into the fiction as a spectator, of making it less authored and so more real, but also of highlighting the questions of understanding and interpretation which the plot continually throws up. To give one notable example, the course of the plot is predicted by an enigmatic oracle at the end of the second book, whose meaning only gradually becomes clear as events unfold: Heliodoros exploits the reader's attempts to understand it to generate a series of expectations which the plot then overthrows, apparently fulfilling the oracle in unforeseen ways, which themselves often turn out to be false trails. Thus the novel is presented from tailing off into stereotypical predictability; only on the very last page is the final detail of the oracle definitively resolved. On a smaller scale, there is a whole series of dreams and predictions in the story, which puzzle reader and character alike. A favourite sequence is for a character to act on an incorrect interpretation with the result that he brings about a fulfilment of the prediction in a way neither he nor the reader had anticipated. A good example of this is provided by the dream of the robber captain Thyamis in Book 1.[9]

From this perspective the long narrative of Calasiris, which occupies more than three books – and Cnemon's response to it – has an emblematic significance: Heliodorus uses this narrative within a narrative to define both his own strategies as a novelist and the desired reception of his story. Even before Calasiris' narration begins, Cnemon comments on his elusiveness, and Calasiris himself apologizes for the apparently gratuitously complex arrangement of his material. Although he sometimes speaks with genuine learning, Calasiris manipulates the whole of the intrigue at Delphi through false appearances, half-truths and play-acting, combining the conventional twin Egyptian personae of sage and charlatan. His narrative is similarly ambivalent, and close reading reveals an apparently irreconcilable inconsistency as to his motives for being in Delphi. Initially he presents Delphi as just one port of call during his self-imposed exile and his meeting with Chariclea as an unforeseen bonus, but later (4.12) divulges that he has been commissioned by Chariclea's mother to seek her out after discovering that she was alive and at Delphi. This is not simply a lapse on the author's part in controlling his own intricately structured plot. Rather the discrepancy is a product of Calasiris' narrative technique. Like Heliodorus, he makes his story more effective by withholding relevant information: he does not tell Cnemon what he now knows about Chariclea, so that Cnemon, and through him the reader, is made to re-enact Calasiris' own discovery of the truth.[10]

The *Ethiopian Story* is set in the real world. All place names are authentic, although two Egyptian towns (Chemmis and Bessa) appear to have wandered from their real geography. The author has gone to some length to anchor his narrative in an historical and geographical setting which would be plausible to a literate reader. Almost every detail he gives of the kingdom of Ethiopia, for instance, can be paralleled in the Greek literary tradition (which is not to say that it is actually correct!). Some elementary mistakes (such as ignorance that the important city of Philae was built on an island in the Nile) suggest that his knowledge of Egypt and Ethiopia is not first-hand. The novel is set at the time of the Persian occupation of Egypt in the sixth and fifth centuries BC, although there are some careless minor anachronisms. The realism of the setting is reinforced by some subtly appropriated mannerisms from writers of history, such as judicious uncertainty over 'facts' that Heliodorus has himself invented, or alternative explanations for fictitious events.[11]

In comparison with the other novels, the sexual ethic of the *Ethiopian Story* is extremely strict, with a very strong emphasis on chastity and physical purity. In Chariton's novel, by way of contrast, the heroine takes a second husband in order to provide her unborn child with a father, but her emotional fidelity is not called into question by her inability to sustain strict physical monogamy. The heroes of Achilles' and Longus' novels both enjoy sex with another woman in the course of the story, and although their heroines retain their virginity until they are married, it is not for want of trying to lose it. Xenophon's protagonists enjoy a night of graphic marital bliss before being separated. Heliodorus' heroine, on the other hand, begins as a ministrant of Artemis, the goddess of virginity, and, even after falling reluctantly in love, would die to protect her chastity, even from her beloved. Very untypically for an ancient Greek male, he shares her rigid code of sexual restraint. The morality of the protagonists is illuminated by the story of Cnemon in Book 1, which presents its exact antithesis, a scenario of selfish, promiscuous and purely physical eroticism with disastrous consequences. While it is tempting to connect the novel's emphasis on sexual purity with the story that its author was a bishop who enforced celibacy on his clergy, we should not read the *Ethiopian Story* as a simple anti-sexual tract; rather it is the paramount value of human love which necessitates that its consummation be reserved so long and so strictly until all the proprieties can be observed.[12]

Religion plays a prominent part in the *Ethiopian Story*. The love of the protagonists originates at one religious ceremony in Delphi and is finally solemnized at another in Ethiopia. The action is distributed around three religious sites, Delphi, Memphis and Meroe, each of which contributes a priest to the cast list to act as father-figure to the heroine. These priests, Charicles, Calasiris and Sisimithres, even form their own internal hierarchy, so that Chariclea's journey back to Ethiopia is articulated as an ascent towards spiritual wisdom. The plot is driven forward by repeated divine intervention in the form of oracles, dreams and theophanies; a god-sent dream is even responsible for Chariclea's conception. Both narrator and characters repeatedly invoke divine agency to explain events, and the climax of the novel is marked by an unequivocal assertion by the wisest of its wise men that 'these events have been thus brought about by the direction of the gods' (10.40). This is not the place to enter into details, especially since translation inevitably obscures the nuances of the vocabulary employed to denote various divine levels, but we can broadly say that Heliodorus gives us a typically late-antique view of the divine world, with an almost abstract level of pure deity mediated to humanity by a plurality of lower powers, or *daimones*, whose activities are often malign. This is not necessarily to say that the divine aspects of the novel are seriously meant as a didactic representation of the workings of the real world, merely that the novel, not surprisingly, employs a representation that was instinctively comprehensible to its intended readers.

It is tempting to look for a connection between the novel and the sun cult of Heliodorus' native city. It has been argued that Chariclea's journey to her homeland is an allegory for the experience of a devotee of the cult, passing through a series of initiation ordeals, which in their turn figure the trials of a soul in its progression through the material world to a reunion with its god. The myth of the fall of the soul is familiar to us from

Plato, and was characteristic of neoplatonist thought. However, to interpret the *Ethiopian Story* exclusively as an allegory of religious initiation is deny importance to the literary innovations by which Heliodorus clearly set great store. Nevertheless it is possible to argue, in a somewhat looser sense, that the sun is presented as the controlling power of the novel, whose story begins in Delphi, sacred site of Apollo, often identified with the sun and ends in Ethiopia, land of the sun *par excellence*. The problem with this line of argument is that we know really very little of the rituals and theologies of the sun cult, whose truths were revealed only to initiates. The picture of orgiastic excesses under Elagabalus, presented by admittedly hostile sources, however, sits very uneasily with the sexual purity on which Heliodorus puts such stress. Although the sun cult was later cleaned up and de-orientalized and given philosophical respectability, there is no evidence that it ever demanded such rigid sexual purity from its adherents as that exhibited by Theagenes and Chariclea.[13]

This element in fact is better explained as philosophically than as religiously derived. The philosophy of neoplatonism and neopythagoreanism, with its rejection of the physical world as mere appearance, has left its clear mark on the *Ethiopian Story*. Calasiris combines aspects of asceticism, such as vegetarianism, and theurgy which are found in neoplatonist thinkers, many of whom looked towards Egypt as a source of revealed wisdom.[14] Heliodorus shows undeniable acquaintance with another important text with Emesan connections, the largely fictional biography of the neopythagorean guru Apollonius of Tyana, written by Philostratus on the commission of Julia Domna, but the specific similarities are matters of detail and diction rather than spiritual profundity. The philosophical background of the novel is still to be thoroughly researched, but we need not expect to find a systematically expounded intellectual system in a work of imaginative fiction. Modern readers need not feel that they are lacking the vital key to unlock the work's meaning.

J. R. MORGAN

References

1. The Hadrianic dating is advocated by E. Feuillâtre, *Études sur les Éthiopiques d'Héliodore* (Presses Universitaires de France 1966) 147-8.

The most influential proponent of a date under Aurelian was E. Rohde, *Der griechische Roman and seine Vorlaüfer*, 3rd edn., ed. W. Schmid (Leipzig 1914) 496–7. The identification with Heliodorus the Arab (given a short biographical notice by Philostratus, *Lives of the Sophists* 2.32) is found as early as the first printed edition of the Greek text in 1534; see F. Altheim, *Literatur und Gesellschaft im ausgehenden Altertum* (Halle 1948) 113; R. Merkelbach, *Roman und Mysterium in der Antike* (Munich and Berlin 1962) 234. The latest support for a fourth-century dating comes from G. W. Bowersock, *Fiction as History* (California UP 1994) 149–60.

2. Socrates Scholasticus, *Historia Ecclesiastica* 5.22.

3. Nicephorus Callistus, *Historia Ecclesiastica* 12.34.

4. For translations of the extant novels and the most important ancillary texts, see B. P. Reardon, *Collected Ancient Greek Novels* (California UP 1989).

5. See Rohde, cited above; B. E. Perry, *The Ancient Romances. A Literary-historical Account of their Origins* (California UP 1967); G. Anderson, *Ancient Fiction. The Novel in the Graeco-Roman World* (Croom Helm 1984) revives the hypothesis of an origin in oriental myth or folktale.

6. Cf. M. Foucault, *The History of Sexuality*, vol. 3: *The Care of the Self*, trans. R. Hurley (Penguin 1988); D. Konstan, *Sexual Symmetry. Love in the Ancient Novel and Related Genres* (Princeton UP 1994).

7. For the readership of the novels, see S. A. Stephens, 'Who Read Ancient Novels?', in J. Tatum ed. *The Search for the Ancient Novel* (Johns Hopkins UP 1994) 405–18; E. L. Bowie, 'The Readership of Greek Novels in the Ancient World', *ibid.* 435–59; J. R. Morgan, 'The Greek Novel: Towards a Sociology of Production and Reception' in A. Powell, ed., *The Greek World* (Routledge 1995) 130–52. For the Second Sophistic, see G. Anderson, *The Second Sophistic. A Cultural Phenomenon in the Roman Empire* (Routledge 1993).

8. On Heliodorus' narrative technique, see J. R. Morgan, 'Reader and Audiences in the *Aithiopika* of Heliodoros', *Groningen Colloquia on the Novel* 4 (1991) 85–103; *id.* 'The *Aithiopika* of Heliodoros. Narrative as Riddle' in J. R. Morgan, R. Stoneman, eds., *Greek Fiction. The Greek Novel in Context* (Routledge 1994) 97–113.

9 On these aspects see J. R. Morgan, 'A Sense of the Ending: the

Conclusion of Heliodoros' *Aithiopika*', *Transactions of the American Philological Association* 119 (1989) 299–320; S. Bartsch, *Decoding the Ancient Novel* (Princeton UP 1989) 109–44.

10. On Calasiris see J. J. Winkler, 'The Mendacity of Kalasiris and the Narrative Strategy of Heliodoros' *Aithiopika*', *Yale Classical Studies* 27 (1982) 93–158.

11. On the novels' relation to the 'real world', see J. R. Morgan, 'History, Romance and Realism in the *Aithiopika* of Heliodoros', *Classical Antiquity* 1 (1982) 221–65.

12. See Konstan, *op.cit.*; J. R. Morgan, 'The Story of Knemon in Heliodoros' *Aithiopika*', *Journal of Hellenic Studies* 109 (1989) 99–113.

13.—The allegorical interpretation is that of R. Merkelbach, *op.cit.*; see also F. Altheim, *op.cit.*

14. For Calasiris as a neoplatonist, see G. N. Sandy, 'Characterization and Philosophical Decor in Heliodorus's *Aethiopica*, *Transactions of the American Philological Association* 112 (1982) 141–67.

ETHIOPIAN STORY

BOOK I

A strange scene around two young lovers, resulting from a feast
and a fray near the mouth of the Nile, is espied by some brigands.

(1) The cheerful smile of day was just appearing, as the rays of the sun began to light up the mountain tops, when some men armed like brigands peered over the ridge that stretches alongside the outlets of the Nile and that mouth of the river which is named after Hercules. They halted there for a little while, scanning with their eyes the sea that lay below them; and when they had cast their first glances over the ocean and found no craft upon it and no promise there of pirates' plunder, they bent their gaze down upon the shore near by. And what it showed was this: a merchant ship was moored there by her stern cables, bereft of her ship's company, but full laden; so much could be inferred even at a distance, for her burthen brought the water as high as the third waling-piece of her timbers. The shore was thickly strewn with newly slain bodies, some quite lifeless, and others half dead whose limbs were still aquiver, thus indicating that the conflict had only just ceased. That it had been no regular engagement was betokened by what was visible; for there lay mingled the pitiful remnants of a feast that had thus come to no happy conclusion. There were tables still laden with their victuals; some others, overturned on the ground, were held in the grasp of those of the vanquished who had used them as armour in the struggle, for it had been a fight on the spur of the moment; and underneath others were men who had crept there in the hope of concealment. Wine-bowls were upset, and some were slipping from the hands of their holders – either drinkers or those who had taken them up to use as missiles instead of stones. The suddenness of the clash enforced innovations in the uses of things and prompted the hurling of drinking-cups. Here lay a man wounded with an axe, there one struck by a stone that the shingle had provided on the spot, another mangled by a piece of timber and another burnt to death by a firebrand; but most had fallen victims to darts and arrows. Countless were the varieties of sights that Fate had produced upon that small area – befouling wine with blood, thrusting battle upon banquet,

with conjunction of killing and swilling, libation and laceration – so strange was the scene thus displayed to the Egyptian brigands. They had taken their places on that mountain height as spectators of this scene but could not apprehend its meaning: they had the vanquished lying there, but nowhere could they see the victors. The conquest was clear as day, but the spoils were unseized; while the vessel deserted and void of men, yet held its cargo intact, as though protected by a strong guard, and it rocked gently at its moorings as in a time of peace. But, although at a loss to know what could have occurred, they looked to the gain to be had in the booty, and assuming the part of victors they dashed on.

(2) When they had advanced to a little way short of the ship and the fallen, they came upon a sight more unaccountable than what they had seen before. A young girl was seated on a rock, so inconceivably beautiful as to convince one that she was a goddess. Though sorely anguished by her present plight, she yet breathed forth a high and noble spirit. Her head was crowned with laurel; a quiver was slung over her shoulder; and her left arm was propped upon her bow, beyond which the hand hung negligently down. The elbow of her other arm she supported on her right thigh, while on its palm she rested her cheek; and with downcast eyes she held her head still, gazing intently on a prostrate youth. He, cruelly wounded, seemed to be faintly awakening as from a deep slumber that was wellnigh death. Yet, for all that, he had upon him the bloom of manly beauty, and his cheek, stained red by the gushing of his blood, showed forth its whiteness all the more brightly. The sufferings of the youth were weighing down his eyes; but the sight of her drew them upward to her, compelled to see by merely seeing her. Then, collecting his breath and heaving a profound sigh, in a weak undertone he said: 'My sweet one, are you truly with me, still alive? Or have you too fallen by chance a victim to the fighting, and cannot any way endure, even after death, to be parted from me, but your wraith and your soul yet show concern for my fortunes?' 'On you,' she answered, 'it rests whether I live or die. Now, do you see this?' she added, showing a sword that lay upon her knees. 'Hitherto it has been idle, withheld by your breathing.' As she spoke she sprang up from the rock: the men on the mountain, struck, with wonder and alarm by the sight, as though by some fiery blast, cowered under bushes here and

there, for she seemed to them to be something greater and more divine when she stood erect. Her arrows rattled with her sudden movement;* the inwoven gold of her dress glistened in the beams of the sun, and her hair, tossing below the wreath like the tresses of a bacchant, flowed widespread over her back. All this and, more than what they saw, their ignorance of what was happening, filled them with terror: they either said she was some goddess – the goddess Artemis, or Isis, the deity of that country* – or supposed her to be a priestess who, in a god-sent frenzy, had wrought the massacre that they saw before them. Thus they opined, as yet unable to form a true opinion. Then the maiden, descending swiftly upon the young man and enfolding his whole person in her arms, wept and kissed him, wiped his wounds and lamented, still in doubt of her holding him. Seeing this, the Egyptians turned their thoughts to other reasonings. 'How could these be the actions of a goddess?' they asked; 'how could a deity kiss a corpse with such fervid passion?' So they urged one another to be brave, and by advancing nearer learn the truth of the matter. They thus recovered themselves, and running down they came upon the maiden as she was still intent on the young man's wounds; then, having come to a halt behind her, they did not venture to say or do anything. The noisy clatter of the men, and their shadows slanting across her view, caused the maiden to raise her head: she looked, then bent it down again, not in the least dismayed by their strange colour and brigand-like appearance – armed as they showed themselves to be – but wholly engaged in tending the prostrate youth. So it is that a true-hearted affection, a genuine love, will despise all pains and pleasures alike that may intrude from without, and will constrain the mind to regard and gratify the beloved one alone.

(3) The brigands moved up, then stopped in front of the girl and seemed to be on the point of taking some action. Again she raised her head and, seeing their sable hue and unkempt appearance, said: 'If you are phantoms of the fallen,* you have no right to molest us, since most of you were slain by each other's hands; while those of you who were killed by us have met your fate through lawful self-defence and in retribution for vile assault on chastity. If you are among the living, your life, it would seem, is one of brigandage; but your coming here is timely. Release us from the sufferings that harass us by killing us and bringing to its close the drama of our destiny.' Thus she

spoke to them, in high tragic vein; but they, unable to understand one word of what she said, left the young couple there,
deeming their weakness a strong enough guard to be set over
them. The brigands then hastened to the ship, which they
proceeded to ransack for her cargo. Despising the rest of her
contents, which were many and various, they bore off as much
as each man could carry of gold, silver, precious stones and
silken attire. When they thought that they had got enough – it
was as much as might satiate even pirates' greed – they laid
down their booty on the shore and divided it up into separate
loads which they apportioned, not according to the value of
each article seized, but to an equality of weight of burdens. As
to what should be done with the maiden and the youth, this
they would leave over to a later time.

*A larger band of brigands arrives on the scene under their leader
Thyamis.*

At this moment another troop of brigands appeared, with two
horsemen at its head. When the former band observed it,
without showing any resistance or carrying off any of their
spoils – so eager were they to evade pursuit – they fled as fast as
they could run: they were but ten in number, and perceived the
newcomers to be thrice as many. Thus were the girl and her
companion a second time made captives before being captured.
These brigands, however, despite their eagerness to be at the
plunder, stayed their steps awhile in amazement at a sight that
passed their comprehension. All that slaughter, they surmised,
had been the work of the former brigands, while they saw the
maiden dressed in resplendent foreign attire and ignoring the
perils that beset her as though they did not even exist, so entirely
concerned she was with the young man's wounds, and pained
by his suffering as if it were her own. They admired her for her
beauty and her spirit, and were amazed at him, wounded though
he was, so fine and tall a figure he made lying there; for by now
he was slightly revived, and was recovering the usual look in his
eyes.

(4) After some little delay the brigand chief took hold of the
girl and bade her rise and follow him. She understood no word
of what he said, but guessing the sense of what he ordered she
drew along with her the young man, who on his part would not

let go of her; then, levelling her sword at her breast, she threatened to kill herself if they did not bring away the two of them. The brigand chief, understanding her not so much by her words as by her gestures, and also expecting to have the youth as an assistant, if he survived, in their major exploits, dismounted his henchman and himself from their horses and placed the prisoners on their saddles. He ordered the others to pack up the booty and follow him, while he ran on foot beside the prisoners and held them up when they might be losing their balance. There was something to count as glory in this proceeding: the master was to be seen acting as a slave, and the victor choosing to do a service to his captives. So it is that a noble presence and the sight of beauty have the secret of subduing even a brigand's nature, and the power to control even the most uncouth of creatures.

The two lovers, Theagenes and Chariclea, are carried off by the later brigands to their habitation on a lagoon, and are put in the charge of a Greek youth.

(5) After passing along the seashore for about two furlongs they turned and made straight for the mountain slopes, having the sea on their right. They climbed over the ridge with some difficulty, and then hastened on to a lagoon, which extended below the far side of the range and was of this nature: the whole region is named by the Egyptians 'Herdsman's Home';* it is a low-lying tract in those parts which receives certain overflows of the Nile, so as to form a lake which is of immense depth at its centre but dwindles towards its edges into a swamp. What shores are to seas, swamps are to lakes. Here it is that Egyptians of the bandit kind have their city: one man has built himself a cabin on a patch of land that may lie above the water level; another makes his dwelling in a boat which serves at once for transport and for habitation; upon this the women spin their wool, and also bring forth their children. When a child is born, it is reared at first on its mother's milk, but thereafter on the fish taken from the lagoon and broiled in the sun. When they observe the child attempting to crawl, they fasten a thong to its ankles which allows it to move to the limits of the boat or the hut, thus singularly making the tethering of their feet serve instead of leading them by the hand.*

(6) Hence many a herdsman has been born on the lagoon and reared in this manner, and so come to regard the lagoon as his homeland; and it fully serves as a strong bastion for brigands. Into it therefore flows a stream of men in that way of life, all relying on the water as a wall, and the abundant growth of reeds in the swamp as a stockade. By cutting a number of winding paths which straggle in many twists and turns, and by contriving exits which, while easy enough for them through their familiarity, are bewildering to strangers, they have ingeniously produced a fastness of surpassing strength to ward off harm that might come upon them from an onslaught. So much for the lagoon and the herdsmen who dwell within it.

(7) Towards the hour of sunset the brigand chief and his troop arrived at the lagoon. They dismounted the young pair from the horses, and placed the booty in their boats; while the main body of the brigands who had remained in the region, emerging from various parts of the swamp, were seen running together to greet their chief with a welcome suited to one who ruled over them like a king. When they saw the vast amount of the spoil and gazed upon the beauty of the girl as on something sublime, they supposed that some temples or gold-enriched shrines had been pillaged by their confederates, who moreover had abducted the priestess herself; or in their boorish simplicity they surmised from the girl's appearance that the living image of a goddess had actually been carried off. Showering praises on their chieftain for his steadfast valour, they escorted him to his dwelling-place: it was an islet lying at some distance from the rest, which had been assigned as a solitary retreat for him and his few companions. On retiring there he ordered the main body to depart to their homes, with the direction that they should all come to him on the morrow. He himself, left alone with his few intimates, treated these to a brief repast, of which he also partook. The young captives he put in the charge of a Greek youth, taken prisoner by the brigands shortly before, through whom he might converse with them and to whom he allotted a cabin close to his own, commanding him to take due care of the young man, but especially to guard the maiden from any outrage. Then he, overborne by the fatigue of his journeying, and feeling the strain of his present concerns, betook himself to sleep.

(8) Silence reigned over the swamp, and night had entered on

the first watch;* the girl and her friend now, in the absence of
any people likely to interfere with them, were given an opportunity for lamentation. Night, I imagine, stirred up their woes
the more, because neither hearing nor sight distracted their
reflections, and free scope was then allowed to their grief alone.
So the girl, after wailing aloud by herself – for by order given
she had been put in a place apart, and was lying on a low pallet
bed – and having shed very many tears – 'Apollo,' she said,
'with what excessive bitterness do you punish us for our
offences! Are not the past events sufficient for your vengeance?
Bereft of our kinsfolk, captured by murderous pirates, and after
a thousand perils on the sea taken prisoners once again by
brigands on the land, we have now the prospect of ordeals more
severe than those that we underwent before. Where will you
stay your hand? If it is to be at a death that I may meet
unravished, sweet will be my end; but if anyone is to know me
vilely, me whom not even Theagenes has yet possessed, I will
forestall the outrage with a noose, having preserved myself then,
as I have done till now, a pure virgin unto death, and taking
with me my chastity as a noble winding-sheet. And I shall have
no judge more severe than you.' As she was yet speaking she
was stopped by Theagenes. 'Enough,' he said, 'my dearest, my
very life, Chariclea! Your laments are natural, but you provoke
the deity more than you are aware. He is not to be reproached,
but entreated; the higher power is appeased by prayers, not by
accusations.' 'You are right,' she said; 'but tell me, how is it
with you?' 'Easier and better since the evening,' he replied,
'thanks to this lad's attentions, which have relieved the inflam-
mation of my wounds.' 'And also,' said the person charged with
their custody, 'you will have even greater relief by the morning.
I will supply you with a kind of herb that in two days' time will
close up those gashes; I have tested its effect in actual use. For
since these people brought me here a prisoner, whenever any of
this chieftain's subjects came in wounded from an affray, their
cure took only a few days' treatment with the herb of which I
speak. My concern for the fortunes of you both should cause
you no surprise: you appear to be sharing the same lot with me,
and besides, being Greeks, you have my pity, since I am myself
a Greek by birth.' 'A Greek? O Heaven!' exclaimed the two
strangers together in delight. 'A Greek in very truth, by birth
and by language! Perhaps we are to have some respite from our

troubles.' 'But by what name are we to call you?' asked
Theagenes. 'Cnemon,' he replied. 'And what citizenship do you
claim?' 'Athenian.' 'What fortune have you met with?' 'Stop,'
he answered; '"why dost batter and unbar" all that? – as they
say in tragedy.* This is no time to thrust in an episode of my
troubles upon the drama of yours. Besides, the remainder of the
night would not suffice for my story to be told, especially as you
are in need of sleep and repose after all your hardships.'

*The Greek youth Cnemon tells his distressful story to the two
lovers, with the wicked devices of his stepmother Demaenete and
her maid Thisbe.*

(9) When they would not give way, but begged him by all
means to speak on, expecting to find no small consolation in
hearing of troubles like their own, Cnemon began his relation
thus: 'My father was Aristippus, an Athenian by birth, a member
of the Senate,* and a man of moderate wealth. When in course
of time my mother died, he let himself lapse into a second
marriage, complaining that he had me as his one and only child
to depend upon. He brought into the house a woman who was
elegant indeed, but a fount of evil, named Demaenete. For from
the moment of her arrival she was getting him entirely into her
power and persuading him to do whatever she wished, by
seducing the old man with her charms and coddling him in one
way or another, as clever a woman as ever lived at making a
man besotted with her, and marvellously expert in the art of
seduction – groaning at my father's goings-out and running to
him at his comings-in, reproaching him for his late return, and
saying that she would have died if he had delayed a moment
longer, with embracements at every word and tears mingled
with her kisses. Ensnared with all these wiles, my father made
her absolutely his life-breath, his eyesight. Me she at first
affected to regard as her son – another trick of hers to captivate
Aristippus. Sometimes she would come and kiss me, and continually begged that she might have enjoyment of me. I bore
with her behaviour, having no suspicion of her real meaning,
but only a feeling of wonder at this display of a motherly
attitude towards me. But when she accosted me more recklessly,
and her kisses were more ardent than was seemly, and her
glances so far passed the bounds of modesty that I began to feel

suspicious, I then made a rule of shunning her and repulsing her advances. For the rest, why should I trouble you with a lengthy account – of the persistent attempts that she made upon me, the promises that she held out, calling me now her little boy, now her sweet dear, and then again, addressing me as her heir and, in the next moment, her very soul? In short, she mingled the choicest terms with her enticements, and was at pains to devise any and every means of drawing me in to her. For, although in her more serious moods she assumed the role of mother, in her more abandoned moments she revealed herself actually in the glaring character of lover.

(10) 'In the end it came to this. The Great Panathenaean Festival* was being held, in which the Athenians carry the ship to Athena in a procession overland. I was a young man, just come of age: after I had sung the customary paean to the goddess and joined in the traditional procession, I made my way home, still dressed up in the particular cloak and garlands of the ceremony. At her first sight of me she became quite demented, and dropped all artful concealment of her love. Laying bare her longing, she ran up to me and embraced me, saying: "My young Hippolytus!"* What, do you suppose, was the effect of this on me? Even now I blush to relate it. Well, when evening came, my father was out dining at the town hall, where the festal assembly with its civic carousel would naturally detain him all night. She then took me unawares in the night time, and tried to obtain from me what was criminal. I made all the resistance in the world, and fought off every blandishment and promise and menace; then, with a deep and heavy groan, she left me and went away. No sooner had the abominable creature passed the night than she put in motion her plots against me. First, without rising that day from her bed, she pretended to my father, when he came to inquire what was the matter, that she was in a feeble state, and made no reply at first. On his pressing her and asking again and again what had happened to her, she said: "That wonderful pious young man, son to us both, whom – the gods are my witnesses – I have often treated with more affection even than you, perceived by some signs that I was with child. For the time I was hiding this from you till I could know it for certain. He watched for your absence and, while I was giving him my usual good advice, and admonishing him to be temperate and keep his thoughts off courtesans and drinking-bouts – for I was

quite aware of these habits of his, but did not mention them to you for fear of being looked upon as a stepmother* – while I was thus speaking to him, alone with me so that I should not put him to the blush, I am ashamed to repeat all the vile insults that he heaped on you as well as me; and then he rushed at me and gave me a kick in the stomach which put me in the condition that you see."

(11) 'After hearing her words he said nothing, he asked no question, he allowed me no chance of defence. Convinced that this woman, so well disposed towards me, could never slander me, in that instant and on the spot where he found me in a part of the house, while I knew nothing of the matter, he struck me with his fists, and summoning servants he had me cruelly flogged, though I lacked even the knowledge, that is commonly given, of the reason for my thrashing. When he had sated his rage, "Oh, now at least, father," I said, "if I could not before, I may fairly be told the reason for this beating." His anger flared up then all the more and – "Ha, playing the innocent!" he said; "he wants me to tell him of his impious doings!" Then turning away he hastened to Demaenete. She, for her wrath was still not glutted, put in hand a second design against me, in this way. She had a young maidservant named Thisbe, who could sing to her own lute-playing and was not uncomely to look upon. This girl she set upon me with orders to make a show of loving me, and Thisbe promptly made love. Having frequently repulsed my advances, she was now seeking in every way to allure me – by glances, motions of the head and other tokens. I, in my vanity, believed that of a sudden I had become good looking, and at length I received her one night in my room. She came to me a second time, and then again, and after that she was continually paying me visits. Once, when I strongly urged her to take good care not to be detected by her mistress, she said: "Cnemon, I find you are too much of a simpleton: if you think it a bad business for me, a maidservant bought with money, to be caught in intercourse with you, what punishment would you say that woman deserves who, claiming to be well born, and having her lawful spouse, and knowing that death is the end in store for such transgression, commits adultery?" "Stop," I said; "I cannot believe you." "I tell you," she went on, "that if you were so minded, I could expose her gallant in the very act." "If only you would care to do so," I said. "To be sure I will," she replied,

"not only for your sake, since she has caused you to be so grossly maltreated, but as much for my own, suffering as I do the vilest usage every day at the hands of that woman, who wreaks her senseless jealousy upon me. Now, mind that you play the man."

(12) 'I promised that I would so acquit myself; she then left me and departed. On the third night following she roused me from sleep and informed me that the adulterer was in the house: my father, she said, had gone on a journey into the country on some sudden call of business, and the gallant, by arrangement with Demaenete, had just then slipped in; I must be prepared to punish them, and must break in upon them, blade in hand, so that the rascal should not make his escape. I did as she bade me. Dagger in hand, with Thisbe guiding me and lighting torches, I approached the bedroom. Stopping there I saw the gleam of some lamplight emanating from within. The door was closed: in the heat of my anger I burst it open, and rushing in I cried: "Where is the criminal, the dashing lover of this spotless chastity?" – and as I spoke I advanced to dispatch them both. From the bed, ye gods! my father, turning round, threw himself at my knees, saying: "My son, stay a moment! Have pity on him who begot you! Spare the hoary head that nurtured you! I have maltreated you, but not so as to deserve the penalty of death. Let not your wrath so possess you, nor pollute your hands with a father's blood!" With these and other appeals added to them he besought my mercy, while I, as though caught in a tornado, stood there, struck senseless as a stone, looking round for Thisbe – who had crept away, I know not how – and casting my eyes all about the bed and the room, utterly at a loss for words and incapable of any action. My weapon fell from my grasp; Demaenete ran forward and eagerly snatched it up; and my father, finding himself out of danger, laid hands on me and ordered me to be bound, while Demaenete continually fomented his rage, crying: "The very thing against which I cautioned you, when I told you to beware of the lad, as he would seize the first opportunity of doing us a mischief! I saw the look in his eyes, and read there his purpose." "You did caution me," he said, "but I did not believe it." For the time he kept me in bonds; I wanted to tell something of the facts, but he would not allow me to do so, or to speak a single word.

(13) 'At break of day he took me, bound as I was, before the

people and, his head all bespattered with ashes,* he said:
"Nothing like this did I anticipate, men of Athens, in nurturing
this person. Looking forward rather to his being a staff for my
old age, I bestowed on him, as soon as he was born to me, a
liberal upbringing. I taught him the rudiments of grammar; I
made him a member of a clan, with the highest rank in it; I
enrolled him in the class of adult students; and having thus
established him as your fellow-citizen I anchored my whole
existence upon him. But he, forgetful of all this, first outraged
me with insults, and my wife here, my lawfully wedded house-
mate, with blows, and ended by attacking us at night, blade in
hand, and was only prevented from committing parricide by the
fortune of a surprise alarm causing his weapon to fall from his
grasp. I have turned to you for protection, and now denounce
him to you. Our laws permit me to kill him myself, but I would
not do it, preferring to leave the whole matter to your judgment,
because I hold it better to punish a son through the law than by
private slaughter." With that he shed tears, while Demaenete on
her part lamented and made a great show, slyly enough, of
grieving deeply over me, calling me a poor wretch now doomed
to die, justly but before his time, who had been driven on by
malignant spirits to assail his parents. So she wailed on – nay
rather, testified against me with her wailing, as though confirming the truth of her accusation with her mournful cries. When I
claimed to be allowed my turn to speak, the clerk came to me
and put to me one bare question – whether I had attacked my
father blade in hand. When I answered "I did attack him, but
hear how this came about," with a great shout they all gave the
verdict that I should not be allowed even to make a defence.
Some were for stoning me, others for handing me over to the
executioner and flinging me into the death-pit.* And I, through
all this uproar, and during the time of their voting to decide
which punishment I was to suffer, kept on shouting: "A stepmother is the cause of my destruction! A stepmother is putting
me to death untried!" My words reached the greater part of the
assembly, and led them to suspect the truth. Even then I was not
granted a hearing, so completely had the people been carried
away by that ungovernable clamour.

(14) 'When the votes for the sentence were counted, those
whose verdict was for death, either by stoning or by flinging
into the death-pit, numbered about one thousand seven

hundred; the rest, about a thousand, being those who inclined to a suspicion of my stepmother, condemned me to perpetual banishment. However, it was the vote of the latter that prevailed: for, although they were fewer than the whole body of the others, the thousand outnumbered either section of the divided vote of the rest. Accordingly I was expelled from the paternal hearth and the land of my birth. Yet Demaenete, with the gods' hatred upon her, did not remain unpunished. The manner of her fate you shall hear some other time; for the present you must take some sleep, since the night is far spent, and you are in need of a long rest.' 'But you will only add to our distress', said Theagenes 'if your story is to leave the pernicious Demaenete unpunished.'

'Well then, listen,' said Cnemon, 'since that is your desire. Immediately after that decision I went down without further ado to the Piraeus, and found there a vessel just putting to sea on which I voyaged to Aegina, because I had information that some cousins of my mother were there. I landed and found the people whom I was seeking, and at first the time went not unpleasantly for me. On the twentieth day of my visit I was strolling about in my usual way, and came down to the harbour, where a skiff was just coming in. So I stopped for a little to observe whence it hailed and what persons it had on board. The gangway had not yet been properly fixed when somebody leapt ashore, ran up to me and embraced me. It was Charias, one of my student group. "Cnemon," he said, "I bring you good news. You are avenged on your enemy. Demaenete is dead." "My best wishes to you Charias," I said; "but why do you scamper so over this good news, as though it were something sinister that you were announcing? Go on and tell me how it happened, for I greatly fear she has met with a natural death, and eluded her deserts." "Not altogether", said Charias, "has Justice forsaken us, as Hesiod says:* at times, indeed, she may disregard some slight matter, drawing out the time for its requital; but sharp is the glance that she turns upon such unlawful acts as these, and so has she called to account the guilt-laden Demaenete. I have full knowledge of what was done or said, since Thisbe, as you are aware, was on intimate terms with me, and she told me the whole story. When that unjust exile had been inflicted upon you, your unhappy father, repenting of his actions, removed to a distant part of the country and there dwelt, 'devouring his

own soul' – to quote the poem.* As for her, the Furies were not
slow to drive her on: she loved you more madly in your absence,
uttering ceaseless laments – over you, seemingly, but really over
herself – and crying out 'Cnemon!' night and day, and calling
you her darling boy, her very life; so that the women of her
acquaintance who came to visit her were full of admiration: they
praised this instance of a stepmother showing the distress of a
mother, and endeavoured to console and reassure her. But she
replied that her misery was beyond consolation, and that other
women could not know what a bitter shaft was infixed in her
heart.

(15) '"Whenever she was alone, she poured out reproaches
against Thisbe for not having served her dutifully, saying 'Intent
on mischief, she has been no helper in my love-suit. She has
shown herself swifter than speech to bereave me of my dearest,
and has not even allowed me a chance of changing my mind.' It
became as clear as day that she would do some injury to Thisbe
who, seeing her so deeply incensed and so sorely wounded that
she was on the point of some action against her, especially as
she was infuriated at once by wrath and by love, decided to
forestall her and ensure her own safety by taking action against
her in advance. So she came to her and said: 'What is the matter,
mistress? Why do you make vain charges against your little
handmaid? I have served you always, in the past as in the
present, according to your wishes: if something has turned out
contrary to your design, that is to be ascribed to Fortune; yet I
am ready, at your bidding, to contrive some solution of the
present trouble.' 'Ah, what could you devise, dear friend,' said
Demaenete, 'when he who is able to solve it is now far from me,
and the unexpected clemency of the judges has undone me? If
he had been stoned, if he had been put to death, then my passion
also would have wholly expired with him. For as soon as an
object is past hoping for it has been withdrawn from one's soul;
and when there can no longer be any looking forward to the
thing desired it enables the sufferer to be relieved of his pain;
whereas now I imagine that I see him, I have the illusion of
hearing his voice near by, shaming me with reprobation of my
criminal plot against him. I fancy to myself that I shall one day
find him come secretly to court me, and that I am to have my
pleasure of him, or that I am about to visit him myself, wherever
in the world he may be. These things inflame one; they drive one

mad. My suffering, ye gods, is deserved! Why did I persecute,
and not rather entreat him? He refused me the first time, as was
fitting; I was a stranger: but beyond that he was ashamed for his
father's bed. Perhaps time and persuasion would have converted
him to a softer mood. But I, with my savage, merciless nature,
more like a task-mistress to him than a lover, took it as an
offence that he did not comply with my command and disdained
Demaenete, whom he far surpassed in beauty. Now, darling
Thisbe, what is the solution that you mentioned?' 'An easy one,
mistress,' she replied. 'It is the general opinion that Cnemon
withdrew from the city and travelled out of Attica in obedience
to the judgment: but I, who seek by every means to serve your
interest, have discovered that he is in hiding somewhere just
outside the city. You must surely have heard, I suppose, of
Arsinoe the flute-player: he had been intimate with her, and
after his misadventure he was taken in by this young woman.
Promising him that she will go along as his fellow-traveller, she
is keeping him concealed in her house until she has packed her
baggage.' 'Happy Arsinoe,' said Demaenete, 'in her former
intercourse with Cnemon and in this prospect of sharing his
exile! But what is the good of all this to us?' 'A great deal,
mistress,' said Thisbe. 'I will make a show of being in love with
Cnemon, and will request Arsinoe, who is an old acquaintance
of mine through her profession, to bring me in to him by night
instead of herself. If this could be arranged, it would be for you
then to personate Arsinoe and visit him in her place. It will be
my business to see that he goes to bed a little drunk. Should you
attain your object, your love will most likely cool off: many a
woman, after the first experience, has found her desire quite
extinguished; for the sating of love is the ending of the trouble.
If your love should still continue – which Heaven forbid! – there
will be, as they say, a second string to your bow, another plan.
Meanwhile, let us make the most of the present chance.'

(16) '"Demaenete approved her plan, and begged her to act
swiftly on their resolve. Thisbe asked her mistress to be allowed
one day for carrying it out. She went to Arsinoe and said: 'You
know Teledemus?' The other assented, and she went on: 'Take
us in here today; I promised I would sleep with him. He will
come first, and I later, when I have put my mistress to bed.'
Then away she ran to Aristippus in the country and said to him:
'Master, I have come to accuse myself; deal with me in what

way you please. I am in part the cause of your losing your son: it was against my will, but yet I was an accomplice. Observing that my mistress, instead of leading an honest life, was defiling your bed, and fearing that trouble might one day come upon myself if another should detect the affair, and also being deeply grieved that in return for all your care bestowed on the wife of your bosom you received this treatment, I shrank indeed from reporting it to you myself; but I went and spoke to the young master at night, so that nobody should know, and told him that an adulterer was sleeping with the mistress. Then he, who as you know had already a grievance against her, thinking that I meant that the adulterer was then in the house, was filled with uncontrollable anger and snatched up his dagger. I tried my best to restrain him, telling him that there was nothing of the sort there at the moment; but he, taking little heed, or else having expected me to back out of my words, rushed in fury to the bedchamber. You know the rest. And now you have the chance, if you want to take it, to excuse yourself to your son, exile though he be now, and to punish her who has done this wrong to you both. For I will show you this day Demaenete lying with her paramour in a house, and that a stranger's house, outside the city.' 'Oh, if you could show it to be as you say,' cried Aristippus, 'the money for the purchase of your freedom shall be kept in reserve for you; and I perhaps could enjoy a new life after avenging myself on my enemy. For a long time now I have had a smouldering doubt in my mind; I suspected that affair, but for want of proofs I kept quiet about it. Now, what is to be done?' 'You know the garden,' she said, 'where stands the Epicureans' monument?* Go there this evening and wait for me.'

(17) '"With these words she at once ran off, and coming to Demaenete she said: 'Make yourself fine; you must be in elegant trim for your visit. I have made all the arrangements for you that I promised.' So she dressed herself in the manner directed by Thisbe. When evening had come Thisbe took charge of her and led her to the place of assignation. As they approached it she bade her mistress wait a moment: she then went ahead and requested Arsinoe to move into another apartment and leave her to herself; for the youth, she told her, was bashful, being a mere novice in the ministry of Aphrodite. Arsinoe complied; then Thisbe returned and fetched Demaenete, brought her inside, saw her into bed, and took away the lamp, so that she should not be

recognized by you – you, forsooth, who were staying in Aegina! After recommending her to satisfy her desire in silence Thisbe said: 'I am off now to the young man, and will bring him to you; he is drinking at a neighbour's house hard by.' She slipped out, picked up Aristippus at the appointed place and incited him to surprise and bind the adulterer. He followed her and suddenly dashed into the room. Making his way with some difficulty to the bed by a slight glimmer of the moon he said: 'I have caught you, accursed woman!' Just as he uttered these words Thisbe knocked on the door with all her might and cried out: 'What a strange thing! The adulterer has escaped us! Take care, master, that you make no mistake this second time!' 'Never fear,' he replied; 'I have got the villainous woman, her whom I wanted most.' He then seized hold of her and began leading her towards the city. Upon her mind, as might be supposed, came crowding all the troubles that beset her – the disappointment of her expectations, the public disgrace in what was in store for her, the punishment ordained by the laws. Aggrieved by being caught in such a situation and enraged at being so duped, when she came near the pit in the Academy garden – you know it, of course, at which the Kings of Arms sacrifice by ancient custom to the heroes* – she suddenly broke from the old man's grasp and threw herself headlong into the pit! As she lay there, in a plight as evil as herself, Aristippus said: 'You have paid me the penalty before the laws could exact it.' On the next day he declared the whole affair to the people and with some difficulty obtained their exoneration. He then made a round of visits to his friends and acquaintances, seeking their advice on the prospect of his procuring your return. Whether anything in that way has been done I cannot say; before it could be I took ship for this place, as you see, on some private business. However, you can fairly count on the people's consent to your return, and on your father's coming here in search of you, for he was proposing to do so.'

Thyamis, the brigand chief, prompted by a dream, announces his intention of marrying Chariclea.

(18) 'This was the report that Charias gave me. What occurred next, how I came here and through what happenings by the way would be too long to tell and take too much time.' Upon this

Cnemon wept and the two strangers wept also, apparently for his experiences, but each of them really reflecting on their own. Nor would they have ceased lamenting, had not a spirit of sleep touched by the charm of their sad plaints, alighted upon them and quelled their tears. And so they slumbered. Meanwhile Thyamis – this being the name of the bandit chief – after taking tranquil repose for most of the night, had been disturbed by fitful dreams which suddenly robbed him of his sleep; and puzzling over their explanation he was kept awake by his anxious thoughts. It was about the hour when cocks crow – whether moved, as they say, to address the sun by an instinctive sense of this god's turning round to our region, or impelled by his warmth, as well as by their desire to be stirring and feeding betimes, to rouse up to work the people with whom they live by their peculiar proclamation – about that time he had this heavensent dream: at Memphis, his native city, he entered the temple of Isis, which seemed to be lit throughout with a blaze of lamps. Altars and braziers were laden with all kinds of animals and were drenched with their blood. The portico and passages outside were thronged with people whose clatter and clamour filled the whole place. When he came within the shrine itself, the goddess advanced to meet him, leading Chariclea by the hand, and said: 'Thyamis, I deliver to you this maiden: you will have her and have her not; you will be a wrongdoer and will slay your guest; yet she will not be slain.' The effect of this vision was to put him in a state of perplexity, in which he kept turning its indications this way and that, as he tried to make out their meaning. Tiring at length of this, he shaped the solution to suit his own desire. The words 'you will have her and have her not' he supposed to mean 'as a woman, and no longer a virgin'; and 'you will slay' he took to signify the wounding to end virginity – which would not be fatal to Chariclea.

(19) This was the sense in which he construed his dream, according to the promptings of his passion. At break of day he called to him the foremost men among his subjects, and ordered the booty, which he dignified with the name of spoils of war, to be brought before them. He then sent for Cnemon, whom he ordered to attend together with the persons held under his guard. As they were being brought: 'Now what turn of fortune are we to encounter next?' they cried, plying Cnemon with appeals for any support that he could give them. He promised his help, and

urged them to be of good cheer, engaging that the bandit chief was not wholly a barbarian in behaviour, but even had something civilized about him; for he belonged to a distinguished family, and had been driven by necessity to adopt his present way of life. When they had been brought to the place, and the main body of brigands had gathered there, Thyamis seated himself in a prominent position above them and declared the island to be in assembly. He directed Cnemon to interpret to the captives what he was about to say; for Cnemon by then understood Egyptian, while Thyamis was not perfect in the Greek tongue. He then spoke as follows: 'Fellow-soldiers, you know well the sort of feeling which I have always had towards you. I was born, as you are aware, a son of the prophet at Memphis; but after my father's retirement I failed to obtain the priestly office, which was unlawfully usurped by my younger brother. I then took refuge with you, for the purpose of avenging myself and recovering my high function. I was deemed worthy by you to be your chieftain, and to this day I have continued without once allotting to myself any larger portion than to each member of our body. If it was money to be shared, I was content with an equal division; if captives were to be sold, I paid all the receipts into the common fund. For I consider that a captain so competent as I ought to take the largest portion of the work, but an equal one of the winnings. As to prisoners, I enlisted in our band all the men among them whose bodily vigour made them likely to be useful recruits, and sold off the weaklings. On women I have committed no outrage, but have released those of good family either on payment made or merely from the pity that I felt for their plight. Those of meaner birth, for whom slavery, rather from habitude than from the fact of captivity, was inevitable, I distributed severally amongst us as servants. In the present case, however, I request of you one part of our booty – this foreign maiden here, whom I could assign to myself; but I consider it better to receive her from our body as a whole. It would be foolish indeed to seize this prisoner by force, and be seen securing an advantage against the will of one's friends. Moreover, I ask this favour of you, not as a free gift but in return for my resigning any share in the rest of the plunder. Since we of the family of the prophets disdain the popular Aphrodite, it is not for the purpose of enjoyment, but to provide offspring for the succession, that I have resolved to have this woman for myself.

(20) 'And I wish to explain to you my reasons for so doing. First, she appears to me to be of high birth, judging by the riches found about her person, and by her steadfastness under her present hardships and her maintenance of a brave spirit in face of all her previous fortunes. Next, I can discern her to be at heart both virtuous and chaste. For if, surpassing all other women in beauty of form, she restrains in awed respect every man who looks upon her by the modesty of her glance, how can she not produce with good reason the most favourable impression of herself? And, what is the most important point of her description, she seems to me to be the priestess of some deity. You can see how even in her calamity she does not think it permissible to put off the sacred vestments and chaplets.

(21) 'What marriage, I ask all here present, could be more appropriate than that of a prophet's son taking to wife the dedicated woman?' All in the assembly shouted their assent, and wished them a propitious wedlock. Then he, resuming his speech, went on: 'I thank you: but it would be reasonable for us to find out what are the maiden's feelings in the matter. For if I had had to avail myself of the chieftain's privilege, my desire alone was fully sufficient, since to those empowered to compel any such inquiry is superfluous. But where the matter in hand is a marriage both parties must give their willing consent.' Then, turning and addressing the girl, he asked her: 'Well then, how do you feel about being my wife?' And with that he requested her to state who she and her companion were, and of what parentage. For a good while she kept her eyes fixed on the ground and shook her head a number of times, as though collecting her words and thoughts. At last, looking Thyamis full in the face and dazzling him more than ever with her beauty – for her cheek had flushed unwontedly from the nature of her reflections, and her glance had quickened to a quite awesome keenness – with Cnemon interpreting she said: 'It would be more fitting for my brother here, Theagenes, to be the speaker; for I think it proper for a woman to be silent,* and for a man to make answer, before a company of men.

Chariclea gives a fictitious account of herself and Theagenes to Thyamis.

(22) 'But since you have granted to myself a part in the speaking, and are tendering this first token of a gentle heart in trying to make good your claims by persuasion rather than by force; and in particular, because the whole matter in debate is centred upon me; I am constrained to depart from the code observed by myself as well as every maiden, and to reply to our conqueror's inquiry about marriage, though it be before such a great assemblage of men. Here then is our story. We are of Ionian descent, born in the first place to Ephesian parents,* and blessed with the affluence of a family from which children are called by law to service in the priesthood. I was assigned to the service of Artemis, and my brother here to that of Apollo. Our ministration was for one year, and when our term was completed we had to conduct a mission to Delos,* where we were to arrange musical and gymnastic contests, and had then to resign our priestly offices in accordance with the national custom. So a ship was laden with gold and silver and vestments and everything else that would be required for the contests and the public banquet. Our parents stayed at home because of their advanced age and their fear of a sea voyage; but a large number of our citizens either embarked with us on the same ship or made use of boats of their own. When our voyage was all but accomplished we were struck by a sudden upsurge of waves and a violent blast of wind, with scurrying squalls and tornadoes that wildly lashed the sea and bore the ship off her course. The helmsman, quailing before this tremendous turmoil, had abandoned all control of the vessel under stress of the storm, and resigned the steering to Fortune. And so we were swept along by the gale, which blew for seven days and as many nights, till at last we were driven ashore at the place where we were captured by you, and where you have seen the great slaughter that was done when the sailors set upon us as we were feasting in celebration of our coming safe to land; it being their purpose to do away with us for the sake of our riches. Huge was the havoc and destruction of all our people, and likewise of the attackers themselves, as they slew and were slain.* In the end the victory fell to us two, surviving as a pitiful remnant – would that it had been otherwise! – out of all that number, with one

sole benefit granted to us in our disasters, of being brought by some deity into your hands and, when we were in fear of death, being invited to consider a marriage which I am by no means disposed to refuse. For that I, a prisoner, should be deemed worthy of my conqueror's bed overtops the best of good fortune; and that a maiden dedicated to the gods should live united with a prophet's son who ere long, with the deity's assent, is to become a prophet, cannot in any wise appear to be other than the doing of divine Providence. One single thing I ask, and you must grant, Thyamis: allow me first to go to a town, or some place where an altar has been consecrated to Apollo, and there deliver up my priesthood and its insignia. It would be preferable to do this at Memphis when you have regained your office of prophet; in this way our marriage would be more joyfully performed, being connected then with victory, and accomplished as the finishing touch to a successful enterprise. Whether it should take place sooner I leave for your consideration: I only ask that I may first enact the rites that are customary in my country. Indeed, I know that you will consent to this, since you have been dedicated, as you say, from childhood to sacred observances, and hold in reverent regard the worship of the gods.'

(23) With these words she ended her speech, and then began to weep. Everyone present approved her request, and urged Thyamis to do as she suggested, with shouts of their readiness for the move. He also gave his approval, half willing and half unwilling. In his desire for Chariclea he found even the present hour an unending period of delay, while her words, holding him with a charm like that of some siren's voice, compelled his assent; and besides, he connected them with his dream, and felt confident that his marriage would take place at Memphis. He dismissed the assembly after distributing the booty, carrying off for himself a quantity of the choicest goods which the others willingly renounced in his favour.

(24) He issued an order to them that they should be fully prepared to make an advance on Memphis in ten days' time. To the Greeks he assigned the same hut as before, which Cnemon was directed to share with them again: his appointed duty was thenceforth not to be their guard, but to keep them company. And Thyamis not only provided them with food more refined than their present fare, but occasionally brought Theagenes in

to partake of a meal with him, out of respect for the youth's sister. Chariclea herself he had decided not even to see at all frequently, lest the sight of her should add fuel to the flame of his insistent longing and he should be driven perforce to disregard the decisions and declarations that he had made. For these reasons then Thyamis declined to see the girl, feeling it impossible to look upon her without losing his self-control. Cnemon, as soon as all the men had departed by slinking away into different parts of the lagoon, went out for a little distance to look for the herb which he had promised to Theagenes on the previous day.

Theagenes, alarmed by Chariclea's show of willingness to marry Thyamis, is reassured by her.

(25) Meanwhile Theagenes applied this vacant hour to weeping and lamenting. He spoke no word to Chariclea, but continually called upon the gods to witness his grief. When she asked him whether he was mourning their common and accustomed situation, or had met with some new misfortune, he replied: 'And what could be newer, what more nefarious, than a violation of oaths and covenants, than Chariclea forgetting me and consenting to wed another?' 'Fie on such words!' said the girl, 'do not distress me more than do my misfortunes nor, when past events provide you with ample proof of my loyalty in my actions, take words uttered in an emergency as matter for suspicion of me; else you yourself, on the contrary, will appear to be changed, instead of your finding a change in me. I on my part do not deny that I am unfortunate; but no force on earth can shake me in my resolve to preserve my virtue. In one instance alone am I conscious of some immodesty – when I felt my passion for you; but even so it was a lawful feeling. For from the first I gave myself, not as yielding to a lover, but as affianced to a husband, and to this day I have continually kept myself pure from any intimacy even with you. Often I have repulsed your attempts, in order to make sure that the marriage agreed between us from the beginning and pledged with our most binding oaths, should eventually be solemnized according to law. It must therefore be absurd for you to believe that I could prefer the barbarian to the Greek, or the brigand to the man whom I love.' 'Then what was your design in all

that fine harangue of yours?' asked Theagenes. 'To represent me as your brother, indeed, was exceedingly clever; it quite cleared Thyamis' mind of jealousy regarding us, and enabled us to keep each other company without anxiety. I also understood about Ionia and our straying to Delos, how this was all a device to conceal the truth and lead your hearers' minds astray.

(26) 'But to be so ready to consent to this marriage, to enter into the contract in definite terms, and to appoint a time – these steps I was neither able nor wishful to comprehend. I could only pray that I might sink into the earth rather than witness such a conclusion to all my endeavours and hopes for you.' Chariclea embraced Theagenes, gave him countless kisses and bedewed him with her tears as she said: 'What a delight to hear you expressing these fears for me! Those words are clear evidence that you have not slackened in your passion for me beneath the stress of so many misfortunes. But I assure you, Theagenes, that we could not at this moment be holding our conversation if those promises had not been made as you heard. For an impulse of dominant desire, you know, is augmented by a stubborn opposition, but words of compliance, meeting the lover's will half way, will repress the first effervescence of passion and lull to sleep the poignancy of his craving with the sweetness of the promise given. Indeed, I believe that lovers of the rustic sort regard such a pledge as an earnest of success; they take the promise as a proof of a conquest and conduct themselves more calmly, buoyed up by their hopes. So I, anticipating this effect, bestowed myself in those words, entrusting the sequel to the gods and to the spirit who from the first was appointed to foster our love. Often have one or two days brought us ample means of deliverance, and Fortune has provided what an abundance of human counsels could not devise. So you see how in my case I have put off immediate action, and have averted certainties with uncertainties. We must be careful then to maintain this pretence as our defence, my darling, and to divulge it to nobody, not even to Cnemon. He is kindly disposed to us, and a Greek; but he is a prisoner, and more likely if he has occasion, to gratify his master than us. Neither duration of friendship nor obligation of kinship is there, to give us an absolute guarantee of his loyalty to our interest; and so, should he ever suspect something and get an inkling of the truth about us, it must be denied at once.

For falsehood can be honourable when it assists the speaker
without doing any real injury to the hearers.'

*On the approach of a hostile force of bandits, Chariclea is
imprisoned in a secret cavern.*

(27) While Chariclea was making these and similar suggestions for their best advantage, Cnemon came running to them in
great haste, and with a look in his eyes that attested much
perturbation. 'Theagenes,' he said, 'I have come with that herb
for you: apply it and cure your sores. But we must hold ourselves
prepared for further wounds and renewed slaughter.' Theagenes
begged him to state his meaning in clearer terms, but he said:
'This is no moment for listening; there is danger of words being
overtaken by deeds. Follow me with all speed, and bring
Chariclea too along with you.' He then took them both and
brought them to Thyamis, whom he found furbishing his helmet
and whetting a javelin. 'This is indeed the moment to be looking
to your arms,' said Cnemon; 'now put on yours, and order the
others to do likewise. A larger body of enemies than you ever
met before is upon us: at so little distance are they that, when I
spied them clambering over the ridge near by, I ran to you to
give you warning of their attack, not once slackening my pace
but also notifying as many men as I could in my passage to you
here that they must make themselves ready.'

(28) At these words Thyamis leapt to his feet and asked again
and again: 'Where is Chariclea?' seeming to fear more for her
than for himself. When Cnemon pointed to where she stood
shyly by the doorway, he said to him aside: 'Cnemon, take this
woman away to the cavern in which our treasure has been
stored for security: lead her down into it, my friend, and after
closing its mouth as usual with the block, come to us as quickly
as you can. The fighting shall be our concern.* He then ordered
his henchman to fetch a victim to be offered as a sacrifice to the
gods of the country before they began the battle. Cnemon went
to carry out his order, and led away Chariclea, who with much
lamentation kept turning back to Theagenes; and so Cnemon
deposited her in the cavern. This place was not a work of nature,
like so many that become hollowed out of themselves either
above or under the ground, but one wrought by the brigands'
skill in imitating nature; it was the mining of Egyptian hands

that had there elaborately scooped out a safe storehouse for
their booty.

(29) It had been contrived after this fashion: it had a narrow,
gloomy entrance situated beneath the door of a secret chamber,
in such a way that the threshold stone served also as a door to
the downward passage in case of need, and easily fell into
position or opened up; and the space just beyond it was divided
irregularly into a number of winding tunnels. The paths and
cuttings that led to the inmost recesses in some parts kept to
separate ways with artful meanderings; while in some they
crossed each other and became intertwined like tree roots until
they converged and opened out in the depths to a single spacious
area, over which a dim light was shed through a small fissure
close to the surface of the lagoon. Into this place Cnemon
brought down Chariclea, leading her by the hand all the way, as
he was acquainted with it, to the furthermost part of the cavern:
there he gave her his best encouragement, and promised to come
and visit her with Theagenes in the evening; he would not allow
him, he said, to engage in combat with the enemy, but would
see that he made his escape from the battle. Chariclea spoke no
word as though mortally wounded by this mischance, and bereft
of life by the loss of Theagenes. Leaving her there in a breathless
and speechless state, he ascended from the cavern, and putting
to the threshold stone he shed some tears both for his own hard
duty and for the fate of her whom he had all but buried alive,
and had thus consigned Chariclea, brightest of human beauties,
to night and darkness. He ran back to Thyamis, and found him
all afire for the fray and clad, himself and Theagenes like him,
in shining armour. The leader was addressing the men already
mustered around him in words calculated to work them up to a
height of furious ardour. Standing in their midst he said: 'Fellow-
soldiers, I hardly think it necessary to exhort you at any length,
when you yourselves need no reminder, being ever wont to
regard warfare as your life. Moreover, this unexpected attack of
the enemy precludes speaking at any length. To see the enemy
moving into action, and not to aim a swift counterstroke in
retaliation, is an absolute dereliction of one's duty. We know
that it is no mere question of defending women and children – a
reason indeed which alone may often suffice to spur one on to
battle – for we shall now be enabled to hold it of less account,
as also all the profit to be gained by victory; our fight being

rather for very existence, for our own lives. A conflict between brigands never ends with a covenant or a treaty, but of necessity one must either survive as victor or die as vanquished. So, in face of our bitterest foes, let us whet the edge of our spirits and our powers, and come to grips with them.'

Thyamis, construing his dream differently, in distraction goes to the cavern and there kills a woman whom he supposes to be Chariclea.

(30) At the end of this speech he looked about him for his henchman, and called him repeatedly by his name, Thermouthis. When the man nowhere appeared Thyamis poured out angry threats against him and betook himself at a run to his boat. The fighting had already broken out, and in the distance it could be seen how the dwellers on the farthest part of the lagoon, near to its inflow, were being overpowered. For the aggressors had set on fire the boats and huts of those who were being struck down or were taking to flight: the flames from these fires were blown far and wide over the adjacent swamp and devoured the huge, compact mass of reeds growing in it, so that an inexpressible, unbearable blaze flared full in men's eyes, while the loud noise of its crackling smote their ears. Every form of fighting was in operation and was resounding there: the inhabitants withstood the onslaught with their utmost zeal and vigour, but the enemy had an overwhelming advantage against them, both in their numbers and in the surprise of their attack, and were killing some on the land and sinking others, together with their boats and their dwellings in the lagoon. From all these happenings a confused rumbling arose in the air, as the battle raged at once ashore and afloat, men killing and being killed,* reddening the lagoon with blood, and grappling with perils of fire and of water. When Thyamis saw and heard these things he reflected on the dream in which he had beheld Isis, and the temple all lit up and full of sacrifices; and supposing it to have signified the present events he construed his vision in a sense quite contrary to what he conceived before. That he 'would have and not have' Chariclea meant that she was destined to be taken from him by war, and his slaying and not wounding her meant that it would be with the sword and not by the usage of Aphrodite. Many were the reproaches that he uttered against the goddess for

being so deceptive, and great his indignation that another man
should gain possession of Chariclea. He ordered the men about
him to halt for a moment, telling them that they must remain in
that spot and continue to fight by lurking in ambush round
about the islet, and from amongst its surrounding marshes
making surprise sorties, well content if in this way they could
hold out against the great numbers of the enemy. He himself, as
though he were going in search of Thermouthis and to offer up
prayers to their guardian deities, permitted no one to accompany
him, and then turned his steps in mad distraction to the cavern
cell. It is hard to withhold the barbarian temperament from any
course on which it has set out: when it despairs of its own
survival, it is wont first to destroy all beloved beings,* either
fondly believing that it will rejoin them after death, or wishing
to rescue them from the danger of outrage at an enemy's hands.
Such thoughts as these caused Thyamis to forget all his immediate concerns, even when the enemy had closed in around him
like a net. Frantic with love and jealousy and wrath, he ran with
all speed to the cavern and leapt down into it, uttering many
loud cries in the Egyptian tongue. Just at the entrance he became
aware of a woman's voice speaking to him in Greek. Following
the guidance of the sound he came up to her, seized her head
with his left hand, and drove his sword into her bosom close to
the breasts.

(31) Thus cruelly was she struck down, as she sent forth a last
pitiful shriek. Then he ran back, closed the doorway with the
stone, and covered it with a small heap of earth. 'There you
have my betrothal gift!' he said, weeping. When he returned to
the boats he found his men just resolving on flight as the enemy
were soon to be close upon them; while Thermouthis had arrived
with a victim which he was holding ready for the sacrifice.
Thyamis reproached him sharply, and said that he had forestalled him by offering up the finest of sacrifices. He then
embarked in his boat with two others, Thermouthis and his
oarsman; for the boats on the lagoon cannot carry more persons,
being rudely hollowed in one piece from a stout tree trunk.
Theagenes and Cnemon set out together in another boat, and all
the rest followed likewise in their several vessels. When they had
rowed a little distance from the island, and voyaged round it
instead of away from it, they ceased rowing and ranged their
boats in line of battle, so as to meet the enemy front to front.

But on seeing their mere nearness to the foe, and finding that the dashing of oars alone was more than they could stomach they all took to flight at first view of the enemy, some even being unable to bear the sound of their battle-cry. Theagenes and Cnemon retreated also, not, however, giving way in the main to fear. Thyamis alone – partly no doubt because he was ashamed to flee, but also perhaps because he could not bear to outlive Chariclea – dashed in among the enemy.

Thyamis is captured alive by the hostile bandits.

(32) As they were in the act of closing in combat someone called out: 'This is the man Thyamis; have a care, everybody!' Immediately the enemy turned their boats to form a circle round him on every side. He was defending himself, wounding some and slaying others with his spear, when a marvel of marvels occurred: not a single one of them either thrust or slashed at the man with his sword, but each endeavoured all he could to take Thyamis alive. He held his own to the utmost, until a number of them together seized hold of him and snatched away his spear; he was also deprived of his henchman, who after battling gallantly at his side had received what seemed to be a mortal wound. Giving way to despair, this man had plunged into the lagoon and, being an expert swimmer, came up to the surface beyond the range of missiles; then, with some difficulty, he swam away to the swamp where, moreover, nobody thought to follow in his pursuit. For now the enemy had possession of Thyamis, and regarded the capture of this single person as a complete victory. Though they had suffered the loss of so many comrades, they delighted more in escorting the slayer of their friends than they sorrowed for their decease. So true it is that brigands esteem riches more highly even than the very lives of men, and the words 'friendship' and 'kinship' have meaning for them only in respect of their profit. Thus it was in the case of these people.

(33) They were in fact a part of the band which had fled before Thyamis and his troop near the river mouth of Hercules. Annoyed at being deprived of the property of others, and as bitterly aggrieved by the loss of the booty as if it had belonged to them, they went and collected at home those of their body who had remained there, and made similar appeals to the

surrounding villages, offering them a fair and equal share in the
spoils that should be taken. They then took the lead in the raid
on Thyamis whom they were now capturing alive for a particular reason. He had a brother Petosiris in Memphis who,
although his junior had treacherously and against tradition
deprived Thyamis of the prophet's priestly office. When he
learnt that his elder brother was a chief of brigands, he feared
that Thyamis might one day seize an opportunity of attacking
him, or else that time might bring disclosure of his treachery;
and besides, he was becoming aware that in the minds of most
people he was under suspicion, as there was nowhere any sign
of Thyamis, of having done away with him. He therefore
proclaimed by messengers sent to the villages of the brigands
that large rewards of money and cattle would be given to those
who brought in Thyamis alive. Prevailed on by these offers, the
brigands did not allow even the ebullience of battle to expel the
memory of the gain to be got, but as soon as he was recognized
they took him alive, at the cost of many deaths. They bound
him and conveyed him ashore, having chosen by lot one half of
their number to be his guard, while he protested against their
apparent humanity, more exasperated by his bonds than by
death. The rest of the brigands went off to the island, expecting
to find there the treasures and spoils that they were seeking.
They ran about all over the place, leaving no part unsearched,
but could discover nothing of what they had hoped for, or only
some trifling remnants that had not been hidden underground
but left lying near the cave. They then set fire to the cabins. As
nightfall was approaching and gave warning against lingering
on the island, lest they should be surprised there by the fugitives
from the fighting, they departed to their kinsfolk at home.

BOOK 2

Theagenes laments the apparent loss of Chariclea in the foray, but is assured by Cnemon that she is alive.

(1) The island was being ravaged thus by fire; but Theagenes and Cnemon, so long as the sun showed above the earth, did not observe the calamity, because the aspect of fire is dimmed in the day time by the rays of the Sun-god shedding their light upon it. When, however, he was setting and drawing on the night, the blaze regained its brilliance in unsubdued vigour, and became visible over an enormous distance. Then the two men, emboldened by the night, peered out from the swamp and saw the island clearly overrun now by the fire. Theagenes smote his head and tore his hair, saying: 'Away now with life, on this day! Let all be brought to conclusion, to dissolution – fears, perils, cares, hopes and loves! Lost is Chariclea; Theagenes has perished! In vain, ill-fated wretch, did I turn coward and sink to unmanly flight, that I might save myself, sweet girl, for you! Nay, no longer will I seek my safety, when you, my dearest, are laid low – not by the common rule of nature – O the bitterness of it! – nor relinquishing your life in the arms that you had wished to hold you. Instead, you have fallen a victim, alas, to fire; such were the strange bridal torches* that the deity lit for you. Squandered is the choicest beauty amongst mankind, so that not a relic of that unfeigned loveliness remains upon her body, now that it is but a corpse. O the cruelty, O the unspeakable malignity of the divine will! I am deprived even of the last embracements, bereft of the farewell, lifeless kisses!'

(2) As he spoke these words and looked for his sword, Cnemon quickly thrust it away from his grasp, saying: 'What is this, Theagenes? Why bewail her who is alive? Chariclea lives, and is safe and sound; have no more fear.' 'That is a tale for idiots or children,' he replied; 'you have undone me, in robbing me of the sweetest death.' Then Cnemon, speaking now on oath, gave him a full account of the order issued by Thyamis, of the cavern, of his own descent into it, and of the nature of the excavation, which precluded any danger of the depths being reached by the fire, baffled as it would be by the countless

windings of the tunnels. At these words Theagenes breathed
again: he hastened away to the island, beholding in his mind his
absent love, and picturing the cavern as his nuptial chamber,
unaware of the lamentation that he was to make in that place.
So they set forward with all speed in their boat, rowing
themselves across the water; for their ferryman in the first clash
of the fight had darted away, scared by the shouting as though
shot off from a spring-board. Thus they went, diverging from a
straight course, first to one side, then to the other, because in
their inexperience they failed to pull together in their strokes,
and were also buffeted by an adverse wind.

*Theagenes and Cnemon enter the cavern in search of Chariclea,
and stumble upon the dead body of a woman.*

(3) But their fervent resolution overcame their lack of skill,
and with great effort and sweat they brought their boat to the
shore of the island and ran up as fast as they could to the cabins.
These they found already burnt to ashes, and traceable only by
their sites; the threshold stone, however, that concealed the
cavern stood out clearly to their view. For the wind, bearing in
that direction, had blown upon the cabins which, constructed of
plaited reeds, and those too of the marsh-grown kind, were
burnt up by the sudden sweep of its passage, and the area where
they had stood now appeared to be almost level ground. The
blaze had quickly died down and subsided into cinders: most of
the embers had been scattered by the strong gusts of wind, and
the small remainder had been almost entirely quenched on the
spot by the draught and had been sufficiently cooled to be
walked upon. The two searchers discovered some half-burnt
torches and ignited some remnants of the reeds; they then
opened the entrance to the cavern and ran down, Cnemon
leading the way. When they had descended a little he cried out.
'O Zeus, what is this? We are undone! Chariclea is destroyed!'
He dropped his torch on the ground, causing it to go out; with
his hands held over his eyes he went down on his knees and
wailed. Theagenes, as if someone had forced him forward, fell
down on the woman's body lying there, clasped it tightly and
enfolded it so completely in his arms as to seem incorporate
with it. Cnemon, observing him totally absorbed in his grief and
overwhelmed by the calamity, from fear lest he should do

himself some mischief, covertly withdrew his sword from its sheath slung at his side, and leaving him alone ran back to relight the torches.

(4) Meanwhile Theagenes was crying out in an agony of tragic distress: 'O unbearable blow! O god-sent disaster! What insatiable Fury can it be that has wildly revelled in our ruin, ejecting us in exile from our native land, subjecting us to perils of the sea and perils of pirate gangs, delivering us up to brigands, and despoiling us again and again of our possessions? A single one of all these yet remained to me, and it has now been snatched away: Chariclea has perished, stricken, she my dearest, by the hand of an enemy, holding fast, it is plain, to her virtue, and seeking to save herself, alas, for me! Yet, after all, the hapless girl has perished, having had no benefit herself of her maiden bloom, nor granted me any enjoyment of it. Ah, sweetheart, do but speak to me the usual last words! Lay on me now your behest, with what little breath still is in you! Alas, you are speechless; silence has hold of those prophetic lips which told of things divine; darkness has enveloped the torchbearer, and chaos the ministrant of the sacred shrine. Light has left the eyes which dazzled all men with their beauty, and which her assassin did not see, I am most certain. But what am I to call you? Bride? But you can have no wedding. Wife? But you have known no marriage bed. Then it must be the sweetest name of all, Chariclea! Ah, Chariclea, be assured; you have a faithful lover. In a little time you will have me again. See, I will offer up to you as libation the flow from my own wounding, and will pour out my own blood so dear to you. This cavern shall be our unintended tomb; at least we shall be allowed our union after death, even if the deity has not vouchsafed it to us in our lives.'

(5) As he was yet speaking he reached with his hand to draw his sword: not finding it, he cried out: 'Cnemon, you have destroyed me! And besides, you have done injury to Chariclea, by depriving her this second time of her greatest pleasure, our companionship.' While he was thus speaking his mind, from the depths of the cavern the sound of a voice seemed to be heard calling 'Theagenes!' He, no whit perturbed, made answer saying: 'I will come, dearest soul; clearly you are still moving about the earth, partly because you could not bear to be separated from that body of yours from which you were by violence expelled, and partly perhaps because owing to your unburied state you

are excluded by the infernal shades.'* By this time Cnemon had
arrived with lighted torches; then again the same sound could
be heard, and the call it gave was 'Theagenes!' Cnemon cried
out: 'Ye gods, is it not the voice of Chariclea? I think she is yet
alive, Theagenes; for it comes from the farthest recess, from the
part of the cave where I know that I left her, this voice that
strikes my ear.' 'Oh, cease deluding me,' said Theagenes, 'as so
often you have done before.' 'Well, then, in deluding you I
delude myself no less,' said Cnemon, 'if we should find this
woman lying here to be Chariclea.' With that he turned over the
body to see its face, and as he looked: 'What is this,' he cried,
'ye wonder-working gods? It is the face of Thisbe!' He stepped
backwards and stood there, trembling all over and
dumbfounded.

*Cnemon recognizes the dead woman as Thisbe, and they are
happily joined by Chariclea.*

(6) At Cnemon's words Theagenes recovered his breath and
turned his thoughts to fresh hope. He roused Cnemon as he was
swooning away, and begged him to lead him on with all speed
to Chariclea. After a brief pause Cnemon came to himself, and
began again to examine the corpse. It was in truth Thisbe, and
he recognized by its hilt the sword, which had fallen out at her
side after Thyamis, having dealt his stroke, in his rage and haste
had left it in the wound. A tablet also was seen protruding from
her bosom beneath the armpit: this he picked up, and then tried
to make out some of the writing upon it. But Theagenes
prevented him with importunate insistence, saying: 'Let us first
retrieve my dearest one, unless some deity even now is making
game of us. We can look into this writing later.' Cnemon agreed
and, taking along the tablet and picking up the sword, they
hurried away to Chariclea. She, having clambered up with hands
as well as feet to the light, came running to Theagenes and clung
round his neck. 'I hold you, Theagenes!' and 'I have you alive,
Chariclea!' they said to each other, again and again, and ended
by falling both at once to the ground, where they lay clasping
one another in a mute embrace, yet seeming to have become but
one person, and were at a point very near to death. True indeed
it is that an excess of joy will often turn to anguish, and an
immoderate pleasure will beget a self-induced pain. So those

two, surviving against all hope, were now endangered; until Cnemon by scraping opened up a spring from which came a trickle of water. Collecting some of it in the hollow of his hands, he brought it to them and, by sprinkling it on their faces and continually stroking their noses, he restored them to their senses.

(7) Then they, suddenly finding themselves prostrate in attitudes so different from those in which they met each other, at once stood upright and blushed – Chariclea especially – for shame that Cnemon should have witnessed such a scene, and besought his pardon. But he smiled at them, and to put them in blither mood he said: 'Your behaviour only merits praise, in my judgment and in that of anyone who, having wrestled with Love, has been pleasingly defeated in the struggle, and has been temperate in taking the inevitable tosses of that god. One thing, however, Theagenes, I could not commend – but was deeply ashamed, in truth, to see – your throwing yourself upon that strange woman, with whom you had no sort of connection, and abjectly bewailing her; and that too when I earnestly insisted that your beloved was still among the living.' 'O Cnemon,' replied Theagenes, 'do cease traducing me to Chariclea, whom I was bewailing in the body of another, supposing that it was she who lay there. But, since some god has graciously shown us what a mistake that was, it is time that you called to mind the surpassing manliness that led you in advance of me to bewail my lot, and then take to your heels on your unexpected recognition of the corpse, as though at the sight of spirits on the stage – you, an armed man, sword in hand, fleeing from a woman, and her a dead body! You, the stalwart Attic infantryman!'

Cnemon relates more about Thisbe to Theagenes and Chariclea.

(8) At these words they laughed, in a somewhat curt, constrained manner, and that not without some tears: indeed, in such a sorry plight as theirs, lamentation could not but claim the larger part. After a short pause Chariclea, chafing her cheek below the ear, said: 'Happy to my mind is she who has been bewailed by Theagenes, perhaps also kissed by him, as Cnemon tells, whoever she may really be. But – if you will not suspect me of being a little piqued by love – who pray was the fortunate person found worthy of Theagenes' tears, and how came it that

you kissed an unknown woman in mistake for me? I should like to be told this, if you happen to know.' 'You will be surprised,' he answered, 'but in fact it was Thisbe, so Cnemon here says – that Athenian woman, the harp-player, and the hatcher of plots against him and against Demaenete.' Chariclea was astonished at his words, and said: 'How was it likely, Cnemon, that a woman from the middle of Greece should be transported into a remote corner of Egypt, as though by a stage-machine?* And how was it that we did not see her as we came down here?' 'Those are questions that I cannot answer,' replied Cnemon; 'but what I do know about her I will tell you. When Demaenete, after she had been beguiled, had flung herself into the pit, and my father had reported the occurrence to the people, in the first place he obtained their exoneration; and he managed to procure from the people the grant of my recall and of his making a voyage in search of me. Then Thisbe, gaining freedom from occupation by his preoccupation, was at liberty to offer herself and her art for hire at banquets. In time she won a greater repute than Arsinoe – whose flute-playing was in slow measure – through the tripping rhythms of her own harp-playing and delicate singing to the lute: she unwittingly aroused against herself an intense jealousy in her comrade, and still more when a merchant of Naucratis,* a man almost made of gold, named Nausicles, took her to his arms. For in doing so he was casting aside Arsinoe, with whom he had been intimate before; but he had seen her cheeks bulged out by her fluting and forced by her vigorous blowing to protrude in an unseemly way to the length of her nose, while her eyes all ablaze, were starting from their proper position.*

(9) 'Swelling with rancour at this treatment and inflamed with jealousy, Arsinoe went to the kinsfolk of Demaenete and informed them of the trap set for her by Thisbe, partly from what she had herself surmised and partly from Thisbe's disclosures to her in the way of companionship. So the relatives of Demaenete combined to attack my father, and with heavy bribes put up the most skilful pleaders to appear as his accusers. They clamoured that Demaenete had been done to death untried and uncondemned; they made out that the adultery was invented to screen her murder, and demanded that the adulterer be produced either alive or dead, or insisted that at least his name should be given. Finally, they called for Thisbe to be put to the torture.*

My father undertook to hand her over, but was unable to do so, since she, foreseeing this proposal while the case was being drawn up, by arrangement with the merchant had made good her escape. The people were so provoked that, although they did not convict him of murder, since his deposition was deemed to be a full and true account, they pronounced him to be an accomplice in the plot against Demaenete and in my unjust banishment, and condemned him to expulsion from the city and confiscation of his property. Such was the joy that he had of his venture upon a second marriage. And thus did the villainous Thisbe sail away from Athens, and has now met this punishment before my eyes. That is all that I have been able to learn from the report of a certain Anticles at Aegina with whom I later voyaged to Egypt, to see if I could find Thisbe somewhere in Naucratis, bring her back to Athens, and not only dispel the suspicions against my father, but also demand the punishment of her machinations against us all. And now here I am, a sharer in your ordeal: the cause of this, and the manner of it, and all that I have undergone in the meantime, you shall hear later on. But how Thisbe came to be in the cavern, and by whose hand she was killed, will require an intimation, I should say, from some deity.

(10) 'But, if you agree, let us examine the tablet that we have found by her bosom; it may well be that we shall get some further information from it.' They agreed, and he opened the leaves of the tablet* and began to read the writing as follows: 'To Cnemon, my master, from his enemy and his avenger, Thisbe. First I give you good tidings of the death of Demaenete, brought about by me for your sake; how – if you will admit me to your presence – I will recount to you in person. Next, I inform you that I have been in this island now for ten days, a captive of one of the brigands dwelling here who boasts of being the henchman of the chief of their band. He also keeps me in confinement, not permitting me so much as to peep out of doors, and imposing this restriction, in his own words, out of kindness to me but, as I conclude, for fear of somebody carrying me off. Yet, by the grace of some god, I have seen you, master, passing by, and recognized you; and I have secretly dispatched to you this tablet by means of the old woman who lives with me. I have bidden her deliver it into the hands of the good-looking Greek who is besides a friend of the Commander. Come then, rescue

me from the brigands' hands, and receive your own little maidservant. Save me, if you will be so good; and understand that
the wrong which I seemed to do was done under duress, while
the vengeance that I took on your enemy was the work of my
own free will. But if you are filled with an implacable wrath,
expend it upon me to your heart's content: only let me return to
your service, even if I should have to die. For it would be better
to perish by your hand, and be granted a Greek funeral, than to
endure a life more grievous than death, and a barbarian's
endearments, more baneful to an Athenian woman than his
enmity.'

(11) Such was the message that came from Thisbe in her
tablet. Then Cnemon said: 'Thisbe, you have done well to die,
and to be yourself the informant of your own misfortunes by
delivering the relation of them to us through the very wound of
which you died. Thus an avenging Fury, it would seem, has
driven you from land to land, not ceasing to ply the scourge of
justice until I, chancing to be in Egypt, am here the injured
person made a witness of your punishment. But what, I wonder
was the further artful scheme which you were devising against
me in writing this letter, and which justice has been quick to
balk of execution? For I, even when you lie dead, still hold you
suspect, and greatly fear that the death of Demaenete is a mere
fiction, and that I was deceived by those who reported it, while
you came far across the ocean to enact even in Egypt another
scene of Attic drama for my undoing.' 'Come, cease overplaying
the unmanly fellow,' said Theagenes, 'with your apprehensions
of spectres and shades. For you cannot say that I too, and these
eyes of mine, have been bewitched by her; I have no part in your
play. Now, in simple fact, she lies there, a lifeless corpse, so on
that score be absolutely reassured, Cnemon; but who could have
done you the good turn of killing her, or when was she brought
here? These are questions that leave me extremely perplexed
and astonished.' 'There is much of which I can see no explanation,' said Cnemon; but, all things considered, her slayer is
Thyamis, if we are to judge by the sword that we found close to
the mortal wound: I recognize it as his by this notable feature of
the hilt, an ivory carving of an eagle.' 'And could you say,'
asked Theagenes, 'how and with what motive he committed this
murder?' 'How could I know that?' he replied. 'This cavern did
not transform me into a soothsayer, as the sanctuary of Pytho

might.'* Suddenly Theagenes and Chariclea wailed aloud and cried out in mournful tones: 'O Pytho! O Delphi!' Cnemon was astonished, and could not guess what it was that so affected them at hearing the name of Pytho.

Thermouthis, henchman of Thyamis, comes to the cave in search of Thisbe, finds her corpse, and meets Theagenes, Chariclea and Cnemon.

(12) While they were thus occupied, Thermouthis, the henchman of Thyamis, after being wounded in the fight had made his escape by swimming to land. At nightfall he happened upon a boat that was drifting through the swamp from among wreckage, and embarking in it he made with all speed for the island in search of Thisbe. She, a few days before, as she was being taken along by her merchant Nausicles, had been carried off from him by Thermouthis, who had ambushed him in narrow pass of the mountain range. When Thermouthis, amid the tumult of the battle that raged as the enemy attacked, was sent by Thyamis to fetch the sacrificial victim, he took her out of the reach of missiles and, purposing to preserve her for himself, brought her down unobserved into the cavern; and there in his distraction and haste he left her at a point just within the entrance. There, in the spot where she had been thrust inside, she remained for the moment, from fear of the perils all about her and from ignorance of the passages leading to the cavern; and there Thyamis came upon her and slew her, Thisbe, supposing her to be Chariclea. To this same woman hastened Thermouthis, in the belief that she had safely evaded the danger of the battle: as soon as he had landed on the island he ran as fast as he could to the cabins. These were now no more than ashes, and he had difficulty in detecting by its stone the entrance to the cavern. He lit some reeds that happened to be left still smouldering, and ran down with all speed calling out Thisbe's name – the only word of Greek that he knew. At the sight of her prostrate body he stood for some length of time dumbfounded till finally he became aware of a sound of voices borne like a murmur from the hollow depths of the cavern; it came from Theagenes and Cnemon talking together, and he surmised that they were the murderers of Thisbe. He was perplexed as to what he should do: his brigand's fierceness and barbarian's rage exasperated

now by the frustration of his love, urged him to close there and then with the supposed authors of the deed; but his lack of armour and sword constrained him against his will to refrain and control himself.

(13) It seemed to him better not to meet them as an enemy but, if he could provide himself with some means of defence, to go then and set about his enemies. With this resolve he halted near Theagenes and his companions, darting wild, wrathful glances from eyes that betrayed the purpose lurking in his heart. When they beheld a naked man suddenly appearing before them wounded and with blood-stained face, Chariclea withdrew into the farther recesses of the cavern, partly, no doubt, as a precaution, but more of course from virgin modesty at the sight of a nudity so indecorous. Cnemon slunk back a little way: he recognized Thermouthis, whose unlooked-for presence suggested that he was bent on some desperate act. But his aspect did not scare Theagenes; it rather provoked him to brandish his sword at the man, in readiness to strike if he should attempt any affront. 'Stop, man,' he said, 'or you will be struck; that you have not been struck already is because I partly recognized you, and because your purpose in coming here is still dubious.' Thermouthis threw himself down before him, entreating him in supplication born of the moment, rather than his mood, and beseeching Cnemon to come to his aid. He said he could rightly claim to be spared his life at their hands, earnestly protesting that he had done them no wrong; that he had always been friendly to them up to the previous day, and had come to them now as his friends.

(14) Moved to pity by these words, Cnemon drew near to him, raised him up from clasping the knees* of Theagenes, and asked him repeatedly where Thyamis was. He then gave a full account of how Thyamis got to grips with the enemy; how rushing into their midst he fought without sparing either them or himself; how he continued to kill whoever came in his way, but was himself safeguarded by an order directing everyone to spare his life. He finally stated that he was unable to tell what had become of him: he himself was wounded, and swam away to land; and he had now come to the cavern in search of Thisbe. They asked him what interest he had in Thisbe, or how he had got hold of her, that he should be searching for her. Thermouthis explained this also, by relating how he had carried her off from

some merchants, had fallen madly in love with her, and had kept her hidden all the time until, on the attack of the enemy, he had taken her down into the cavern. He now found her slain by some persons of whom he had no knowledge but whom he would much like to discover, that he might learn the reason of their action. Then Cnemon, speaking with extreme earnestness, so eager was he to clear himself of possible suspicion, said 'Thyamis is her slayer', and showed him as evidence the sword which they had found by the body of the slain. When Thermouthis saw it still dripping with her blood – the steel spitting it yet warm from the recent slaughter – he recognized it as Thyamis' sword, and heaved a deep and long-drawn sigh. At a loss to comprehend the truth of the affair, smitten with misted sight and muteness, he crept up to the mouth of the cave, and coming beside the dead woman he laid his head upon her bosom and said: 'O Thisbe!' – and repeatedly spoke the name, and nothing more, till he began to curtail it somewhat, and so, his voice gradually failing, insensibly he fell asleep.

(15) The thoughts of Theagenes and Chariclea, and of Cnemon also, turned quickly to the general state of their concerns. While they seemed wishful to give this some consideration, yet the multitude of their sufferings in the past, the perplexities of their present misfortunes, and the uncertainty of what the future held for them in prospect, obscured the light of reason in their minds. For a great while they looked at one another; each of them, expecting someone else to speak and being disappointed, turned eyes to the ground, and then lifted head again to take fresh breath and relieve emotion with a sigh. At length Cnemon lay down on the ground; Theagenes sank down on a rock; and Chariclea flung herself upon him. For no little time they repelled the onset of sleep, in their desire to settle on some expedient for their present straits; but yielding to faintness and exhaustion they obeyed, despite themselves, the law of nature, as the excess of their grief caused them to slide into a pleasing slumber. Thus it is that at times even the intelligence of the soul is content to come to terms with the sensations of the body.

(16) When they had snatched a little sleep – just enough to close up smoothly the rims of their eyelids – Chariclea was visited by a dream of this tenor: a man with shaggy hair, stealthy looks and blood-stained hand struck at her with his sword and

cut out her right eye. At that moment she screamed and she
called to Theagenes, telling him that her eye had been plucked
away. He turned to her in the instant of hearing her call, and
was deeply distressed by her suffering, as though he shared even
the sensations that she had from visions in sleep. She clapped
her hand to her face and felt it all over, searching for the feature
that she had lost in her dream. Finding that it was a dream she
said: 'It was a dream. I have my eye. Do not be alarmed,
Theagenes.' Hearing this, Theagenes breathed again and said:
'How fortunate that you have preserved those rays of sunshine!
But tell me, what was it that happened to you? What was that
sudden fright about yourself?' 'A violent, reckless man,' she
said, 'undeterred by even your irresistible strength, made a
savage assault on me, sword in hand, as I rested upon your
knees, and I thought that he robbed me of my right eye. Would
that it had been a waking reality and no dream, Theagenes, that
I beheld!' 'Fie on such words!' he said, and asked her why she
said that. 'Because it were better,' she replied, 'that I should be
deprived of one of my eyes than be anxious on your account;
for I greatly fear that the dream points to you, whom I have
come to regard as my eye, my soul, my all.' 'No more of that,'
said Cnemon, who had been roused from sleep by Chariclea's
first outcry and had overheard everything. 'To my mind the
dream is plainly to be construed in another way. Tell me, are
your parents still alive?' She told him that they were and asked:
'And what if they should be?' 'Well then,' he said, 'you must
take it that your father has died; and this is how I make it out.
We owe our coming forth into this life on earth and our sharing
in the light of day to those who begat us; so it is likely that our
dreams subtly present our father and mother in our wedded pair
of eyes – our luminous sense, enabling our perception of the
visible world.'* 'A grievous meaning, this also,' said Chariclea.
'Yet I would rather it were true than the other. May the tripod
of your oracle* prove to be the more accurate, and I a false
prophetess!' 'So it will turn out; only have faith,' said Cnemon;
'but we, in truth, seem to be dreaming, since we inquire into
visions and apparitions instead of advancing some kind of
scheme for our own future – and that too while we are free to
do so in the absence of that Egyptian' (meaning Thermouthis)
'while he is refashioning and lamenting loves that are dead and
gone.'

It is decided that Cnemon and Thermouthis shall go in search of Thyamis.

(17) Theagenes then spoke up. 'Well, Cnemon,' he said, 'since some deity has linked you with us, and made you a fellow-voyager through our misfortunes, you shall be the opener of our consultation. You have a good knowledge of this region and of languages, whereas our wits are altogether too addled to devise what ought to be done; for we are overwhelmed by a huger surge of troubles.' After a short pause Cnemon answered him thus: 'Of troubles, Theagenes, it is doubtful who can claim to have the larger share, because the deity has deluged me also with a profusion of disasters. But since you both request me, as your senior, to speak of our present situation, this island, as you see, is deserted, having nobody on it but ourselves. Of gold, silver and apparel it has an abundance; many articles are stored here in this cavern, stolen from you and stripped from others by Thyamis and his men; but of grain and other provisions not the merest hint remains. There is a danger, if we stay on here, of perishing from starvation, or of perishing in an onslaught either of the enemy, should they return to the attack, or of the band with whom we were, if they should join up together again and, mindful of the treasure hidden here, come in search of this wealth. In that event we should inevitably be destroyed out of hand, or exposed to their maltreatment, if some humaner feeling prevailed. For in general these herdsmen are a faithless race, and more so than ever now, when they are deprived of the leader who restrained their minds to more temperate measures. We must therefore abandon this island, and avoid it as we would some snare or jail, having first dispatched Thermouthis on the alleged errand of inquiring far and wide for any news that he may gather of Thyamis. For it will be easier for us, when we are by ourselves, to consider and carry out our plan of action; and besides, it will be well to rid ourselves of a man who is by nature unreliable and a brigand of quarrelsome temper; one who is also inclined to have some suspicion of us on account of Thisbe, and who will surely not rest until he can find an opportunity of discomfiting us.'

(18) His advice was approved, and they resolved to act upon it. They advanced to the mouth of the cavern – for they reckoned that it was now day time – and roused up Thermouthis, who

was wholly sunk in slumber. They explained to him as much as
was suitable of the plans that they had made, and found it easy
to persuade his somewhat volatile mind. They laid the body of
Thisbe in a cavity, and heaped over it, instead of earth, some of
the ashes from the cabins; and they performed all the customary
funeral rites that were possible on the occasion, paying the
tribute of their tears and lamentations in default of the full
honours of the traditional offerings. Then they dispatched
Thermouthis on the errand that they had arranged for him. He
went off on his way for a short distance, and then turned back.
He said that he would not travel alone, nor would venture upon
such a dangerous investigation, unless Cnemon agreed to bear a
share in the undertaking. Theagenes, observing that Cnemon
shrank from this proposal – for, while reporting what the
Egyptian had said, he was obviously in great trepidation –
remarked: 'I see; you are sturdy enough in opinion, but rather
feeble in resolution: I have noted some signs of your character,
and most clearly in this present instance. Come now, whet the
edge of your spirit, and raise your mind to more manly thoughts.
At this moment it seems necessary to agree to his terms, that he
may not conceive some suspicion of our intended flight, and to
accompany him for the first part of his journey. Surely there is
no danger in going along with an unarmed man, when one has
a sword in one's hand and armour on one's body, and then, at
a favourable moment, quietly giving him the slip and coming to
join us at an agreed place. Let us agree, if you like, on some
village near by, which may be known to you as a civilized one.'
Cnemon thought well of his suggestion, and mentioned a village
named Chemmis, a wealthy place and populous, built along the
banks of the Nile on high ground, so as to be fortified against
the herdsmen. The distance, he said, after one crossed the
swamp, was a little under a hundred furlongs, and they must
make for it with faces turned due south.

(19) 'Hard going,' rejoined Theagenes, 'at least for Chariclea,
for she is unaccustomed to walking any great distance. Nevertheless we will make the journey, assuming the guise of beggars
and strollers who show tricks to get food.' 'Yes, by Zeus,' said
Cnemon, 'you both do look grossly disfigured, especially Chariclea since she had her eye knocked out, just lately. In your
present state, I should say, you will be asking, not for scraps,
but for falchions and cauldrons.'* At this they smiled a faint,

forced smile, that merely flitted over their lips; then, after confirming with oaths their joint resolve, and calling the gods to witness that never of their own will would they forsake one another, they proceeded to do as their plan required. Cnemon and Thermouthis crossed over the swamp at sunrise, and made their way through a dense forest whose tangled growth much impeded their passage. Thermouthis led the way, at the request purposely made by Cnemon, who gave as his pretext the other's acquaintance with that difficult region, and his reliance on Thermouthis as guide; but more truly he was concerned to ensure his own safety, and wished to prearrange an opportunity of making his escape. As they progressed they came upon some flocks of sheep – the shepherds ran away and lay hidden in the denser part of the forest. They slaughtered one of the rams and set it to roast over the fire prearranged by the shepherds; and they gorged themselves on the meat without waiting for it to be properly roasted, so hard pressed by hunger were their bellies. Like wolves or jackals* they devoured the pieces of flesh as they were cut off, only slightly scorched by the fire, and the half-roasted meat, as they ate, dripped its blood down their cheeks. When they had gorged their fill, they gulped down some milk, and then pursued their intended route. The time was now about the hour of the unyoking of oxen. As they were ascending a ridge, Thermouthis stated that below it was the village in which he guessed that Thyamis, after his capture, was confined or had been put to death. Cnemon began complaining that his belly was disordered by his overeating, and said that the milk had brought on a troublesome flux of the bowels: he bade Thermouthis go on ahead, saying that he would soon overtake him. When he had made this move once, twice and thrice, he was judged to have spoken the truth; and he added that he had difficulty in catching up. Having brought the Egyptian to the point of being used to his halts, he finally stayed behind, well out of sight, and by dashing headlong down the hill into the more difficult parts of the undergrowth he made good his escape.

(20) When the Egyptian reached the crest of the ridge, he rested awhile on a rock, awaiting the evening and nightfall, after which they had agreed to enter the village and inquire up and down for Thyamis. At the same time he looked about to see if Cnemon were coming up from anywhere, for the fellow was forming a sinister plan against him. The suspicion rankled in his

mind that Cnemon was the slayer of Thisbe, and he was
considering how he might at some time take his life; while his
fury impelled him, after dealing with Cnemon, to make an
attack also on Theagenes. As Cnemon nowhere appeared, and it
was now the dead of night, Thermouthis betook himself to sleep
– a sleep heavy as bronze, so prolonged as to become his last,
through the bite of an asp; and thus by the will, no doubt, of
the Fates he sank to a sudden end not inappropriate to his
character.* Cnemon, from the moment of parting from Thermouthis, sped away in his flight without pausing for breath, till
the darkness of night came on and hindered his further progress.
On the spot where he was thus overtaken he hid himself beneath
as large a pile of leaves as he could heap together. As he lay
beneath the pile he passed most of the time without sleeping and
in sore distress, supposing every sound, a gust of wind or a stir
of leaves to be Thermouthis; and when he had yielded a little to
the onset of sleep, he seemed to be fleeing, and kept turning
round to look behind him to see if he could spy a pursuer who
was not anywhere. He wanted to sleep, yet prayed to be spared
what he wanted, since the dreams that visited him were more
dire than the truth of his case. He felt like being angry with the
night, accounting this a longer one than any others. Gladdened
by the sight of day, he first cut off so much of the overgrowth of
his hair as he had purposely produced to accord with a brigand-
like appearance among the herdsmen, in order that he might not
arouse aversion or suspicion in anyone who came across him.
For herdsmen, among various ways of presenting a formidable
aspect, draw their hair down upon their eyebrows, and toss it
about as it falls over their shoulders, well knowing that the hair
makes love-makers more winsome, but freebooters more
fearsome.

*Cnemon, having parted from Thermouthis and come to the Nile,
meets with the Egyptian sage Calasiris at Chemmis.*

(21) So Cnemon cut away enough of his locks to reduce them
from the brigands' style to one of some refinement; and he then
made haste to reach the village of Chemmis, where he had
appointed to meet Theagenes. As he drew near the Nile, and
was about to cross over to Chemmis, he observed an old man
roaming along the bank: he was continually running up and

down for quite a distance beside the flowing water, and seemed
to be imparting to the river some matters preying on his mind.
His hair hung down in the priestly fashion, and was perfectly
white: his chin had a bushy beard of venerable length; and his
gown and other attire tended somewhat to the Grecian style.
Cnemon halted for a moment: the old man ran past him again
and again, without seeming to notice that anyone was there, so
completely, in fact, was he absorbed in his train of thought, his
mind being occupied solely with his meditation. Cnemon
advanced to meet him face to face, and began by bidding him
good day. The man replied that it could not be such for him,
since he was not being so treated by Fortune. Surprised at his
words, Cnemon asked if the stranger were a Greek. 'Not a
Greek,' he answered, 'but an Egyptian of these parts.' 'How
comes it then that you are wearing Greek dress?' 'Calamities,'
he said, 'have put me in this brilliant change of costume.'
Cnemon wondered that a man should brighten his appearance
on account of calamities, and requested to be informed of these.
'You summon me from Troy,'* answered the old man, 'and stir
up against yourself a swarm of troubles and their incessant
buzzing. But whither are you bound, young man, and whence?
Why this Greek speech in Egypt?' 'How absurd!' said Cnemon.
'You explain nothing of your own business, though the first to
be questioned about it and seek information of mine.' 'Well
then,' said the other, 'since you look like a Greek man, and
some turn of Fortune, belike, is disguising you also, and you are
filled with a desire to hear my story, and I on my part am with
child to relate it to somebody – I would perhaps have told it to
these reeds here, like the fellow in the legend,* if I had not met
with you – well now, let us leave these banks of the Nile, and
the Nile itself, for there can be no pleasure in listening to
narrations of some length in a place that is being burnt up by
the midday sun. Let us go to the village that you see situated
just opposite, unless you have some more pressing affair on
hand. I will lodge you, not in a house of my own, but in that of
an honest man who took me in myself at my entreaty. Under his
roof you shall hear as much of my tale as you desire, and in
your turn shall recount your own adventures.' 'Let us go,' said
Cnemon; 'for in any case I am anxious to make my way to that
village, as I have an appointment to wait there for some special
friends of mine.'

(22) So they embarked in one of the boats that lay moored by the bank in readiness for travellers who paid to be ferried over. They made the passage to the village, and arrived at the lodging where the old man stayed. They did not find there the master of the house, but were cordially welcomed by a daughter of their host – a young woman of marriageable age – and by all the maidservants in the house, who treated their lodger just as they would a father, on instructions, I conceive, from the proprietor. One of them washed his feet and wiped away the dust from his shanks; another attended to his bed, and got ready a soft couch on which he could recline; another fetched a jug of water and kindled a fire; while another brought in a table laden with wheaten bread and all sorts of the season's fruits. Marvelling at all this, Cnemon said: 'Surely we have come to the abode of Zeus the Hospitaller – so it would seem from these open-handed attentions, revealing a disposition of such warm kindliness.' 'Not the abode of Zeus,' said the other, 'but of a man exact in his devotions to Zeus the Hospitaller and Patron of Suppliants. His life also, my son, is a roving one: he is a merchant, whose experience of many cities and the behaviour and cast of mind of many people has taught him, it would seem, to receive strangers under his roof, as he received me a few days ago, restless wanderer that I am.' 'And why all this wandering, father, that you mention?' 'Robbed of my children by brigands,' he replied, 'and knowing the offenders but unable to obtain my rights, I roam around this region and utter forth my grief in moaning, like some bird, I imagine, whose nest is ravaged by a snake and, while her brood is being devoured before her eyes, is afraid to go near, yet cannot bear to flee away. Affection and affright do battle in her breast, and with shrill cries she flutters about her beleaguered young, addressing to savage ears, that nature has not made acquainted with pity, the ineffectual appeal of a mother's laments.'* 'Then will you please relate,' said Cnemon, 'how and when you were a victim of this grievous assault?' 'Later on,' he replied; 'for it is time now for us to attend to the stomach – which Homer, glancing at the fact that it makes all things wait upon its pleasure, admirably called 'baneful'.* But first let us follow the rule of the Egyptian sages, and pour libations to the gods; for even the belly shall not induce me to transgress, or ever let any suffering succeed in dispelling the memory of one's duty towards the divine.'

(23) Having thus spoken he poured from his drinking-bowl some pure water, for that was his habitual drink, and said: 'Let us offer libation to the gods of this land, and to those of Greece besides, and especially to the Pythian Apollo; also to Theagenes and Chariclea, those most excellent persons, seeing that I number them too in the company of the gods.' With that he shed some tears, as though rendering to that pair, in those mournful drops, an additional libation. Cnemon was astounded at hearing their names and, after gazing up and down at the old man, he asked: 'What is this you say? Are Theagenes and Chariclea in very truth your children?' 'Children, good sir,' he replied, 'born to me motherless. It was my fortune that the gods presented them to me: they were brought forth by the travail of my soul; my inclination towards them was regarded as natural affection; and this led to their both regarding and addressing me as their father. But tell me, how came you to know them?' 'Not only have I come to know them,' said Cnemon, 'but I can give you the happy news of their being still alive.' 'Apollo!' cried out the other; 'ye gods! Where on earth are they? Oh, tell me! I will look upon you as my saviour, and esteem you as on a par with the gods!' 'And what will be my reward?' said Cnemon. 'For the present,' he replied, 'gratitude, which to my mind is the hand-somest guest-offering to a man of good sense; I know many a one who has laid up this gift as a treasure in his soul. But if we should once set foot in our native land – an event which the gods foreshadow to me – you will have your fill of a plentiful draught of riches.' 'These are future, uncertain things that you promise me,' said Cnemon, 'while you have the means of requiting me here and now.' 'Point out to me anything that you see here and now, for I am ready to give up even a part of my body.' 'No need of any amputation: I shall consider myself amply repaid if you will please make clear to me whence that pair came, of what parentage they are, how they arrived here, and what manner of experiences have been their lot.' 'You shall have your reward,' replied the old man, 'in good measure, such as you would not get even if you went so far as to ask for all the money in the possession of mankind. But for the moment let us taste a few morsels of food; for the tale will require a lengthy spell of listening on your part and of relating on mine.' They then ate heartily of nuts, figs, fresh-gathered dates and other such things as the old man had for his daily food, for he never

killed any animal for a meal; and for his drink he had water, while Cnemon took some wine. The latter, after a little while, said – 'Dionysus, as you know, father, delights in tales, and loves comedies: he has now taken up his abode in me,* and disposes me to be a hearer of something, and he impels me to claim the payment that you promised me; so now it is time for you to produce the drama of your story, as it were, upon the stage.' 'You shall hear it,' he said; 'but would that we chanced to have here the worthy Nausicles, who many a time has pestered me to unfold my narrative to him, but whom I have fobbed off each time by one shift or another.'

(24) 'And where might he be now?' asked Cnemon, as he called to mind the name of Nausicles. 'He has gone a-hunting,' he said. To Cnemon's next question: 'After what sort of quarry? 'Wild beasts,' replied the other, 'of the most dangerous kind: they are called men, and herdsmen, but they are brigands in their way of life, and extremely hard to catch in the swamp which provides them with lairs and hollow places.' 'And with what offence does he charge them?' 'The seizure of an Attic woman,' he answered, 'whom he loved, and whom he called Thisbe.' 'Alack!' said Cnemon, and of a sudden fell silent, as though checking himself. 'What ails you?' asked the old man; but Cnemon changed the subject and said: 'I wonder how, or relying on what support, he was moved to make this attack.' To which the other answered: 'The Great King,* sir, has as his satrap over Egypt Oroondates, by whose authority Mitranes has been assigned the command of the garrison of this village. Now this man has been paid a great sum by Nausicles to accompany him with a strong body of cavalry and men-at-arms. Nausicles is aggrieved by the abduction of the Attic girl, not merely as being the object of his love and a most admirable singer, but because he intended, in his own words, to convey her actually to the King of Ethiopia, to be the future play-fellow and companion of his consort, after the Grecian fashion. Deprived of the very handsome price which he was expecting to be paid for her, he is casting about for any expedient that will assist him. I myself have incited him to this action, in the hope that he might also be the means of preserving my children's lives.' Here Cnemon broke in, saying: 'Enough of herdsmen and satraps, yes, and even of kings! Before I was aware of it, you were almost leading me on and on to the end with such talk. Here you have

trundled in this old scene which, as they say, has "nothing to do with Dionysus".* So bring back your story to its promised course. I find you behaving like Proteus of Pharos* – not assuming as he did, a delusive, fluid form, but still attempting to lead me astray.' 'You shall be told the tale,' said the old man; 'I will relate to you my own history first, quite briefly, not complicating my narrative as you imagine, but providing an orderly, consecutive account for your hearing.

Calasiris recounts his adventures to Cnemon.

'I belong to the city of Memphis. My father, and I myself, were named Calasiris.* My life is now a wandering one, but was not such aforetime, for in the past I was a prophet. I took to me a wife according to my country's law; I lost her by the ordinance of nature. After her dissolution and passage into her next allotted state, I lived for some time unmolested by troubles, priding myself on two children that I had by her. But a few years later the fated revolution of the luminaries of heaven caused a change in my fortunes. The eye of Cronos* cast a glance upon my house which brought upon me the alteration for the worse that my learning had foreshadowed, but had not enabled me to escape. For, while it is possible to foresee the inflexible determinations of the Fates, to evade them is beyond our reach. Yet foreknowledge in such matters is an advantage, since it mitigates the fiery effect of the dread event. An unexpected disaster, my son, is intolerable, but one foreknown is more easily borne: for in the former case the mind, gripped by fear, cowers down; in the latter, habituation reconciles us through cool calculation.

(25) 'What befell me was this: a Thracian woman, in the full bloom of her age, in beauty second only to Chariclea, whose name was Rhodopis,* but who was sent forth, I know not whence or how, by a Fate intent on harming all who came acquainted with her, went roaming about Egypt and paraded herself even as far as Memphis. She was escorted by a great train of attendants, was possessed of great wealth, and was a perfect adept in all amatory seductions. It was impossible to meet her and not be captivated, so inescapable and irresistible was the kind of lascivious drag-net that she trailed with the glances of her eyes. She often visited the temple of Isis, whose priest-in-charge I was, and constantly made offerings of sacri-

fices and votive gifts of great price. I am ashamed to tell it, but
it shall be spoken: the frequent sight of her came to be too much
for me; she began to break down my lifelong practice of
continence. For some time I opposed the eyes of the soul to
those of the body, but at last I had to own my defeat and submit
to the burden of amorous passion. I discerned in that woman
the origin of the future distresses foretold to me by the divine
power, and understood that there my destiny was producing a
scene in which the spirit then appointed to play the part had
seemingly assumed the character of Rhodopis. I resolved not to
disgrace the priestly service in which I had been reared from
childhood – and I did resist – nor to profane the rites and the
shrines of the gods. On my offence – not one of acts, which
Heaven forbid! – but only of appetite, I imposed a fitting
penalty. Setting up my reason as my judge, I punished my lust
with exile. Ill-starred wretch that I was, I went forth from my
native land, submitting to the constraints of the Fates and
resigning my life to whatever treatment they might choose to
give it, and at the same time escaping from the accursed
Rhodopis. For I feared, good sir, that under the oppression of
the star then dominant over me I might be reduced even to the
viler course. But what more than all and on all accounts drove
me forth was my children, of whom the inexpressible wisdom
vouchsafed to me by the gods often gave me forewarning that
they would clash with one another in armed conflict. So, to
exclude from my eyes such a cruel sight – one which I imagine
the very sun would avoid by veiling his rays in a cloud – and to
deliver a father's vision from the spectacle of his children's
slaughter, I expelled myself from the land and home of my
fathers, without speaking a word to anyone of my departure. I
made a pretext of voyaging to Great Thebes,* in order to see
the elder of my two sons, who dwelt there at that time with his
maternal grandfather. That son's name, good sir, was Thyamis.'
Once again Cnemon started back, as though his ears had been
struck a blow by the name of Thyamis: while he refrained from
speech so as to hear the sequel, the other completed his story
thus:

Calasiris relates how he visited Delphi, received a prophecy from the oracle, and met Charicles, the priest of Apollo, who told his story to Calasiris.

(26) 'I pass over the middle stages of my wanderings, young man, since they contribute nothing towards your inquiry. I learnt that there was a city in Greece named Delphi, sacred to Apollo and containing shrines of other gods; and that it was a centre for the work of learned men in a situation apart from the madding crowd. Thither I betook me, deciding on it as a suitable resort for a prophet, dedicated as it was to sacred rites and ceremonies. I crossed the Crisaean Gulf, and putting in at Cirrha I hastened from shipboard to the city. As I halted before it, a holy voice, in tones truly divine, came to my ears on the very spot; and the city impressed me in general as an abode of the higher powers, but especially from the nature of its site. For, precisely like a fortress, the inartificial acropolis of Mount Parnassus, impending aloft, closely enfolds the city within its flanks.' 'Admirably spoken,' said Cnemon, 'as by one who actually felt upon him the Pythian afflatus. So it was that my father used to describe the position of Delphi, after the citizens of Athens had sent him as recorder to oversee the ceremonies.'* 'Are you then an Athenian, my son?' 'Yes,' he said. 'And your name?' 'Cnemon,' he replied, and added: 'As for my story, you shall hear it another time: for the moment, continue with yours.' 'I will do so,' said the old man, and resumed the account of his ascent to the city. 'Highly pleased with the city's public walks and squares and fountains, and with the Castalian spring itself, from which I duly besprinkled myself, I hastened on to the temple, incited by the talk of the crowd, who were saying that it was the time for the prophetess to have her tremor. I entered in, and prostrate before her I was uttering some words of private prayer, when the Pythia pronounced these words:

> "Thou hast brought thy footsteps from the fruitful land
>   beside the Nile,
> In flight from the spinnings of the predominant Fates.
> Persevere, for I will give thee soon the soil
> Of dark-furrowed Egypt. Meanwhile, be thou my friend."

(27) 'When she had delivered this oracle, I flung myself prone upon the steps of the altar, and besought the god to be gracious

to me in all things. The large gathering of bystanders loudly praised the god for the prophecy vouchsafed to me on my first appeal to him; and they congratulated me and paid me thenceforward all manner of kindly attentions, saying that I was the first man to be received by the god as a friend since a certain Lycurgus of Sparta.* They gave their consent to my dwelling at my pleasure within the precincts of the temple, and decreed that I be provided with sustenance at the public expense. In short, I enjoyed every advantage without stint. I either took part in the ceremonies or officiated at the sacrifices daily offered by foreign as well as native peoples in great number and variety to gratify the god, or else I held converse with philosophers; for not a few in that walk of life gather about the temple of the Pythian Apollo. Indeed, the city is quite a school of the Muses, being inspired by Phoebus, divine leader of the Muses. For some time at first these persons plied me with questions on various matters. One would ask how we Egyptians worship our country's gods, while another wished to know how it came about that different animals were adored by different sections of our people, and what was the reason of each cult. Some wished to know about the construction of the Pyramids, others about the subterranean mazes.* In brief, they omitted not a single point of interest in their inquiries concerning Egypt; for listening to any accounts of Egypt is what appeals most strongly to Greek ears.

(28) 'At length a day came when one of the more accomplished of them brought me a query concerning the Nile – as to what are its sources, and what is the peculiarity distinguishing it from other rivers, whereby it alone of them all overflows in the summer season.* I told him what I knew of these matters, giving him all the information which is recorded in sacred books about this river and which prophets alone may read and learn. I described how it has its sources in the highlands of Ethiopia on the borders of Libya – that is, in the region where the zone of the East has its end and that of the South its beginning. The river increases its height in the summer season not, as some have supposed, because its flow is repelled by opposing currents of the monsoons, but through the action of these same winds which, about the summer solstice, drive and hustle all the clouds from the north to the south until they are crowded into the torrid zone. There they are repelled in their onward course by the extreme fieriness of that region: all the moisture that until

then has been gradually collected and condensed is evaporated, with the result that heavy rains are precipitated. The Nile then swells up and, disdaining to be a river, rebels against its banks and transforms Egypt into a sea, fertilizing in its passage all the arable land. That is why its water is so very sweet to drink, being furnished forth by the showers of heaven, and so very agreeable to the touch, being no longer so hot as at its outset, though still tepid from its earlier warmth. For this reason it alone of rivers gives off no vapours, as it doubtless might be expected to do if, as some persons, I am informed, of high repute in Greece have held,* it derives its brimming flood from the melting of snows.

(29) 'While I was expounding these and other such matters, the priest of the Pythian god, with whom I had become intimate, and whose name was Charicles, said to me: "A most excellent statement, with which I am myself in agreement; for I have had the same information from the priests at Catadoupa* on the Nile." "Then, Charicles," I said to him, "you have been there?" "I have, learned Calasiris," he replied. When I asked him next "What purpose drew you thither?" he answered: "Ill fortune in my domestic affairs, which yet has been a cause of good fortune also for me." When I showed surprise at this inconsequence he went on: "You will not be surprised if you learn the course of events; and you can learn it whenever you wish." "Then it is time that you told me," I said; "for I wish to hear it now." "Listen then," said Charicles, after he had dismissed the rest of the company; "indeed, I have long been wishing to let you hear my experiences, for a certain benefit that it may bring to me. I married, but had no children, until at long last, when I was advanced in years, my many entreaties to the god were answered: I was declared father of a daughter, who according to the forewarning of the god would be born under no fair auspices. She came to be of marriageable age, and I bestowed her upon the man among her suitors – and they were many – whom I judged to be of the highest merit. On the very night of her going to bed with her bridegroom, the unfortunate girl met her death from a thunderbolt, or a fire caused by man, that seized on our sleeping-quarters. The nuptial song was suddenly succeeded by lamentation; from her bride-chamber she was escorted to her tomb; and the same torches that had so brightly lit up her wedding feast now kindled her funeral pyre.* My Fate

added a further woeful scene to this tragedy, by carrying off my
girl's mother, worn out by her mourning. This divine visitation
of misery was too much for me. I did not remove myself from
life, in deference to the theologians' opinion that such a course
is unlawful, but crept away from my native land, fleeing from
the desolation of my house. For it is a great help towards
oblivion of one's troubles to screen from one's soul any visual
reminders of them. I wandered in many regions, and came at
length to your Egypt, and even to Catadoupa, seeking knowledge of the Cataracts of the Nile.

(30) '"So there, my friend, you have the explanation of my
travelling thither. But there is something incidental to my
account, or rather, to speak more truly, the main point in it,
which I would have you know. As I was strolling about the city
and availing myself of my leisure for buying some articles that
are scarce in Greece – for by then the severity of my grief was
being softened down by time, and I was feeling an eagerness to
return to my native country – I was approached by a man of
serious mien whose eyes shone with a quick intelligence. He had
but newly emerged from adolescence; his colour was perfectly
black. He greeted me, and stated in halting Greek that he wished
to tell me something in private. I readily complied, and having
led me into a temple near by he said: 'I have seen you buying
leaves and roots of Indian, Ethiopian and Egyptian plants. Now,
if you should have a mind to buy things that I have of pure
quality, with no deception about them, I am ready to supply
them.' 'I am so minded,' I said; 'show me some.' 'You shall see
them,' he went on; 'but you must not be a haggler over their
purchase.' 'On your part,' I said, 'you must pledge yourself not
to put too high a price on them for their sale.' Then he drew
forth a small pouch that he had under his arm, and showed me
some marvellous specimens of precious stones: in it were pearls
of the size of a small nut, developed to a perfect roundness and
shining with the whitest lustre; also emeralds, hyacinths – some
green like corn in the spring, and gleaming with a smooth polish
like drops of olive oil, while others suggested the colour of the
sea shivering slightly beneath some sheer headland and showing
in its depths a violet tinge. In brief, they combined to make such
a sparkling medley of various colours as was highly delightful
to the eye. When I saw them I said: 'You had better go, sir, and
find other purchasers of these things; for I and all my resources

could hardly balance in value a single one of the stones that I see there.' 'But even if unable to buy,' he said, 'you can at least accept a gift.' 'I am not incapable,' I replied, 'of accepting a gift, but for some purpose or other you are jesting with me.' 'I am not jesting,' he said; 'I am quite serious; and I swear by the god who has his abode in this place that I will give you all these things if, besides them, you consent to take possession of another gift much more precious than these.' At this I laughed: when he asked me why, I answered: 'Because it is laughable that, while gravely promising me gifts of such great value, you propose in addition to enrich me with something far more valuable even than those.' 'Only trust me,' he said. 'Come, swear that you on your part will make the best use of my gift, in the way which I myself shall indicate to you.' Surprised and bewildered, I yet swore to this, in the hope of acquiring such fine things. When I had taken the oath in the terms that he required, he took me to his house and showed me a girl of inconceivable, celestial beauty. He said that she was seven years old, but to me she seemed to be approaching the marriageable age – so much, you know, does exquisite beauty tend to magnify one's impression of stature. I stood dumbfounded, alike from incomprehension of the whole proceeding and from a desire to feast my eyes more and more on what I was beholding.

(31) '"The man then started to tell this story: 'The girl whom you see here, sir, was still in her swaddling-clothes when her mother exposed her, for a reason that you will learn a little later, committing her life to the vacillations of Fortune. I discovered her and took her up; for it had been a wrongful thing for me to suffer a soul once invested with human existence to remain in peril – this being one great precept of our Naked Sages,* a disciple of whom I have lately been counted worthy to become. Besides, I was there and then aware of a radiant, heavenly light that shone from the infant's eyes, so awe-inspiring, and at the same time so fascinating, was the gaze that it turned on me as I was inspecting it. Exposed with the child was a necklace of stones – that which I showed you just now – and a swathe of spun silk in which were inwoven characters of our native script so pricked out as to relate the child's story: the mother, I suppose, had the forethought to provide these tokens for her daughter's identification. When I had read the writing and learnt where and to whom the infant belonged, I carried it

to a farm in a situation remote from the city, and handed it over
to my shepherds to rear, sternly warning them not to tell anyone.
The articles exposed with it I kept in my hands, lest they should
occasion an attempt upon the girl. At first she continued in this
way unnoticed; but when with the passage of time the fullness
of her maidenhood was seen to display a more than ordinary
bloom, and her beauty, even if hidden underground, could not
have escaped notice, but would, I believe, have shone forth even
thence, I feared that knowledge of her might come to light; she
might be put to death, and I in turn might be faced with some
unpleasant consequences. I therefore contrived to be dispatched
as an envoy to the Satrap of Egypt, and came here, bringing her
along with me in the hope of settling her in life. I am to speak
with the satrap forthwith on the business of my mission: he has
notified me that I am to have an audience today. To you, and to
the gods who have so ordained, I commit the girl on the terms
of the sworn agreement between us: that you will keep this girl
free, and give her in marriage to a free man, together with this
swathe which I convey to you from my own hands, or rather
from those of the mother who exposed her. I have confidence
that you will carry out in full the purpose of this transaction;
for I take courage from the oaths that you have sworn, and I
have also been at pains during the many days of your sojourn
here to take note of your character as one that is truly Greek.
This is what I had to tell you, in concise terms at this moment
of my being called away by the duties of my mission. A clearer
and more particular account of the girl shall be given you
tomorrow, when I meet you at the temple of Isis.'

(32) '"Proceeding as had been agreed. I took charge of the
girl and brought her veiled to my house. During that day I
tended her with care and constant kindliness, and rendering
many thanks to the gods I have ever since considered and called
her my own daughter. The next day, at dawn, I went off in great
haste to the temple of Isis, where I had the appointment to meet
the stranger. After walking about there for a great while and
failing to see him anywhere, I presented myself at the satrap's
palace and inquired whether anyone had seen the envoy from
Ethiopia. I was informed that he had departed, or rather, had
been expelled, the satrap having threatened him with death if he
had not passed over the frontier before sunset. When I asked the
reason of this my informant replied: 'Because he ordered the

satrap to keep his hands off the emerald mines,* since they belonged to Ethiopia.' I returned, greatly annoyed, like one who had received a heavy blow, at not having obtained any knowledge concerning the girl – as to who she was, whence she came and what was her parentage."' 'You ought not to wonder at that,' said Cnemon. 'I too am vexed at having heard nothing, but perhaps I shall hear.' 'You shall hear,' said Calasiris.

Calasiris continues the story told to him by Charicles.

(33) 'I will now relate,' he went on, 'how Charicles continued with the rest of his story. "When I arrived at my dwelling," he said, "the young girl came to meet me and, without saying a word – for she was not yet familiar with the Greek tongue – gave me her hand in greeting. The mere sight of her relaxed my mind to a more cheerful mood. I marvelled also that, just as fine, well-bred dogs will fawn upon everyone, even at a short acquaintance, this girl was so quick to perceive my goodwill towards her, and honoured me as a father. So I resolved not to linger on at Catadoupa, for fear lest some malign visitation should bereave me of this my second daughter; and I voyaged down the length of the Nile to the sea, where I found a vessel that took me on my homeward way. And now the child is here with me, as my own child, bearing my name; for my life is anchored upon her, and in every respect she excels, surpassing even all that I could pray for, so rapidly has she absorbed the Greek language, and rapidly also sprung up to her prime like a shoot of some thriving plant.* And so far has she outstripped all the other girls in the fresh bloom of her person, that every eye, Greek or foreign, is turned upon her; and wherever she appears, in temples, walks or squares, like some statue upheld as an exemplar of beauty she attracts to herself the sight and mind of everybody. Yet, with all this excellence, she afflicts me with a harassing distress: for she has renounced marriage, and is intent on remaining a virgin all her life; and having devoted herself as a ministrant to Artemis she spends most of her time in hunting and practising archery. My life is now a misery, because I hoped to give her in marriage to my sister's son, a youth of rare refinement and charm in both speech and disposition; but I am now frustrated by the girl's heartless decision. Neither by kind attentions, nor by promises, nor by appeals to reason, have

I been able to persuade her. Hardest blow of all, she has aimed, as they say, my own shafts against me, and brandishes over me her accomplishment in the arts of speech – the subtleties of which I have imparted to her – to demonstrate that she has chosen for herself the best life – glorifying the virgin state which, she declares, is next to the immortal, and calling it unspotted, untainted, incorruptible. Love, Aphrodite, and all nuptial celebration she utterly consigns to the crows! In this situation I appeal to you for your help; and it was for this reason that I seized an opportunity, a happy chance that somehow came my way of its own accord, and so was led to tell you my story at this undue length. And now indulge me, my good Calasiris: bring to bear on her something of the Egyptian lore and enchantment.* Persuade her, whether by words or by works, to know her own nature and to be conscious of her womanhood. If you consent you will find it an easy matter; for she is one who has not lacked converse with learned men, but has come to maidenhood in constant company with them. She shares the same dwelling with you there, I mean within the precincts and shadow of the temple. Do not disregard my entreaty; do not assent to my continuing a childless and disconsolate man, to live out a burdensome old age bereft of descendants. I beseech you by Apollo and by the gods of your country!" I wept, Cnemon, at hearing those words; for he too shed some tears as he pressed his petition, and I promised to give him any succour that I could.

(34) 'While we were still considering the matter, a man came running to us and reported that the leader of the Aenianes' mission had been waiting a long time at the door, and was loudly calling for the priest to attend and begin the sacred ceremony. When I asked Charicles who the Aenianes were and what was their mission and their sacrificial oblation, he replied: "The Aenianes are the noblest people in the region of Thessaly, having a distinct Hellenic descent from Hellen, son of Deucalion.* Altogether they are spread along the whole extent of the Malian Gulf; but they take especial pride in their capital, Hypate, so named, they will have it, from its supremacy and authority, but according to others because it is situated below Mount Oeta.*The sacrifice and pious mission take place in every fourth year, when the Pythian Games are being held, as they are now, to your knowledge. The Aenianes do this in honour of Neoptolemus, son of Achilles; for it was here that he was

treacherously murdered, close to the very altar of the Pythian Apollo, by Orestes, son of Agamemnon.* The present mission surpasses all that have come before, as its leader prides himself on being a descendant of Achilles. I met the young man yesterday, and truly I thought him worthy of the lineage of Achilles, so distinguished he is in form and stature, which visibly attest his kinship." I wondered at this, and asked how, belonging to the clan of the Aenianes, he could declare himself to be a descendant of Achilles, seeing that the Egyptian Homer's poem informs us that Achilles was of Phthiotis. "This young man," said Charicles, "contends that the hero was entirely of the stock of the Aenianes, insisting that Thetis came from the Malian Gulf to be wedded to Peleus; that of old the region bordering on the gulf was named Phthia; and that the other peoples, because of Achilles' great renown, fictitiously appropriated him.* And, apart from this, the youth accounts himself one of the Aeacidae,* adducing as his forefather Menesthius, son of Spercheius and Polydora, daughter of Peleus – Menesthius, who with Achilles was a leader in the expedition against Troy and, as being his kinsman, commanded the first rank of the Myrmidons. And he clasps and clings tightly to Achilles, and tries in every way to embody him among the Aenianes; citing as proof, besides other grounds that he alleges, this sacrificial offering to the spirit of Neoptolemus, in which service the Thessalians, he says, gave the preference to the Aenianes, thus attesting their close kinship with the hero." "One can have no objection, Charicles," I said, "either to their being thus favoured or to their claim being vindicated. Now, order the leader of the mission to be called in here, for I am in quite a mad flutter of eagerness to see him."

(35) 'Charicles made a sign to have him called, and the youth came in, diffusing something truly Achillean about him. His looks and spirit recalled the hero: his neck was held erect,* and his hair was thrown back from his forehead and tossed up high like a mane; his nose bespoke courage, and its nostrils had a gallant way of respiring the air; while his eyes, not quite a light blue, but darkish with a light blue gleam, gave glances at once haughty and apt for love, like the sea when it is just beginning to settle down from a swell into a calm. After giving us the usual greeting and receiving ours in return, he told us that the moment had arrived to offer the sacrifice to the god, so that there might be time enough thereafter for the rite of atonement to the hero

and the procession in his honour. "It shall be done," said Charicles. He then stood up and said to me: "You will see Chariclea also today, if you have not seen her already: precedent requires that the ministrant of Artemis shall take part in the procession and the propitiation of Neoptolemus." Now, Cnemon, I had often seen the girl before, when she joined me in conducting sacrifices, and sometimes sought to learn parts of the liturgy: however, I was silent, in eager expectation of what would ensue. Meanwhile we made our way towards the temple, where all the preparations for the sacrifice had already been made by the Thessalians. When we reached the altars, and the young man was beginning the performance of the ritual, and when the priest had offered the opening prayer, from the inmost sanctuary the Pythian priestess delivered these words:

"Mark well, ye Delphians, her who hath first, Grace and last, Glory;
Also him, the Goddess-born.*
These shall depart from my fane and, after cleaving the waves, Shall arrive at the swarthy land of the Sun.
There they shall win and wear about their temples, as the noble prize of virtuous lives,
A white coronal from darkling brows."

(36) 'When the god had thus pronounced, a deep perplexity possessed the company gathered there, who were at a loss to tell what was the meaning of the oracle. Each of them strained the message to a different sense, making some conjecture to suit his own desire; but none at that time could apprehend the truth of it, for oracles and dreams in general are tested only by the event. And besides, the Delphians were in a flutter of excitement to see the procession, which had been magnificently equipped, and they would not trouble themselves to search out the exact meaning of the oracle.'

BOOK 3

*Calasiris describes to Cnemon the solemnities at Delphi in honour
of the hero Neoptolemus, and how Theagenes and Chariclea
became enamoured there.*

(1) 'When the procession and the whole ceremony of the
propitiation had been performed—' 'Stay, father,' interrupted
Cnemon, 'not all performed: at least, your account has not yet
made me a viewer of the spectacle. Here I am, utterly consumed
with impatience to hear your recital, and am all ardour to be an
actual witness of the festival; and there you go rushing past me,
so that I arrive, as they say, too late for the party. No sooner
have you opened your theatre than you close it!' 'I am far from
wishing, Cnemon,' said Calasiris, 'to pester you with incidental
matters such as these; I am for pressing on to the more
momentous points in my relation, and to the questions that you
raised with me at the beginning. But since you have set your
heart on being a casual spectator, revealing thereby your Attic
character,* I will give you a concise description of that procession – a famous one as few have ever been, both on its own
account and for its consequences. It was headed by a hecatomb,
brought along by male initiates of a somewhat rustic way of life
and attire: each had a white tunic trussed up into a looped fold
by a girdle; and his right hand, bared – as also were his shoulder
and breast – waved on high a two-edged axe. The oxen were all
black, with brawny necks rising in a gentle curve; their horns
were sharp-pointed but not overlarge or crooked, some having
them gilded, while others had them entwined with garlands of
flowers; their forelegs were stocky, and their dewlaps hung
down as low as their knees. The hecatomb numbered exactly
one hundred, fulfilling the true sense of the term.* These were
followed by a varied assortment of other victims, each kind of
animal being made to proceed in a separately marshalled troop,
while flute and syrinx struck up a mystic air in announcement
of the sacrifice.

(2) 'The cattle and their herdsmen were succeeded by Thessalian maidens with handsome girdles worn low in the waist* and
their hair flowing loose. They were divided into two companies.

In the first they carried small baskets full of flowers and fruits; in the other they bore large baskets containing cakes and incense balms that breathed sweet fragrance about the place. In this group they kept their hands disengaged, bearing their burdens on their heads, and they went linked together in a figure of oblique lines, so that they were able to pace onward and dance at the same time. The other group marked the time for them with the keynotes of the tune, it being enjoined on this group to chant the whole of the hymn, the theme of which was praise of Thetis and Peleus, and also of their son Achilles and his son Neoptolemus. After the maidens, Cnemon—' 'Why "Cnemon?"' asked the other, 'when you are going to deprive me once more, father, of a rare pleasure, by omitting to recite the hymn, as though you had invited me to be only a spectator and not also a hearer of this procession?' 'You shall hear it,' replied Calasiris, 'since you so desire. The chant went somewhat like this:

> Thetis I sing, golden-haired Thetis,
> Immortal daughter of Nereus of the briny wave,
> Wedded to Peleus on the prompting of Zeus,*
> Bright glory of the waves, our own Lady of Paphos;*
> Who from her womb brought forth
> The furious spearman, the god of battles,
> The thunderbolt of Greece,
> Divine Achilles, whose glory rose to heaven;
> To him Pyrrha* bore a son, Neoptolemus,
> Destroyer of the Trojans' city, saviour of the cities of the Greeks;
> Be gracious unto us, O hero Neoptolemus,
> Thou who art blest in lying now beneath the earth of the
>   Pythian;*
> Receive with favour this mystic sacrifice,
> And ward off all threatened peril from our city.
> Thetis I sing, golden-haired Thetis.

(3) 'Somewhat after this fashion was the hymn, Cnemon, so far as I can recollect it. So harmonious was the music accompanying the dancers, and so exactly did the beat of their footfalls accord with the rhythm of the tune, that one's eyes were induced by one's ears to neglect what one was beholding; and those present followed along with the maidens as they passed on from point to point, seeming to be impelled by the ringing tones of their

chant, until close behind them a mounted troop of youths with their captain flashed forth, presenting a vision of beauty that prevailed over any charm of hearing. In number the young men amounted altogether to fifty: they were divided into two companies of twenty-five, escorting the leader of the mission as he rode midway between them. They were shod with boots of red leather strapping interlaced and fastened above the ankle, and they wore white cloaks gathered into their chests by gold clasps and edged all round with a border tinted blue. Their mounts were all from Thessaly, with the gallant glance of steeds bred in the plains of that country: they chafed at the bit as a tyrannous master, spitting upon it and foaming amain; and yet they suffered themselves to be guided by the rider's intent. They were richly adorned with silver or gilded head-bosses and frontlets, as though the youths had made this a matter of emulation amongst them. But their splendid appearance, Cnemon, was disregarded and forsaken by the eyes of the onlookers, which were all turned upon the captain of the troop – upon my heart's darling, Theagenes; and you might have supposed that a lightning flash had bedimmed all that had appeared before, so brightly did the sight of him illumine us. He too was mounted indeed, but armed like a foot-soldier he brandished an ashen spear tipped with bronze:* he did not wear his helmet, but rode gravely along bare-headed, and clad in a cloak of purple dye which was embroidered at large with gold thread depicting the Lapithae in combat with the Centaurs,* while its clasp was in the form of a wreath encircling an Athene of amber, showing forth to shield her the Gorgon's head upon her breast. A special grace was added to the scene by some fresh puffs of wind; for blowing lightly upon him they softly dispersed his hair over his neck while they drew his locks away from his forehead, and trailed the border of his cloak over the back and haunches of his horse. One would have said that the horse himself was sensible of the bloom and beauty of his master, and felt the glory of bearing so glorious a rider, to see the undulation of his neck as he tossed up his head with ears pricked, and haughtily twirled his brows above his eyes. Exulting in him whom he bore and in his own bearing, he paced onward obedient to the rein: balancing himself on either shoulder in turn, and lightly tapping the ground with the tips of his hoofs, he adapted his paces to the rhythm of a gentle motion. All were astonished at the spectacle, and all accorded to the youth the prize for pre-eminence in manliness and beauty. And promptly the women of the common folk, such as were unable to restrain and conceal their emotion, tossed to him apples* and flowers, thinking thus to attract to them some sign of his favour. For this single verdict prevailed amongst all present – that nothing could be found in all mankind to surpass the beauty of Theagenes.

(4) '"But when the daughter of the morning, rosy-fingered Dawn, appeared," as Homer would have said* – when from the temple of Artemis drove forth the fair and sagacious Chariclea, we were then made aware that even Theagenes could happen to be excelled, though only inasmuch as the purest feminine beauty has a stronger attraction than the greatest comeliness to be found amongst men. For she rode in a covered car drawn by a pair of white oxen in charge of a driver; and she was attired in a purple robe reaching to her feet and bespangled with golden rays. She wore a girdle set close up to her bosom, on which the craftsman had brought to bear the full power of his craft: never before had he fabricated its like, nor would be able ever to repeat it.* For he wrought two serpents so that they twined their tails behind her back, while their necks crossed below her breasts and were plaited into a complex knot from which their heads were allowed to emerge and hang down on either side as the loose ends of the girdle. You would have said that the snakes not merely seemed to creep, but were actually creeping; they struck no terror with grim and cruel looks, but were relaxed in a melting languor, as though lulled to repose by the sweet charm of the maiden's bosom. Their material was gold, but their colour was dark; for the gold had been skilfully so blackened that the mingled yellow and black should represent the rough surface and varying sheen of the scales. Such was the maiden's girdle. Her hair was neither wholly plaited nor flowing loose; the greater part of it, behind her neck, fell in waves over her shoulders and her back, while the rest, on her crown and forehead, was held by a garland of tender sprays of laurel, binding it close as it gleamed like roses amid sunbeams, and keeping it from being tossed about more than was seemly by the breeze. In her left hand she bore a gilded bow, and the attachment of her quiver passed over her right shoulder; in her other hand she held a small lighted torch, yet even so she flashed from her eyes a brighter light than any torch could shed.' 'It is

they – Chariclea and Theagenes!' cried Cnemon. 'And where in the world are they? By the gods I beg you, tell me!' said Calasiris, fancying that they were visible to Cnemon. 'I thought that I had sight of them, father,' he replied, 'although they were not there, so vividly, so truly as I recall seeing them, has your description brought them before me.' 'I doubt,' said Calasiris, 'if you saw them as they were beheld on that day by Greece and the sun – so admired by all, so kindly congratulated, answering the dearest wish, she of men and he of women. A union with either of those two they deemed equal to immortality, except that the people of that country admired more the young man, and the Thessalians the maiden, each more impressed by what he saw for the first time; for a strange sight is more apt to astonish than a familiar one. But oh, the pleasing deception! Oh, the sweet idea! How wildly you excited me with the fancy that you saw and could point out my darlings, Cnemon! And indeed it seems that you are altogether deceiving me: at the beginning of my relation you undertook that they would be coming and showing themselves at any moment, and on those terms you claimed the reward of my informing you about them; evening has now come on, and night also, and nowhere can you indicate their presence.' 'Bear up,' said Cnemon, 'and be of good heart, for in truth they will come. It may be the fact that some hindrance has arisen, and they may arrive rather behind the appointed time. In any case, even were they here, I would not have pointed them out before I had obtained my full reward. So, if you are eager for the sight of them, make good your promise, and complete your narration.' 'I shrink in any case,' said Calasiris, 'from a subject that recalls painful events to my mind; but I also considered that I must be wearing you out with such an overdose of garrulity. Since, however, I find that you are so fond of listening, and have an insatiable appetite for good discourses, come now, let us step into the story where I quitted it, first lighting a lamp and pouring our bedtime libation to the gods of night, so that after performance of the customary rites we may pursue our night-hour narrative with our minds at ease.'

(5) After the old man had thus spoken, a lighted lamp was brought in by a young maidservant at his bidding. He poured the libations, invoking several gods and especially Hermes;* he asked for a night of pleasant dreams, and entreated that his dearest ones might appear to him, if only in his sleep. Having

finished his prayers he said: 'Now, when the procession, Cnemon, had made a circuit round the tomb of Neoptolemus, and the young horsemen had ridden around thrice, the women raised the ritual call, and the men the martial chant. Then, as at one concerted signal, oxen, lambs and goats were sacrificed; it was as though the slaughter of them all were done by the stroke of a single hand. On an altar of great size they heaped a vast amount of cleft wood and placed upon that, according to custom, all the extremities of the victims; they then called upon the priest of Pythian Apollo to begin the libation and kindle the altar fire. Charicles replied that it was his office to perform the libations, but he said: "The leader of the mission must kindle the altar fire with the torch handed to him by the ministrant; that is the practice ordained by ancestral custom." So saying he began to pour the libations; and Theagenes was about to take the torch, when, my dear Cnemon, we were convinced by what occurred of the divinity of the soul and its kinship with the powers on high. For at the moment of meeting the young pair looked and loved, as though the soul of each at the first encounter recognized its fellow and leapt towards that which deserved to belong to it. At first they stopped short, in consternation; then, with a lingering motion, she proffered and he received the torch, with eyes intently fixed on each other, as if they had had some previous knowledge or sight which they were recalling to memory.* Next, they smiled slightly and furtively, a smile traceable only by the light shed forth by their eyes. Then, as though ashamed of what they did, they blushed; and again, their passion, I conceive, having seized hold also of their hearts, they turned pale and, in short, a thousand changes of expression in that brief moment spread over the features of them both, as every variation of hue and look declared the agitation of their souls. These effects, naturally enough, escaped the notice of the multitude, since everyone was absorbed in one or another interest or consideration of his own: they escaped even Charicles, who was pronouncing the traditional prayer and invocation. I was occupied solely with my observation of the young pair, ever since, Cnemon, the oracle was chanted concerning Theagenes as he sacrificed in the temple; and I had been moved by hearing their names to speculate on what would befall them. But I still could not make out any distinct meaning of the latter part of the prophecy.

(6) 'At length and, it seemed, with a struggle, Theagenes tore himself away from the young girl. When he had applied the torch and ignited the altar, the procession was disbanded. The Thessalians then betook themselves to feasting; the rest of the people departed, each one to his own home. Chariclea clad herself in a white robe and made her way with her few female companions to her lodging in the temple precincts; for she was not dwelling with her supposed father, since the sanctity of her office obliged her to keep herself entirely apart. So then, my curiosity keenly aroused by what I had both heard and seen, I chanced to fall in with Charicles – just what I had been intending. "Have you seen," he asked me, "my glory, and the glory also of the Delphians – Chariclea?" "Not now for the first time," I answered. "Many a time before have I seen her, whenever she met me in the temple, and not just, as it were, by the way. And besides, I have sacrificed with her not a few times, and she has questioned me and received my instruction on various divine and human matters that happened to perplex her." "And what was your opinion of her on the present occasion, my good Calasiris? Did she add some grace to the procession?" "Fie on such words, Charicles," I said; "as well ask me whether the moon outshines the other stars." "Well, you know," he said, "there were some who praised the Thessalian youth also." "Awarding him the second or the third prize," I said; "but the crowning glory, indeed the bright eye, of the procession was acknowledged to be your daughter." Charicles was delighted with this, while I by speaking the truth was attaining the object that I had in view – of getting the man in some way or other to feel at ease with me. He smiled and said: "I am going to her now: if you like, come, share my solicitude and my observation as to any unpleasantness from the crowd that may have discomposed her." I gladly nodded my assent, and made it clear to him that I accounted no other business so important to me as his.

(7) 'When we arrived at her dwelling, we entered and found her lying listless on her bed, with her eyes all bedewed with love. She greeted her father with her habitual embrace: when he asked what ailed her, she replied that she was suffering from a severe headache, and would like to keep quiet, if this could be allowed her. Charicles was greatly disturbed by her words; he stole out of the room with me, directing the maidservant to leave her in

peace. When he had passed outside the house he said: "What can this be, my good Calasiris? What is the meaning of this weakness that has stricken my little daughter?" "Do not be surprised," I answered, "that by her figuring in a procession before so great a concourse she has drawn upon her a glance of the evil eye." He laughed ironically and said: "Why, you too, like the multitude, have come to believe that there is such a thing as the power of the evil eye!" There is nothing more real," I said; "it works in this way.* This air enveloping us makes an entrance through our eyes, our nose, our windpipe and our other apertures into our inmost parts, and brings in with it portions of the external qualities, and there it implants in the recipients a passion of like quality to that which it has when it flows in. Hence whenever anyone looks with envy upon beautiful objects, the ambient air becomes charged with a malignant quality, and that person's breath, laden with bitterness, blows hard upon the person near him. This breath, made up of the finest particles, penetrates to the very bones and marrow, and engenders in many cases the disease of envy, which has received the appropriate name of the influence of the evil eye. With that too you should consider, Charicles, the many instances of people who have been infected with ophthalmia or symptoms of the plague, without having touched diseased persons at all, or even shared bed or board with any such, but have only partaken of the same air. And to give you good proof of this theory, let me cite in particular the generation of love – how things taken in by our sight produce in us its beginning by shooting the passionate feelings like wind-borne shafts through our eyes into our souls. That this should be so is reasonable enough: for of all our bodily vents and senses the most constantly mobile and fervid is our sight, and hence is especially receptive of the effluences of things, attracting by its igneous fume the transits of the feelings of love.

(8) '"I can also adduce for you, if you require it, by way of example, a fact of natural history, set forth in the sacred books on the subject of animals.* The plover cures sufferers from jaundice: the patient has only to look at this bird, and it turns away, fleeing from him, with its eyes shut – not, as some suppose, that it begrudges him the relief it can give, but because its gaze has the property of attracting and transferring his disease in a sort of flux to itself; and hence it shuns the sight of him like the infliction of a wound. And you have doubtless

heard how the serpent called 'the basilisk' by its mere breath and glance will shrivel and cripple whatever comes in its way. Nor is it surprising that some people cast a spell over others who are most dear to them and to whom they wish well; for being naturally inclined to jealousy they act thus, not from their will, but from their nature."

(9) 'At this Charicles paused for a while; then he said: "You have cleared up the question in a most sagacious and convincing way. May she likewise feel one day in herself a lover's longing! I should then have satisfied myself that she was in good instead of ill health: you know it was to this end that I called upon you for help. But as things are, there is no risk of her being affected – this enemy of wedlock, this stranger to love! Rather I should say, she is in fact labouring under a malignant spell, and I am sure that you will wish to clear up this trouble also, being my friend and a man of comprehensive knowledge." I promised to do my utmost to relieve her of whatever malady I might find afflicting her.

(10) 'While we were still discussing the matter a man hurried up to us and said: "Gentlemen, you are loitering as though you had been summoned to the field of battle instead of a banquet which is being provided by that most handsome of youths Theagenes, and presided over by that greatest of heroes Neoptolemus. Come along; do not stretch out the festivity till evening, for you are the only ones missing from the party.' Charicles leant over to me and said in my ear: "This fellow has come with an invitation backed by a cudgel: how very unDionysiac he is, although in a fairly tipsy condition! But let us go, for I fear he may end by treating us to a drubbing." "You are joking," I said; "however, let us go." When we had arrived Theagenes seated Charicles next to himself, and put me also, I may say, in a place of honour, on Charicles' account. There is no need for me to overburden you with all that passed at the banquet – the maidens' dances, the flute-girls, the war-dance of young men under arms* and other performances with which Theagenes enhanced the sumptuous provision of victuals, and so rendered the festivity a sociable and unusually joyous carousal. But there was one particular feature of it which you must be told, and which will be more pleasant for me to mention: it was this. Theagenes made a show of gaiety, and constrained himself to pay kind attentions to the guests; but I detected the direction in

which his mind was working. At one time his eyes rolled to and fro, at another he heaved a deep sigh for no apparent reason; now he was downcast and seemed lost in thought, now of a sudden he changed to a more cheerful expression, as though recovering his senses and recollecting himself, thus easily passing from one variation into another. For the mind of a lover, not unlike that of a drunken man, is mutable and intolerant of any settled state: both alike have their souls tossing on the tide of passion; and hence it is that the lover is inclined to drinking, and the drunkard to loving.

(11) 'When he was seen to be seized with an oppressive fit of yawning, it became obvious to the rest of the company that he was unwell; so that Charicles, having observed his disorder, said quietly to me: "I do believe that he too has been looked upon by the evil eye; he seems to me to have met with the same misfortune as Chariclea." "Yes," I said, "the same, by Isis; quite rightly and reasonably too, since in the procession he came second to her in distinction." These remarks we made to each other. When the time came for the cups to circulate, Theagenes drank to each person from the loving-cup, though unwillingly. As it came round to me I said that I welcomed his friendly compliment, but I declined the offer of the cup. He gave me a sharp, heated look, conceiving himself to be slighted. Charicles understood, and told him: "He abstains from wine and the flesh of animate creatures." Theagenes asked the reason, and he replied: "He is of Memphis, an Egyptian, and a prophet of Isis." When Theagenes heard mention of Egyptian and prophet, he was at once filled with delight and, like one who had discovered some treasure, stood up, called for water, drank some and said: "O paragon of wisdom, please accept this toast that I have drunk to you with the liquor most agreeable to you; and may this table solemnize our pact of friendship!" "So be it," I said, "handsome Theagenes; it is a friendship that I have long felt on my part for you." I received the cup and drank. With this incident the festivity came to an end. We took our departure, each to his own home, after Theagenes had embraced me repeatedly, with remarkable fervour considering the time in which he had come to know me. On reaching my dwelling I lay awake for a while on my bed, turning over and over in my mind the concern that I felt for the young pair, and trying to make out the meaning of the last part of the oracle. When midnight

came I saw Apollo and Artemis – so I thought, if I was merely thinking so, and not really seeing them – the one leading up to me Theagenes, and the other Chariclea. They called me by name and said: "It is time now for you to return to your native land: this is the dictate issued by the Fates. Depart hence, therefore, and take these twain with you in your charge, to be your fellow-travellers, and to be treated as your children; and then conduct them out of Egypt to such region and in such wise as may be pleasing to the gods."

Calasiris, after having a vision in the night, discusses its meaning with Cnemon.

(12) 'Thus they spoke, and then departed, leaving me in no doubt that what I had seen was no dream, but a waking vision. In the main I grasped the meaning of the apparition; but I was at a loss to know to what people or to what country it pleased the gods that the young pair should be conducted.' 'You acquired that knowledge yourself later on, father,' said Cnemon, 'and later too you will tell it to me: but in what way did the gods convince you, as you said, that they came, not in a dream, but in visible presence?' 'In the way, my son,' he answered, 'which sapient Homer expresses, in a riddling fashion over-looked by ordinary folk:

> "The traces left behind him" (he says somewhere) "of his
>   feet and legs
> I easily discerned as he departed; the gods are not hard to
>   discern."*

'It seems, in truth,' said Cnemon, 'that I too am one of the ordinary folk, and it was doubtless with the purpose of exposing me as such, Calasiris, that you have recalled those verses. Their superficial sense I have known ever since I was taught to know the words; but the theological lesson implanted in them I have not comprehended.'*

(13) After a brief pause, in which Calasiris uplifted his mind to the mystic aspect of things, he said: 'Gods and divine spirits, Cnemon, in their comings and goings on visits to us, assume but rarely the forms of common animals, and most frequently those of human beings, so that their likeness to us may aid in producing in us the impression of their presence. The uninitiated

must fail to observe them, but they will not escape the perfection
of the sage: he will recognize them by their eyes, with which
they maintain a steady gaze, never closing their eyelids; and still
more by their gait, which does not proceed with the feet parted,
or one before the other, but in a sort of aerial gliding, with an
unimpeded motion, as they cleave rather than tread the atmos-
phere. For this reason the images of the gods are fashioned with
the feet joined together, as though forming a single limb. All this
was well known to Homer, as he was an Egyptian and was well
schooled in the sacred lore; and he wrapped it up in symbolical
verses, leaving it to be discerned by persons able to understand.
He says of Athene:

> "Her two eyes shone forth,"*

and of Poseidon:

> "The traces left behind him of his feet and legs
> I discerned as he departed *flowing*,"

as it were, flowing in his onward motion; for so should the
words to be taken, and not, as some do in error, "I *easily*
discerned."'*

(14) 'You have admitted me here to a mystery, most reverend
sir,' said Cnemon, 'and as you keep calling Homer an Egyptian
– a thing which I dare say nobody in the world has heard until
this day – I cannot venture to disbelieve you. At the same time I
am so struck with surprise that I beg you not to pass on without
giving me the precise reason for this statement.' 'Cnemon,' he
said, 'although this is not the moment for a detailed exposition
of the matter, I will nevertheless give you a summary of the case.
Let Homer be styled, my friend, a native of this or that country
by different people, and let any city claim to be the birthplace of
the sage;* but in truth he was our countryman, an Egyptian,
and his city was Thebes, "which hath a hundred gates", as he
himself tells us.* His reputed father was a prophet, but was
actually Hermes, whose prophet that reputed father was. For,
when the prophet's wife had the duty of performing some
traditional rite, and was sleeping in the temple, the god lay with
her and begot Homer, who bore upon him a mark attesting this
unequal union. From the time of her delivery one of his thighs
was overspread with hairs of great length, whence he received
his name* as he wandered and chanted his poems among various

nations, and especially among the Greeks. He himself did not mention his real name, or even that of his city or of his race; but those who knew of that growth affecting his body fabricated his name from it.' 'And what was his object, father, in keeping silence about his native land?' 'It was either because he was ashamed of being an exile – for he was cast out by his father when he was about to be selected as one of the young men consecrated to divine service, the blemish on his body having caused him to be deemed a bastard – or else it was a skilful expedient that enabled him, in concealing his real city, to win favour in every place.'

(15) 'I have accepted your statement of the matter as sound and true,' said Cnemon, 'judging by the man's quite Egyptian way of giving us in his poems dark sayings mingled with all kinds of delight, and also by the pre-eminence of his natural powers, which could never have set him above everyone else if he had not partaken, in truth, of some divine, some supernal influence. But after you had caught sight of the gods in person, Calasiris, as they appear in Homer, what happened next?' 'The same kind of thing as before, Cnemon: more wakefulness, more speculations and more anxieties – those friends of Night. I felt very glad, hoping that I had been granted an unlooked-for boon, and looking forward to my return to my own country; but I was also pained by the thought that Charicles would be deprived of his daughter; and I was perplexed as I bethought me in what manner I should take the young people along with me and contrive our departure. I was harassed with doubts as to how we could make our escape unobserved, in what direction we should travel and whether by land or by sea. In short, I was tossed on a surge of anxieties, and had no sleep during the remainder of an exhausting night.

(16) 'Day had not fully dawned when there came a knocking at the inner door, and I heard someone calling "Boy!" When my servant asked who knocked and what he wanted, the caller answered: "Announce that it is Theagenes the Thessalian." I was delighted to hear the young man announced, and ordered that he be invited in; for I conceived that here of itself was coming my way an inception of the scheme that I had in hand. I surmised that, having heard at the banquet that I was an Egyptian and a prophet, he had come to obtain my assistance in his love-affair – labouring, I imagine, under the common,

ignorant misapprehension that the lore of the Egyptians is a single, invariable knowledge. Now, one kind of it is popular – moving, one might say, along the ground, ministrant to images, and wallowing among corpses; addicted to simples, and relying on incantations. It neither attains any good end itself, nor brings any good to those who use it; most often it finds itself at fault, such successes as it may achieve being painful and meagre – merely the presentation of unrealities as realities, and the disappointment of hopes; a deviser of unlawful actions and purveyor of licentious pleasures. But the other knowledge, my son, the true wisdom, of which this has spuriously assumed the name, and in which we priests of the prophetic line are trained from our youth, looks upward to the heavenly region: companion of the gods, partaker of the nature of the higher powers, it traces the motions of the stars and gleans foreknowledge of the future. Standing aloof from all our earthly evils, it devotes itself to the pursuit of what is honourable and beneficial to mankind. It was the cause of my absenting myself from my native land in time for me to see if I could give a wide berth to the events that it foretold to me, as I have already recounted to you, and the conflict between my two sons. So now I must commit these matters to the care of the gods, and especially of the Fates that have power to decide our doing or not doing: for they enjoined on me this exile from my native land, not merely, it would seem, because of those events, but equally for my discovery of Chariclea, the manner of which you will learn in the next part of my story.

Theagenes confesses to Calasiris his love for Chariclea.

(17) 'When Theagenes came in I exchanged greetings with him, and seated him beside me on the bed. "What business brings you so early to see me?" I asked. He stroked his face for some length of time, and then said: "I am in great anxiety about my whole position, but I blush to explain why," and was silent. I decided that the moment had come for me to play the mountebank with him, and appear to divine what I actually knew. Looking at him with a more cheerful expression I said: "Though you are shy of speaking, still nothing is unknown to our wisdom and to the gods." I paused for a little, arranging on my fingers some counters that bore no numbers, tossing out my

hair and imitating some person possessed by a spirit; then I said: "You are in love, my child." He started up at my divination, and when I added "With Chariclea", he believed these words to be the very promptings of a god: and he was on the point of falling down and worshipping me. When I prevented this he stepped up to me, covered my head with kisses, gave thanks to the gods for not having been disappointed, as he said, of what he expected, and besought me to be his saviour: his life could not be saved, he declared, if he failed to get help, and that quickly, so serious was the attack from which he suffered and so fierce the flame of his passion, in what was, moreover, his first experience of love. He affirmed with many oaths that he had never yet had intimacy with a woman. He had spurned all women, and marriage itself, and any love-affairs that were mentioned to him, until the beauty of Chariclea had proved to him that he was not by nature obdurate; but up to the previous day he had never beheld a woman worthy of being loved. With these words he wept, as though for his thus confessing himself overcome against his will by a girl. Wishing to reassure him I said: "Take courage, now that you have turned to me for succour: she will not win a similar victory over our wisdom. She is indeed somewhat austere, and stubbornly resists subjection to the sway of love; for she despises Aphrodite and marriage – nay, the mere mention of their names. But to help you every means must be tried; art can find a way to compel even nature. Only be of good cheer, and follow the advice that I shall give you on what is to be done." He promised to comply with all directions that I gave him, even if I bade him walk over swords.

(18) 'He was still entreating me about his affair, and promising to reward me with his whole fortune, when a messenger came from Charicles and said: "Charicles requests you to come to him: he is there, near at hand, in the temple of Apollo, where he is offering up a hymn to the god, after being alarmed by something in his sleep." I rose at once, sent Theagenes away and repaired to the temple, where I found Charicles seated in a stall, overcome with grief and uttering groan upon groan. I went up to him and asked: "Why so gloomy and doleful?" "How should I be otherwise," he replied, "when dreams have filled me with alarm, and my daughter's condition, as I have heard, has taken a more serious turn, and she has not had a wink of sleep all night? And I am the more distressed by her ill health because

the occasion for the contest has been fixed for tomorrow: it is the custom then for the female ministrant of the goddess to present torches to the armed runners and award the prize. One of two things must happen: either her failure to appear will be an outrage on the tradition, or by attending under constraint she will greatly aggravate her illness. So, if you have not already done so, pray go now to her aid, and bring her some remedy; you will be doing what we and our friendship may fairly claim of you, and it will be a pious service to the gods. I know that it would mean no great effort to you, if you were so minded, to cure what you yourself called a case of the evil eye: prophets do not lack the power to deal successfully with even the greatest difficulties." I acknowledged my remissness, artfully dissembling with him also; and I requested him to allow me the space of that day, since I had to concoct something to apply as a remedy. "Meanwhile," I said, "let us go to the girl, in order to examine her more closely, and comfort her as much as we can. At the same time, Charicles, I should like you to use such language about me to the girl, as will make it plain that you commend me to her better acquaintance, so that, having become familiar with me, she may receive my curative treatment with the greater confidence." "Agreed," he said; "now let us go."

(19) 'When we had come in to Chariclea – why tell it all at length? She had become completely subjugated by her passion, and the bloom was now banished from her cheeks, the fire in her eye seemed to have been quenched, as it were, in the flood of her tears. Nevertheless she tried to recover herself on seeing us, and strove her utmost to resume her wonted looks and speech. Charicles embraced her, gave her countless kisses, and lavished on her every mark of tenderness. "My little daughter, my child," he said, "will you hide your trouble from me, your father? You have fallen under a malign influence, and will you keep silent, as though you had done wrong, and were not rather wronged by the evil eye that has looked upon you? Come, have no fear: this wise man, Calasiris, has been called in to provide us with a remedy. He is an adept, excelling all others in divine science; for prophecy is his vocation, and he has been dedicated to the sacred service from childhood; more important than all, he has in addition the most affectionate regard for us. It is only reasonable, then, that you should welcome him without reserve, and submit yourself to the spells and other remedies that he

proposes to apply: it is not your habit to shun converse with men of the learned sort." Chariclea was silent, but nodded her assent, however, seeming glad to accept consultation with me. This settled, we parted from each other, after Charicles had reminded me that I would give careful attention to the subject of his previous appeal to me, and take thought how I could produce in Chariclea some appetite for marriage and male company. So I sent him off in good spirits, having promised him that it would not be long before his wish was fulfilled.'

BOOK 4

Calasiris continues his story to Cnemon, telling him what occurred on the last day of the Pythian Games at Delphi.

(1) 'On the following day the Pythian contest was to end; but the contest of the young couple was then coming to its height. The god of love, I imagine, was acting as their marshal and umpire, and was determined to prove, through the particular case of these two athletes, paired off by him, that his own kind of contest is the greatest of all. What came to pass in chief was this. All Greece was present to see the games, and these were managed by the leagues of the various states. When the other events had been duly performed in magnificent style – close-run races, clinches of wrestling and buffets of boxing – at the end the herald called out: "Forward, the armed men!" The ministrant of the goddess, Chariclea, then shone forth at the far limit of the stadium, having come, though reluctantly, in obedience to tradition – or rather, I should suppose, in the hope of somewhere getting sight of Theagenes. In her left hand she bore a flaming torch, in the other she held before her a branch of palm;* and as she appeared she attracted to herself the gaze of the whole assembly, but of no one, I should say, more quickly than that of Theagenes; for a lover has sharp sight for the object of his desire. And he of course having already heard what was to take place, had his whole mind so intent on his first glimpse of her that he could no longer be silent, but said to me softly – for he had purposely seated himself close to me – "That is she, Chariclea!" I requested him to keep quiet.

(2) 'At the herald's call there came forward a man in light armour, of haughty mien and, it seemed, of particular distinction. He had already been crowned in a number of contests, and now he had no competitor to challenge him, since no one, I suppose, was bold enough to encounter him. So the leagues' officers were for sending him away on the ground that the law did not grant a crown to one who had not engaged in a contest. But he claimed that the herald should call for anyone who offered to come and contend with him. The managers gave the order, and the herald announced that any intending competitor

should come forward. Then Theagenes said to me: "He is calling me." "How do you mean?" I asked. "Just as it shall be, father," he said; "for no one else, in my presence and in my sight, shall obtain the victor's crown from the hands of Chariclea." "But failure," I asked him, "and the consequent disgrace, are those of no account to you?" "And who," he said, "is so madly eager to behold and approach Chariclea as to outstrip me? Who, like me, can be so elated by the sight of her as almost to take wing and be borne into the upper air? Do you not know that Love himself is given wings by painters, who thus allude to the mobility of those whom he has mastered? And, if I am to add a little boast to my remarks, nobody to this day has plumed himself on outrunning me in a race."*

(3) 'With these words he started up, and advancing into their midst announced his name and stated his nationality; he was allotted his position on the course, and then put on a complete suit of armour, and took his stand at the starting line, panting and barely able in his impatience to wait for the signal call of the trumpet. It was a grand and impressive spectacle such as Homer presents in Achilles' feats of arms at the River Scamander.* Thrilled by this unlooked-for challenge, the whole of Greece there prayed for the victory of Theagenes, as though each man present were himself engaged in the contest; for beauty has something that compels goodwill in one at the very first sight. Chariclea's excitement knew no bounds; and I, who had been observing her for some time, saw continual changes occurring in her demeanour. When, for all to hear, the herald had proclaimed the names of the entrants for the race, calling out "Ormenus* of Arcadia and Theagenes of Thessaly", and when the cord was let fall and the race was started at a speed which almost defeated the quickest vision, then the young girl was no longer able to keep still: her legs quivered, her feet danced, as if, to my thinking, her soul were floating away with Theagenes and were zealously supporting him in the race. The spectators, to a man, were in suspense to see the outcome, and filled with a great anxiety – and I more than any, since I had made up my mind to be concerned for him as for a son.' 'No wonder,' said Cnemon, 'that the spectators on the spot were anxious when I am myself in fear now for Theagenes; so I beg you to go on and tell me quickly whether he was declared the winner.'

(4) 'When he had completed half the course, Cnemon, he turned a little and looked askance at Ormenus; he then lifted up his shield on high, threw back his head, and fixing his gaze full on Chariclea he sped onward like a dart to its mark, and came in so many yards ahead of the Arcadian that the measure of the interval was taken afterwards. He ran up to Chariclea, flung himself with intense energy into her bosom, as though he were unable to check the impetus of his pace; and as he received the palm I observed that he kissed the girl's hand.' 'You have brought me back to life,' said Cnemon, 'by telling of his victory and his kiss; but what happened next?' 'Ah, Cnemon, you are not only an insatiable listener to tales, but also an elusive truant from sleep: already no small portion of the night has gone by, and you hold out, wide awake, while my narration, for all its long continuance, does not exasperate you.' 'I blame Homer, father, for saying that one becomes sated with love as with other things.* In my opinion it is a thing that induces no repletion, either when its pleasures are being enjoyed or when a tale of it is told. If anyone should relate the love of Theagenes and Chariclea, what heart of steel or iron would not be charmed by the story, even should it last for a year? So please continue with the sequel.'

'Theagenes, as I said, Cnemon, was crowned and proclaimed the victor, and he was applauded, as he passed along, by the whole assembly; while his conquest of Chariclea was decisive, and she was now in greater subjection to her passion than before, from having this second view of Theagenes. For the exchange of looks between lovers revives the fervour in their souls, and sight can rekindle their minds like logs upon a hearth. The girl, when she returned home, passed the same sort of night as those preceding, or one even more anguished; while I again lay sleepless, considering in what direction we should take our flight to avoid being observed, and wondering to what country the god intended the young couple to be conducted. I could only conclude that our escape must be made by sea, taking as a clue the words of the oracle:

> "After cleaving the waves they shall arrive at the swarthy land
>   of the Sun."

(5) 'But for the problem of where I should conduct them I could see but one solution – to discover, if somehow I could, the

swathe which was exposed with Chariclea, and on which was embroidered the statement about her, as Charicles said he had been told; for it was likely that I should ascertain from it what the girl's country was, and who were the parents already guessed at by me as hers; most probably it was there that the young people were being sent by Destiny. So at an early hour I went to see Chariclea. I found the whole household in tears, especially Charicles. I went up to him and asked: "What means all this upset?" He replied: "The malady has been increasing its hold on my daughter, and she has found the past night a more troublous one than the former." "You must withdraw," I said, "and all the others must go away too. I wish only to be provided with a tripod, some laurel, fire and incense, and to be disturbed by nobody whatever, until I call for someone to come in." Charicles gave orders accordingly, which were carried out. When I was left in peace I began what you might call a piece of play-acting business. I burnt the incense and, after muttering some pretended prayers with my lips, I shook the laurel briskly over Chariclea, up and down, from head to foot; then, yawning at her in a drowsy, or rather, an old-womanish fashion,* at long last I ended my performance, having bespattered both myself and the girl with a fine lot of twaddle. She kept on shaking her head, with a wry sort of smile, to signify that I was hopelessly adrift, with no inkling of her sickness. I sat down beside her and said: "Have no fear, daughter; your disease is a slight matter, easily cured. The evil eye lighted upon you, no doubt when you were in the procession, and still more when you were presenting the prize. And I guess who chiefly cast the spell – Theagenes, he who raced in armour: I noticed how he was constantly watching you and turning on you an ardent glance." "Whether that person looked at me as you say, or not," she said, "much good may it do him. What is his parentage or his country? I saw indeed that many people were in a flutter about him." "That he is a Thessalian by birth," I said, "you have already heard, by the herald's announcement of him. He traces his ancestry back to Achilles, and there, I dare say, he speaks the truth, to judge by the youth's stature and beauty, which seem to attest his exalted kinship with Achilles – except that he is not haughty or headstrong like that hero,* but has a sweetness that tempers the high dignity of his mind. Yet, with all these qualities, may he suffer severer pains than those which he has inflicted on you, for the envious vision that he possesses and the spell of an evil eye that he has cast upon you." "Father," she said, "my thanks to you for your sympathy in my sore distress; but why curse at random a man who may well have done no wrong? My sickness comes from no evil spell; it is seemingly some other disease." "And so you hide it away, my child," I said, "and will not be brave and tell it me, so that we might find some effective means of relieving you. Am I not a father to you in years, and still more in affection? Am I not well known to your father and at one with him in mind? Reveal what it is that ails you. You can take me into your confidence – if you wish, under oath. Be brave and tell me; do not augment your pain by your silence. For every disorder, if quickly recognized, is amenable to treatment; but, neglected for a time, it is wellnigh incurable. Silence is a nourisher of disease; trouble divulged is quickly assuaged."

(6) 'At this she paused for a moment, showing by her looks the countless rapid changes and impulses of her mind. Then she said: "Grant me this day, and you shall be told afterwards, if you do not learn the truth meanwhile by the divination that you profess." I rose at once and went out, to allow the girl in the interval to come to terms with her maiden modesty. I was met by Charicles, who asked: "What news have you?" "All favourable," I replied; "tomorrow she will be rid of the trouble that so oppresses her, and then another effect very agreeable to you will follow. And there is nothing to prevent us from calling in a doctor." So saying I ran off, to stop Charicles asking any more questions. I had not proceeded far after leaving the house when I saw Theagenes there by the temple, pacing about the precinct and talking to himself, as though he were content merely to be observing the dwelling-place of Chariclea. So I turned aside and went past him, as if I had not seen him. "Good day, Calasiris," he said, "now listen: I was waiting for you." I turned round quickly and said: "Ah, the handsome Theagenes! I did not see you." "How can he be handsome," he said, "who is not agreeable to Chariclea?" I assumed an air of annoyance and said "You must cease insulting me and my science, by which she has already been captivated, and compelled to love you and pray for a sight of you, as if you were a visitant from on high." "What is that you say, father? Does Chariclea love me? Why then do you not at once lead me to her?" And as he spoke he was dashing away. I got hold of his cape and said: "Stop now,

swift runner though you be. This affair is no catch, or a thing to snatch up like a cheap bargain laid out for sale to anyone who may fancy it; rather it is something that requires much consideration for its suitable accomplishment, and much prearrangement to avoid mishap in carrying it through. You must surely know that the girl's father has the highest position in Delphi, and keep in mind the laws that visit such attempts with death?" "To me," he replied, "even loss of life is indifferent, if I have obtained Chariclea: however, if you think fit, let us go to her father and ask her in marriage; for I surely am no unworthy person to become a kinsman of Charicles." "We should not obtain her," I said; "not that any fault can be found with you, but Charicles has promised the girl some time ago to his sister's son." "He shall rue it", said Theagenes, "whoever he may be; for no other man, while I live, shall take to bed Chariclea. This arm of mine, and this my sword, will not be so indolent as to suffer that." "Peace!" I said; "there will be no need of such action. Only obey me and do as I direct you. For the present go away, and take care not to be seen continually in my company: see that you meet me in quiet and alone." He went away downcast.

(7) 'Charicles met with me on the following day. As soon as he saw me he ran to me and kissed me on the head many times, exclaiming repeatedly: "Here is wisdom, here friendship! You have achieved a great work; she is caught who defied capture, she, the invincible, is vanquished! Chariclea is in love!" At these words I bridled up, raised my eyebrows, and moving at a sauntering pace I said: "It was clear enough that she would not withstand even my first onset, without any harassing action by my stronger forces. But how, Charicles, have you discovered that she is in love?" "By following your advice," he replied. "I summoned, on your own suggestion, the most renowned physicians and brought them in to examine her, promising to reward them with my whole fortune if they succeeded in curing her. As soon as they came in they asked her what ailed her. She turned away from them, and would not answer them, and would not answer them a single word, but kept loudly repeating the verse of Homer:

'O Achilles, son of Peleus, most valiant of the Achaeans!'*

The learned Akesinus* – you doubtless know the man – seized hold of her wrist despite her resistance, and seemed to be diagnosing her illness from her pulse and its indication, I conceive, of the beating of her heart. For some length of time he pursued his accurate investigation, thoroughly observing her condition in one part after another, and then said: 'Charicles, it was superfluous to call us in to this case; medicine can do nothing at all to help her.' 'Ye gods!' I cried, 'what do you say? Then I have lost my daughter, lost her beyond all hope?' 'No need for agitation,' he replied; 'listen to me.' And taking me aside, at some distance from the girl and the others, he said: 'Our science undertakes to treat disorders of the body, not those of the soul particularly, but only when the soul suffers together with an afflicted body and is relieved equally with it under the treatment. The condition of this girl is one of disease, but not in the body; there is no excess of fluids, no oppressive headache, no burning fever, and no other bodily ailment, either local or general, so it seems. This, and this alone, is the correct opinion.' At my earnest entreaty that he would tell me if he had discovered anything he said: 'Why, a child could perceive that the trouble is in her soul, and that her malady is obviously love.* Do you not see how her eyelids are swollen, her glances distracted, her face pallid, while she complains of no internal pain; whereas she wanders in her mind, utters whatever comes into her head, suffers from an unaccountable insomnia, and has suddenly lost flesh? You must go in search of her healer, Charicles; and he can only be the man of whom she is enamoured.'

'"This said he departed; and here I have come running to you, my saviour, my god, who alone are able to assist us, as the girl herself understands. For indeed, when I begged and pressed her to tell me what ailed her, she merely answered that she did not know her disorder, but felt sure that Calasiris alone could cure her; and she besought me to call you in to see her. This inevitably led me to the conclusion that she has been captivated by your wisdom." "Then can you tell me, besides the fact of her being in love," I asked, "who it is that she loves?" "No, by Apollo," he said; "how and by what means could I know that? Rather than all the wealth in the world I was longing to have her in love with Alcamenes, my sister's son, whom this long time I have intended to be her future husband, so far as my own wishes are concerned." I suggested that he might easily try the effect of bringing the lad to her dwelling and showing him to her. He approved and went off. Later on, about noontide, he met me again and said: "I have painful news to give you: the girl seems to be possessed, her manner is so very strange. I brought Alcamenes in to her, as you bade me, and presented him in attire of due elegance: but she, as though she had looked on the Gorgon's head* or something yet more monstrous, uttered a loud and piercing shriek, and averted her eyes to the other side of the room. Pressing her hands like a noose around her throat, she threatened, and swore an oath, to destroy herself if we did not instantly depart. We removed ourselves from her presence more speedily than words can tell; for what in fact was to be done when we saw such extraordinary behaviour? To you I come once more with an entreaty – that you will neither allow her to perish, nor suffer me to be disappointed of my earnest hopes." "Charicles," I said, "you were not far wrong in stating that the girl is possessed; for she is irritated by the powers that I myself drew down upon her – powers of no little influence, but such as might be expected to force her into actions prompted neither by her nature nor by her inclination. It seems, however, that some hostile deity is hindering my operation and contending with my assistants; so now the right moment has come for you to show me the swathe that was exposed with the girl child and which you said you had received with the other means of identification. For I fear the thing may be full fraught with sorceries and perhaps inscribed with cabbalistic signs which are turning her heart to a savage harshness, through some device of an enemy aimed at her living through all her days a stranger to love and offspring."

Charicles brings to Calasiris the swathe which was found with the infant Chariclea, and which bears an inscription worked upon it by her mother, Persinna, queen consort of Ethiopia.

(8) 'He assented, and came soon after with the swathe. I asked him to grant me some leisure and, as I found him agreeable, I went to my lodging. Without losing a moment I began reading the script on the swathe. It was pricked out in Ethiopian characters, not in the popular but in the royal hand, which resembles that of the so-called sacred writings of the Egyptians.* As I proceeded I made out this statement from the script: "I, Persinna, Queen of Ethiopia, to her who has yet to bear a name, my daughter only until the travail of her birth, I inscribe as my

parting gift these letters of lamentation." I was astounded, Cnemon, at the mention of that name, Persinna; but yet I went on and read what followed: "It was owing to no guilt of mine, my child, that I exposed you thus at your birth, and concealed you from the sight of your father, Hydaspes; as witness to this I would invoke the founder of our family, the Sun.* I can, however, justify myself to you one day, my daughter, should you survive, to him who may be divinely appointed to take you up, and indeed to the whole of mankind then alive, by revealing my motive in exposing you. Our ancestors were, among the gods, the Sun and Dionysus, and among demigods, Perseus and Andromeda, and also Memnon.* Now those who from time to time constructed the several parts of the royal palace adorned them with pictures relating to those ancestors; representations of them and their deeds were depicted in the men's apartments and the galleries, and the bed-chambers were decorated with the love-making of Andromeda and Perseus. There one day it chanced that Hydaspes and I, having had no children born to us after the passage of ten years since our marriage, were taking our noonday rest, relaxed in summer-time slumber. Your father then had intercourse with me, as he had been bidden to do, he solemnly averred, in a dream; and immediately I was aware that I was pregnant by his engendering. The period from that day to my delivery was devoted to public festival and sacrifices of thanksgiving to the gods for the king's expectation of a successor in his line. But when I brought you forth white, gleaming with a light complexion alien to the Ethiopian race, I understood the cause.* During the intercourse with my husband the picture of Andromeda presented her image to my eyes, showing her entirely nude, just as Perseus was taking her down from the rock, and it had thus by ill fortune given to the seed a form similar in appearance to that of the heroine. I therefore decided to save myself from a shameful death, being convinced that your colour would subject me to a charge of adultery – for nobody would believe my account of that miraculous change – and that it was better to give you the advantage of the hazard of fortune than the certainty of death or, in any case, of being called a bastard. I pretended to my husband that you had died at the moment of birth, and I exposed you in complete and utter secrecy, placing with you as large a store of riches as I could, to be a reward for whoever should preserve your life.* I decked

you out finely, and wound this swathe about you, to tell your
pitiful story, yours and my own, with the marks that I made on
it of the tears and blood shed over you by me, whose first child
labour brought me so much lamentation. But, my sweet daughter of only an hour, if you should survive, be mindful of your
noble descent; honour chastity, the distinguishing mark of
woman's virtue; and cultivate a regal spirit that will bespeak
your parentage. Remember, from all the treasures exposed with
you, to select and cherish especially for yourself a ring which
your father presented to me at my betrothal: it has the royal
emblem engraved round it, and is hallowed by a stone, pantarbe,* set in a bezel, which exerts a secret influence. This
account I have given you, availing myself of the service of script
since the deity has deprived me of living and visual converse
with you. Perchance my words will be mute and futile, perchance they will one day stand you in good stead; the hidden
issues of fortune are not to be known by men. You, whose
charms are wasted, you, whose beauty smirched me with
imputation, will have in this writing, if you should survive, the
means of your recognition. But if that befalls which I pray may
never come to my hearing, it will serve as your epitaph and your
mother's funeral tribute of her tears."

(9) 'When I had read these words, Cnemon, I recognized and
admired the wise dispensation of the gods. Filled with mingled
feelings of pleasure and pain, I went through the singular
experience of weeping and rejoicing at the same moment. My
soul felt relaxed by the discovery of the unknown facts and the
conclusive explanation of the oracle; but it was greatly harassed
with thoughts of what result the future might bring, and stirred
with pity for the instability and infirmity of human life, swayed
now towards one thing and now towards another – as was then
supremely evidenced in the fortunes of Chariclea. My mind was
beset by many reflections: what an origin was hers, and with
what parentage had she been credited! How great a distance
had she been brought from her native land, she to whom Destiny
had allotted a spurious daughterhood after being deprived of
her genuine one in Ethiopia and in the royal house! For some
time I stood there with my mind divided – inclined to feel pity
for the past, yet not daring to be happy about the future – until,
recalling my reason to sober thought, I decided that I must set
to work without further dallying. I went to see Chariclea; I

found her alone, quite prostrated now by her passion. Her spirit urged her to recover herself, but her body bore her down altogether by yielding to her malady and failing through weakness to hold out against its attack.

(10) 'I therefore dismissed the persons who were with her, and ordered that no one should disturb us, pretending that I wished to resort to some prayers and invocations for the girl. "It is time now, Chariclea," I said, "that you told me what ails you, as you promised to do yesterday, and that you ceased to conceal it from a man who is your well-wisher and is quite able to know all about it, even if you keep silence. She took my hand and kissed it, shedding some tears; then she said: "O wise Calasiris, let your first kind service be to leave me to bear my sad lot in silence, after taking such note as you wish of the nature of my sickness; and let me at least profit enough from my sense of shame to conceal what is shameful to feel, and more shameful to utter. For I am suffering from the full pressure of my disease, and still more from my failure to subdue it in its first onset and my surrender to a passion which I have continually renounced hitherto, and which defiles by its mere mention the proud name of virgin." Then, to encourage her, I said: "Daughter, on two accounts you do well to conceal your condition: I on my part have no need to be told what I have long known through my special skill, while you, from a natural feeling, blush to speak what it is more seemly for women to conceal. But now that you have experienced the passion of love, and at first sight Theagenes has captivated you – for so much has been imparted to me by the divine voice – be assured that you are not the only or the first woman to submit to this passion, but are sharing the experience with many women of distinction and with many a maiden of irreproachable virtue. Love is the mightiest of gods; indeed, he is even said to vanquish at times the gods themselves. Now, consider what is best to be done in regard to your present case. There is happiness in having remained altogether free from experience of love; but if once you have been caught, the wisest course is to guide your desire safely into the way of sobriety. And so, if you agree to trust this advice, it is feasible for you to fend off the shameful repute of mere lust and, by deciding on a legal contract of union, convert your malady into marriage."

(11) 'At these words of mine she perspired profusely, Cnemon,

and was evidently moved by a great mixture of feelings – of joy over what she heard me say, anxiety for the chances of her hopes and bashful shame for being so captivated. For some time she remained silent; then: "Father," she said, "you mention marriage, and urge me to decide on it, as though one were certain that it will meet with my father's consent, or with my enemy's aspirations." "As to the young man," I replied, "we can depend upon him: he on his side is probably more captivated than you, and has been stirred by feelings similar to yours. It seems that your souls, at your first meeting, had somehow a cognisance of each other's quality, and were swept along into a mutual affection. Out of kindness to you I have applied my skill to heightening his desire. But your supposed father is providing you with another husband, Alcamenes, who is not unknown to you." "For Alcamenes," she said, "let him provide rather a tomb than wedlock with me: I shall either be bride to Theagenes or be overtaken by my destined fate. But, as to your remark that Charicles is not my real but my supposed father, tell me, I beseech you, how you discovered that." "By means of this," I replied, displaying the swathe. "From whom, and how, did you get it? For ever since he received me from my foster-parent in Egypt and brought me – how, I cannot tell – to this place, he has taken and kept it from me, stowed in a casket, to save it from suffering injury in the course of time." "How I procured it," I replied, "you shall hear later on; for the moment tell me if you are aware of what is inscribed on it." She owned that she did not know. "How could I? "she asked. "It declares your family,' I went on, "your nation and what befell you." She implored me to disclose everything that I was able to learn, and I told her all, going through phrase after phrase of the script and translating it word for word.

Calasiris tells Chariclea of his acquaintance with her mother, and how he undertook to search for her.

(12) 'When she had learnt who she was and, her spirit now raised more in keeping with her birth, she stepped up to me quickly, asking "What now is to be done?" I then and there entered on a more open kind of counsel, revealing to her all the facts of the matter. "I had gone, daughter," I said, "as far as to the Ethiopians, from a longing to acquire their wisdom. I became

acquainted with your mother, Persinna, for that royal court always welcomes the learned sort of men, and besides, I enjoyed there the enhanced credit of sanctifying my Egyptian wisdom by adding to it the Ethiopian.* When the Queen understood that I was about to depart for home, she related to me the whole of what happened to you, after obtaining my sworn pledge of silence, for she said that she dared not tell it to the sages of her country. She begged me to ask the gods first, whether you had survived your exposure, and next, in what part of the world you were living: she could not hear of any girl like you in her nation, despite her many persistent inquiries. I was informed of everything by the gods, and told her that you were alive and where you were. She then besought me to seek you out and induce you to come to your native land; not once, she said, had she conceived or borne any child since the travail of your birth, and she was prepared, if you should one day appear, to confess to your father what had happened. She knew that he would believe her story, as he had tested her integrity in the years of their wedded life, and would then be attaining beyond all expectation his ambition of being succeeded by offspring of his own.

(13) '"That is what in her talk with me she begged me to do, conjuring me repeatedly by the Sun, an oath that may not be violated by any of the sages. I have come here in order to perform the duty laid on me by the vow that I took at her supplication; not that this was the actual cause of my hastening to reach this place. It was through an intimation from the gods that I have reaped this richest gain from my travels, and for a long time now, as you are aware, I have been close to you here, without ever neglecting any careful attention that I ought to pay to you. I have been silent about the truth, waiting for the right moment and means for obtaining the swathe that should attest the statement which I was to make to you. So now, if you will be persuaded, and decide to join us in our flight from here before you are forced to submit to some arrangement contrary to your own choice – for Charicles even now is busied with your marriage to Alcamenes – you have the prospect of regaining your kinsfolk, your native land and your parents, and of being united to Theagenes, who is prepared to accompany us wherever we may go. Thus you may exchange the life of a stranger beneath an alien roof for one that is truly your own in a ruling house, where you will share the royal throne with him whom you love

best, if we are to place any confidence in the gods, and especially
in the oracle of the Pythian Apollo." And with that I reminded
her of the oracle's words and explained to her their meaning:
Chariclea was not ignorant of them, as they were chanted and
discussed by many of the people. She was petrified by my words,
and said: "Since that is the purpose of the gods, as you say, and
I believe it, what then are we to do, father?" "Make pretence,"
I replied, "of consenting to the marriage with Alcamenes." "It
would be a burdensome, and besides a degrading, thing for me,"
she said, "merely to profess my preference of another to Theagenes; but yet, as I have committed myself to the gods and to
you, father, what is the object of such pretence, and by what
means could one be disentangled before the fact is upon one?"
"The facts will inform you," I said; "it sometimes happens that
the prediction of them causes a certain wavering in women, but
the performance of them on the spur of the moment often results
in a quite gallant achievement. Only follow my instructions in
all things and, just for the present, concur in Charicles' plan for
your marriage; for he has done nothing without my guidance."
She consented to this, and I left her in tears.

(14) 'Hardly had I come out of the house when I saw Charicles
in a state of extreme distress and utterly sunk in dejection. "You
marvellous man!" I said. "When you ought to be wearing a
crown, and rejoicing, and offering up sacrifices of gratitude to
the gods for granting your oft-repeated prayer – now that
Chariclea has been at long last converted to a desire for marriage
by my powerful art and my lore, you choose this moment to be
gloomy and despondent, and all but lamenting over goodness
knows what trouble." "And why should I not," he asked,
"when she who is dearest to me is ready, it seems, to rid herself
of life sooner than enter, as you say she will, into the bond of
wedlock – if one is to have regard to dreams, and particularly to
those which have terrified me last night? It appeared to me that
an eagle was released from the hand of Apollo, and swooped
down and suddenly snatched up my darling daughter, alas! from
my embrace, and then bore her away to the farthest corner of
the earth, a place all crowded with dusky, shadow-like phantoms. In the end I failed to make out what the bird could have
done with her, because the immense distance that separated it
from me baffled the efforts of my sight to keep up with it in its
course."

(15) 'After he had told me this I understood the intention of his dream; but to recall him from his despondency and to make sure that he would be far from suspecting what was to ensue I said: "For a priest, and one moreover who serves the most prophetic of the gods, you seem to me no adept at construing dreams. These visions in your sleep foretell to you the future marriage of your daughter: by the eagle they darkly intimate the husband who will take her to himself, and they announce to you the good tidings that so it will befall, with Apollo approving and almost leading to her by the hand her destined spouse; and you are distressed by this vision, and make your dream a reason for being despondent! Now, Charicles, let us keep our lips from uttering inauspicious words, and concur in the purpose of the higher powers by applying ourselves with still greater zeal to persuasion of the girl." He asked me what he should do to make her amenable. "If you have some precious article that you treasure," I said, "a robe inwoven with gold, or a valuable necklace, bring it to her as a wedding gift from her bridegroom, and by its presentation conciliate Chariclea. Indefeasible is the spell cast by gold or gems upon a woman. And now you must get everything in readiness for the celebration: it will be best to clinch the marriage while the girl is still feeling the unabated urgency of the desire effected by my treatment." "You may take it that I shall neglect nothing that lies in my power," said Charicles, as he ran off in joyful haste to act upon his words. He did indeed, as I learnt later, just what I had put to him, without any putting off: he brought to Chariclea not only garments of great price, but also the very Ethiopian necklaces that had been exposed with her by Persinna for her identitication – all represented to be wedding gifts from Alcamenes.

Calasiris tells of his meeting with some Phoenician traders, and how he planned to escape from Delphi with Theagenes and Chariclea.

(16) 'Then, meeting with Theagenes, I asked him where the persons who formed the procession with him had their dwelling. He replied that the girls had taken their departure, having been sent on in advance because of their less speedy rate of walking; while the youths were showing their impatience by making a disturbance as they mustered in a body to start their return

journey. On learning this I enjoined on him what he should say
to them and what he was to do; and I bade him be on the alert
for the signal that I would give him when the right time and
moment had arrived. I then left him, and was making my way
towards the temple of Apollo, intending to entreat the god to
guide me by an oracle on my flight with the young pair. But in
truth the divine nature moves more quickly than any human
mind in coming to the support of what is done in accord with
its will, and often anticipating one's prayer with an unsolicited
benignity. And so it was then; for Apollo gave the answer to my
inquiry before I could present it, and signified his guidance of
me by the incidents that followed. For, while I was busied with
the matters that weighed upon my mind, and was hastening, as
I have said, to consult the prophetess, I was stopped on my way
by some visitors calling out to me: "Join us in our libations dear
sir." They were, it seemed, about to hold a ceremonial banquet
with some flute-playing, in honour of Hercules. I stopped in my
onward course when I perceived what this was, for it was not
permissible for me to disregard a sacred call. When I took some
incense and offered it up, and poured libation of water, they
showed surprise at the costliness of my offering;* but still they
accepted me as a worthy partaker of their banquet. I complied
in this also, and reclined on the couch strewn for their guests
with myrtle and laurel; and I tasted such portions of the fare as
were habitual with me. "Now, my good sirs," I said to them, "I
have here no lack of delectable dishes but as yet I am uninformed
of your repute in the world; so it is time for you to tell me who
you are and whence you come. For I look upon it as the vulgar
way of uncultivated people when, after sharing in the libations
and the meal at table, they part without becoming acquainted
with one another – after they have partaken of the salt that is
sacred to the forming of friendship." So then they told me that
they were Phoenicians of Tyre, and were sea-traders voyaging
to Carthage in Libya,* in a vessel of very large tonnage freighted
with Indian, Ethiopian and Phoenician wares. At the moment
they were dedicating their banquet to the Tyrian Hercules* in
celebration of a victory; for the young man there – they showed
him reclining there opposite to me – had won the garland in the
wrestling at Delphi, and had made Tyre renowned among the
Greeks for its victory. "This man," they said, "when we had
passed by Cape Malea* and, meeting with contrary winds, had

put in at Cephallenia, declared to us on oath taken in the name of this our national god that a dream foretold to him his coming victory in the Pythian Games; and he persuaded us to turn aside from our intended route and put in at this place. By his exploits he has proved the truth of the prophecy, and he who till now was a mere merchant stands forth a glorious victor. And he makes this feast-offering to the god who gave him that intimation, to signalize both his victory and his gratitude, and also to obtain a blessing on our voyage. For at dawn tomorrow, my very good friend, we mean to set sail, if the winds should blow in favour of our wishes." "You really mean to do so?" I asked. "Yes, we do," they replied. "Then will it be agreeable to you to have me as your passenger? I intend to make the voyage to Sicily about some business: that island, you know, lies on your route, as you are bound for Libya." To which they answered: "If it should be your pleasure, we shall consider ourselves most fortunate in having with us a man who is a sage and a Greek and who, as our impression indicates, is probably in high favour with the gods." "It will be my pleasure," I told them, "if you will allow me a single day to make ready." "You shall have tomorrow," they said; "only be by the waterside, at any rate, by the evening: for the night time is most advantageous for sailing, because vessels are then sped on their way by land breezes which raise no great swell." I agreed to do as they said, after I had made them pledge their word on oath that they would not put to sea before the appointed time.

(17) 'I left them there at their flute music and their dancing, in which they frisked to a tripping time given out by pipes in an Assyrian measure; now lightly springing aloft, and now crouching close to the ground and spinning the entire body round and round like possessed persons. I went and visited Chariclea: she was still holding in a fold of her dress and examining the heirlooms that she had received from Charicles. From her I passed on to Theagenes, and having imparted to them what each had to do and at what hour, I went home and meditated on what lay before us. On the following day things fell out thus: while midnight steeped the city in sleep an armed band invaded the dwelling of Chariclea; the leader of this amorous foray was Theagenes, who had formed the young men of the procession into a fighting troop. With a sudden uproar of shouting and a clashing of shields, which utterly dismayed even those who

heard it but faintly, they dashed with lighted torches into the house, breaking their way through the outer door without difficulty, since the bolts had been purposely tampered with in order to facilitate an opening. They snatched up Chariclea, who was in readiness and had knowledge beforehand of the whole plan, and willingly submitted to this violent proceeding; and they also carried away such belongings as the girl desired them to take. As soon as they came outside the house they raised loud shouts of victory, made a mighty clatter by beating on their shields, and marched through the length of the city, filling its inhabitants with inexpressible alarm; for it had been their plan to cause a thorough panic by doing this in the dead of night, Parnassus* the while re-echoing their outcry together with the brazen clang. In this manner they traversed Delphi, continually calling out in quick reiteration the name of Chariclea.

(18) 'When they had got outside the town they took horse and rode at full speed to the heights of Locris and Oeta. Theagenes and Chariclea, acting on the prearranged plan, parted from the Thessalians and took refuge in secret with me: together they fell down at my knees and clung to them for a long time, trembling all over and exclaiming again and again: "Save us, father!" Chariclea indeed said this and no more, bowing her head to the ground and blushing for the strange action that had just been taken; but Theagenes went on to make a further appeal, saying: "Calasiris, save suppliants who are in a foreign land, stateless, dispossessed of everything, so that having lost all else they may gain only each other! Save two creatures left as chattels to the disposal of Fortune, two captives of chaste love! Save two fugitives, voluntary but guiltless, who rest on you all their hopes of salvation!" I was confounded by this appeal, and wept more in my mind than with my eyes over the young pair, so much as, unobserved by them, might relieve my own feelings. I raised them up and encouraged them; then, having advised them of the good hopes we should have of our coming adventure, undertaken from the start with the god's blessing, I said to them: "I leave you now, and go to see to the next steps to be taken. You two must wait for me in this spot, taking the utmost care that nobody shall see you." With these words I was hurrying away. But Chariclea took hold of my cloak and stopped me, saying: "Father, you are heading for wrongdoing, nay, even betrayal, if you go away and leave me here alone, with

my fortunes committed to Theagenes, and do not reflect how untrustworthy a guardian is the lover who is dominant in the love-making, especially when he is freed from the presence of those who could give him a feeling of shame. For his ardour blazes up the more, I conceive, when he sees the object of his longing at his mercy, with none there to defend her. So I will not let you go before assurance is obtained from Theagenes under a binding oath, as a safeguard for the present, and still more for the times to come, that he will have no amorous connection with me before I regain my family and home; or, if this is denied me by Fate, at least until he can take me with my full consent to be his wife; otherwise, not at all." I admired this speech of hers, and decided that we should certainly proceed as she wished. I lit a fire on the hearth, using it as an altar, and burnt on it some incense. Theagenes then swore an oath, stating indeed that it was an injustice to take this solemn precaution whereby the fidelity of his character was discredited in advance, since he was now unable to prove that he could do of his own choice what he was regarded as forced to do by fear of a supernal power. However, he swore by the Pythian Apollo and Artemis, and by Aphrodite herself and the Loves,* that he would in all things act according to the wishes and bidding of Chariclea.

(19) 'To this mutual agreement they added some others besides, praying the gods to be witnesses to their vows. I then hurried off to see Charicles, and found the house full of tribulation and wailing. The servants had already come to him with reports of the girl's abduction, and a great throng of citizens was streaming in. Charicles, as he lamented, was hemmed in on all sides by these people, who were bewildered by ignorance of what had happened and perplexity as to what should be done. Thereupon with a loud voice I called out to them: "You poor wretches, how long will you remain sitting here like senseless creatures, speechless and inert, as though in the presence of misfortune you had suffered the loss of your wits! Why not arm yourselves forthwith and go in pursuit of the enemy? Why not capture and punish the ruffians?" "Surely it is useless," said Charicles, "to struggle against this disaster; for I can see that it is the wrath of the gods that has brought upon me this penalty, of which I had warning from Apollo for having once entered his sanctuary at an incorrect time, and having

allowed my eyes to behold a forbidden sight: such an improper
view was to be requited by my losing sight of my darling.
Nevertheless there is nothing to prevent us from battling, as the
saying goes, even against divinity,* if we could but know whom
we are to pursue, and who it is that has launched this grievous
assault." "It is the Thessalian," I said, "so greatly admired by
you, whom you would have me also accept as a friend; it is
Theagenes and his young companions. You will not find in the
city now a single one of that troop who were staying in it up to
last evening, so you must rise and call on the people to assemble
for a consultation." This was done, and the commandants
proclaimed by trumpet throughout the city the summoning of a
special assembly. The people attended immediately in the
theatre, putting it in use for their nocturnal debate. Charicles
came forward in the view of all; the mere sight of him at once
moved the multitude to cries of grief. He stood there clothed in
black, his face and head bespattered with ashes,* and said:
"You may well suppose, people of Delphi, that I have come
before you, and have convened this assembly, in order to make
some announcement concerning myself; so much may be suggested to you by my extraordinary misfortunes. But that is not
the case. My fate indeed is tantamount to many deaths: I am
destitute, and am pursued by divine rancour; my house henceforth is desolate, being emptied all at once of my dearest
intimates. However, hope, that vain illusion shared by all
mankind, persuades me still to hold on to life, suggesting to me
the possibility that my daughter may be found; and even more
than this, the city bids me stay, that I may see it take vengeance
on those who have committed this gross outrage – that is, if
your spirit of liberty, and your indignation for your native and
ancestral gods, have not been abducted also by these Thessalian
youngsters. For the most grievous feature of the affair is that a
handful of young dancers, attendants on a sacred mission, have
got away after trampling on the first city of Greece, and robbing
Apollo's temple of its most precious treasure, Chariclea – the
light, too, alas, of mine eyes! Oh, the implacable enmity of Fate
against us! It extinguished my first, my own begotten daughter,
as you know, together with her wedding torches; it carried off
from me her mother at the first shock of her grief; and it drove
me forth from my native land. Yet all these things could be
borne after I had found Chariclea. Chariclea was my life, the

hope of succession in my family; Chariclea, my only solace and, one may say, my sheet-anchor. And now this anchor has been cut loose and swept away by whatever may be the destined tempest that, in no light or casual manner, but in its wonted course, has chosen this untimely moment to make cruel sport of me, by snatching her almost from her very bridal chamber, just when her coming marriage had been announced to you all."

(20) 'While he was yet speaking these words, completely carried away by his grief, the commandant Hegesias* stopped him and, thrusting him aside, said: "Hear me, all present: Charicles will be at full liberty to lament, both now and hereafter; but let us not be engulfed with him in the depths of his distress, nor be unwarily swept along, as it were, in the torrent of his tears, thus throwing away opportunity, a thing which in every affair, and especially in war, tips the scale. For if we now leave this assembly there is hope of the enemy being taken by surprise, in a time when their expectation of our being still engaged in our preparations causes them to be quite leisurely in their progress. But if, in pitying ourselves, or rather playing the woman's part, we allow our delay to put them farther ahead of us, the only result must be that we shall be laughed to scorn, and that too by a number of lads whom, in my opinion, we should capture with all speed and crucify, and then, by outlawing their descendants, carry over our retribution to the whole of their posterity. This could easily be done if we were to excite the indignation of the Thessalian people against any of these same persons who might escape us, and against their descendants, by our decreeing that Thessalians be forbidden to perform the sacred mission and sacrifice to the hero, and resolving that this service shall be maintained from our public funds."

(21) 'These proposals were no sooner approved and sanctioned by resolution of the people than the commandant went on to say: "Let this also be voted by show of hands, if it be thought fit – that henceforth the ministrant maiden shall not be brought into view of the runners in the armed race; for I see reason to suppose that it was from such view that Theagenes derived the impulse to his sacrilege and, from his first sight of the maiden, apparently, conceived the idea of her abduction. It will be well, therefore, to preclude any similar enterprise on future occasions."* When this resolution also had been passed unanimously by show of hands, Hegesias gave the signal for

departure. The trumpet sounded the call to arms, and the meeting in the theatre broke up to go to battle. All made a headlong rush from the assembly to engage in the fight; not only men at arms of robust age, but many boys also and youths just on the threshold of manhood, who made up the tale of years with their zeal, and thus emboldened themselves to join in that expedition. Many women besides showed a more manly spirit than beseemed their nature and, snatching up any weapon that came to hand, ran after them – in vain, for falling behind in the race they had to acknowedge the inherent weakness of their sex. One could have seen also, struggling against his senility, an old man whose mind seemed in his zeal to drag his body along and upbraid its feebleness. Thus the whole city showed its deep resentment of the abduction of Chariclea: all, as if stirred by a single emotion, launched themselves in one body upon the pursuit at the first call to battle, without waiting for daylight.

BOOK 5

After hearing Calasiris' story Cnemon discovers Chariclea in the house at Chemmis where Calasiris and he are staying.

(1) 'Such then was the state of things in the city of Delphi, and such the action that it took; with what result I am unable to tell. But to me that pursuit of theirs indicated the moment for our flight. I took the young pair with me in the direction of the sea just as they were, while it was still night, and put them on board the Phoenician ship, finding her on the very point of casting off. For indeed, as a glimmer of dawn was already appearing, the Phoenicians did not consider that they were breaking their sworn agreement with me – that they would wait for a day and a night only. They greeted our arrival with much pleasure, and immediately moved out of harbour, at first by rowing; but as a gentle breeze began to blow from the land, and low waves came running under the stern, seeming to smile at it, they then handed over the ship to the power of the sails. The gulf of Cirrha, the foothills of Parnassus, the headlands of Aetolia and Calydon in turn passed by the vessel as she almost flew along; and the Pointed Isles, so named from their shape, and the sea of Zacynthus came into view just as the sun dipped to its setting. But why am I relating all this at such length and out of season? Why do I heedlessly send my narrative sailing out upon the veritable ocean of what ensued? Here, I think, we may well halt my story and snatch a little sleep; for however resolute a listener you may be, and however stoutly you may fend off sleep, Cnemon, I fancy you are already beginning to sink down under the tale of my experiences, drawn out by me to such a late hour of the night. And besides, I on my part, my son, am feeling now the weight of my many years, while the recollection of my misfortunes prostrates my mind and inclines it to sleep.' 'Stay, father,' said Cnemon; 'it is not that I wish to jettison your narrative, for I believe that even if you were to continue for a long string of nights, and a longer one of days, I should never come to that, so uncloying, so bewitching, is the matter of your story. But for some time now I have heard a kind of murmur, like the buzzing of a crowd, resounding through the house: I

could not help being disturbed by it, but I refrained from saying anything, I was so enticed by my desire to hear each new incident that you had to tell me.' 'I did not notice it,' said Calasiris, 'I dare say because my old age has made me somewhat hard of hearing – for deafness is one of the ailments of advanced years – and also, I suppose, because I was preoccupied with my narration. I should think it will be Nausicles, the master of the house, who has come in; but, O ye gods, what has he succeeded in doing.' 'Everything as I wished,' said Nausicles, suddenly appearing before them. 'I did not fail to observe, my good Calasiris, that my operations were much on your mind, and that in a sense you were adventuring abroad with me in your thoughts; and now, apart from what I have perceived in your general behaviour towards me, I have come upon clear evidence of your feeling in those words that I caught you uttering here, as I entered. But who is this stranger?' 'A Greek,' said Calasiris. 'You shall hear more about him later on. If your efforts have happily succeeded, make haste to let us know, so that you may bring us in to share your joy.' 'Well,' said Nausicles, 'you shall hear about it all at daybreak; but for the moment it will suffice you to know that I have got hold of Thisbe, now in better trim. As for me, I must have at least a short sleep, to relieve the fatigue of my journeying and my many anxieties.'

(2) With these words he hurried away to do as he had said. Cnemon had been stunned when he heard the name of Thisbe, and in his helpless bewilderment was revolving thought after thought in his mind. Continually heaving deep sighs, he spent the rest of the night in great distress, so that at length even Calasiris, sunk though he was in a deep slumber, became aware of his trouble. The old man then raised himself up and, leaning on his elbow, asked Cnemon what ailed him, and what was the cause of his being so strangely distracted in a manner hardly differing from that of mad people. To this Cnemon replied: 'How should I not be mad, when I have heard that Thisbe is still alive?' 'And who is that Thisbe?' said Calasiris; 'how come you to know her name, or be concerned at the report of her being alive?' To which he answered: 'You shall have a full account later on, when the time comes for me to tell you my own story; but with these eyes I discovered that woman lying dead, and with these hands of mine I buried her in the herdsmen's haunt.' 'Go to sleep,' said Calasiris; 'we shall know quite soon how it

may have happened.' 'That I cannot do,' he said; 'you must have quiet rest; but I feel that I cannot live if I do not slip away immediately and search out by hook or by crook what illusion has taken hold of Nausicles, or how it is that only among Egyptians do the dead come to life again.' Calasiris showed a slight smile at this, and betook himself to sleep once more. But Cnemon left the room, and found himself in the natural difficulty of one who wanders in the darkness of night about an unknown house. Yet he went on undeterred, so eager was he to rid himself of his terror of Thisbe and the imaginings of his mind. At length, as he took many turns through the same parts of the house, which seemed to him each time to be different, he became aware of a woman weeping and wailing in secret, like the nightingale when it sobs out its nocturnal song of woe in the spring time.* Guided by this mournful sound, he made his way towards the room whence it came and, on applying his ear to where the doors met and listening, he caught these words of the woman's continuing lamentation: 'What boundless misery is mine! I thought that I had escaped from the clutches of the brigands and evaded the brutal murder that I was expecting, so that I could live thenceforth with my darling the life indeed of a wandering exile, yet made delightful by his company; for no burden could be so irksome that I would not be able to bear it with him at my side. But now the Fate-appointed spirit, still unsated, though in charge of me from the first, has allowed me a little taste of pleasure only to disappoint me. I thought that I had escaped from slavery, and I am a slave once more; from prison, and I am in custody. I was held in an island, and in darkness; my present lot is no better than the former or, to speak more truly, more painful, now that he who has both the will and the power to assuage my pain is parted from me. Till yesterday a brigands' cave was my lodging: an awesome chasm, a veritable tomb, was my dwelling. Yet even these hardships were relieved by the presence of him who is dearer to me than all the world. There he lamented over me while I lived, and bewept me when as he supposed, I was dead; he mourned for me as perished from the earth. Now I am deprived even of his plaints; gone is my comrade in misfortune, he who shared with me the burden of my sufferings. I am alone, deserted, a captive ever in tears, a prey to the designs of a bitter Destiny, only enduring life itself because I hope that my darling may still be alive. But, O my soul, where, where can you be? What fortune has befallen you? Can it be that you yourself, alas, are enslaved – the one high spirit that was free and unenslaved, except by love? Oh, if only you may remain alive, and behold one day your own Thisbe! For by this name shall you call me, even though it be against your will.'

(3) Cnemon, on hearing these words, lost all power to restrain himself any longer. He did not wait to hear what else might be said; for, although the first words had given him a different impression, the last that he heard convinced him that it was in truth Thisbe, and he came near collapsing close to the very door. With a great effort he held himself up; then, in fear of being caught there by someone – for the cocks were already crowing for the second time – he hurried away, stumbling as he went, now getting his feet tripped up, now suddenly running into the walls: here it was against a lintel, there against some utensil hanging by chance from the roof, that he knocked his head; till after much wandering he reached the apartment where they were lodged, and there flung himself prone upon his bed. His body was quivering, his teeth chattered aloud,* and he would probably have sunk into a most critical condition had not Calasiris, on perceiving his disorder, hastened to chafe him assiduously and done all that he could to rouse him with words. When Cnemon had a little recovered himself, Calasiris earnestly asked him to say what was the cause of his trouble. 'I am done for, I tell you,' he replied; 'that vile creature, Thisbe, is in truth alive!' With these words he swooned away again.

How it came about that Chariclea was separated from Theagenes and was found in the same house as Calasiris and Cnemon.

(4) Calasiris once more was hard put to it in efforts to revive him. And indeed it seemed that Cnemon had become the plaything of some divinity that makes a practice of treating human affairs altogether as a jest and a sport. It would not permit him to enjoy even his greatest pleasures without incurring some pain, but promptly interwove a strand of anguish with what was ere long to bring him delight; and belike it was giving an example of its practice in this instance, though perhaps the truth is that human nature is incapable of any joy unmixed and pure. And so on this occasion Cnemon shrank from that which

he preferred to all the world, and viewed with terror what gave him most delight. For the wailing woman was not Thisbe, but Chariclèa. Now, what had happened to her was this. When Thyamis had been captured alive and was held as a prisoner, and the island had been set ablaze and had been evacuated by its herdsmen inhabitants, Cnemon and Thermouthis, the henchman of Thyamis, crossed over the lagoon at dawn to discover in what way the enemy had dealt with the brigand chief. How it fared with them has already been told. Theagenes and Chariclea were left alone in the cavern, and turned their extremely perilous situation to the best advantage. For this was the first time that they found themselves together in private, freed from any irksome presence; and they took their fill of unhindered ardent embraces and kisses. In a moment they were plunged in oblivion of everything: for a long time they clung to each other as though grown into one person, satiating themselves with a devout, virginal love, communing with one another through the flow of hot tears, and commingling only by the chaste means of their kisses. For Chariclea, when she found Theagenes making some too impulsive advance of manly ardour, restrained him by recalling his oaths, and his attempt was easily checked. It was a light matter for him to be temperate, for although mastered by love he could be master of his pleasures. But when at long last they came to reflect on what they had to do, and were forced into thinking that they had had their fill, Theagenes began their consultation thus: 'To be united with each other, Chariclea, and to possess what we have deemed more precious than anything else, and for which we have endured all things – that is the object of our prayers, and may the gods of Greece bestow it. But human nature is an unstable thing, ever veering this way and that: we have undergone much, and expect to undergo more. It is now our duty, under our agreement with Cnemon, to go with all speed to the village of Chemmis. There is no knowing what kind of fortune will next attend us, and we have a long, a seemingly infinite distance yet to travel before we reach the land of our hopes. So come, let us devise some tokens by which we can convey information without speech when we are together, and if we should ever chance to be separated we can search for each other. For it is a wise provision, in case of going astray, to have a sign agreed between friends as a ready means of finding themselves again.'

(5) Chariclea approved his suggestion, and they resolved, if they should be separated, to inscribe on temples, notable statues, boundary pillars or stones set at partings of the ways, these words: The Pythian man (for Theagenes) or The Pythian woman (for Chariclea) has passed on to the right, or to the left, making for such and such a town or village or people; and besides this to specify the day and hour. If they should meet at some place it would be enough for them merely to be seen by each other; for no lapse of time could avail to erase from their souls the marks of identity made by love. Nevertheless Chariclea showed her father's ring that was exposed with her, and Theagenes the scar on his knee that he had from a boar hunt;* and to save words they agreed to use two emblems, she a torch and he a palm. Upon this they embraced one another again, and again they wept, offering up their tears, I conceive, as libations and their kisses as solemn vows. Their compact thus made, they crept out of the cavern, not touching any of the treasure stored within it, since they regarded as unclean those riches gained by rapine. But the articles which they had themselves brought from Delphi, and which the brigands had taken from them, these they packed up for their journey. Chariclea changed her dress, putting away in a small satchel her necklaces, her garlands and her sacred robe and, to hide these from view, placing on top some other articles of small value. Her bow and quiver she handed to Theagenes to carry – a most pleasant burden to him, as they were the arms associated with the god who was his master.* Then, just as they reached the lagoon and were about to embark in a boat, they saw a large body of armed men crossing over towards the island.

(6) Staggered by this sight, they stood for a great while dumbfounded, as if they had become insensible to the despiteful treatment that they received unceasingly from Fortune. At length, however, when the newcomers were just on the point of putting in to land, Chariclea urged that they should take to flight and hide themselves in the cavern, on the chance of avoiding discovery, and she started at once to run off. But Theagenes stopped her, saying: 'How far are we to continue fleeing from the Fate that everywhere pursues us? Let us yield to Fortune, and meet half way the flood that would sweep us along. Let us spare ourselves these futile strayings of a nomad life, and the deity's persistent mockery of us. Do you not see

how eagerly he endeavours to lengthen the chain, linking ordeals to exile and adding to misadventures at sea the greater hardships of the land, and now, in quick succession, producing battles after brigands? But lately he had us in captivity; then he returned us to solitude; and after giving promise of deliverance and freedom in flight, he sets our destroyers upon us. Thus he diverts himself with battling against us, as though he had made our fortunes the plot of a drama on the stage. Why then do we not cut short his tragic scheme, and give ourselves up to men intent on our destruction, lest in his eagerness to bring his play to some monstrous conclusion he should drive us to laying violent hands on ourselves?

(7) Chariclea did not agree with everything that he had said. His upbraiding of Fortune, she said, was just; but she did not approve of voluntarily yielding themselves up to the enemy, since there was no evidence to show that they would be put to death when taken. The divinity against whom they were contending was not so kind as to grant them a quick deliverance from their troubles. Nay, rather, it was possible that he might desire to preserve them for a life of slavery; and what death would not be less bitter than that? To be subjected to the infamous and abominable outrages of murderous barbarians – 'that we must avoid by every means in our power,' she said 'counting our past trials as so many hopes of success, since we have often come through still more desperate straits.' 'Let us do as you wish,' said Theagenes, following her lead as though drawn along by her. However, they were unable to reach the cavern in time. While they were observing the advance of the men in front of them, they failed to see that they had been enveloped by a detachment of the enemy which had disembarked behind them in another part of the island. They both stood still in consternation; Chariclea had crept close to Theagenes so that if indeed she had to die it should be in his arms. Some of the assailants pressed forward as if about to strike at them; but when the gaze of the young pair shed its radiance on them as they dashed up, the spirit of each man sank down and his right hand fell limp by his side; for even a barbarian's arm, it seems, will falter in the presence of human beauty, and the sight of loveliness can pacify even an alien's eye.

(8) So they seized hold of the pair and led them before their commander, full of eagerness to be the first to bring in the finest

piece of plunder. But in fact this was the only piece that they were to bring, because not a man of them found anything else about the place, although they scoured the island from end to end, sweeping it thoroughly in every direction, as it were, with the drag-net of their weapons. It had been altogether devastated by fire that arose in the previous fighting; only the cavern remained, and it was not discovered. The two captives were thus hurried before the commanding officer. Now he was Mitranes, a prefect under Oroondates, the satrap set by the Great King over Egypt. This officer, for a large sum paid to him by Nausicles, as has been related, had invaded the island in search of Thisbe. When Theagenes and Chariclea, continually calling aloud for divine deliverance, were seen approaching under guard, Nausicles, conceiving a commercial and practical plan, started up and ran to them, crying out: 'This is the woman Thisbe, whom those pestilent herdsmen stole from me, and whom I now hold, thanks to you, Mitranes, and the gods!' He took firm grasp of Chariclea, making a show of extreme delight, and urged her to acknowledge that she was Thisbe, if she wished to save her life, speaking aside to her in a low voice and in Greek, so as not to be understood by the persons there present. His ruse was successful: for Chariclea, hearing the Greek language, and surmising that she might obtain some advantage from this man, became an accomplice in his scheme and, when Mitranes asked her what her name might be, she agreed that it was Thisbe. Thereupon Nausicles ran to Mitranes and kissed his head again and again. He expressed immense admiration of the commander's good fortune, puffing up the barbarian with praises of his numerous successes in war, and especially of the happy result of his present expedition. The other, swollen with pride by these compliments, was at the same time deluded by the name into believing the case to be really as pretended; for, although astonished at the girl's beauty, which shone forth even in her simple attire like a moonbeam from among clouds, he yet had his shallow mind so overborne by the swiftness of the deception that he left himself no time to reconsider, and said: 'This girl is yours: receive her again, and take her away.' So saying he handed her over to Nausicles, gazing fixedly at her the while and clearly signifying that his renunciation of the girl was against his will and on account of the prepayment made to him. 'As for this fellow, whoever he may be,' he said, referring to

Theagenes, 'he must be our booty, and be brought along under guard. He is to be sent up to Babylon, for he is suitable for the service of the King's table.'

(9) After this parley they all crossed over the lagoon and then separated, Nausicles proceeding to Chemmis with Chariclea, while Mitranes diverged to visit other villages in his domain; and without a moment's delay he dispatched Theagenes together with a letter to Oroondates, who was then at Memphis. The terms of his message were these: 'To Oroondates, satrap, Mitranes, his prefect: this young Greek, superior to the quality of persons in my service, and worthy to be in personal attendance on the celestial Great King alone, I have taken prisoner and now send over to you, yielding to you the presentation to our common master of this fine and valuable gift – an adornment such as the royal court has never seen before nor will ever see again.'

The Egyptian merchant Nausicles offers a sacrifice and holds a feast, at which Calasiris presents him with a marvellous jewel.

(10) These were the terms of his message. Day had not yet fully dawned when Calasiris went together with Cnemon to see Nausicles, in quest of some news of doings as yet unknown to him. On being asked what he had accomplished, Nausicles told the whole story: how he went to the island and found it deserted; how at first he met with nobody; how he beguiled Mitranes with a pretence and received, claiming her as Thisbe, a girl who had been discovered; and how he had done much better for himself by happening upon her than if he had found the girl whom he had been seeking. For there was no small difference between them: it was as much as set a god above a man, so incomparable was this girl's beauty, so beyond any power of his to describe in words; moreover, she was there at hand: he could readily show her to them.

(11) On hearing his words they at once conceived a notion of the truth, and begged him to have her summoned as quickly as possible; for they called to mind the indescribable beauty of Chariclea. When she was brought in she at first kept her head bent down and her face covered to her eyebrows. Nausicles urged her to have no fear; she raised her head a little, and saw and was seen by them, to the great surprise of both parties. At

once all three gave way to tearful sobbing and doleful cries, as
though at one signal or the shock of a single blow. One could
hear, for the most part, only the words 'O father!' 'O daughter!'
and 'It is really Chariclea, and not Thisbe!' Nausicles was struck
dumb, as he gazed at Calasiris embracing Chariclea and continuing to weep over her for so long; he wondered what to make of
this recognition scene, enacted as though in a drama.* At length
Calasiris said to him, after saluting him for a great while with
kisses: 'O best of men, for this deed may the gods grant you all
the desires of your heart, to its full contentment!* You are the
saviour of my daughter when I had abandoned all hope of her;
you have enabled me to behold what is to me the sweetest sight
in all the world. But O daughter, O Chariclea, where have you
left Theagenes?' She uttered a wail at this question and, after
pausing awhile said: 'He has been captured and taken away by
whoever the man may be that handed me over to this person.'
Calasiris then begged Nausicles to relate what he knew about
Theagenes – who was now his master, and whither he was being
taken. Nausicles told him everything, for he now understood
that the young pair were the persons of whom the old man had
so often spoken to him, and in search of whom he knew
Calasiris to be pursuing his sorrowful wanderings. But he added
that their case was none the better for this intelligence, as they
were without any resources; it would be astonishing if Mitranes
should be willing to give up the young man for even a large sum
of money. 'We have money,' said Chariclea aside to Calasiris;
'promise as large a sum as you please. I have preserved the
necklace that you know of, and have it here with me.'

(12) Calasiris was encouraged by these words; but he feared
lest Nausicles should get some suspicion of the facts and of the
articles that Chariclea carried with her. 'My good Nausicles,' he
said, 'a sage is never in want: he confines his desires to what is
essential, and obtains from the highest powers only so much as
he can honourably ask. So now, just tell us where is the master
of Theagenes; for the divine power will not ignore us, but will
succour us as fully as we desire, to the discomfiture of the
Persian love of money.' Nausicles smiled at this and said: 'You
will induce me to believe that you are able to become wealthy
all of a sudden, as by some miracle, if and when you pay me
first the ransom of this girl: you must in any case bear in mind
that merchants, no less than Persians, are lovers of riches.' 'I am

aware of that,' said Calasiris, 'and you shall be paid. Why should you not, indeed, when you show no lack of generosity, and even forestall my appeals by your spontaneous assent to the restoration of my daughter? But first I must offer up a prayer.' 'No objection,' said Nausicles; 'or rather, come now, if you will – for I am about to offer a thanksgiving sacrifice to the gods – and speak the prayer at this oblation, as one dedicated to the service: ask the gift of riches for us, and then receive it for yourself.' 'Do not jest or be so unbelieving,' Calasiris said to him; 'go on ahead and make the preparations for your sacrifice: we will attend when all has been got ready.'

(13) They proceeded accordingly: a little later a messenger from Nausicles bade them come without delay to the sacrifice. They had by now agreed on what they should do; and they set forth in joyful mood, the two men along with Nausicles and a company of others whom he had invited, for it had been arranged as a public sacrifice. Chariclea went with the daughter of Nausicles and the other women, whose many appeals and requests had with some difficulty prevailed on her to walk along with them. It is probable that they would never have succeeded if she had not bethought her of using the ceremony as a cover for her intercession for Theagenes. When they arrived at the temple of Hermes – to whom Nausicles was offering the sacrifice as the god of commerce and traders, and whom he singled out from all the gods for his personal devotion – and as soon as the victims had been slain, Calasiris briefly inspected the entrails,* and indicated by his facial expressions an intimation of future fortunes chequered with both pleasures and pains. He then reached out with his hands over the altars, uttering some words and making pretence of having drawn out of the fire what he had all the time been carrying with him. 'Here,' he said, 'you have the ransom of Chariclea, Nausicles; the gods bestow it through me.' Therewith he put into the merchant's hands a ring of regal splendour, a miraculous work of divine art. The circlet was a hoop of amber, and in the bezel blazed an Ethiopian amethyst, as large in contour as a maiden's eye, and in beauty far surpassing the stones to be found in Spain or Britain,* which have a faint reddish bloom like that of a rose just opening out its petals from the bud and beginning to blush under the rays of the sun. But the amethyst of Ethiopia glows in its depths with a pure gleam that has a fresh, spring-like charm: if you turn it

round in your hand it gives forth a golden beam which, instead of dazzling your eyes with a fierce glare, sheds all around it a gladdening light. And yet there also resides in it a potency more sovereign than is found in many of those that come from the West: for it does not falsify the import of its name, but is in truth preventive of intoxication in its wearer, and preserves his sobriety in wine parties.*

(14) This is the quality of all amethysts coming from India and Ethiopia; but that which Calasiris then offered Nausicles far excelled even those in merit. For it was finely worked with a design which had been carved into a representation of live creatures. The subject was a young boy tending sheep; he stood on a low rock, so that he could look all around him, and he was regulating the pasture of his flock with the music of cross-fluting. They appeared to be submitting obediently to the guidance of their feeding given by the keynotes of his flute. One would have said that they were heavy-laden with fleeces of gold: not that this was a happy effect of the artist's skill; it was rather that the amethyst shed over their backs the flower-like brightness of its natural flush. The design included the limber friskings of the lambs: some were running upwards in troops at the rock, while others wheeled in stately circles round their shepherd, treating this outcrop of stone as the platform of a pastoral theatre; while others, delighting in the sun-like blaze of the amethyst, scraped the rock with the tips of their hoofs as they bounded against it. Those of earliest birth, bolder than the rest, seemed eager to leap outside the circle of the gem, but to be prevented by the art with which the bezel had been made to enclose both them and the rock as in a golden fold. The rock was a real stone, and no imitation of one; for the artist, to make it real, had so marked off a portion of the gem's border as to produce his effect in the actual material, considering it over-curious to impose by craft one stone upon another. Such was his ring.

(15) Nausicles, besides being quite taken aback by the surprise of the jewel, was even more delighted with its great value, which he judged to be equal to that of a man's entire fortune. 'I was jesting, my good Calasiris,' he said; 'my request for her ransom was mere talk, whereas my purpose was to deliver your daughter to you free of any payment. But since, as you say, "not to be cast aside are the glorious gifts of the gods"*, I accept this

heaven-sent jewel, convinced that it has come to me from Hermes, best and kindest of the gods, in his wonted manner. He has in fact conveyed this treasure trove to you through that fire – indeed, one can see it beaming far and wide with the flame. And besides, I judge the finest kind of gain to be that which enriches the recipient without causing a loss to the donor.' When he had thus spoken and acted he bade the whole company join him at the banquet: he disposed the women by themselves in the interior of the temple, while the men he set at table in the vestibule. When they had taken their fill of enjoyment of the viands, the pleasures of the table gave place to those of the wine-bowl; the men poured libations singing a hymn to Dionysus for a blessing on their voyage, while the women danced to a chant of thanksgiving to Demeter. But Chariclea withdrew for her own devotions, and prayed that she might survive for Thea-genes, and he be preserved for her.

(16) The drinking-bout was now in the full flow of its gaiety, and each man was making merry as he felt inclined, when Nausicles offered a cup of water free from any admixture to Calasiris, saying: 'My good Calasiris, we drink to you this virgin draught, as being congenial to you; it has had no association with Dionysus, and is still truly in its maiden state.* If you would respond to our toast with the story that we are longing to hear, you would be entertaining us with a draught of the most exquisite of liquors. You hear how the women have arranged for a dance as their pastime during our potations; but for us your adventures, if you would be so good as to relate them, would make a most admirable accompaniment to our festivity, pleasanter than any dancing or piping. You have often, you know, put off recounting them to me, as you were still immersed in the flood of your experiences; but you could not possibly reserve them for a fitter occasion than the present, when of your two children the daughter here is saved and visible to your eyes, and the son will at any moment, with the gods' aid, appear before you – the more surely, if you do not annoy me by a further deferment of your story.' 'A thousand blessings light upon you, Nausicles,' interjected Cnemon; 'for, after having called in all manner of musical instruments for our banquet, you despise them at this moment, renouncing the more popular kinds of entertainment, and show yourself eager to hear of matters truly mystical and, in fact, imbued with heavenly

pleasure. To me you seem to have the finest understanding of the divine nature, linking as you do the cult of Hermes* with that of Dionysus, and mingling the flow of sweet-savoured words with the draughts of our wine. I have been filled with admiration of the whole of your sumptuous celebration of this sacrifice; but how could one better propitiate Hermes than by raising from among the company some discourses as a festive contribution most appropriate to the god?' Calasiris complied, since he wished to gratify Cnemon, and also to oblige Nausicles, with an eye to what the future might bring. He told them the whole story, but abridged the first part, already told to Cnemon, only giving it in a sort of summary, and purposely omitting portions which he did not consider advantageous for Nausicles to know. When he came to the yet untold sequel of what he had related, he thus took up the tale.

Calasiris tells how he, Theagenes and Chariclea sailed with the Phoenicians to Zacynthus, and lodged there with a deaf fisherman named Tyrrhenus.

(17) When they had got on board the Phoenician vessel, he said, in their flight from Delphi, the beginning of their voyage was quite agreeable, as they were borne along by a following wind of moderate strength. But when they entered the strait of Calydon* they were subjected to a severe tossing by the naturally turbulent waters that they met with there. Cnemon requested him not to pass over this fact itself, but to tell of any particular observation that he might have made of the cause of the sea's prevailing roughness in that part. 'The Ionian Sea,' he answered, 'is there contracted from a wide expanse and, pouring through a sort of bottle-neck into the Crisaean Gulf* and speeding on to meet the Aegean Sea, is thrust back from its onward flow by the Peloponnesian Isthmus: Divine Providence, it would seem, has erected the bulwark of this neck of land as a barrier against inundation of the lands confronting the current. Thence arises, of course, a reflux of the waters, which are more constricted in this passage than in the rest of the gulf. It often happens that the main stream, still moving on, meets the returning flow, and causes the water to boil up as it is roused into a seething surge and piled up by the clash of currents into high-crested billows.' This account of his was warmly applauded

and approved by his hearers, who testified to the truth of his explanation. Calasiris then pursued his narrative thus: 'We made our way through the strait,' he said, 'and when we had lost sight of the Pointed Isles we fancied that we could distinguish the headland of Zacynthus creeping into our view like a dark cloud. The pilot ordered some sails to be furled: when we asked him why he was slackening the ship's motion when she was running so well before a fair wind – "Because," he answered, "if we continued under full sail before this breeze, we should be coming to anchor by the island about the first watch, and in the dark there is a risk of running our ship aground in a place full of hidden and rugged reefs. So it will be best to pass the night well out to sea, and make now but a moderate use of the breeze, calculated so as to suffice us for a landing at daybreak."

(18) 'These words of the pilot, Nausicles, were not confuted by the event; for the sun was rising at the moment when we dropped anchor. The people of the island dwelling about the harbour, which is not far distant from the town, came streaming towards us as though to some strange new sight. They were evidently filled with wonder at the easy management of our vessel and the combined beauty and loftiness of the lines which her builders had given her. They recognized, they said, the subtle skill of the Phoenicians, but wondered more at the singular good fortune which had enabled us to make a tranquil and unharassed voyage in the winter time, and just as the Pleiads had begun to set.* Hardly had the hawsers been made fast when almost all the passengers left the ship and hurried to the town of Zacynthus to do their marketing. But I, having chanced to hear the pilot say that they were going to make the island their winter quarters, went to look for a lodging somewhere near the shore; for I rejected the ship as a dwelling-place, made unsuitable as it was by the rowdiness of the sailors, and the town as unsafe in view of the young couple being refugees. After proceeding for a little way I saw an elderly fisherman seated in front of his door and at work on the repair of some broken meshes of a net. I went up to him and said: "Good day, my friend; tell me, where can one find a lodging?" "By that near headland," he replied; "it was caught on a sunken rock yesterday and was badly torn." Then I told him: "That is not what I wished to know; it would, however, be good of you, and I should take it kindly if you would either provide a lodging

yourself, or direct me to someone else who would." "It was not I," he said; "I was not in the boat: may Tyrrhenus never make such a bad mistake, or be so broken down by old age! No, it was a blunder of my little boys who, unacquainted with the reefs, put down the nets where they should not have done." At last I understood that he was somewhat hard of hearing; so I raised my voice and shouted: "I bid you good day, sir; and would you tell us strangers of a lodging?" "Oh, good day to you too," he answered; "do stay with us, if you will, unless mayhap you are one of the sort who go looking for houses with many beds, or bring along with them a train of attendants." When I told him that we were three – my two children and myself – "The quota is agreeable," he said, "for you will find us but one more than that. I also have still two children boarding with me; my elder sons are married and heads of their own households; and my children's nurse makes the fourth in mine. Their mother died not long ago. So, my very good sir, do not hesitate, or be in any doubt of our giving a warm welcome to a man who, from the moment of one's meeting with him, shows the marks of good breeding." I took him at his word, and after a brief interval I came along with Theagenes and Chariclea. The old man received us gladly, and allotted to us the sunnier side of the house; and, I may say, we passed quite pleasantly there the first part of the winter season. Our rule was to spend the day time together, but to separate at bed time: Chariclea took her rest with the nurse, and I and Theagenes ours by ourselves; while Tyrrhenus retired with his children to another room. We shared common table with them, and we provided most of the food; but Tyrrhenus brought in from the sea abundance of fish for his young guests' entertainment, in part the product of his personal fishing, but some also caught at times when we employed our leisure in assisting at the haul. In this pursuit he had become a perfect adept, varying his method to suit the changes of the seasons. This brought him such happy success in securing great catches that the skill which he had acquired by long practice was commonly accounted to a special benignity of Fortune.

(19) 'But it was not possible, as the saying is,* for unfortunates to avoid misfortune anywhere; and even in her lonely retreat Chariclea's beauty was not without its embarrassments. That merchant of Tyre, who had been victorious in the Pythian

Games and our fellow-voyager, frequently pestered me with coming to see me in private and wearying me with importunate requests that, as her apparent father, I would let him have Chariclea in marriage. He gave himself great airs, first pointing out the distinction of his family, and then recounting in detail the riches that he had with him; how the ship was his own property and the main part of the wares that she carried belonged to him – gold, stones of many talents' worth and silken stuffs; and, as no small enhancement of his fair fame, he spoke of his victory at Delphi and many other successes besides. I pleaded my present poverty, and said that I would never consent to give my dear daughter to anyone residing in a foreign land, and among people so far remote from Egypt. "No more of that, father!" he said; "I shall regard the girl herself as a fully paid dowry of many talents' value, amounting to absolute opulence; and I will adopt your people and your country as my own. I will abandon my voyage to Carthage, and will be your shipmate wheresoever you may choose to go."

Tyrrhenus warns Calasiris against a threatened attack of pirates.

(20) 'Seeing that the Phoenician, instead of relinquishing his purpose, continued to pursue it with the utmost fervour, and did not cease for a single day from pestering me on the same subject, I decided to put him off for the present with fair promises, lest we should become victims of some act of violence in the island. So I promised that I would do all that he desired when I arrived in Egypt. Hardly had I thus disposed of the man for a while, when Fate drove one wave after another, as they say,* upon me. For Tyrrhenus, a few days later, drew me apart into a little cove in the coast and said: "Calasiris, I swear to you by Poseidon, lord of the ocean, and all the other deities of the sea, that I truly look upon yourself as a brother, and upon your children quite as though they were my own. I have come now to tell you of a certain matter that is raising its head – a troublesome affair, but such as I could not rightly keep to myself, since I have had you sharing my hearth and home, and such as it is absolutely necessary for you to know. A gang of pirates, lurking in the hollow fold of the flank of this headland, is lying in wait for the Phoenician vessel, and is posting scouts in relays to watch for her departure. Look out then; be on your

guard, and think out your plan of action; for it is on your account, or rather on that of your daughter, that they are meditating this stroke – so brutal, but common enough among those people." "May the gods reward you," I said to him, "as you deserve, for doing this! But how, Tyrrhenus, have you got hold of their design?" "Through my business," he said, "I have become known to those men: I supply them with fish, and they pay me more for it than I get from any other people. Yesterday, as I was collecting some wicker creels round the cliffs, the pirate chief met me and questioned me earnestly, saying: 'Tell me, have you heard when the Phoenicians intend to sail?' I, perceiving the hidden purpose of his question, replied: 'Trachinus,* I cannot say exactly; but I believe they will depart about the beginning of spring.' 'Well, and will that girl,' he asked, 'who is staying with you, accompany them on the voyage? 'That is uncertain,' I replied; 'but why are you so curious?' 'Because I am madly in love with her,' he said, 'from a single sight that I had of her. I do not recall having come across such beauty before, though I have made many girls my prisoners who were not unattractive.' Then, that I might induce him to reveal the whole of his design, I said: 'Now why should you get yourself embroiled with these Phoenicians, instead of possessing yourself of the girl without bloodshed, before she goes to sea, by abducting her from my house?' 'Even among brigands,' he replied, 'there still survives something of conscience and kindly feeling towards their acquaintance. So, besides sparing you the trouble caused to you by an inquiry being made concerning your guests, I propose to achieve at one blow two paramount objects – possession of the riches in the ship and marriage with the girl. I must certainly fail of attaining one of these if I set about the action on land; and besides, any such proceeding so close to the town would be exposed to a real risk of immediate detection and pursuit.' After complimenting him profusely on his sagacity I parted from him; and, in bringing you this information of the plot which is being hatched by those accursed villains, I beseech you to take serious thought for the safety of both yourself and yours."

(21) 'I went away depressed by this news, and was turning over all manner of plans in my mind, when by sheer chance the merchant met me again: as he kept on conversing in the same strain, he gave me my cue for a certain plan of action. I

concealed from him part of the information that I had from Tyrrhenus, as seemed best to me, and disclosed only the news that an abduction of the girl was contemplated by a local inhabitant by whom he was sure to be outmatched in a conflict. "I would much prefer," I told him, "to betroth her to you, because of what I already know of you as well as your affluence; above all, for your prompt undertaking, if you had her to wife, that you would live in our country. So, if this is absolutely your desire, we must hasten our voyage hence before we are surprised by some very unwelcome experience." He was overjoyed at hearing this and: "That is fine, father!" he said, as he came and kissed my head; then he asked me what time I appointed for putting to sea. Although the season might be too early yet for navigation, he said, we might shift to another anchorage where we could both avoid the suspected attack and await the full advent of spring. "Well then," I said, "if my order is to decide it, I should like to sail away this coming night." "So shall it be," he said, and went off. I returned to the house and, without saying a word to Tyrrhenus, told my children that after nightfall we had to re-embark in the ship. They wondered at this sudden resolve and asked me the reason of it. I put off telling them till later and only said: "This is the best course for us in the circumstances."

(22) 'After having a little supper together we betook ourselves to sleep. Then in a dream an old man appeared to me whose form was withered away, except that where his doublet was trussed up he showed in his thigh muscles some relics of the robustness of his prime. On his head he wore a leathern cap; he looked about him with glances at once sagacious and wily; and he dragged a limping leg, as though he had been wounded.* He drew near to me and said with a cunning kind of smile: "Reverend sir, you alone have treated us as persons of no account. From all who have voyaged past the island of the Cephallenians, and who have taken note of my house and made it their concern to acquaint themselves with my renown, you alone have distinguished yourself by such disdain that you did not show me even the courtesy of an ordinary greeting, although I was dwelling in the neighbourhood. Consequently it will not be long before you pay the penalty of this behaviour. You will meet with sufferings similar to mine, at the hands of enemies on both sea and land. Give this message from my wife to the girl

who accompanies you: she blesses her for prizing chastity above all things, and assures her that all will end happily for her." I started up trembling with fright at this vision. When Theagenes asked what had so affected me, I said: "Surely we are too late now for the ship's departure – the thought of this has upset me when I awoke. Come, get up yourself, and help to pack our things; I will go and fetch Chariclea." My daughter appeared at my call, and Tyrrhenus, on hearing it, rose also and asked what was happening. "It is the happening," I told him, "that you recommended. We are trying to elude our would-be assailants. May the gods preserve you also, who have proved yourself such an excellent friend to us. Now do us this final favour: sail over to Ithaca,* and sacrifice to Odysseus on our behalf, begging him to abate his wrath against us. He appeared to me this night to declare his resentment of our negligence." He promised to do this, and accompanied us to the ship, shedding abundant tears and praying that we might have a prosperous and satisfactory voyage.

'Why weary you with a drawn-out tale? The morning star was just beginning to shine out when we put to sea. The crew at first made many objections to sailing, but were at length persuaded by the Tyrian merchant telling them that he was evading an attack of pirates, of which he had had warning – little knowing how true was his feigned explanation. We then met with such boisterous winds, and had to contend with such an overwhelming surge of billows, beyond all description, that after nearly losing our lives we ran the ship inshore by a promontory of Crete. One of our rudders* had been carried away and most of the yard-arm shattered. We therefore decided to remain in that island for a few days, in order to repair the vessel and refresh ourselves. When we had done so word was given for setting sail again on the first day of the new moon's shining after its conjunction with the sun. We put out to sea and, to the humming sound of the vernal zephyrs, were borne along night and day, the pilot setting the vessel's course for the Libyan coast. For he declared that with this favouring breeze he could cross the sea on a direct line throughout, and that he was making all haste to reach a harbour in some mainland, since he suspected the small boat showing astern of us to be a pirate craft. "Ever since we left the Cretan headland," he said, "it has been following in our wake and persistently running along the line of our course, just as though by some connection it were sharing the same motive power. I frequently detected it varying its movement in accord with ours, whenever I purposely turned our ship, now and then, off her straight course."

The ship bearing Calasiris and the young lovers from Zacynthus is chased and captured by pirates led by Trachinus. Nearly overwhelmed by a storm, they land at length near the mouth of the Nile.

(23) 'The effect of his words was to spur some of the men to action, and these called for measures to be taken for resistance: but others made light of the matter, asserting that it was usual in the open seas for lesser craft to follow those of greater size, as though to have the guidance of their more expert navigation. The contest between these two opinions continued till the day had advanced to the hour when the husbandman unyokes his oxen from the plough. The wind was abating its vehemence, and gradually gave way to a breeze of ineffectual feebleness which, as it came upon the sails, rather stirred than propelled the canvas, and at last subsided into a calm. It was as though the wind were setting in company with the sun or, in words nearer to the truth, were bent on serving the ends of our pursuers. For the people in the boat, so long as the wind sufficed to keep us on our course, naturally lagged a good distance behind our ship, since her larger sails took the wind in greater strength; but when the calm had smoothed the sea, and there was need to employ the oars, they made up to us faster than words can tell, all of those on board, I suppose, being oarsmen and working a light craft that was more responsive to their strokes.

(24) 'When they were coming quite close to us one of the persons who had embarked with us at Zacynthus cried out: "There you are, friends, we are done for! It is a pirate craft; I recognize the boat of Trachinus." A great tremor ran through our ship at this news and, although becalmed, it was filled now with a storm of the men's clamours, laments and hurry-scurry that burst upon it; some hiding themselves below in the hold, some calling on each other to stand and fight on the deck, while others urged that they should jump into the cockboat and make

their escape; till the conflict caught and held them as they were
hesitating and shrinking, and forced them to take up any chance
objects as weapons for their defence. I and Chariclea held
Theagenes enclosed in our arms; he was in a frantic state,
boiling with desire to fight, and we were hardly able to restrain
him; she was striving, as she declared, not to be parted from
him even in death, and in that to share with him a like fate by
the same stroke of the same sword; while I, aware that our
assailant was Trachinus, was devising a plan that would serve
us well in what might follow. And so in fact it turned out to do.
For the pirates came close up to us and, passing athwart our
bows, reconnoitred to see whether they might be able to get
possession of our ship without bloodshed. While they refrained
from launching any missile, they circled round us in a manner
that kept us from making progress in any direction, just as
though they had us under siege and were desirous of taking the
ship by capitulation. "You hapless creatures," they said, "why
be so mad as to lift your hands in resistance to such invincible
and preponderant force, and at the hazard of evident death? We
still prefer the humaner part; we permit you to take to your
cockboat and make off with your lives to wheresoever you
please." These were the terms that they offered: yet the men in
our vessel, so long as they were in a conflict free from danger, a
bloodless war, made bold to say that they would not quit the
ship.

(25) 'But one of the pirates, the most daring among them,
leapt aboard our ship, and striking with his sword at those who
came in his way gave proof that war is decided by slaughter and
death. Then all the rest of his fellows leapt aboard after him.
This quickly brought the Phoenicians to their senses, and on
their knees they begged the enemy to spare them in return for
their compliance with any terms that might be imposed on them.
The pirates, though now at their work of slaughter – for the
sight of blood is a hardener of valour – on the order of
Trachinus, and beyond all hope, had mercy on the prostrate
suppliants. An unstipulated armistice ensued by which, under
the false appellation of peace, the bitterest war was in fact
unleashed, with conditions imposed which were more distressing
than any battle. For command went out that each man was to
quit the vessel wearing only a single short tunic, under threat of
death to any who disobeyed. But it would seem that men value

life above all else;* and so, for its sake, on this occasion, the
Phoenicians, while they were cheated of the riches that they
hoped to gain from their ship, seemed as though instead of being
robbed they were in the way to make a profit. They pressed
forward to get before one another in embarking in the cockboat,
everyone struggling to be the quickest in making sure of saving
his life.

(26) 'As soon as in obedience to his order we came before
Trachinus, he seized hold of Chariclea and said: "It was not at
all against you, dearest one, but for you, that this battle has
been fought; all this time I have been following you, ever since
you left Zacynthus, and it is for your sake that I have undertaken this long voyage with all its perils. Take heart, then,
and know that with me you will be mistress of all this booty."
At these words of his she, as clever a creature as ever lived,
with her quickness in turning a situation to the best account,
and also getting some advantage from my promptings, threw
off the downcast look caused by her present predicament and,
forcing herself to show a more engaging expression, said: "Ah,
thanks be to the gods for inclining your mind to humaner
intentions towards us! But if you wish to have and keep me
truly enheartened, give me the first impression of your goodwill by saving the lives of this brother of mine, and of my
father here, and do not allow them to leave the ship; for it
will not be possible to live if they are parted from me." With
these words she threw herself down at his knees and clung to
them for a long time in supplication, while Trachinus, luxuriat-
ing in the clasp of her entwining arms, purposely delayed in
giving his promise. Moved at length to pity by her tears, and
subdued by her glances to absolute compliance, he raised up the
girl and said: "I grant you your brother, with the greatest
pleasure, for I see that the young man is full of valour and
competent to play his part in our way of life. As for this old
man, he is a useless burden; but, solely as a favour to you, he
may remain."

(27) 'While all this was being spoken and enacted, the sun
completed his round and came to his setting, thus bringing on
the hour of twilight, that limbo betwixt day and night.* The sea
then suddenly became rough, perhaps affected by the change of
hour, or perhaps unsettled by the design of some Fate. One
heard a booming of the wind as it swept down, and instantly a

blast of unprecedented fury and force struck us, and filled the
pirates with all the confusion caused by a sudden surprise. They
had left their own boat, and were caught as they were busied
with pillaging the cargo of the merchant ship, and they lacked
any experience of managing a vessel of her large size. Consequently the several tasks of her navigation were taken up
casually by each man as he chanced to be at hand, and each
made bold to improvise what skill he could for his task. Some
tugged distractedly at the sails, others ignorantly handled the
ropes; one, quite unqualified, was posted in the prow, while
another in the stern had charge of the tiller. Indeed, what chiefly
exposed us to extreme peril was not the violence of the storm,
which had not yet reached the full height of its tumult, but the
inexpertness of the pilot, who held out as long as the beams of
daylight continued to shine around us, but resigned his task
when darkness prevailed. Finding themselves now all awash
and on the point of foundering, some of the pirates at first
attempted to transfer themselves to their own boat. But they
quickly desisted when they were beaten back by the surge, and
were also persuaded by Trachinus that they could be wealthier
by the value of a multitude of such boats if they preserved the
merchant ship and her rich cargo; and he ended by cutting the
cable with which their boat was attached to the ship, averring
that it was like dragging another storm along after them. He
also pointed out that they must take thought for their future
safety; for suspicions would be aroused by their sailing into
any place with both of the vessels, and inquiry would surely
be made after the passengers embarked on one of them. His
words carried conviction, and at one stroke he gained credit,
for the moment, on both counts. They were sensible of some
little relief as soon as their boat was parted from them, though
they were still not wholly clear of their danger. Huge waves,
one close upon another, drove them hard; they jettisoned much
of the cargo, and were menaced with every kind of danger
until, having barely survived the passing of that night and the
following day also, towards evening we ran the ship in to land
by the Herculean mouth of the Nile. There we, unhappy
creatures, set foot by no wish of ours on Egyptian soil: while
the pirates did so gladly enough, we in our sore distress poured
out reproaches against the sea for preserving our lives. For its
waves had begrudged us a death clear of human outrage, and

had abandoned us to the greater terrors of the land and what it held for us in prospect, exposed as we were to the lawless purposes of pirates. Such in fact were the dealings of those miscreants from the moment of their stepping ashore. Professing a specious desire to sacrifice in thanksgiving to Poseidon, they fetched some Tyrian wine with other fare from the ship, and dispatched a party of men to purchase cattle from the inhabitants of the district: these men were amply supplied with money, and were ordered to pay the first price that was demanded.

Calasiris finally tells how the pirate chief Trachinus held feast to celebrate his intended marriage with Chariclea; how Pelorus, his second-in-command, quarrelled with him over possession of the girl; and how a murderous fight ensued between partisans of the two men, the result of which was described at the beginning of Book I.

(28) 'The men returned very soon, driving a whole flock of sheep and pigs. The pirates who had stayed behind met them, lit an altar fire, flayed the victims, and were preparing the banquet, when Trachinus took me aside privately, so as not to be overheard by the others, and said: "Father, I have set my heart on taking your daughter to wife and, as you see, I am going to hold the marriage feast this day, thereby combining with this sacrifice to the gods the sweetest of festivities. So, in order that you on your part should not, from lack of this information, cut a somewhat sullen figure at our banquet, and that your child, by learning it from you, should welcome with joy her new condition, I have thought it right to tell you my intention beforehand. It is not that I desire to have it confirmed by you, since I hold full warranty for my purpose in my freedom of action; but I consider that in any case it is propitious and seemly to secure the ready compliance of one's bride by having her informed of it beforehand by her parent." I warmly commended his statement, and made a show of being delighted; and I rendered a thousand thanks to the gods for having vouchsafed that the absolute master of my daughter should become her husband.

(29) 'I retired for a little while and tried to think out by myself some plan for what had next to be done. I then returned and

begged of him that a greater solemnity be given to the performance of the ceremony by using the merchant ship as the girl's
bridal apartment, and ordering that no one else should enter it
or disturb her there, so that she might be able to attend in good
time to her wedding attire and her other adornment befitting the
occasion. "For it would be most extraordinary," I said, "if with
the pride that she takes in her high birth and great fortune and,
above all, with this prospect of being the wife of Trachinus, she
should not even bedeck herself with the things available to her,
when we are deprived by time and place of the more brilliant
equipage of a bridal procession." At these words Trachinus'
features relaxed, and he assured me that he would gladly issue
this command. So he then commanded his men to fetch at once
everything that they required from the ship, and thereafter not
to go near it. They carried out his orders, and brought away
tables, wine-bowls, carpets, hangings – handiworks from Sidon
and Tyre* – and everything else in abundance for furnishing
forth a banquet, all displayed in a jumble on their shoulders;
and so the rich store amassed by long, parsimonious industry
was abandoned now by Fortune to the rude ill usage of a party
of dissolute revellers. Taking Theagenes with me, I went to look
for Chariclea, whom I found all in tears. "Daughter," I said,
"you have here nothing unusual or strange. But tell me now, are
you, however, lamenting old bygones or something quite new?"
"Everything," she replied, "and most of all, the prospect that I
have of Trachinus' repugnant affection, which the luck of the
moment, no doubt, has heightened in him; for it is the way of
unexpected success to call forth acts of insolence. But Trachinus
and Trachinus' odious passion will have a bitter blow, forestalled and thwarted by my death. My lamenting arose from the
thought that I shall be parted from you and Theagenes before
my death." "The facts are as you surmise," I said; "Trachinus
intends, after the sacrifice, to turn the customary banquet into
your marriage feast. He has explained his purpose to me as your
father. I have long known the frantic ardour of his feeling
towards you, ever since a conversation that I had with Tyrrhenus
in the isle of Zacynthus. But I said no word about it to either of
you, that your minds might not be distressed by fears of
impending troubles while there was a possibility of our evading
the plot laid against us. But, my children, since the divine power
has worked against us in this affair, and we are now bound on

a course through a sea of dangers, come, let us make a gallant,
an impetuous attempt, and advance to meet the onset of our
danger, resolved either to achieve life with gallantry and freedom
or to gain death with probity and valour."

(30) 'They promised to do whatever I bade them, and after
informing them of the steps we were to take I left them busied
with their preparations. I then went to the pirate who was
second-in-command to Trachinus – his name, I think, was
Pelorus* – and told him that I had something greatly to his
advantage to impart to him. He readily gave me his attention,
and took me apart, where none could overhear us. "You shall
be told it, my son," I said, "in concise form, since limits of time
prevent our talking at large. My daughter is in love with you,
and no wonder: she has been captivated by your superior
character. She suspects that the chief of your band is preparing
this feast to celebrate his marriage with her; indeed he has
intimated as much by ordering her to appear in attire of special
elegance. So look to it and, if you can, avert this event, and
rather get possession of the girl for yourself; for she says that
she will die sooner than be married to Trachinus." "Have no
fear," he said. "I myself have for some time past had a tender
feeling for her, and have been longing to hit on some expedient;
so now Trachinus shall either freely resign his bride to me as the
prize to which I am entitled for having led the boarding party
on to the merchant ship, or he shall find that he has had a
woeful wedding, when this right hand has dealt him his deserts."
I ran off after hearing his words, to avoid raising any suspicion,
and went and reassured my children with the good news that
the scheme was making some progress.

(31) 'A little after that we were at dinner; and when I
perceived that the men were far gone in liquor and were tending to be in a roistering mood, I said softly to Pelorus, close
to whom I had taken care to be placed: "Have you seen how
the girl has arrayed herself?" "No, I have not," he replied.
"Well, you could do so," I went on, "if you crept secretly into
the ship: you know that this is what Trachinus has forbidden.
There you will behold Artemis herself, seated before your eyes.
But at present be prudent in your looking, lest you draw down
death on both yourself and her." He made not a moment's
delay; as though pressed by some necessity, he arose and
hurried unobserved on board the vessel, where he saw Chariclea

wearing a garland of laurel on her head and glittering in her gold-inwoven robe. For she had dressed herself in her sacred vesture brought from Delphi, so as to be in fitting garb for either a triumph or a tomb. Her whole attire was radiant, and had an aspect well adapted to the bridal chamber. He, fired, as was natural, by this sight, and assailed at once by desire and jealousy, plainly showed in his eyes, when he returned from his visit, that he meditated some frantic act. Hardly had he resumed his seat when he said: "And I, why do not I obtain the reward due to the man who led the boarding party?" "Because," said Trachinus, "you have not asked for it. Besides, the time for distributing the booty has not yet been fixed." "Then I demand," he said, "the girl who is among the prisoners." When Trachinus answered "Take anything you please except her," Pelorus rejoined: "Then you are violating the pirates' law which assigns to the first man who boards an enemy ship – to him who has been foremost in facing the danger of a combat fought for all the rest – the choice of whatever he desires." "That law, my gallant friend," replied Trachinus, "I am not violating. I rely on another which requires subordinates to give way to their leaders. True, I have a certain affection for this girl, and in taking her as my wife I lay claim to precedence. If you disobey my command you will soon howl for it – feeling the weight of this wine-bowl!" Then Pelorus, glancing round at the company, said: "You see, this is the wage of all my labours!* Thus each man among you will be cheated of his reward, and know the quality of this tyrannical law."

(32) 'What a scene then ensued, Nausicles! Just like a sea convulsed by a sudden squall, those men were stirred up by an unreasoning impulse to an indescribable commotion, crazed as they were with wine and wrath. Taking sides with one or the other of the disputants, some clamoured for deference to their chief, and some against infringement of their law. At length Trachinus made a threatening motion, as though about to strike Pelorus with the wine-bowl; but he, already holding himself on the alert, forestalled the blow by stabbing the other in the breast with his dagger. Trachinus fell, mortally wounded; the rest of them were grappled in a truceless conflict, fighting hand to hand and raining blows without stint, some to avenge their chief, and others in defence of Pelorus and the right. With the sound of one dismal outcry they struck and in turn were stricken with

billets of wood, stones, bowls, torches and tables. I had removed myself as far away as I could, and from a rising ground I treated myself to a spectacle void of danger. But Theagenes, for his part, did not refrain from fighting, nor did Chariclea. Acting as had been agreed, he from the start plied his sword in support of one side, appearing for all the world like one possessed; and she, when she perceived that the fighting had broken out, shot from the ship well-directed arrows that spared only Theagenes. She did not strike at one party only in the struggle, but brought down whoever first came into her view. Herself unseen, she easily descried the enemy by the light of their blazing fire, while they were unable to tell what was wreaking the mischief, and some suspected that these strokes were dealt them by some superhuman power. In time all of them were laid low, except that Theagenes was left fighting in single combat with Pelorus, who was a man of boundless valour, since he had practised his hand in a vast number of butcheries. And Chariclea's archery was now no longer able to give its aid: her heart ached with longing to assist but she was afraid of missing her mark, as the fight had now come to close quarters, the two men pressing each other hard in hand to hand combat. At last, however, Pelorus could bear up no longer. Chariclea, though without power of giving active support to Theagenes, sent a volley of words to his aid, calling out: "Bravely now, dearest one!" From that moment Theagenes clearly had the upper hand of Pelorus, as though her voice supplied him with fresh strength and courage, and indicated that the prize for which they fought was still alive. Rousing up his spirit from the stress of his now numerous wounds, he leapt upon Pelorus and drove his blade at the man's head, which he missed as the other bent his body aside, but grazing the top of his shoulder he cut off his arm at the elbow joint; whereupon the man took to flight, pursued by Theagenes.

(33) 'I am unable to relate what happened next, except that I could see no sign of Theagenes' return, since I had stayed where I was on the rising ground, and had shrunk from making my way by night through the battle area. With Chariclea it was quite otherwise. When the dawn came I saw Theagenes lying prostrate like a dead man, and Chariclea seated by his side, lamenting and making as though she intended to slay herself over his body, yet restrained by a faint hope that the youth might haply survive. By ill fortune I had no time to speak to them and

hear from them, or to relieve their distress with comforting words, or to tend them in any way practicable; for our calamities at sea were now so immediately succeeded by others on land. At the moment when, on seeing daylight, I was descending the hillock, a band of Egyptian brigands came running down, as it seemed, from the mountain range that overlooked the area. They at once laid hold on the young pair, and shortly after led them away, carrying with them as much as they could of the ship's cargo. As for me, I tried in vain to follow after them at a distance bewailing my own and my children's fate: I could neither protect them nor think it well that I should join them, since I had rather reserve myself for some better prospect of assisting them. In truth, I had not the strength to do it: how could I? At that moment I was forlorn, and my age prevented me from rushing along with the Egyptians over the mountain heights; and now I owe it to the grace of the gods and your kindness, Nausicles, that I have meanwhile recovered my daughter. To this I have contributed nothing, but have been liberal only in bestowing tears and laments for her.' With these words he wept himself and his hearers wept with him, and so the banqueting was changed to lamenting, mingled with a certain pleasure; for wine disposes one somewhat to tears. At length Nausicles, to encourage Calasiris, said to him: 'Father, from now onwards at least you can be in good spirits: you have already recovered this daughter of yours, and only the night time hinders you from seeing your son. At daybreak we shall go to Mitranes and try by all possible means to have the excellent Theagenes released to you.' 'That will be my desire,' said Calasiris; 'but it is now time to break up the party. Let us be mindful of the divine power, and let the libations for deliverance be brought round.'

(34) Thereupon the libations were handed round, and the banquet broke up. Calasiris looked out for Chariclea, and when, as he carefully watched the company passing by, he failed to discover her, he finally made his way on the advice of a woman into the sanctuary. There he found Chariclea clasping close the feet of the statue: her prolonged praying and exhausting grief had caused her to slide into a deep slumber. He wept for a little while at the sight, and implored the god to give a happier turn to her affairs; he then gently roused her and led her to their dwelling, her face blushing, as it seemed, for her

inadvertent surrender to sleep. She withdrew into the women's quarters, and lay down with the young daughter of Nausicles, but spent a wakeful night, her mind occupied by the cares that beset her.

BOOK 6

*Cnemon marries the daughter of Nausicles at Chemmis, and
Calasiris and Chariclea, disguised as beggars, go in search of
Theagenes.*

(1) Calasiris and Cnemon had gone to take their rest in a room
of the men's quarters. There they passed the remainder of the
night, more slowly than they wished, but yet more quickly than
they expected, since the greater part of it had been spent at the
feast and in the narration whose length gave no feeling of surfeit.
Without waiting for full daylight they went to see Nausicles,
whom they pressed to tell them where he thought Theagenes
might be, and to take them to him with all speed. He agreed to
this, and conducted them on their way. Chariclea earnestly
begged that she might accompany them, but was prevailed on
to stay where she was, Nausicles assuring her that they would
not be proceeding any great distance, and would return with
Theagenes immediately. So they left her behind, with a heart
wavering between sorrow over this separation and joy over its
hoped-for outcome. They had just quitted the village, and were
passing along by the banks of the Nile, when they saw a
crocodile which crawled across their path from right to left, and
with a sudden dash plunged into the flowing waters of the river.
While the others took this sight with composure as something
ordinary – though Calasiris differed in pronouncing it to portend
an obstacle awaiting them on their way – Cnemon was greatly
alarmed when he saw it. The creature had not shown itself
clearly to him, but rather slipped past him like a shadow along
the ground, and he was even on the point of taking to flight. At
this, while Nausicles laughed consumedly, Calasiris remarked:
'Cnemon, I thought it was only in the night that you had your
attacks of cowardice, and only darkness made you start with
fright at every sound; and here you are, in broad daylight,
showing yourself, it seems, a prodigy of courage! Not only the
mention of names, but now sights of a commonplace and
harmless kind strike you with dismay.' 'And what god or spirit
is it,' asked Nausicles, 'whose naming our gallant friend cannot
bear to hear?' 'Whether a god or a spirit might so affect him,'

replied Calasiris, 'I cannot say; but a human being and, what is stranger, not even a man or someone renowned for valour, but a woman – and that, as he himself says, a dead one – makes him shudder with fear if one utters her name. On that night, for instance, when you arrived, my good sir, as the deliverer of our Chariclea from the herdsmen, after he had somehow overheard somebody or other mention this name that I tell of, he did not permit me to snatch so much as a wink of sleep: he was continually swooning away with his terror, and I was hard put to it to bring him round. If I could do so without annoying or scaring him, I would have told you the name just now, Nausi-cles, to make you laugh still more.' And with that he added: 'Thisbe.'

(2) But this time Nausicles did not laugh. Withdrawn into himself at what he had heard, he stood pensive for a long time, at a loss to know for what sort of reason, through what connection or in what degree Cnemon was affected by the name of Thisbe. Observing this, Cnemon broke into a peal of laughter and said: 'My good Calasiris, do you see what mighty power this name possesses, and what a bugbear it is, not only to me, as you yourself, say, but now to Nausicles as well? Or rather, we see here a complete change-over of its effect. It is now my turn to laugh, since I know that she no longer exists; while our doughty friend Nausicles, who so merrily laughs others to scorn, has assumed a gloomy look.' 'Enough of that,' said Nausicles; 'you have your revenge on me in full measure, Cnemon. But by the gods of hospitality and friendship, and by the share of salt and board that you both have received, I think, with kindly courtesy in my house, will you please explain how you know the name of Thisbe, how you have come to fear it, or why you have been making fun of me?' Then Calasiris said: 'It is your turn now, Cnemon, to give us the story which you have so often promised to relate to me, and which will acquaint us with your own adventures, but which you have hitherto put off each time with artful subterfuges. The right moment has now arrived for you to tell it, and so gratify Nausicles here, relieving as well the tedium of our journey with the welcome aid of its recital. Cnemon complied, and related in brief all the events which he had before described to Theagenes and Chariclea. He told them that he was a native of Athens, that his father was Aristippus, and that Demaenete became his stepmother. He then recounted

her illicit love for him, and how on failing of her object she hatched a plot against him, employing Thisbe as her accomplice; and he added the circumstances of his exile from his native land, the people having imposed this penalty upon him as a parricide; and how, during his stay in Aegina, he first had from Charias, a youth of his own standing, the news of Demaenete's death, and the manner of it, Thisbe having set a trap for her also; and that he later learnt from Anticles how his father had suffered the confiscation of his estate, through the blood-relations of Demaenete combining against him to arouse in the people a suspicion of his being her murderer; and that Thisbe eloped from Athens with her lover, the merchant of Naucratis.* Cnemon finally added that, after taking ship for Egypt with Anticles to search for Thisbe, in the hope that if he could find her and bring her to Athens he might clear his father of that calumnious charge, and at the same time punish her, he had encountered a host of dangers and happenings, until he was captured by a band of murderous pirates. From these he managed to escape, and landed in Egypt, where he was captured again by the robber herdsmen; and there it was that he met with Theagenes and Chariclea. He also related the violent end of Thisbe and the events that ensued, up to those which were all known to Calasiris and Nausicles.

(3) On hearing this story Nausicles revolved in his mind a multitude of questions, now being minded to relate what had passed between him and Thisbe, now thinking it well to defer the story to some other time. At length, though with an effort, he refrained, partly because he thought it the better way, and partly because a fresh incident gave him pause. They had just travelled about sixty furlongs, and were already approaching the village where Mitranes was staying, when they met with an acquaintance of Nausicles, and asked him whither he was bound in such urgent haste. 'Nausicles,' he answered, 'you question me as though you did not know that all my efforts just now are directed to one object – compliance with the commands of Isias of Chemmis. For her I till the soil, I supply all her needs; because of her I pass sleepless nights and days that I may deny her nothing – though it be at my heavy cost and pains – nothing, great or small that Isias there may demand of me. So now I am running, as you see, to bring this bird, a flamingo of the Nile, which my beloved had demanded of me.' 'What a considerate

mistress,' said Nausicles, 'you have taken to your bosom! How very slight her requirements are, if she has demanded of you a flamingo, and not the Phoenix itself,* which comes to us from Ethiopia or India!' 'That is just her way,' he replied; 'it is her regular practice to make sport of me and my efforts. But you, whither are you bound, and on what business?' 'We are hastening to see Mitranes,' they said. 'You hasten in vain, to no purpose,' he said, 'for Mitranes is not there at present: he has set out this night on an expedition against the herdsmen inhabiting the village of Bessa. For he had dispatched a young Greek prisoner to Oroondates at Memphis, to be forwarded thence, I believe, as a gift to the Great King; and the men of Bessa, led by Thyamis, whom they have lately appointed their chief, captured the youth in a surprise attack, and now have him in their possession.'

(4) He continued, as he started to run past them, with these words: 'But I must hurry on to Isias, who I suppose is all eyes now watching for me, and not let my delay produce a lovers' quarrel: she is a terror for working up, on no good grounds, accusations and a show of indignation against me.' After hearing his words they stood for a long time speechless at this surprising disappointment of their expectations. At length Nausicles rallied their spirits by representing that they should not be led by a passing moment of disappointment to abandon their undertaking altogether; they ought now to return to Chemmis, consider carefully what steps they had to take and, after putting up provisions in quantity for a lengthy excursion, devote themselves to the search for Theagenes, whether he might be heard of among the herdsmen or among some other people, maintaining everywhere a good hope of discovering him. For at this moment it seemed to be not without divine aid that they had met with a man who was an acquaintance and whose report had served to guide them to the quarter in which they should seek out Theagenes, keeping the course of their journey pointed directly upon the herdsman's village.

(5) They were quickly convinced by his words and, methinks, a fresh hope too was born in them at the hearing of that report; while Cnemon privately encouraged Calasiris by assuring him that Thyamis would see to the safety of Theagenes. They therefore decided to return, and did so, and descried Chariclea in the front porch of the house looking out for them in the

distance and in every quarter. When she saw no sign of Theagenes coming with them, with a loud and dismal wail she exclaimed: 'Can it be, father, that you three come back to me alone, as you were when you set out from here? Theagenes then, it seems, is dead! If you have something to tell, speak out quickly, for heaven's sake; do not increase my misfortune by delaying your news. It is an act of kindly feeling to be prompt in disclosing a calamity: one's soul is thus made ready to encounter the dread fact, and is given early relief from its pain.' To cut short her extreme anxiety Cnemon said: 'What a depressing way this is of yours, Chariclea! Ever showing yourself prone to presaging the worst, and that too a delusion – which is just as well. For in fact Theagenes is alive; he is safe and sound, by the gods' grace.' How this had come about, and with whom he then was, Cnemon told her briefly. Then Calasiris said to him: 'You have never yet been in love by your way of speaking; else you would know that even unfearful things are terrible to lovers, and that they trust only the evidence of their eyes in regard to their sweethearts, whose absence is sheer terror and anguish to their amorous souls. The cause of this is that they have persuaded themselves that their darlings can never be parted from them save by some grievous hindrance barring their way. So, my friend, let us indulge Chariclea in her deep and genuine suffering from the pangs of love, and ourselves go indoors and bethink us what we are to do.'

(6) So saying he took Chariclea by the hand with the tender care of a father and led her into the house. Nausicles, who wished from that moment to dispel their anxieties, and had a new purpose astir in his mind, made arrangements for holding a more splendid banquet than usual for a party of themselves only and his daughter, whose appearance he enhanced with a special elegance and choice adornments of great price. When they considered that they had had their fill of feasting, he entered on a parley with them in these words: 'My good guests, the gods be my witness when I tell you that it would suit me well if you chose to remain here, in this very place, and live with me permanently, sharing alike my means and all that I hold most dear. For I have come to regard you, not as guests merely paying me a visit, but as affectionate, genuine friends of mine henceforward; and I shall look upon all the services that I may render to you as anything but a burden. I am ready, should you wish to

go in search of your kinsfolk, to assist you with all my power for so long as I may happen to be with you. But you on your part must understand that I lead the life of a merchant; that is the skill that I cultivate. Fair west winds have been blowing now for some time, and have opened the sea to navigation; they give good promise of easy passages to traders, and my business summons me as with a trumpet call to set out for Greece. It would therefore be right and proper for you to impart to me what in time you propose to do, so that I may adapt my plans to suit the end that you have in view.'

(7) Calasiris pondered his words for a moment or two, and then said: 'Nausicles, may your voyaging hence go off with fair auspices; may Hermes the Gaingiver and Poseidon the Safeguarder be your companions and conductors, and speed you on your course through every sea with gentle waves and winds, and render every harbour · secure for you and every city accommodating and friendly towards merchants! You treat us so handsomely during our stay, and send us forth so courteously when we wish to depart, with such careful observance of the laws of hospitality and friendship!* We feel some pain, it may be, at our parting from you and your house, which your attentions have led us to look upon as our own; but we are under an inexorable necessity of giving our utmost efforts to the discovery of those who are dearest to us. This is the case with me and Chariclea here; as to Cnemon, and what his purpose may be – whether he is willing to gratify us by sharing in our wanderings or has decided on some other course – he might tell us here and now.'

Cnemon was intending to make reply, and was on the point of speaking when suddenly he broke into sobs, and a flood of tears gushed forth and muffled his tongue; until at length he recovered his breath and deeply groaning said: 'O Destiny of man, whose workings abound in continual turns, and are so utterly inconstant! What a huge upsurge of troubles you have determined to raise against me, as indeed you have against many more, time and again! You have bereft me of my family and my father's house, and have banished me from my native land and city which held all that was dearest to me; you have cast me up on the land of Egypt, to say nothing of all that befell me by the way; and you have delivered me into the hands of brigand herdsmen. You have vouchsafed me a gleam of good hope in granting me chance companions, as unfortunate as myself, but yet Greeks, with whom I was hoping to spend the remaining days of my life. And this consolation, it seems, you are now cutting off. Which way am I to turn? What is it my duty to do? Can I desert Chariclea, when she has not yet discovered Theagenes? A monstrous act, O Earth,* and criminal! Should I then accompany her and help her in her search? If one could be sure of finding him the labour would be welcome, buoyed up by the hope of success; but if the prospect is uncertain, and the difficulties increase, there is no certainty as to where my wandering steps will come to rest. Why should I not, after begging your indulgence and that of the gods of friendship, propose at this very moment my return to my native land and my family – at this opportune juncture that has occurred, it would seem, by the grace of some god, when Nausicles here, as 'he has told us, is about to leave for Greece – so that, even if something in the meantime should have happened to my father, his house might not remain bereft of an heir to succeed him? For even if I should have to be a pauper, the survival in my person of at least some relic of my family would be of real value in itself.

'O Chariclea, it is principally to you that I make my excuses, your indulgence that I beg and crave; O grant it to me! I will accompany you as far as the herdsmen's haunt, and will entreat Nausicles to delay for a little, hard pressed for time though he be. My hope is that by handing you over in person to Theagenes I may prove myself a steadfast guardian of the treasure entrusted to my care, and that I may part from you with a like steadfast confidence in what the future will bring, and a good conscience. If, however, we should fail at that point – which Heaven forbid! – I still should be forgiven, since I should not even then have left you desolate, but would have transferred my charge of you to Calasiris here, as your devoted guardian and father.' Now Chariclea had already guessed from numerous signs that Cnemon had been deeply impressed by the daughter of Nausicles; for a lover is quick to detect the sway of the same strong feeling over another. She had understood from words dropped by Nausicles that this alliance would be agreeable to him, and that he had long been scheming for it and subtly contriving to entice Cnemon into a profitable bit of business. At the same time she did not regard Cnemon as a suitable or trustworthy companion for their intended journey. She therefore said to him:

'As you please; for I am under an obligation to you, which I now acknowledge, for your past good services to us: but as for your help in the future, there is no necessity at all for you to be preoccupied with our interests, or to share against your will the perils attendant on fortunes other than your own. You should go and regain your city of Athens, your family and your home, and not on any account reject Nausicles and the occasion that has presented itself, as you say, for doing all this by his means. Calasiris and I will continue to struggle with events until we reach the end of our wanderings. Even if no human being should strike up with us, we shall be confident of having the gods as companions on our way.'

(8) Nausicles now took part and said: 'May Chariclea's prayers be granted; may the gods accompany her as she desires; and may she regain her kinsfolk – so stalwart a spirit is hers, and so sagacious a mind. And you, Cnemon, must not take it too hard that you are not bringing Thisbe to Athens, now that you have me here as the person responsible for her seizure and abduction from Athens; for the merchant of Naucratis, the lover of Thisbe, is none other than I. Nor should you lament your poverty, or expect any longer to be a beggar; for if you should find it acceptable, as it would be to me, that I brought you back again, you will there be in possession of ample wealth and will regain your home and your native land. And if you desire to marry, I affiance to you my daughter here, with the addition on my part of the richest dowry that my means can provide, while I regard the settlement on your part as already discharged since I came to know your family, your home and your nation.' On hearing this Cnemon did not hesitate for a moment: he was obtaining what he had long prayed for and desired without any hope, and what he now unexpectedly found to be more than his prayers had sought. 'I gladly accept at once all that you propose,' he said, and thereupon held out his right hand: Nausicles placed it in that of his daughter and confirmed their espousal. He then called on his kinsfolk to chant the nuptial song and led up the first dance, having designated the banquet of the day as the feast in celebration of this improvised marriage. All the guests were now engaged in dancing and an impromptu performance of the nuptial song about the inner chambers, and all night long the bridal torches lit up the house. But Chariclea alone, apart from the rest, entered her private room and securely closed the door.

There, assured of being undisturbed, she raged as in a bacchic frenzy, letting her hair float loose and wild; then, after rending her clothes, she said: 'Come, let us also dance, in honour of the Fate assigned to us, a measure suited to its nature. Let us sing to it dirges, and perform the tragic motions of lamentation. Let gloomy shade overspread us, and rayless night direct our rites, as this lamp has now been dashed to the ground. What kind of bridal bed has Fate devised for me? What nuptial chamber is appointed for me? Here Fate holds me alone, with no husband, widowed, alas! of him who is my husband only in name, Theagenes. Cnemon is marrying; Theagenes is a vagabond, and one who is a prisoner, perhaps even in fetters. This might yet be a piece of good fortune, if only his life could be saved. Nausiclea is being wedded, and is dissevered from me after sharing her bed with me till the past night: but Chariclea is alone and derelict. It is not of their lot, O Fortune and Fates, that I complain; no, let them fare as their hearts desire: it is that in deciding mine you have not put me on a level with them. You have drawn out my drama to such an inordinate length that its story transcends all that are told on any stages in the world. But why do I at such an hour thus rail against the dealings of the gods? Let the issue be determined according to their pleasure. But, O Theagenes, my sole, my darling care, if you are dead, if I should have to believe that which I pray I may never know, I shall not hesitate to join you. Meanwhile I tender you these offerings' – and with that she plucked out some of her hair and threw it on the bed* – 'and I pour these libations from the eyes that you cherish,' and as she spoke the bedding was all bedewed with her tears. 'But if happily your life is preserved for me, come now, my dear one, and repose yourself by my side, though it be but in the vision of a dream. Yet even so, of your goodness restrain yourself, and reserve your own virgin bride for the lawful bond of marriage. Ah, look now, I do clasp you in my arms, imagining that you are here with me and see me.'

(9) As she spoke these words she suddenly flung herself prone on the bed, and spreading out her arms embraced it with sobs and heavy sighs, until from the excess of her grief a misty dizziness crept upon her, overclouding her mental faculties, and insensibly drawing her into a sleep which held her until broad daylight had come. Calasiris, surprised that he did not see her at the usual time, went in search of her. Coming to her room, he

knocked loudly and repeatedly called her name, till he roused her from slumber. Chariclea, alarmed by this sudden call, darted to the door in the state in which she was disturbed, drew back the bolt and opened for the old man to enter. When he saw her dishevelled hair, her dress all tattered on her bosom, and her eyes still swollen and showing traces of the frenzy that held her before she fell asleep, he understood the cause. He led her back to the bed, seated her and put a cloak about her. Having her thus more suitably attired, he asked: 'What is this, Chariclea? Why such excessive, such immoderate dismay? Why this senseless subjection to circumstances? I do not recognize you at this moment, you whom I have hitherto found so gallant always and sagacious under the strokes of Fortune. Come now, have done with this extravagant folly! Recollect that you are human, a thing unstable, wont to swerve of a sudden this way and that. Why hasten to destroy yourself, when better prospects may well be just appearing? And be considerate of us, my child; be considerate, if not of yourself yet at least of Theagenes, to whom only life with you is desirable, and existence has value only if you survive.' Chariclea blushed as she heard these words and did so the more when she thought of the state in which she had been surprised. For a long time she was silent; then, as Calasiris kept on pressing her for a reply, she said: 'There is truth in your remonstrances; yet I may perhaps be excused, father; for it is no vulgar or riotous desire that drives me to such behaviour in my misery, but a pure and sober longing for one who, having had no union with me, is yet to me a husband, and who is, moreover, Theagenes. That he is not with me is painful but more fearful is the doubt whether he survives or not.' 'On that score,' said Calasiris, 'take comfort; the gods assent to his living now and rejoining you hereafter, if we are to put faith – and we must – in the predictions of the oracle about you both, and in the man who yesterday reported that Theagenes had been captured by Thyamis as he was being sent up to Memphis. If he has been captured he is evidently safe, because of the friendly terms of acquaintance between him and Thyamis. So the time has now come for us to act without delay, and to go with all possible speed to the village of Bessa and search, you for Theagenes, and me not only for him but for my son also. You are aware, I believe, from what you have surely heard already, that Thyamis is my son.' Chariclea showed some anxiety at this, and said: 'If

Thyamis is indeed your son, your own and not another's, a different person, then am I heading straight for a situation of extreme danger.' Calasiris wondered at this, and asked her the meaning of it. 'You know,' she replied, 'that I was taken prisoner by the herdsmen. And so in that place Thyamis was drawn into a longing for me by the fresh beauty of my looks, which seems to have brought me nothing but misfortune; and my fear is that, if in our search we should light upon him, he would recognize me as the maiden whom he saw there, and would effect by force the marriage which he then proffered to me and which I artfully contrived to evade.' 'I hope,' said Calasiris, 'that his passion would never so overmaster him that he would disregard his father's presence before his eyes, and that the glance of his parent would not shame him into the repression of a longing which, if really felt, is not permissible. Nevertheless, since there is nothing to hinder you, why not contrive some artifice to circumvent the dangers that alarm you? It seems that you are skilful enough in the invention of evasions and deferments of your assailants' devices.'

(10) Somewhat composed by his words, Chariclea said: 'Whether you are speaking sincerely, or have been making game of me, let it pass for the moment. I did once before devise a scheme with Theagenes, but it was debarred by events that befell at the time. I will have recourse to it now, with better chances of success. When we resolved to escape from the herdsmen's island we decided to change the character of our dress to one of utter squalor, and to go thus disguised as beggars on our visits to villages and towns. So, if you are agreeable, let us assume that character and go abegging, for in this way we shall be less likely to be molested by people who fall in with us. The simple life is a security in such encounters, and "Poverty finds Pity instead of Envy at its side." And we shall the more easily obtain our necessary supply of daily food; for in a strange land it is hard for the unacquainted to find what they can buy, whereas a dole that is asked is readily bestowed out of compassion.'

(11) Calasiris commended her plan, and was for setting out promptly on their travels. Meeting with Nausicles and Cnemon, they made known to them their departure, and two days later they started out, after declining to take a pack-animal, though one was offered to them, or any person as a fellow-traveller. Nausicles and Cnemon, with all the household, escorted them

on their way. Nausiclea also, having obtained her father's
permission after pressing entreaties, joined in escorting them;
for the charm of Chariclea's company had quite overcome the
bashfulness of a recent bride. After they had proceeded about
five furlongs, they bade a final farewell to one another, those of
the same sex embracing each other, shaking hands, shedding
abundant tears, and wishing each other the best of fortune as
they parted. Cnemon begged to be excused from accompanying
the travellers, being newly bound in wedlock, and professed his
intention of following and overtaking them at the first opportunity. And so they parted: while the rest returned to Chemmis,
Chariclea and Calasiris first changed into their beggars' disguise,
pauperizing their appearance with rags which they had previously provided; then Chariclea disfigured her face, besmirching
it by rubbing it with soot and smearing it with mud. She also
flung over her head a filthy veil whose hem straggled down from
her forehead and covered one of her eyes. Under her arm she
slung a wallet, seemingly for holding their store of scraps of
meat and bread; but its actual purpose was to be the receptacle
for her sacred robe and her garlands from Delphi, and also the
heirlooms and tokens for identification exposed with her by her
mother. Calasiris carried across his shoulders the quiver of
Chariclea, which he had wrapped in some old, worn sheepskin,
as though it were some ordinary bundle; her bow he unstrung
and, as soon as it straightened itself, grasped it as a staff on
which he leant heavily with much of his weight; and whenever
he got sight in advance of people whom he was about to meet
he made himself more of a humpback than was the mere effect
of old age, dragged along one of his legs, and at times had
Chariclea leading him by the hand.

*Calasiris and Chariclea come upon a battlefield strewn with
corpses near the village of Bessa, and witness the gruesome
practices of a nocturnal sorceress.*

(12) When they had quite fitted themselves for the parts that
they were to play, they exchanged a little banter, each flattering
the other on being so becomingly costumed. They then besought
the deity concerned with their fortunes to cease at this point, if
ever, from afflicting them and to be satisfied; and so they
hastened on their way to Bessa, the village in which they hoped

to find Theagenes and Thyamis: but in this they were disappointed. For just as they were nearing Bessa, about sunset, they
saw a multitude of men lying dead who had been but lately
slain: the greater number of them were Persians, as was evident
from their dress and armour, while a few were natives of the
country. They surmised that a battle scene had there been
enacted, but could not tell who were the contending parties.
They moved about among the corpses, looking everywhere in
fear that a relative of their own might be lying among them; for
human souls, apprehensive for their dearest ones, are apt to
forbode the worst. They came upon an elderly woman who was
clinging to the body of a native and giving vent to all manner of
doleful cries. They therefore resolved to see if they could possibly
gather some information from the old dame; so they seated
themselves near to her, and tried first to console her and restrain
her miserable wailing. Then, as she yielded to their efforts, they
asked her for whom she was mourning, and what the fighting
was, Calasiris asking his questions in Egyptian. She gave them a
brief account of all that had occurred: it was over her son's
body that she mourned, and she had purposely come among the
corpses in the hope that someone would run her through and
rid her of life; but meanwhile she was rendering to her son the
customary tribute in the only form left to her, that of her tears
and lamentation.

(13) Of the fighting she gave them this account: 'A young
stranger, of singular beauty and stature, was being taken to
Memphis for Oroondates, the lieutenant-governor of the Great
King. He had been dispatched, I believe, by Mitranes, a garrison
commander, after being taken prisoner, and was offered as a
gift of particular value, so they say. The people of our village
here,' she went on, pointing to the place near by, 'waylaid the
party and carried him off, stating – it may have been the truth,
or perhaps just a made-up pretext – that they knew him.
Mitranes, learning this and being naturally annoyed, led an
expedition against the village two days ago. Now, our villagers
are an extremely warlike race, having always made their living
by brigandage, and are quite regardless of death; hence it is that
they have so often bereft many women, like me in this instance,
of husbands or children. When they had reason to expect the
coming of this attack, they set well-concealed ambuscades in
advance and, meeting the onset of the enemy, they gained the

upper hand. While some faced the Persians in direct combat, others assailed them from ambushes in their rear, shouting as they caught them off their guard. Mitranes fell fighting in the front line, and with him fell nearly all the rest, since they were encircled and had no chance even of finding a way of escape. A few of our people fell also; and among those few, by a grievous disposition of Fate, was my son, wounded in the breast, as you see, by a Persian javelin. And now, woe is me! I lament over his dead body; and seemingly I shall have to lament over my other son, who alone is left to me, since he has joined in the expedition of our remaining men which set out yesterday against the city of Memphis.' When Calasiris inquired what was the cause of this expedition, the old woman went on to tell him – what she had heard from her surviving son – that having killed some soldiers of the Great King and his majesty's garrison commander, they saw full well that the outcome of deeds ill done would be no slight matter for them, but the risk of losing their all. Oroondates, the lieutenant-governor at Memphis, was equipped with abundant forces, and would act on the instant of receiving the news; at the first attack he would make a clean sweep of the village,* and would inflict the punishment of complete destruction upon its inhabitants. 'Seeing therefore that they must put their all to the hazard,' she said, 'they decided, if possible, "to remedy ventures brave with braver," and forestall the intended operations of Oroondates by making an unexpected attack on him. Thus they would either destroy him as well as Mitranes, if they should catch him at Memphis or, if he happened to be absent through being engaged, according to report, in an Ethiopian campaign, they would the more easily get possession of the city while it was deprived of its defenders; while they would place themselves out of danger for the present, and could also re-establish Thyamis, their brigand chief, in his sacred office of prophet, which is now illegally held by his younger brother. Otherwise, if they should meet with failure in their enterprise, they would at any rate fall as victims of war, and would avoid the alternative of being captured and subjected to tortures and outrages at the hands of the Persians.* But you strangers, what place are you making for now?' 'The village,' said Calasiris. 'It would not be safe for you,' she said, 'at this late hour, unknown too as you are, to have dealings with the people who remain there.' 'But if you would conduct us,' said Calasiris, 'we should not be without hope of our being in safety.' 'I have not the time,' replied the old woman, 'for I propose during the night to offer up some sacrifices to the departed spirits. But if it is not disagreeable to you – but indeed it is a necessity for you, though you may not like it – retire here a little, where you will be clear of the corpses: at daybreak I will conduct you, and as my guest friends you will be quite secure.'

(14) Calasiris explained all that the woman had said to Chariclea, and taking her with him he moved away. When they had walked a little distance apart from the corpses, they came upon a low mound; there the sage lay down, resting his head on the quiver, while Chariclea seated herself as well as she could on her wallet. The moon was just coming up, and was shedding a bright light on everything around – it chanced to be the third day after the full moon. Calasiris, advanced in years as he was, felt much fatigued by his journeying, and was overcome by sleep; but Chariclea, kept awake by the anxieties that pressed upon her, became a witness of a scene which, although unholy, was familiar enough to the women of Egypt. The old dame, thinking that she had now secured a quiet time, free from any disturbance or observation, proceeded first to dig a hole in the ground, and then on either side of it to light a fire. Between these she laid the body of her son and, taking an earthenware bowl from a tripod set near by, she poured some honey into the hole; from another bowl she poured some milk, and from a third a libation of wine.* Then she took a cake of spelt fashioned in the likeness of a man, and having wreathed it with laurel and fennel she cast it into the hole. Last of all she took up a sword and, in a state of frenzied agitation, uttered outlandish and foreign-sounding words of invocation to the moon. She then made a cut in her arm, smeared some of her blood on a spray of laurel and sprinkled it on the fire. After adding to these a number of other magical acts she crouched down over her son's body and, uttering some incantation in his ear, aroused him, and by the power of her sorcery compelled him to stand upright. Chariclea, who had watched even her first doings with no little alarm, was now trembling with terror at such uncouth proceedings. She awakened Calasiris, and made him a witness of the scene that was being enacted. They themselves remained in darkness and could not be seen; but they could clearly observe what was passing in the light shed by the fires, and could also

overhear what was spoken at so little distance from them. For
the old woman was now questioning the corpse in louder tones:
her inquiry was, whether his brother, the son still left to her,
would return safe and sound. He spoke no word in reply, but
only gave a nod which yielded his mother a doubtful hope of
contentment; then he suddenly sank down and lay prone on his
face. She turned the body over on to its back and, without
desisting from her inquiry, but even pouring into his ears what
seemed to be still more powerfully compelling incantations, she
went leaping about, sword in hand, now to the fire and now to
the pit, till she aroused him once more. When he was standing
up she plied him with the same question, and was forcing him
to impart him occult knowledge, not by merely nodding, but
distinctly by word of mouth. While the old dame was thus
occupied, Chariclea earnestly entreated Calasiris that they might
draw near to her operations and make inquiry for themselves
about Theagenes: but he declined, telling her that the scene was
an unholy one, although they might be obliged to tolerate its
performance. For it was not right for prophets either to perform
or to countenance such practices: their divination proceeded
from lawful sacrifice and righteous prayers, whereas profane
persons obtained theirs by actually crawling about the ground
among corpses,* after the manner which a fortuitous occasion
had revealed to them in the case of this Egyptian woman.

(15) While he was still speaking the corpse muttered out these
words in deep and dismal tones, as though from a chasm or
the inmost recesses of a cavern: 'I was for sparing you at first
mother, and bore with you when you were offending against
human nature, violating the ordinances of the Fates, and moving
the immovable by magical arts, because reverence for parents is
maintained, so far as may be, even among the departed. But
since of your own motion you are destroying that respect, and
are pressing on from the impious methods that you used at first
to an extravagance of impiety without limit; since you compel
my dead body, not merely to stand erect and nod, but also to
speak; since you are neglecting my burial and so preventing me
from commingling with the other souls of the departed, and are
bent only upon your own concerns; hear now what hitherto I
have scrupled to declare to you. Your son will not return to you
safe and sound, nor will you yourself escape death by the sword.
You have continually squandered your years on these unholy

practices, and will meet ere long the violent death appointed for all such offenders, you who, moreover, instead of waiting to perform these abominable mysteries by yourself apart, things which are properly kept in the secrecy of silence and darkness, now disgracefully expose what may be the lot of the deceased before such witnesses as these! One of them indeed is a prophet and there less harm is done; for he has the wisdom to keep silence on such things, his lips sealed against their disclosure; besides, he is dear to the gods. So, although his two sons are preparing to face the bloody ordeal of the sword in single combat, he will intervene and prevail on them to desist, if he makes haste. But it is a graver matter that a young girl should come to behold and overhear all that has passed in relation to me – this poor woman, distracted with love and wandering the world over, one may say, in search of her beloved; with whom, after she has undergone countless toils and countless perils, and reached "the utmost borders of the earth",* she will live united in the splendour of regal state.' Having thus spoken he collapsed and lay prostrate; while the old woman, comprehending that those eye-witnesses must be the two strangers, dashed away after them just as she was, sword in hand and raving mad. She rushed about, wherever the slain were lying, with the suspicion that they had concealed themselves among the corpses, and the determination to dispatch them, if she could discover them, for having spied upon her sorceries with insidious and hostile intent. At length, as she pursued her search among the corpses with the unwary haste of rage, she failed to avoid an upright fragment of a spear-shaft which transfixed her in the groin. There she lay dead, having thus quickly fulfilled her son's prediction of her just punishment.

The sons of Calasiris, Thyamis and Petosiris, contend in single, combat for the priesthood of Memphis, and are pacified by their father. Chariclea finds Theagenes at Memphis.

(1) Calasiris and Chariclea, after an experience of such grave danger, were eager to remove themselves from the horrors of that scene, while they were also urged on by the prophetic message there received by them; so they went along the road to Memphis in hot haste. And indeed, as they were nearing the city, the events predicted by the corpse were already being brought about there. For when Thyamis arrived at the head of his brigands from Bessa, the people of Memphis had just had enough time to close the gates, upon a warning given to the citizens by a soldier in Mitranes' force who had escaped from the battle at Bessa and had foreseen this attack. Thyamis then ordered his men to ground arms at a certain part of the city wall, and rested them there after the forced march that they had made, while he also produced the impression of being about to besiege the place. The people in the city, who at first were struck with terror from the supposition that the approaching force was a large one, but learnt by looking down from the wall that those who had actually advanced against them were but few in number, hastened immediately to call out the few archers and mounted men who had been left on guard in the city, and also armed the townsfolk with whatever weapons were available, intending to sally forth and join battle with the enemy. But an elderly man of high standing opposed their doing so, explaining that although the satrap Oroondates happened to be absent on the Ethiopian campaign, it would be proper at least to inform his wife Arsace* of their proposed action. 'If her consent is given,' he said, 'we shall have the more prompt and zealous support of the troops that are to be found in the city.' His advice was approved, and they all proceeded to the royal palace which was used by the satraps as their residence in the absence of the King.

(2) Arsace was a tall and beautiful woman, of lively intelligence and with a spirit that presumed greatly on her high birth,

as might be expected in the sister of the Great King. But in general she was given to a disreputable way of life, abandoning herself to illicit and dissolute pleasure; and in fact, among other misdeeds, she had been accessory to the previous exile of Thyamis from Memphis. For shortly after Calasiris, in consequence of the divine warning about his two sons, had migrated in complete secrecy from Memphis, and had disappeared and was even thought to have died, Thyamis as his elder son had been called to the prophetic ministry. While he was solemnizing with public sacrifice his induction into the office, Arsace chanced to meet him at the temple of Isis in all the charming bloom of his youth, made more attractive by the fine vestments of the ceremonial in which he was engaged; and she plied him with immodest glances and signs that darkly hinted at her disgraceful purpose. These advances met with not the slightest response from Thyamis, whose nature and upbringing alike had endowed him with a temperate mind, and he was far from suspecting the drift of her behaviour: he supposed that it might have some other explanation, so preoccupied he was with the sacred rites. His brother Petosiris, however, who had long been consumed with jealousy of his priestly function, had closely observed the overtures of Arsace, and availed himself of her licentious attempt as a means of undermining his brother. He approached Oroondates in secret, and not only informed him of his wife's amorous desire, but went so far as to add the slander that Thyamis was consenting to it. The satrap was the more easily convinced because of some grounds that he already had for suspecting Arsace. He did nothing to disquiet her, since he had no certain proof; and besides, fear and respect for the royal family constrained him to bear patiently any suspicion that he might have on his mind. But Thyamis he openly denounced, with continual threats of taking his life, until he forced him to flee the country and installed Petosiris in the office of prophet.

(3) So much then for that affair, which had occurred in an earlier time. Now when Arsace found the crowd of people pressing into her residence, telling her of the enemy's aggression – of which she already had intelligence – and demanding that all the available troops be ordered to sally out with them, she stated that she could not give that order offhand, since she had not yet learnt the numbers of the enemy, nor who they were, nor whence they came; neither did she understand the reason of

their attack. She advised the people to go over to the walls and from them observe everything; then, with the support of other forces, they could take such measures as might be possible and advantageous. Her proposal was approved, and they all promptly marched off to the walls. There Arsace gave directions for an awning to be set up, formed of purple hangings inwoven with gold: beneath this she sat, richly adorned, on a lofty throne, and round her stood a bodyguard clad in gilded armour; and she displayed a caduceus* as the symbol of peaceful parley, and requested the leaders and notables of the enemy to come close up to the wall. When Thyamis and Theagenes, as delegates of the main body, arrived and halted below the wall, fully armed but bareheaded, the herald made this announcement: 'Arsace, wife of Oroondates the premier satrap, and sister of the Great King, sends you word saying: "What would you? Who are you? What reason do you allege for venturing on this aggression?"' They replied that they were a body of Bessans; but Thyamis explained who he was, how he had been unlawfully dispossessed of his prophetic office through the machinations of his brother Petosiris and Oroondates, and that he was to have it restored to him by the Bessans. If he recovered his priesthood peace would be made, and the Bessans would return home without doing the least injury to anyone; if he did not they would commit their cause to the arbitrament of armed conflict. If Arsace had any true conception of what was proper in the case, she ought to seize this opportunity of inflicting on Petosiris the due penalty for his malicious treatment of her and the nefarious slanders of his report to Oroondates, by which falsehoods he had aggrieved her with her husband's suspicion of an illicit and depraved passion and him, Thyamis, with exile from his native land.

(4) At this declaration the people of Memphis were one and all confounded; for they recognized Thyamis, and they had never understood, from the first moment of the transaction, what could be the reason of his unexpected exile. This they now began to suspect from what had been said, and they believed his account to be true. More than any of the rest Arsace was perturbed in mind amid the harassing tempest of her reflections. Filled with wrath against Petosiris and, moreover, reviewing in her mind all that had occurred in the past, she set about devising some means of wreaking her vengeance. Looking upon Thyamis and then upon Theagenes, she felt her mind torn asunder by her

equal desire for each of them, drawn to both at once, to the one by a love that she was reviving, to the other by a more poignant passion that she was newly implanting in her heart. Her state was such that even those around her perceived her deep discomposure. However, after a short pause, she collected herself, like one coming out of an epilepsy, and said: 'My good friends, war is a madness that has seized all the Bessans, and especially you two young men, so well grown and handsome, and of such good birth, as I apprehend and can readily believe. For the sake of some brigands you have rashly exposed yourselves to manifest danger, and will not be able to withstand the first onset, if it comes to a battle. The forces of the Great King could never be so weak that, even though the satrap happens to be absent, the mere remnant of our army stationed here would not suffice to make a clean sweep of you all. But there is no call, I conceive, for the main mass of you to be cut to pieces. Since the grounds for this aggression are the private concern of certain persons, and not a cause affecting the public in general, why should not their dispute be decided between themselves alone, and they be bound to accept whatever outcome may be determined by the gods and by justice? I accordingly resolve,' she said, 'and command that all the people of both Memphis and Bessa shall keep still, and refrain from reasonless hostilities against each other, whilst those who are disputing the position of prophet between themselves shall engage in single combat and contend for the priesthood as the victor's prize.'

(5) As she ended this speech Arsace was acclaimed by the whole population of the city, with full approval of her order, both because they were now strongly inclined to suspect Petosiris of dishonest practices, and also because each man deemed it expedient to avert an obvious and all but inevitable danger by means of a contest between others than himself. The Bessans in the main, seemed dissatisfied and unwilling to allow their leader to imperil himself on their behalf; till at length Thyamis persuaded them to give their assent by pointing out Petosiris' lack of strength and military experience, and reassuring them with the solid advantage that this would give him in the fight. It was on this very fact, it would seem, that Arsace had reckoned in proposing the single combat, as she quickly perceived that her object would be successfully attained without suspicion being aroused; it would be a convenient way of taking her revenge on

Petosiris, if he had to fight to the death with the much more valiant Thyamis.

Then it could be seen how more swiftly than words can tell her commands were carried out. Thyamis, all eagerness in his haste to meet the challenge, was duly methodical and cheerful in spirit as he completed his equipment of armour, Theagenes the while giving him many words of encouragement and fastening on his head the helmet, which was adorned with a fine crest and ablaze with the glitter of gold, and finally buckling on his other pieces of armour to ensure his full protection. But Petosiris, at Arsace's command, was being pushed by main force outside the gates – loud and long were his shouts of protest – and was being armed under compulsion. At the sight of him Thyamis remarked: 'My dear Theagenes, do you not see how Petosiris is quaking with fear?'* 'I see that,' he replied; 'but how are you going to deal with the situation? For it is not just an enemy, but one who is also a brother here opposed to you.' 'You are right,' said Thyamis; 'your words have sped direct to the mark of mine own thought. I have indeed resolved to vanquish him, if the deity permits, but not to kill him; for I trust that wrath and resentment over my past maltreatment would never prevail on me to incur the pollution of the bloodshed of my own brother, the slaughter of one born of the same womb, as the price of requiting the wrongs of the past and gaining a dignity in the future.' 'Your words reveal a noble spirit,' said Theagenes, 'and a mind sensible of the claims of nature. But pray now, what duty do you commit to my care?' 'The combat before me,' he replied, 'is a trifle of little account; but the chances of human life are wont to spring many a strange surprise upon us. So, if I should win, you shall come with me into the city, and shall share my hearth and home on equal terms; but if my hopes should be disappointed, you shall be the leader of these Bessans, who are most kindly disposed towards you; and you shall carry on the struggles of the brigands' way of life until the deity intimates to you some more propitious aim for your activities.'

(6) Thereupon they embraced each other with mingled tears and kisses; and Theagenes sat there, just as he was, on the watch for what should happen. To Arsace he thus unconsciously afforded the luxury of beholding him, as she watched intently his every motion and indulged her eyes for the while in some

gratification of her desire. Thyamis advanced upon Petosiris, who, however, did not stand to face his onset, but at his first movement took to flight and made for the gates, his one concern being to gain an entrance into the city. But he was foiled in his purpose, for he was repulsed by the guards at the gates and, finding that the people on the walls were urging them to deny him admission at whatever point he might attempt it, he fled away for a time as fast as he could round the circuit of the city, having already cast away his arms. Theagenes ran along behind, in his anxiety for Thyamis, and from a feeling that he could not bear to miss seeing every incident of the action: but he went quite unarmed, so that he should not be suspected of aiming to support Thyamis in the fight. He had laid down his shield and spear at that part of the wall where he had sat under the eyes of Arsace, and had left them for her to gaze upon, this time instead of himself, before he started to follow the course of the race. Petosiris was neither being overtaken nor getting far ahead in his flight, ever and anon seeming on the point of being caught, yet escaping by just so much as Thyamis in his armour could naturally be outrun by his unarmed rival. In this manner they once, and then twice, sped round the walls;* but as they were completing their third circuit, Thyamis lunged downward with his spear at his brother's back and threatened that he would transfix him if he did not stop. The citizens, ranged along the wall as in a theatre, were observing and appraising the spectacle below.* At this point either some divine Power or Fortune in control of human affairs appended a new scene to this tragic performance by introducing, as a counter-interest, the opening of another drama. On that day, and at that moment, it suddenly produced Calasiris, as it were, upon the stage, joining in this race and unhappily beholding the mortal combat of his sons. After enduring so many trials, essaying every expedient, and submitting himself to exile and wanderings among strangers, in order somehow to evade so atrocious a sight, he was now defeated by Destiny, and constrained to see what the gods had long before presaged to him. So, espying from afar the progress of the pursuit, and comprehending from the repeated predictions that these were his own children, he forced even his old age into the effort of running at a pace more strenuous than his years warranted, in the hope of being in time to prevent their final grapple.

(7) Then, as he came up with them, and was running along with them, he kept calling out: 'What is this, Thyamis and Petosiris?' Again and again he cried out to them: 'What is this, my children?' But as yet they did not recognize their father's features, for he was still wearing the beggar's rags: themselves wholly intent on their contest, they disregarded him as some mendicant or poor lunatic. Of the spectators on the walls, some wondered at his flinging himself so recklessly between men committed to armed combat, while others laughed at a madman rushing on a futile errand. But when the old man understood that the meanness of his clothing prevented his recognition, he stripped himself of his ragged attire, loosened and let down his reverend locks, and cast away the burden from his shoulders and the staff from his hand. Standing face to face with them, he was beheld in his own majestic and venerable mien. Then gently he knelt down and stretched forth his hands in entreaty, weeping and sobbing out these words: 'My children, it is I, Calasiris; it is your father! Stop where you are, and stay your fated frenzy! Your parent is before you: show him the reverence that is his due.' At his words they were unnerved and nearly sank to the ground; both threw themselves down before their father, and clasping his knees first gazed at him intently to make sure of their recognizing him. When they perceived that it was he in very truth and not an apparition, a number of contrary feelings came over them in the same moment. They rejoiced to find their parent alive, beyond all hope; they were pained and ashamed at being surprised in such an action; and they were possessed by a harassing doubt as to what the sequel was to be. Moreover, the people of the city in their astonishment neither said nor did anything, but, mute from their ignorance, and comparable to figures in a painting, they were standing there, thrilled by the spectacle alone, when another person made an appearance on the scene – Chariclea. Following closely in the footsteps of Calasiris, she had at some distance recognized Theagenes; for lovers are quick of sight to perceive one another, and often the movement or the bearing alone of someone observed at a distance or even from behind, can impress them with the resemblance. As though distracted by the sight of him, she rushed with frantic speed at Theagenes, enfolded him in her arms, clung tightly about his neck and, hanging there, greeted him with sobs of anguished weeping. He, as was natural at the

sight of her features all besmirched and deliberately disfigured, and her attire all threadbare and tattered, tried to thrust her off and elbow her aside, taking her for one of the mendicant tribe, a very vagabond. At length, when she would not let go, to stop her molesting him and hindering his view of Calasiris, he cuffed her sharply. 'O Pythian!' she said softly to him; 'and do you not remember the torch?' Then Theagenes, as if transfixed by those words, recalled the torch as one of the emblems agreed between them. He gazed intently at Chariclea and, enlightened by the rays shot forth from her eyes as by a sunbeam breaking from a cloud, he clasped her fondly in his encircling arms. And lastly, all the people at that part of the walls where Arsace sat in state and was swelling now with no little jealousy as she observed Chariclea, took their fill of the wondrous spectacle presented by the scene.

Arsace, wife of the Persian satrap Oroondates, becomes enamoured of Theagenes.

(8) Thus was composed an impious strife between brothers, and a contest that was expected to be decided by bloodshed ended in a change from the tragic to a joyful mood. A father beheld his sons armed against each other for single combat; after facing the imminent disaster of the children's death occurring before the parental eyes, he himself became the dispenser of peace. He proved indeed unable to evade the conjuncture foreordained by Destiny; but he had the happiness of attending in the nick of time at the issue appointed for it. Sons now regained their parent after his ten years' time of wandering, and him who had been the cause of their sanguinary dispute over the office of prophet they were soon crowning with their own hands and escorting in the dignity of the priestly insignia with which they now invested him. But, above all, the love scene gave the finishing touch of charm to the drama. Chariclea and Theagenes, in all the beauty and grace of their youth, who beyond all hope had found each other again, more than anyone else attracted the gaze of the citizens. Indeed, the whole population poured out through the gates and filled the outlying plain. Persons of every age were there: the adolescents of the city, just entering on their manhood, ran up to Theagenes; while men of mature years, in the full possession of manly vigour, surrounded Thyamis, whom they

were of an age to recognize. The young maidens of the city, with minds already envisaging the bride-chamber, attended on Chariclea, while old men and everyone of the religious order escorted Calasiris. Thus a sort of sacerdotal procession was formed on the spur of the moment. Thyamis had dismissed the Bessans with assurances of the gratitude that he felt for their generous support, and a promise to send them, a little later, at the full moon, a hundred oxen, a thousand sheep, and for each man a gift of ten drachmas. He now set his neck beneath his father's arm, so as to lighten the old man's effort in walking and bear up his steps, which were somewhat enfeebled by such an unexpected access of joy. On his other side Petosiris did likewise; and so, by the light of torches, the old man was conducted to the temple of Isis, amid sounds of general applause and felicitation; while the tones of many Panpipes and sacred flutes incited the more impetuous of the young folk to wild transports of dancing. Nor indeed did Arsace lag behind in taking her part in the proceedings. Parading with her bodyguard in a specially pompous progress of her own, she brought necklaces and a quantity of gold into the temple of Isis, making as if she came for the same reason as the rest of the people, but in fact keeping her eyes fixed solely on Theagenes and feasting more than anybody else on the sight of him. Yet her pleasure was not unalloyed. Theagenes was leading Chariclea with his hand on her arm, and as he cleared their way through the jostling throng he stung Arsace to the quick with jealousy. When Calasiris arrived in the inner sanctuary, he prostrated himself and, clasping the feet of the statue, remained thus for a great length of time, in which he came very near to expiring. The bystanders brought him to himself again; with some difficulty he stood up, poured a libation and offered prayers to the goddess. He then removed from his head the sacerdotal crown and set it on the head of his son Thyamis, telling the assembled people that he was now much advanced in years, and foresaw by other signs that his end was approaching; but that his son, the elder of his children, could lawfully claim the prophet's insignia, and was qualified in both soul and body to undertake the public functions of the priesthood.

(9) The people loudly acclaimed his statement, and praised him in terms intimating their full approval of his action. He then, together with his sons and Theagenes, entered a part of

the temple assigned to the prophets for their use, and there they remained. Arsace departed also, after much hesitation: ever and anon she would turn back and vaguely linger, as though intending some further worship of the goddess. However, at long last she did depart, turning round again and again towards Theagenes while he was still visible. When she finally arrived at the royal palace, she went straight to her chamber, threw herself, dressed as she was, upon her bed and lay there uttering no word – a female ever prone to ignoble pleasure, but at that moment fiercely inflamed by the overmastering impression of Theagenes, which outrivalled all others that she had ever experienced. There she lay all night long, continually turning over on this side and on that, and continually sending forth deep groans. Now she sat up, and now she sank down on the bed-sheets, and stripping off part of her clothing flung herself suddenly upon the bed again; at times she summoned her maidservant for no reason, and dismissed her without giving any order.* In short, her passion was insensibly descending into eventual madness, had not an old woman named Cybele, one of the attendants of her bed-chamber who ministered confidentially to her amours, run into the room. There she was able at once to perceive the whole state of affairs, since a lamp revealed everything and seemed to be adding its flame to the fire of Arsace's love. 'What is this, mistress?' she asked; 'what new, what strange passion is it that afflicts you? Who is it this time, the sight of whom distracts my own nursling? Who is so arrogant, so senseless, as to withstand the power of your great beauty, and not to see his happiness in your rapturous embraces, but only to despise your beck and bidding? Do but tell me who, my precious child.* No heart is so flinty that it cannot be defeated by my enticements. Tell me, and you can go straight to the achievement of your purpose. My services, I think, have often given you good proof of my skill.'

(10) These and other suchlike words were the burden of her talk as she fawned on Arsace, crouching at her feet and seeking by all manner of flatteries to induce her to confess her trouble. Then Arsace, after a few moments' silence, said: 'I am smitten, mother, as never before. Many a time and oft you have served me well in affairs of this kind, but I doubt if this time I can count on your being successful. For the battle that today was almost joined before the walls, and was then so suddenly arrested, has for those others turned out a bloodless one, and

was concluded in peace; but for me it has started a more real
sort of battle, in which I have received a wound, not in a mere
limb or other part of my body, but in my very soul, through the
sight that it unfortunately presented to me of that young stranger
who ran along with Thyamis during the single combat. You
know quite well, I am sure, dear mother, who it is that I mean.
For by such a marked distinction did he far outshine all the
other men with his beauty that even a boor devoid of any love
of the beautiful must have remarked it, and still more must you,
with your wide and expert knowledge. So now you, dear friend,
are apprised of the shaft that has pierced me: lose no time in
applying every artifice, every magic spell and wheedling address
that you have acquired in the long span of your life, if you truly
wish your nursling's life to be saved. For it is not possible for
me to live, unless by some means or other I can possess that
man.' 'I remarked the youth,' said the old dame: 'he was broad
in chest and shoulders, and he held his head erect with a gallant
air that singled him out from the rest, while in stature he
overtopped everyone else. He had an ardent gleam in his eyes,
and his glance was at once amiable and awe-inspiring; he it was,
to be sure, with the flowing locks, and cheeks just beginning to
show a golden ornament of down.* It was at him that a foreign
woman, not uncomely but, as it seemed, impetuous in manner,
suddenly rushed up and hung upon him, locked in close
embrace. Was not this the man whom you mean, mistress?' 'It
was he, little mother,' she replied. 'You have done well to
remind me of the demonstrative act of that depraved creature
from some brothel, so highly presuming on a paltry, a vulgar, a
factitious beauty; but yet, more fortunate is she than I, in having
had the luck to win such a lover!' At these words the old woman
smiled at her in a sly, smirking manner and said: 'Take heart,
mistress; until today our stranger has thought her beautiful, but
if I could contrive to face him with you and your beauty, he will
take gold, as they say, in exchange for bronze,* and will thrust
aside that little mincing courtesan with all her futile affecta-
tions.' 'If you do that, my darling Cybele, you will at one stroke
cure me of two diseases, love and jealousy, by satisfying the one
and expelling the other.' 'It shall be done,' said the old woman,
'so far as in me lies. Now I would have you revive yourself by
keeping quiet for the moment: do not let despondency enfeeble
you beforehand; rather cheer yourself with hope.'

*Calasiris dies. Arsace endeavours to seduce Theagenes with the
aid of her serving-woman Cybele.*

(11) So saying, she took away the lamp, closed the door of
the room and went off. When she perceived that day was just
dawning, she took with her one of the eunuchs of the palace,
and also a maidservant whom she ordered to follow along with
some cakes and other offerings, and hastened to the temple of
Isis. On arriving at the doors, she stated that she wished to offer
a sacrifice to the goddess on behalf of her mistress Arsace, who
had been much disturbed by certain dreams, and so desired tò
avert by these offerings the evils revealed to her. One of the
sacristans objected and sent her away, declaring that the temple
was now given up entirely to mourning. For the prophet
Calasiris, he said, on returning to his residence after prolonged
absence, had on that evening enjoyed a fine feast in company
with his dearest ones, and had indulged in complete relaxation
and geniality. At the end of the banquet he had offered up
libations and a number of prayers to the goddess; he had then
told his sons that only up to that hour would they be seeing
their father, and he repeatedly adjured them to devote their best
efforts to caring for the young Greeks who had arrived there
with him, and to give them all possible assistance in whatever
plans they might adopt. He retired to take his rest; then, whether
it were that by the fullness of his joy the channels of respiration
had been too greatly distended and slackened, and so his body,
aged as it was, had suddenly broken down, or that the gods had
granted him this end at his request, at cock-crow it was
discovered that he was dead, while his sons were keeping night-
long watch over the old man on the hint of his warning. 'So
now,' said the sacristan, 'we have issued a summons for the
attendance of the rest of the prophets and priests in the town,
that they may conduct his funeral with the customary rites of
their ancestral tradition. You must therefore depart, since it is
not right that anyone except the persons invested with the holy
functions should offer sacrifice or even set foot in the temple,
during these seven whole days succeeding the decease.' 'Then
how will they fare in the meantime, those strangers whom you
mentioned?' asked Cybele. 'A lodging has been prepared for
them,' he replied, 'near by, just outside the temple, on the order
of the new prophet Thyamis; and, as you see, here come those

very persons, removing themselves from the holy place for the present, in obedience to the rule.' Then Cybele, seizing on the circumstance like a hunter grasping his quarry, said: 'Well now, sacristan most beloved of the gods, here is your chance to render a service both to these strangers and to us, above all to Arsace, sister of the Great King. You know how she loves the Greeks, and what an aptitude she has for entertaining guests. Tell these young people that by Thyamis' command it is in our house that arrangements for their accommodation have been made.' The sacristan did as Cybele requested, having no suspicion of her deep-laid designs, but only thinking to show kindness to the strangers by introducing them into the satrap's court, and at the same time to concede this favour to the persons desiring it, as one in particular that could entail no harm or penalty. When he saw Theagenes and Chariclea, now close at hand, dejected and tearful, the sacristan said to them: 'This is no lawful behaviour, nor agreeable to our ancestral tradition – indeed, you have been told already of its prohibition – to be weeping and wailing over a prophet. Our duty, enjoined on us by the divine and hallowed teaching, is to attend him to his grave with gladness and felicitation,* as having obtained the better portion allotted to him by the higher powers. However, you may be pardoned, since you have been bereft, as you say, of your father, your protector and your only hope. Yet you must not yield utterly to despair, since Thyamis, it seems, is succeeding, not only to his father's priesthood, but also to his regard for you. In fact, he has begun by giving orders for due care to be taken of you, and a lodging has been prepared for you in handsome style, such as might be hoped for by one of the most prosperous persons in our country, and not by mere strangers whose means appear to be so reduced at present. Follow this woman,' he said, pointing to Cybele; 'regard her as a mother to you both, and accept her as your helpful guide.'

(12) Theagenes and his companion did as the man advised; for, while their spirits were sunk to the depths by the unexpected blows that they had sustained, they were thankful to find for the moment some sort of lodging that offered them a refuge. More cautious, no doubt, they would have been, had they suspected the tragic significance of that abode, so imposing and so fraught with mischief for them. At this moment the Fortune that imposed their toils and trials, having allowed them a respite of

a few hours and indulged them with a transient joy, was promptly loading them with fresh affliction, and bringing them like selfmade slaves into the presence of their enemy. With the pretence of kindly hospitality it was now leading captive a pair of young strangers who were all unwary of what might be in store for them. Thus it is that a wandering life inflicts ignorance, like a kind of blindness, on those who visit foreign parts. And so, as soon as they arrived at the residence of the satrap, and faced the imposing portico, erected on a larger scale than that of any private dwelling, and thronged with a great parade of bodyguards and array of domestic servants, the sight of an establishment so disproportionate to their present condition filled them with bewilderment and consternation. Nevertheless, they followed Cybele, who kept urging them to come on and bidding them have no fear; she continually called them her little children, her darlings, and insisted that they should look forward with gladness to the experience that awaited them. At length the old woman, having brought them into the apartment where she lodged, in a specially private and retired part of the palace, dismissed the other persons in it and, sitting alone with the young pair, said to them: 'My children, I have perceived the cause of the dejection that at present affects you, and how the death of the prophet Calasiris has filled you with grief, for he had come to be as a father to you. Now, it is proper that you should tell me who you are and whence you came. I know that you are Greeks, and besides, by your looks one may well surmise that you are persons of good family: the brightness of your eyes, and the comeliness and charm of your whole appearance, produce a clear impression of gentle birth. But of what region of Greece, of what city are you? Who are you, and by what sort of wanderings have you made your way here? Tell me all this; I wish to learn it for your own future benefit, that I may be able to give a full account of you to my mistress Arsace, sister of the Great King, and consort of Oroondates, greatest of all satraps. She is a lover of the Greeks, a lover too of their refinement, and a benefactress of foreigners; and through me you would be treated with the special honour that is your due. You will be informing a woman who is not altogether alien to you; for I also, mark you, am a Greek by birth, a citizen of Lesbos* who was brought here as a captive, but who fares better than my countryfolk at home. I am everything, I may say, to my mistress;

she almost breathes and sees through me. I am her mind, her ears, her all; I am constantly bringing her acquainted with persons of the best quality, and am her trustworthy confidant in all her secret concerns.' Theagenes then brought up for comparison together in his mind these words spoken by Cybele and the behaviour of Arsace on the previous day. He recalled with what an intent, immodest gaze she had looked upon him, continually and clearly indicative of her unchaste thoughts; and he augured nothing good in what was to ensue. He was about to speak to the old woman, when Chariclea leant over and whispered in his ear: 'Remember "your sister" in what you may say.'

(13) He understood to what she was referring, and said: 'Mother, that we are Greeks you have, it seems, found for yourself the means of knowing. We are brother and sister; our parents were captured by brigands. We set out in search of them, and have met with even worse misfortunes than they; for we fell in with men more cruel still, by whom we were stripped of all our possessions, and they were many. We narrowly escaped with our lives, and by some happy disposition of the deity we happened upon Calasiris of blessed memory. We came here intending to live with him thenceforward; but now, as you see, we are left utterly destitute and alone, having lost, besides those parents of ours, him whom we considered and who was indeed our father. This then is our story: we are most grateful to you for your present welcome and kind attentions; but you would gratify us still more if you would arrange for us to live by ourselves apart and in seclusion, and defer the favour that you proposed for us just now, of introducing us to Arsace, rather than disturb the splendour and wellbeing of her state with the alien and forbidding intrusion of our vagabond existence. For, as you know, it is best to have acquaintance and contact with persons of similar condition to one's own.'

(14) After this speech Cybele could not forbear revealing by the look of relief in her face how highly delighted she was to hear the words 'brother and sister', as she reflected that Chariclea would present no hindrance or impediment to the lovemaking of Arsace. 'Young man of surpassing beauty,' she said, 'you will not speak thus of Arsace when you have had some experience of that lady. She is a person familiar with every sort and condition, and is prompt to assist those who are undeservedly less prosperous. A Persian by birth, she is very much a

Grecian at heart, delighting in people from that country and quick to give them a welcome. For the manners and society of Greeks she has an immense affection. Take heart then from the thought that you will be treated as handsomely and honourably as befits a man, while your sister will give the lady her entertaining companionship. But by what names am I to announce you?' When she had been told that they were Theagenes and Chariclea, she bade them await her there, and hurried away to Arsace, after charging the portress – herself also an old woman – not to admit anyone who might try to gain an entrance, and not to allow the young couple to go out. 'Not even your son Achaemenes,* if he should appear?' asked the portress; 'just after you set out for the temple he went away to have his eyes treated for the ailment which still, as you know, is giving him some trouble.' 'Not even him,' replied Cybele. 'Shut the door, keep the key to yourself and tell him that I have taken it with me.' Her order was obeyed. Then, hardly a moment after Cybele had departed, their solitude suggested to Theagenes and Chariclea that they had this opportunity for lamenting and reflecting on their situation. They bewailed themselves, each giving nearly the same expression to the same thoughts; the one continually sighing forth 'O Theagenes!' and the other 'O Chariclea!' He would ask: 'What fresh mischance has overtaken us?' and she: 'What sort of trouble is it that we shall have to face?' And each time they would fondly embrace and weep and kiss each other once more. At length the memory of Calasiris caused a conversion of their lamenting to mourning for him, especially on Chariclea's part, because she had for a longer time experienced his solicitude and kindness. 'O Calasiris,' she exclaimed in woeful tones, 'I am debarred from calling you by the most honoured name of father, since my Destiny has in jealousy cut me off from all hope of addressing you with that word. My natural father I have never known, and him who adopted Chariclea, alas, I have deserted; while him who took charge of me, reared me and preserved me I have lost, and the customary lamentation over his corpse still lying there is denied me by the prophets' rule. But see now, to you, my supporter and saviour – and I will add, my father also, despite the will of Destiny – here at least, where I can, and in such manner as I can, to you I pour libation of my tears, and tender the pious tribute of my locks.' With that she began to tear out large tresses of her hair. Theagenes restrained her, grasping her hands and pleading with her; but she went on speaking in tragic vein: 'What call have we now to go on living? On what hope can we turn our eyes? The guide to lead us through a strange land, the staff to aid our wandering steps, our safe conduct to our native country and recognition of our parents, our consolation in calamity, our resource and deliverance in perplexities, the anchor of all our ventures, Calasiris, has perished, and has left us like a lost pair in harness to stumble blind and baffled on this alien soil. To us all wayfaring, all sea-voyaging, are impeded by our ignorance. Gone is the holy and gentle, the wise and truly venerable heart which itself has failed of achieving the fulfilment of its good offices towards us.

(15) As she was continuing to utter these and other mournful plaints, and as Theagenes, while tending to swell the lamentation with plaints of his own, yet strove to restrain them out of tenderness for Chariclea, Achaemenes arrived and, finding the door bolted and barred, asked the portress what was the meaning of it. When he learnt that it was the doing of his mother, he came up close to the door and, curious to know her motive, caught the sound of Chariclea's lamentation. He stooped down, peered through the holes through which the chains securing the bolts had been passed, and espied the scene within. Again he questioned the portress as to who were the persons in the place. She replied that she knew nothing more of the matter than that they were a girl and a youth, strangers so far as she could guess, who had just been lodged in the house by his mother. He stooped down once more and tried to get a clear impression of the persons who he saw in the room. Chariclea was completely unknown to him; none the less he was utterly amazed at her beauty, and imagined how fine and lovely she would look if she were not weeping, so that his admiration drew him insensibly into the passion of love. Theagenes he fancied that he recognized, in a dim and dubious manner. Then, while Achaemenes was absorbed in his inspection, Cybele arrived, having returned from making a full report of her talk with the young pair. She had warmly congratulated Arsace on her good fortune, which had brought her unsolicited so great a success, beyond anything that could have been looked for from all the planning and contriving in the world – so great, that now she had the beloved one an inmate of her house, where he could see

her and be seen by her with nothing at all to fear. When with many such assurances she had inflamed Arsace, she had some difficulty in restraining her mistress's impulse to go at once and gaze on Theagenes: she told her she would not have her seen by the young man all pale and swollen-eyed from sleeplessness; she should rather take a rest for that day and recover her usual beauty. By plying her with suchlike counsels Cybele at length brought her to a cheerful and hopeful view of her heart's desire, and went on to prescribe her most suitable procedure and the demeanour that she should adopt towards her guests.

(16) After that, when Cybele arrived at her own door, she said: 'Why this curiosity, child?' 'It is about the strangers in the house,' he replied, 'to know who and whence they are.' 'That is forbidden, my son,' she told him; 'hold your tongue, keep this to yourself, tell nobody; and have little or nothing to do with the strangers. This is my mistress's decision.' He went away in prompt obedience to his mother, surmising that Theagenes was just an ordinary accessory to one of Arsace's amours. As he departed he said to himself: 'Is not this the man whom I received from Mitranes the commandant to take to Oroondates for dispatch to the Great King, and whom the Bessans under Thyamis carried off from me, when I came within an ace of losing my life and was the only one of the escort who succeeded in getting away? Can it be that my eyes are deceiving me? But I am recovering my sight, and already it is nearly as clear as it used to be. What is more, I have heard that Thyamis was here yesterday, and that after fighting it out in single combat with his brother he has regained the priestly office. Yes, this is the man. But for the present I must say no word of my recognition of him, and must also be on the look-out for what the mistress's intentions may be regarding these strangers.' Thus did he speak to himself.

(17) Cybele, running in upon the young pair, detected traces of their lamenting. For although at the sound of the door being opened they began to compose themselves and strove to reassume their normal poise and looks, they yet failed to delude the old woman, since their eyes were still bedewed with tears. So she called out: 'Sweetest children, why this untimely lamenting when you ought to be rejoicing; when you should be congratulating yourselves on the happy turn in your fortunes? Arsace has the best intentions towards you that your hearts

could desire: she has consented to give you an audience
tomorrow, and in the meantime she has accorded to you the
warmest welcome and kindest attentions. Come now, you must
cast aside these silly, these truly childish bewailings; the time has
now come for you to bring yourselves to order and comply
obediently with the wishes of Arsace.' To this Theagenes
answered: 'It was the memory, mother, of the death of Calasiris
that aroused in us such anguish, and compelled our tears for the
loss of his fatherly concern for our welfare.' 'What nonsense!'
she said. 'Calasiris, a merely fictitious father, an old man, who
had to yield to our common nature and the period of his years.
Everything is yours to have, as the gift of a single person –
distinction, wealth, luxury and enjoyment of the flowering time
of your years; in short, you are to regard her as your Fortune,
and do homage to Arsace.* Only you must take my advice as to
how you should approach and behold her when she gives the
command, and how you are to set about any service that she
may require of you; for her spirit, as you know, is high and
mighty, indeed queenly, being specially exalted by her youth
and beauty, and will not brook any slighting of her orders.'

(18) At these words Theagenes remained silent, reflecting on
their disagreeable and sinister import. Shortly after, some eunuchs appeared bearing on golden dishes what might seem to be
remnants from the satrap's table, but in fact were dainties of
surpassing costliness and refinement. 'These dishes,' they said,
'Her Highness sends to welcome and honour her guests on this
occasion.' They set down the dishes before the young pair and
immediately withdrew. Moved not only by the urgings of Cybele
but equally by a prudent desire not to appear to flout this
courtesy, they tasted a little of the fare set before them. The
same thing occurred in the evening and on each following day.
On the morrow, however, in the first hour or so, the eunuchs on
the same duty stood before Theagenes and said: 'You have been
summoned, most fortunate sir, by our mistress, and we have
received an order for your presentation. So come now and enjoy
that happiness of which she permits but few, and that but rarely,
to partake.' For a brief space he made no motion; then, as
though he were haled away by main force, he rose and said to
them: 'Is it commanded that I come alone, or with my sister
here?' They replied that he was to come alone, and that she
would be presented separately; for at present Arsace had with

her some Persian officers of state; and besides, it was customary to grant interviews to men by themselves and to women on another occasion. Theagenes leant over to Chariclea and said to her in a low voice: 'This is neither honourable nor above suspicion.' After hearing her answer that they must not run counter but concur at first, and make a show of readiness to do everything to content the lady, he followed his conductors.

Theagenes is received in audience by Arsace.

(19) These men instructed him on the proper manner of meeting and addressing her, and said that it was customary to prostrate oneself on entering: to this he made no response. He entered and found her seated on a lofty throne. She was resplendent in a purple robe shot with gold, and was gorgeously adorned with costly necklaces and a magnificent tiara, while her face had the full luxurious bloom produced by an ample assortment of cosmetics. Close to her stood the bodyguard, and on either side sat the high officers of her council. Theagenes' spirit did not quail. As though unmindful of his agreement with Chariclea to make pretence of humble service, he was moved to all the prouder defiance by this arrogant Persian display. Without the bending of a knee or any prostration, he held his head high as he said: 'Greetings to the lady of the blood royal, Arsace.' The company were annoyed, and raised a murmur that Theagenes' refusal to prostrate himself showed the seditious spirit of a reckless adventurer; but Arsace smiled and said: 'You must forgive him as an ignorant foreigner – in a word, a Greek, infected with that nation's contempt of us.' And with that she removed her tiara from her head, despite vehement remonstrances from the company, since with the Persians this gesture is the regular sign of returning a salutation. Then she said through an interpreter – for while she understood the Greek language she did not speak it – 'Have no fear, stranger: tell us what you would have; you will not be disappointed.' She then dismissed him, indicating her wish to the eunuchs with a nod of her head. He was being conducted by some of the bodyguard, when Achaemenes, catching sight of him again, recognized him more exactly and, suspecting the cause of the extraordinary honour done to him, was struck with wonder; however, he kept silence, adhering to the course on which he had resolved.

Arsace entertained the Persian dignitaries at a banquet, ostensibly in customary compliment to them, but really in celebration of her meeting with Theagenes. To him and his companion she sent, not merely the usual share of her repast, but also some carpets and embroidered coverlets made by the craftsmen of Sidon and Lydia. She sent besides two slaves to wait upon them – a young girl for Chariclea and a young boy for Theagenes, both being of Ionian race* and tender years. Repeatedly she requested Cybele to make haste and achieve her object with all possible speed, as she felt herself no longer able to endure the ardour of her passion; and Cybele was to spare no effort in trying by all possible means to inveigle Theagenes. Cybele, to be sure, did not openly declare Arsace's design, but with circuitous and insinuating talk she sought to draw him into comprehension of it. She made much of her mistress's kindly feeling towards him, and with some fair-sounding representations offered him the sight, not only of her apparent beauty, but also that concealed by her clothing. She spoke of her charming and companionable nature, and how she delighted in young men of specially refined and noble character: in fact, by her whole description she was testing him to see if he were amenable to the lure of love. Theagenes concurred in praising the kindness of Arsace, her affection for the Greeks, and all her other such qualities, and he avowed his gratitude to her; but those which incited him to wantonness he preferred to pass over, as though he had not so much as understood them from the first. The old dame in consequence felt a choking in her throat, and her heart seemed to gasp when, just as she was assuming that he understood her enticements, she perceived him to be so audaciously spurning her temptation. And Arsace, she found, was becoming unbearable; she harassed her with declaring that her patience was exhausted, and demanded fulfilment of the promise made to her. This Cybele each time found some excuse or other for putting off, now asserting that the youth, though desirous, was overawed, and now inventing the sudden attack of some disorder.

(20) When about the next five or six days had passed by, in which Arsace had once or twice summoned Chariclea before her and, to gratify Theagenes, received her with honour and graciousness, Cybele was forced to speak more plainly to Theagenes and declare her mistress's love to him without further

disguise, promising him an infinite abundance of benefits if he complied with her desire, and adding: 'What is this timidity? Why are you so averse from love? A man so young and handsome, in his very prime, to repulse a woman who is his match, and entirely devoted to him! Not to seize on this affair as a prize, as a windfall, when no fear attaches to its doing, and when her husband is away, and you have me who nurtured her and am the keeper of all her secrets, to procure this union! And you, who have no hindrance in your way, with no bride or wife! Yet many a time have numbers of men ignored these impediments, if they were such as had the sense to perceive that their action would in no way harm their kindred, and would advantage themselves by the acquisition of ampler means, along with the enjoyment of that pleasure.' She ended by mingling some threats with her arguments. 'Well-bred women,' she said, 'who love young men, become hard-hearted and rancorous from disappointment, and avenge themselves, with good reason, on any who slight them, as outrageous offenders. This lady, mark you, is of the Persian race and the blood royal – to use the words of your own greeting to her. Reflect that she is invested with great authority and power, whence she possesses full and free licence to honour the well disposed and chastise the recalcitrant; whereas you are a foreigner, all alone, with no one to protect you. Spare yourself for your sake, spare her for hers. She deserves this indulgence from you, for her misconduct arises from the madness of her longing for you. Be on your guard, and beware of a lover's resentment, the vengeful wrath of a woman spurned. Many a man, to my knowledge, has had to recant: I have more experience than you of the ways of Aphrodite. These white hairs that you see have had their part in many such encounters; but a man so insensible, so uncouth, I have never met before.' She next directed her words to Chariclea – for of necessity she had the hardihood to argue as she had done in the girl's hearing. 'Add your voice to mine, daughter,' she said, 'in persuading this man – I know not by what name I ought properly to call him – your brother. You will have your portion of profit from this affair: you will be treated with no less affection, and with greater honour; enriched to your heart's content, you will procure a brilliant marriage for yourself. These are things to be envied even by the prosperous; how much more by strangers who are plainly at present in a state of destitution?'

(21) Chariclea, with a wry smile and glowering eyes, replied: 'It would be desirable, indeed the best thing of all, that the most excellent Arsace should not be so enthralled. Failing that, the next best thing would be to endure her trouble with self-restraint. But since a human weakness has affected her, and she has been conquered, as you say, and has succumbed to her desire, I too would advise Theagenes here not to reject the affair, if he could safely undertake it, and there were no fear of inadvertently causing some harm to himself and to her, through the facts coming to light and the satrap by some means learning of their illicit conduct.' At these words Cybele started up, embraced Chariclea with repeated kisses, and said: 'Well done, child! You have not merely taken pity on a woman of like nature to your own, but have also taken thought for your brother's safety. But have no fear on that score; for the sun himself, as the saying is,* will not get knowledge of it.' 'Enough of this for the present,' said Theagenes; 'now leave us to consider.' Cybele thereupon departed, and Chariclea said: 'O Theagenes, Destiny procures for us the sort of successes in which there is more of adversity than any apparent prosperity. Nevertheless, persons of intelligence ought to turn even their misfortunes to the best account possible in the circumstances. Now, I cannot tell whether your intention is to carry through this affair to the full; and indeed I should not have felt greatly upset, if our deliverance depends entirely on that and on that alone. But if, to your honour, you find the proposal repugnant, see that you make a pretence of compliance. Foster with promises this barbarian woman's yearning; frustrate with deferments any sharp measures that she may meditate against us; soothe with hope, and allay with assurances, the fiery heat of her indignation. It may well be that the respite thus gained will even, by the gods' design, bring forth a solution. But, Theagenes, do not let your mere rehearsal send you sliding down to the vileness of performance.' At this Theagenes smiled and said: 'Ha, so you now, even in the midst of danger, have not escaped that innate malady of women, jealousy! I, you may be sure, cannot so much as simulate such things; for shameful words and deeds are equally depraved. Besides, the discomfiture of Arsace brings us at once the boon of an end to her pestering us. If I should have to suffer, my fortune and my judgment have already taught me, in many trials, how to bear whatever may befall.' 'Take care lest you

unwittingly plunge us into grievous trouble,' Chariclea replied, and said no more.

(22) While they were engaged in these speculations, Cybele had sent the hopes of Arsace soaring high, by telling her to expect a more favourable turn in the affair, because Theagenes had shown certain signs of this. She then returned to her quarters where, after letting the evening go by, she spent the night in making constant appeals to Chariclea, who had continued from the first to be her bedfellow, to aid her in her task; then, in the morning, she again asked Theagenes what decision he had made. His answer was a point-blank refusal, and a declaration that nothing at all was to be expected of him. In dismay she ran back to Arsace who, on hearing her report of Theagenes' perverseness, ordered the old woman to be hustled headlong out of the room. Then, hastening to her chamber, she lay down on her bed and took to lacerating herself. Hardly had Cybele left the women's apartments when her son Achaemenes, seeing her downcast and tearful, asked her: 'Has something untoward, something vexatious, mother, befallen? Has some report annoyed your mistress? Has news of some disaster arrived from the army? Is it that the Ethiopians in the present campaign are gaining the upper hand of our master Oroondates?' And so he went on, with a string of similar questions. But Cybele merely said 'Your talk is nonsense,' and ran away. But he was not to be so put off: following after her, he grasped her hands, fondled her and begged her to explain to her very own son what it was that distressed her.

Cybele's son Achaemenes seeks Chariclea in marriage.

(23) So then she led him by the hand to a secluded part of the gardens and said: 'To no one else would I have related my own and my lady's misfortunes; but she is in desperate straits, and I expect to be in mortal peril – for I know that Arsace's distress and distraction will swoop down on me – and so I am compelled to speak, on the chance that you can devise some deliverance for her who bore you, brought you forth to the light of day and nurtured you at these breasts. Madam is in love with the young man now staying with us. It is no tolerable or ordinary love, but one that is incurable. We had hopes, she and I till now, that it might prosper, but we have been utterly frustrated. Thus it was

that all those kindly thoughts and ingenious courtesies were bestowed on the strangers. But since this young booby has the hardihood and cruelty to set his face against us, she, I know, will lose her life, while I shall be destroyed, as having deluded and deceived her with my promises. That is the position, child. If you can bring some relief, give me your support; if not, then you have to perform the last rites for your deceased mother.' 'And what reward shall I have, mother?' he asked; 'for this is no time for me to mince matters with you, or to use devious circumloctions in promising you my aid, when you are in such extreme anguish and on the very verge of giving up the ghost.' 'Anything that you desire,' Cybele replied, 'you can count upon. At present she has made you one of the chief cupbearers, to do me honour. If you have in mind some higher dignity, declare it: riches you will gain to an incalculable amount, if you can be the saviour of this unhappy lady.' 'I have long suspected this affair, mother,' he said, 'and have kept my cognizance of it to myself, awaiting the outcome with much concern. But I lay claim to no distinction or riches. Only let Arsace bestow that girl on me in marriage, the so-called sister of Theagenes, and she will accomplish all that she has at heart. I am in love with the girl, mother, very deeply: Madam knows from her own case the force and nature of this passion, and she may fairly lend her aid to one who is labouring under the same infection as herself, and who, moreover, promises her such a gratifying success.' 'Do not hesitate,' said Cybele. 'Madam will show her gratitude to you in no ambiguous manner for having been her benefactor and saviour; besides, we may well be able by ourselves to persuade the girl. But tell me, by what means can you relieve us?' 'I shall not answer that,' he replied, 'until Madam has pledged herself by oath to keep her promises. But you must not make trial of the girl in advance, because I see that she has some high and mighty notions, and you might unwittingly upset the whole business.' 'Everything shall be as you wish,' she said, and then ran in to see Arsace in her chamber. There she fell down at her knees and said: 'Be comforted: everything is turning out well, by Heaven's will; only command that my son Achaemenes be summoned before you.' 'Let him be summoned,' said Arsace, 'if you are not intending to deceive me again.'

(24) Achaemenes entered: Arsace, having now heard all the terms from the old woman, swore that she would procure his

marriage with the sister of Theagenes. 'Madam,' said Achaemenes, 'let Theagenes, who is your slave, cease henceforth to
play the fine gallant with his chosen mistress.' 'What mean you
by that?' she asked. He then related the whole story: how
Theagenes was taken prisoner in the ordinary way of war and
fell into captivity; how Mitranes had dispatched him to Oroondates for delivery to the Great King; and how he himself, put in
charge of the youth for his transmission, had lost him through a
daring onslaught of Bessans and Thyamis, from which he himself
had barely succeeded in escaping. He ended by showing Arsace
the letter of Mitranes to Oroondates, which he had been careful
to have ready with him, and said that, if further proof were
needed, he would produce Thyamis also as witness. Arsace was
greatly inspirited by his words, and without a moment's delay
she quitted her chamber, passed into the suite in which she was
accustomed to sit in state for official business and ordered that
Theagenes be brought in. When he appeared she asked him
whether he knew Achaemenes, pointing him out where he stood
near at hand. He replied that he did. She then put a second
question: 'And did he not take you away as a prisoner in his
charge?' Theagenes assented to this also. 'Know then,' she said,
'that you are our slave. You will work as one of our servants,
obedient to our beck and call, however much against your will.
Your sister I am bestowing in marriage upon Achaemenes here,
who holds one of the highest offices in our household, both for
his mother's sake and for his general regard for our interests.
This event only awaits the appointment of the day and the
arrangements for holding the festivity in duly magnificent style.'
Theagenes, though wounded to the quick by her words, nevertheless resolved not to show fight, but to evade the savage
creature's onset. 'Mistress,' he said, 'thanks be to the gods that
we, who are of the noblest birth, have at least this blessing in our
misfortunes, that we are become slaves to you and to none other
– you who have looked upon us, mere aliens and strangers in
your eyes, with such mildness and kindly favour. As for my sister,
she is no prisoner, and hence no slave: but she chooses to attend
on you and to go by such designation as you may be pleased to
give her. Consider well, and do exactly what you judge to be
correct.' 'Let him be placed,' she said, 'among the table attendants, and be instructed in the serving of wine by Achaemenes, so
as to be well trained in advance for his attendance on the King.'

(25) The two young men accordingly withdrew – Theagenes in gloomy mood and with a look of absorption in thinking of what he had to do, while Achaemenes mocked and jeered at Theagenes, saying: 'So you, sir, who were swaggering of late so haughtily,* you who could not bend your neck, who alone were free, who could not bear to bow your head in obeisance, will now perhaps incline it, or else by fisticuffs be disciplined to hold it down.' Arsace then dismissed all the rest of the company, retaining only Cybele, to whom she said: 'You see now, Cybele, every excuse has been stripped off: go, tell the haughty fellow that, if he obeys us and falls in with our purpose, he will be given his freedom, and will have the ample enjoyment of a life of affluence; but if he persists in his opposition to us, he will learn what it is to deal with a woman whose love is spurned, and who is, moreover, his deeply offended mistress, and he will have to submit to the meanest and most ignominious servitude, and suffer every kind of punishment.' Cybele went and delivered Arsace's message, adding not a few such exhortations of her own as seemed expedient. Theagenes requested her to wait a little while. Left alone with Chariclea, he said to her: 'All is over with us, Chariclea: every cable, as they say,* has been severed, every anchor of hope has been completely torn away, and we are unable now even to call ourselves free in our misfortune, but have become slaves once more' – and here he added the kind of slavery that it was. 'Henceforth we are exposed to barbarous cruelties, and we must either subserve the humours of our lords and masters or be numbered amongst the condemned. All this could yet be borne; but, more grievous still, Arsace has promised to bestow you in marriage on Cybele's son, Achaemenes. This event, of a certainty, will not take place, or I shall not see it occur, so long as life can provide me with a sword and armour to prevent it. But what is to be done, what contrivance can we devise, to frustrate these abominable unions, mine with Arsace and yours with Achaemenes?' 'One only,' replied Chariclea; 'assent to yours, and you will prevent mine.' 'Fie on such words!' he said; 'may the persecutions of our Destiny never prevail on me, who have refrained from attempt on Chariclea, to pollute myself by unlawful intimacy with another woman! But I think I have devised an effectual scheme: necessity is indeed an inventor of expedients.' With that he went off to Cybele and said: 'Go, tell your mistress that I wish to see her alone and unattended.

Theagenes tells Arsace that Chariclea is not his sister, but his affianced bride.

(26) Conceiving that the great point was gained, and that Theagenes had submitted, the old woman went and informed Arsace. She was bidden to fetch the young man after dinner; and this she did. After ordering the retinue to leave Madam undisturbed and to do nothing likely to give serious annoyance to the occupants of the chamber, she privily brought in Theagenes. The rest of the house was plunged in what seemed a nocturnal darkness, which enabled one to pass along unseen, the chamber alone being illuminated by a lamp. She showed him in, and was about to withdraw; but Theagenes stopped her, saying: 'Let Cybele stay here at present, mistress: I know that she is the faithful keeper of your secrets.' So saying he took hold of Arsace's hands and said: 'Mistress, it was in no spirit of insolent defiance of your will that I deferred complying with your order before, but because I had to deliberate with myself how it could be done in safety. But now that by what seems a happy turn of fortune I have become your slave, I am much more ready to obey you in all things. One boon only be pleased to grant me over and above the many benefits that you have promised me: countermand the marriage of Chariclea to Achaemenes. Not to speak of other reasons, for a girl who prides herself on the noblest birth to cohabit with a menial would be scandalous: otherwise, I swear to you by the Sun, fairest of the gods, and by all the other gods, that I will not yield to your desire; and if any violence should be offered to Chariclea, you will see me first done to death by my own hand.' 'Be in no doubt,' said Arsace, 'of my desire to grant you every favour, prepared as I am to bestow myself on you. But I am pre-engaged, and bound by oath, to bestow your sister upon Achaemenes.' 'Very well, mistress,' he said; 'then bestow on him my sister, whatever she may be; but my affianced bride, in fact no other than my wife – her you will neither wish, I am sure, to bestow on him nor, though you may wish it, will you do so.' 'What do you mean?' she asked. 'The plain fact,' he replied; 'for in Chariclea I have, not a sister, but a bride, as I said, so that you are released from your oath; and it is possible for you, if you choose, to obtain full proof of the fact, by celebrating at your own good time my marriage with her.' Though somewhat

pricked with jealousy at hearing that Chariclea was his bride
and not his sister, Arsace was yet able to say: 'So shall it be; and
we will arrange another marriage for Achaemenes' consolation.'
'And so it shall be, as between me and you,' he said, 'now that
the matter is settled'; and with that he advanced to kiss her
hands. But she leant forward and, presenting her mouth instead
of her hands, she kissed him. Theagenes then departed without
having kissed her in return. He took the next opportunity of
relating everything to Chariclea, when she also felt some jealousy over one part of what she heard. He went on to explain
the purpose of his obnoxious promise, and how much he
achieved by it at a single stroke. 'Your marriage with Achaemenes,' he said, 'has been scared off, and a pretext has been
devised to balk the desire of Arsace for the present. Best of all,
it is likely that Achaemenes will raise a mighty commotion in
his annoyance at having his hopes frustrated, and in his resentment of my being favoured by Arsace at his expense. He will
come to know the whole truth through his mother's disclosures:
I purposely took care to have her present at our conversation,
because I wished it to be reported to Achaemenes, while I also
secured her witness that my interview with Arsace went no
further than words. It may suffice a man with no misdeed upon
his conscience to count on the kindness of the supernal powers;
but it is desirable also that he convince his human associates of
his innocence, so as to have open-hearted converse with them in
his passage through this mortal life.' He further pointed out that
it was to be anticipated for certain that Achaemenes would even
plot against Arsace, being a man of servile condition – for in
general the subordinate was inimical to the master – and
suffering injury as the victim of a broken oath, and being a lover
also who found that others had been preferred to himself. Privy
to the most depraved and criminal practices, he had no need of
any fabrication for the furtherance of his design, such as many
a man commonly made bold to use under the smart of injury,
but found in the plain facts a ready means for his revenge.

*Theagenes serves the wine at Arsace's table, and Achaemenes is
prevented from marrying Chariclea.*

(27) By these and many other such observations Theagenes
succeeded in restoring some degree of confidence in Chariclea's

mind. On the next day he was taken by Achaemenes to begin
his service at table, as had been directed by Arsace. She had sent
him some costly Persian clothing, in which he now attired
himself; and he also adorned his person, half willing and half
unwilling, with gold torques and necklaces set with gems. When
Achaemenes tried to give him some practical guidance in the
duties of the wine-servers,* Theagenes went quickly to one of
the tripods that held the drinking-cups, took up a vessel of great
price and said: 'I need no teachers; of my self-taught knowledge
I will attend on Madam, without making a foppery of such
simple services. You, my good sir, are compelled by your
condition to be skilled in them, but the promptings of my nature
and the occasion tell me how they are to be performed.' So
saying he mixed a delectable draught for Arsace and bore it to
her, moving with graceful ease and holding the vessel with his
finger-tips. This drink then excited her more wildly than ever: as
she quaffed it she fixed her gaze intently on Theagenes, and
imbibed a larger draught of love than of liquor. Instead of
draining the cup, she designedly left a little wine within it as an
artful toast to Theagenes.* Achaemenes, seated opposite to her,
felt the wound thus inflicted on himself, and was filled with
mingled wrath and jealousy, so that Arsace herself observed his
grim look and his mutterings under his breath to the company.
When the party began to break up Theagenes said to her: 'The
first favour that I beg, mistress, is that you bid me dress in this
costume only for the time of my attendance.' Arsace signed her
assent, and after changing into his ordinary clothes he went
away. With him went Achaemenes, who heaped reproaches on
him for his indiscreet behaviour and his puerile forwardness,
which for that first time Madam had overlooked in a foreigner
of no experience; but, if he persisted in such presumption, he
would be sorry for it. He added that he was giving Theagenes
this advice as a friend, but especially because in a short time he
was to become his kinsman as the husband of his sister, in
accordance with the promise given by Madam. While he kept
on talking a great deal more in this strain, Theagenes marched
along on his way, seeming not to listen and holding his head
bent down, until Cybele met them as she was hastening to put
her mistress to bed for her noontide repose. Seeing her son's
gloomy looks, she asked him the cause. 'The foreign boy,' he
replied, 'has been preferred to us. Having crept in here hardly a

day ago, he has been appointed a wine-server; he bids us, the stewards of the banquet and the wine-service, go our ways, hands the wine-cup and places himself close to her royal person, thus elbowing us into a position of merely nominal importance. That this fellow should be dignified with superior functions, and participation in even the most confidential business, as a result of our ill-advised silence and collaboration, is not so disastrous, disaster though it be; but it was quite possible for us, assistants and servants in honourable occupations, to be at least exempt from gross insult in the course of such services.

(28) 'But more on these matters some other time. For the moment, mother, it is my bride, my best and sweetest Chariclea whom I was wishing to see, in the hope that I might salve the deep wound in my soul with the sight of her.' 'What bride, my child?' said Cybele; 'you seem to me, in your vexation at the most trivial things that affect you, to be blindly unaware of your major grievances. No longer are you to obtain Chariclea in marriage.' 'What is that you say?' he cried; 'am I not worthy to wed a fellow-slave? What is the cause, mother?' 'We are the cause,' she replied, 'with our inordinate kindness and loyalty to Arsace. Esteeming her above our own security, and placing her passion before our preservation, we have assisted her in every fond desire; and then this noble, this brilliant lover of hers, having once found his way into her chamber, has only to be seen to seduce her into violating the oaths sworn to you and betrothing Chariclea to him, while he stoutly alleges that she is not his sister but his bride.' 'And Arsace has given him this promise, mother?' 'She has, dear boy,' replied Cybele, 'in my presence and hearing, and she is to celebrate their wedding in splendid style within the next few days. To you she has promised another to be your spouse.' At this Achaemenes gave a deep groan, and wringing his hands he said: 'I shall make marriage a bitter thing for them all! Only help me to deferment of the wedding for an adequate space of time, and if any should inquire after me, report that I am indisposed by a bad fall somewhere in the country. That fine fellow calls his sister bride, as though one failed to perceive that this is a device aimed solely at ousting me! For if he should embrace her, if he should kiss her as is usual, nay, even if he slept with her, would that be certain proof of her being, not his sister, but his bride? This affair shall be my concern, as it will be also of the oaths and of the gods that have been flouted.'

(29) After he had thus spoken Achaemenes, driven frantic with mingled anger, jealousy, love and frustration – all sufficiently strong to distract any man, let alone a barbarian – took up an idea that crossed his mind and, without any reasoned judgment of it, adopted it on the spur of the moment. When evening had drawn on he contrived to purloin an Armenian horse from the mounts kept in stall for the satrap's use in processions and public celebrations, and rode off to find Oroondates, who was actively preparing at Great Thebes his campaign against the Ethiopians; for this he was assembling a mass of varied war material and all kinds of troops, and he was just making ready to start on the expedition.

BOOK 8

The war between Hydaspes, King of Ethiopia, and Oroondates, Persian governor of Egypt, for possession of Philae and the emerald mines. Achaemenes has an interview with Oroondates.

(1) The King of Ethiopia had cunningly circumvented Oroondates, and had gained possession of one of the two prizes of the war: by a sudden advance he had reduced the city of Philae, which was constantly a bone of contention between them. He thus drove Oroondates into the extreme embarrassment of having to launch his expedition in great haste and largely by improvisation. For the city of Philae lies on the Nile,* a little above the Lesser Cataracts, and about a hundred furlongs' distance from Syene and Elephantine. Egyptian exiles had at one time seized and occupied it, thus making it a subject of dispute between Ethiopia and Egypt, since the former set the Cataracts as the boundary of Ethiopia, while the Egyptians claimed that the previous settlement there of exiles from their country gave them possession of the place no less than if it had been taken by force of arms.* It changed hands continually, becoming the property of successive victors in surprise attacks, and at this time it was held by a garrison of Egyptians and Persians. The King of Ethiopia dispatched a delegation to Oroondates demanding not only Philae but the emerald mines besides: a long time before, as has been related, he had sent an envoy to make representations, but without avail. He now ordered his envoys to precede him by a few days, and followed after them with a force which he had got ready long before as though for a campaign elsewhere, and had let no one know the purpose of this expedition. When he calculated that his envoys had passed by Philae, and had put the inhabitants and the garrison in a careless mood by a message stating that they were on an embassy of peace and friendship, he suddenly appeared and drove out the garrison after it had resisted for two or three days, but had to yield to superior numbers and the use of siege engines against the walls. He thus got possession of the city without injury done to any of the inhabitants. Oroondates, greatly disconcerted by this action and by full accounts of it from men who had made

their escape, was still further disturbed by the arrival of Achaemenes, appearing unexpectedly with no order given for his
admission. When he asked whether something serious had
happened to Arsace or his household, Achaemenes answered
that this was so, and that he wished to speak to him in private.
When they had withdrawn to where they were alone, he gave an
account of all that had occurred: how Theagenes, taken prisoner
by Mitranes, had been dispatched to Oroondates for delivery, at
his discretion, as a gift to the Great King, since he was the sort
of young man who was worthy to serve at the royal court and
table; how he was carried off by the Bessans after they had left
Mitranes among the slain; how he had later arrived at Memphis
– and here he inserted the events connected with Thyamis.
Achaemenes ended by recounting the love of Arsace for Theagenes and his installation in the palace; the kind treatment given
to him, and his attendance and cupbearing service; how up to
the present it was probable that no unlawful act had been
committed, as the young man had maintained a resolute resistance. But it was to be feared that such an act might occur
through forcible coercion of the stranger, or perhaps his weakening under the effect of time, if measures were not quickly
taken to snatch him away forthwith from Memphis and so
entirely eradicate the cause of Arsace's love. It was for these
reasons that he had made haste to slip away unobserved and
make this report; for his loyalty to his master was such that he
could not bear to conceal the injury that was being done to his
honour.

(2) When by his account he had filled Oroondates with wrath,
so that the satrap abandoned himself to indignation and
thoughts of vengeance, he sought next to inflame him with a
passion 'for Chariclea, by adding a description of her in which
he exalted her merits to their real height, and applied all his art
to investing the girl's beauty and grace with a divine charm,
such as had never been seen before nor could ever be seen again.
'Regard as of little worth compared with her,' he said, 'all your
concubines, not merely those at Memphis, but those also who
travel in your train'; and much more Achaemenes told him, in
the hope that, after having intercourse with Chariclea, Oroondates would, a little later at any rate, grant his request for her as
the reward for his information, and would bestow her on him
in marriage. The satrap was altogether highly excited now and

inflamed, as though entangled in the twofold toils of anger and desire. Without a moment's delay he summoned Bagoas,* one of his confidential eunuchs, and dispatched him at the head of fifty horsemen to Memphis, with orders to bring Theagenes and Chariclea to him immediately, wherever Bagoas himself might get hold of them.

On the information given him by Achaemenes, Oroondates sends stern messages to Memphis. Thyamis tries to obtain Theagenes and Chariclea from Arsace, whose passion makes her fiercely resent Theagenes' obduracy.

(3) The man was charged besides with letters, one of which was for Arsace, and was couched in these terms: 'Oroondates to Arsace: send me Theagenes and Chariclea, the brother and sister who are prisoners, and slaves of the King who are to be consigned to the King. Send them willingly, for they will be fetched away, even against your will, and so Achaemenes' information will be credited.' The other letter was for Euphrates, chief of the eunuchs at Memphis, telling him: 'For your disregard of affairs in my house you will be held to account. At this moment hand over the Greek strangers who are prisoners to Bagoas for him to bring to me, whether Arsace is willing or unwilling. Hand them over without fail: otherwise, be it known to you that order has been given that you yourself be brought in fetters to be flayed alive.' Bagoas and his troops set out to execute their commission, with the missives from the satrap bearing his seal, so that the staff at Memphis should be completely convinced of their genuineness, and should readily hand over the young pair. Meanwhile, Oroondates set out on his campaign against the Ethiopians. He had ordered Achaemenes to accompany him, and kept him unawares under secret guard until he should establish the truth of his report.

During these same days affairs at Memphis took the following course. Just after the disappearance of Achaemenes Thyamis, who had now regained the full possession of his prophetic office and held in consequence a leading position in the city, performed the obsequies of Calasiris, and paid to his father all the customary honours during the prescribed number of days. He next bethought him of making a search for Theagenes and Chariclea as soon as he was permitted by the ordinance of the prophets' law to associate with the laity. When by dint of persistent inquiries he learnt of their lodgment in the satrap's palace, he went in hot haste to Arsace and laid claim to the young strangers, stating that on many grounds they were his personal concern, but that his chief reason was that his father Calasiris in his dying words had charged him with the particular guardianship and protection of the pair. He avowed his gratitude to her for having received these young people, foreigners and Greeks though they were, and shown them so much kind attention during the space of those days in which unconsecrated persons were forbidden to frequent the temple; but he considered it his right to regain possession of the wards entrusted to his personal care. 'I wonder,' said Arsace, 'that on the one hand you bear witness to our goodness and humanity while on the other you convict us of inhumanity, if we are to be thought unable or unwilling to provide for these strangers and accord them fitting treatment.' 'It is not that,' said Thyamis; 'I know that they will fare more plenteously here than they would with me, if they should choose to stay where they are. But the fact is that, being persons of distinguished family, they have in their life met with such a series of various molestations from Fortune that they are now reduced to mendicancy, and above all things they desire to regain their kin and re-enter their native land. To help them in this aim my father has left me the inheritor of his care; and there are other grounds on which these strangers can rightly claim my friendship.' 'It is well,' Arsace said to him, 'that you have done with humble pleading, and put forward the claim of right, which tells the more strongly on my side, since the authority of a lord and master has a firmer hold than that of an ineffectual guardian.' Surprised at these words, Thyamis asked: 'You, mistress of these persons! How is that?' 'By the law of war,' she replied, 'which declares those taken prisoner to be slaves.'

(4) Then Thyamis, perceiving that she meant to advert to the affair of Mitranes, said: 'But, Arsace, we are now in a state, not of war, but of peace: the one aims to enslave, the other to liberate; one is the pursuit of a tyrant, the other is the decree of a sovereign. The truth about peace and war is to be apprehended, not so much from the accepted meaning of those terms, as from the disposition of the persons employing them. By adding justice to them you would find that you had them better

defined. But propriety and advantage do not even enter into the question; for how can it be honourable or profitable for you to appear, and also confess yourself, to be so ardently devoted to a couple of young foreigners?'

(5) At these words Arsace could restrain herself no longer, and her behaviour took a turn which may be seen commonly in lovers; while they believe that their case is unobserved, they blush for it, but when detected they cast away all shame; unnoticed they are quite timid, but discovered they show a bold self-disclosure. Guessing that Thyamis had formed a suspicion of her conduct, she took no account of the prophet and the prophetic distinction, and thrust aside all the modesty of her sex. 'Ah, you people will live to regret what you have done to Mitranes,' she said. 'A time will come when Oroondates will inflict condign punishment on those who murdered him and his party. I will not let these strangers go: for the present they are my slaves, and a little later they will be sent up to my brother, the Great King, in accordance with Persian law. So now bestow your eloquence on vain definitions of justice, propriety and advantage: the possessor of power needs no aid of that kind, for in place of each one of those notions he has his own set purpose. Now, get you gone from our court immediately and willingly, if you would not find yourself made to go, however unwilling.' Thyamis then departed, after calling the gods to witness, and merely protesting that the affair would come to no good in the end; his intention was to divulge it to the citizens and to solicit their support. 'I make no account,' said Arsace, 'of your prophetic function: love recognizes but one prophecy – possession.' She then retired to her chamber. There she sent for Cybele and consulted with her on the situation. She was now beginning to suspect the flight of Achaemenes, who was nowhere to be seen. Cybele, in answer to her insistent inquiries after Achaemenes, kept inventing one ingenious reason after another, aimed at inducing her to believe anything rather than the fact of his visit to Oroondates. But finally she was unable fully to convince Arsace, for his continued absence was now beginning to discredit her suggestions. Yet even so Arsace said to her: 'What are we to do, Cybele? How shall I extricate myself from this contingency? My love, instead of weakening, grows more intense; the young man is so much fuel for its raging flame. He is hard and ruthless; he seemed at first to have some kindlier

feeling than he has now, and he sought to console me, at least for the while, with delusive promises; but now his response is downright, undisguised refusal. And what disturbs me still more is that he on his part may have discovered something of what I suspect regarding Achaemenes, and is thus the more inclined to shrink from the venture. But Achaemenes above all distresses me. Has he not gone off to denounce me to Oroondates, or perhaps to persuade him, or just to make mention of things that seem not altogether improbable? If only I could see Oroondates! One caress, a single tear, of his Arsace will be more than he can withstand. The glances of a woman's, of a helpmate's, eyes have a magical power of persuading a man. Most awful of all would it be if, not having had my will of Theagenes, I were forestalled by the accusation – it might even be by the punishment – of an intimacy not yet attained, but believed by Oroondates to have occurred. Go therefore, Cybele, leave no stone unturned or device untried: you see how things have turned out for me and have brought me to the very verge, to the decisive turning-point. Reflect also that, if my case becomes desperate, there is no possible chance of my sparing others. Why, you will be the first to share the consequences of your son's enterprises which, I cannot guess how, you have failed to detect.' To this Cybele answered: 'Of my son, and my loyalty to you, mistress, you have formed a false opinion, as you will learn from the facts. You, who on your part deal so supinely with your love, and show a real slackness, must not throw the blame on others who are blameless. Unlike a mistress who controls, you make much of this stripling as though you were his slave. At the beginning this was perhaps the right way, when he was thought to be of a tender and tractable disposition; but, as soon as he puts up a resistance to you as his lover, he should feel what it is to have you as his mistress, and by the lash and the rack he should be subdued to your desires. For the nature of young men inclines them to be haughty when they are made much of, but to be submissive when they are coerced. So will this fellow perform, when flagellated, that which he refused when flattered.' 'I believe you are in the right,' said Arsace; 'but how could I bear, ye gods, to behold with my eyes that body of his being lacerated or in any way chastised?' 'There you are again, showing your slackness,' she replied, 'as though it will not be for his good, after some slight tormenting, to choose the wiser course, and for

yours, after feeling a little distress, to gain what you have at
heart. And you can easily spare your eyes the pain of seeing the
thing done: hand him over to Euphrates, with instruction to
punish him for some blunder, and so avoid the distressing sight;
for hearing affects one less painfully than seeing. Then, if we
should see signs of his conversion, you could relent and reprieve
him, as having received adequate correction.'

*Cruel maltreatment of Theagenes. Cybele accidentally drinks the
poisoned wine with which she sought to kill Chariclea.*

(6) Arsace was now persuaded; for love that has lost all hope
has no mercy on the beloved, and readily turns frustration into
vengeance. She sent for the chief eunuch, and ordered him to
carry out her resolve. He, naturally infected with the jealousy
common among eunuchs, had besides for long been smouldering
in spite against Theagenes on account of what he both saw and
suspected. He immediately put him in fetters, and oppressed hin
with starvation and blows in a gloomy cell, where he kept him
under lock and key. To Theagenes, who feigned ignorance of
what he well knew, and made a show of asking the reason of all
this, he made no reply, but each day increased his punishments
to a severity of vengeance beyond what Arsace intended or had
enjoined. He allowed no one to visit the prisoner, except only
Cybele, on particular order given to him. She made frequent
visits, with the pretended purpose of bringing in secret some
additional food, as though she were full of pity for him, and
owing to their late association deeply distressed; but in fact she
came to test Theagenes' state of mind under this treatment, and
to see whether he was giving way and becoming amenable as a
result of his torments. But he played the man more than ever,
and fought still more stoutly against these efforts. With his body
sinking in exhaustion, but his spirit firmly braced in defence of
chastity, he both prided himself and gloried in the Fortune
which, hurtful to him in the extreme, was favouring him with
the happiest of lots, in affording him the means of proving his
faithful attachment to Chariclea. If only she herself could know
of this he would consider it his greatest boon; and he called
aloud on Chariclea as 'his life, his light, his soul'. Cybele,
observing this, and informed though she was of Arsace's desire
that only a mild pressure was to be put on Theagenes, since she

had consigned him, not to destruction, but to compulsion, took the contrary course of announcing to Euphrates that he was to increase the young man's punishments. But when she found that she was achieving nothing, and that even this expedient had failed to realize her hopes, she perceived the grievous pass to which she had come. On the one hand she must expect the undelaying vengeance of Oroondates if he learnt of the affair from Achaemenes; while on the other Arsace might well strike first and destroy her for having made game of her mistress in her advancement of the intrigue. She therefore decided to grapple with her embarrassments and accomplish some great mischief by which she would either bring to fruition the desire of Arsace, and so evade for the present the peril in which she stood with her, or else abolish the evidences of the whole affair by contriving the deaths at one swoop of all the persons involved. So she went to Arsace and said: 'Our labours are of no avail, mistress; that hard-hearted youth will not give in, but grows ever more impudent. He has the name of Chariclea continually on his lips, and comforts himself with his invocations of her, as though they could relieve his pain. Let us then drop our last anchor, as they say,* and clear from our course her who impedes us. If he should learn that she was no more, he would probably be converted to our design, having relinquished his desire for her as hopeless.'

(7) Arsace snatched eagerly at this advice and, her longstanding jealousy now heightened by annoyance at Cybele's report, she said: 'You are right; and it is for me now to order the destruction of that pestilent creature.' 'But who will obey your order?' asked Cybele. 'All else is within your power; but to take a life without judgment passed by Persian magistrates is forbidden by the laws. And thus you would be involved in the troublesome business of fabricating charges and accusations against the girl, with the uncertainty besides of our allegations being believed. But, if you agree, I in my readiness to do and undergo everything for you will carry out the scheme by means of poison, and will remove your opponent from your path with a magic potion.' Arsace approved her proposal and bade her act upon it. Cybele set out at once, and found Chariclea lamenting and weeping, utterly abandoned to her grief and to considering how she could rid herself of her life. For by now she had formed some notion of what had befallen Theagenes, despite the crafty

beguilements at first tried on her by Cybele and the various excuses which she invented each time that he failed to appear for his usual visit to their apartment. 'Wretched girl,' she said, 'will you never cease wasting and exhausting yourself to no purpose? Theagenes, I tell you, has been released, and will come here this evening. My mistress, a little irritated by some blunder of his in his service, ordered him to be locked up; but she promised to release him today on account of an ancestral festival which she is about to celebrate, and also in response to my entreaties. So now arise, pluck up your spirits a little and, for this occasion at least, take some food with me.' 'How can I believe you?' said Chariclea. 'Your continual deception of me undermines all confidence in words that you utter.' To which Cybele replied: 'I swear by all the gods that your troubles shall all be dispersed this day, and you shall be freed from all anxiety. Only be in less haste to do away with yourself; it is so many days now that you have fasted! Come, be persuaded, and taste the dishes that have been so opportunely provided.' Chariclea complied, though with much hesitation, suspecting as usual some deception, but then again putting her trust in oaths, and gladly welcoming the prospect held out by Cybele; for the heart is apt to believe that which it desires. So they placed themselves at table and partook of the fine fare. The favourite handmaid who waited on them served cups of diluted wine: Cybele signed to her to hand a cup first to Chariclea, and then took one herself and drank after her. Before the old woman had quite drained hers she was seen to grow dizzy: she poured out the few drops of drink that remained, shot a piercing glance at the maid and fell a prey to violent spasms and convulsions.

Chariclea, falsely accused of giving the poison to Cybele which caused her death, is condemned to be burnt, but escapes unhurt from the flames.

(8) Chariclea herself was utterly confounded, and tried to bring her to her senses, while all present were thrown into no less confusion. For the noxious drug, it seemed, working more swiftly than any arrow dipped in deadly venom, and potent enough to kill even a young person in the full vigour of life, had laid hold on a body that in time had become withered, and more swiftly than words could tell had made its way to the more vital

parts. The old woman's eyes were aflame; her limbs, after the spasms had passed off, lapsed into immobility, and a sable hue overspread her skin. Yet I conceive that her guileful soul was even more malignant than that baneful potion. Cybele, in fact, even at the moment of death, would not relinquish her villainies, but partly by signs and partly by muttered words she indicated Chariclea as the contriver of the deed. The old dame expired; and at the same instant Chariclea was put in fetters and hurried before Arsace, who asked her whether she was the preparer of the poison, and threatened her, if she declined to avow the truth, with castigation and torture. Then Chariclea surprised the onlookers with a singular spectacle. Showing no sign of dismay or ignoble temper, she plainly regarded the situation as matter for laughter and jesting. While her clear conscience enabled her to ignore the calumny, she rejoiced that she was to die now that Theagenes was no more, and to be saved the abominable act that she had decided to commit upon herself, since it was to be perpetrated by others. 'Your Highness,' she said, 'if Theagenes is alive I am as guiltless as he is of this murder; but if he has fallen a victim to your pious purposes, you have no need to put me to the torture. Here I am, the poisoner of her who nurtured you and instructed you in exemplary conduct: now slay me out of hand. Nothing could be so pleasing to Theagenes, the loyal contemner of your disloyal designs.'

(9) Infuriated by her words, Arsace ordered her to be smartly cuffed. 'Take the pestilent wretch,' she said, 'fettered as she is, and let her behold her marvellous lover suffering the same treatment, befitting his case. Load her limbs with chains, and deliver her likewise to Euphrates, for him to keep in his custody till tomorrow, when she will be sentenced by the court of Persian magistrates to the punishment of death.' While Chariclea was being taken away, the young girl who had served the wine to Cybele – she was one of the two Ionian maids whom Arsace had at first assigned to the young pair as their personal attendants – whether moved by some kind feeling for Chariclea, derived from familiar association with her, or by divine intent, shed some tears, and moaned, and said: 'Alas, poor lady! She is not to blame.' The bystanders were surprised, and pressed her to explain precisely what she meant by this. She then confessed that it was she who had given the poison to Cybele: she had received it from the old woman herself, with the order to give it

to Chariclea; but, either seized with a sudden confusion at the baseness of the proceeding, or else flustered by Cybele's signing to her that she was to hand it first to Chariclea, she had changed over the cups and had presented the one containing the poison to the old woman. She was immediately brought before Arsace, and all present accounted it a godsend that Chariclea was thus cleared of the charge against her; for nobility of character and aspect induces pity in even a barbarous people. The declaration of the handmaid resulted only in Arsace's remarking. 'Why, she is an accomplice, it would seem,' and commanding that she be fettered and kept under guard for the trial. She then issued an order for the Persian officers of state, who were empowered to deliberate on public affairs, judge causes and assess due penalties, to be convoked for holding the trial on the following day. When they met the next morning and went into session, Arsace delivered her accusation. She gave information of the poisoning, recounting it in every particular: continually she shed tears for her nurse, in whom she had lost the most precious and affectionate member of her household; and she called on the judges to be witnesses to this repayment that she had received from the stranger woman for the welcome that she had given her and the extreme kindness with which she had treated her. In short, she couched her accusation in the bitterest terms. Chariclea put forward nothing in her defence, but again admitted the charge, and acknowledged that she had administered the poison, adding that she would gladly have destroyed Arsace also if she had not been prevented: she even went so far as to abuse Arsace to her face, and to do everything that she could to provoke the judges to impose the penalty. For during the night, in the prison, she had imparted to Theagenes her whole design, and had in turn been fully informed of his plans. It was agreed between them that they must voluntarily accept whatever kind of death was inflicted on them, so that they might be rid once for all of a desperate existence, endless wandering and an implacably adverse Fortune. She had then given him what was regarded as her last fond embrace. Always careful to carry secretly on her person the necklaces that were exposed with her, she then fastened them within her clothing about her loins, so as to have them upon her, in a sort, as her burial ornaments. She admitted every charge brought against her, and invented others that were not brought. The judges in consequence made no delay over their decision, and came very near consigning her to one of the more savage punishments inflicted in Persia; but affected no doubt by the sight of her youth and her irresistible beauty, they condemned her to be burnt to ashes on a pyre. She was immediately seized by the executioners and removed to a little distance outside the city walls, a herald all the while proclaiming that she was to be burnt as a poisoner. A large crowd besides followed after them from the city: some had been eye-witnesses of her being taken along, and others, on hearing the news as it spread swiftly through the town, hurried out to view the spectacle. Arsace also appeared as a spectator on the walls, for it would have been dreadful for her to miss feasting her eyes on Chariclea's punishment.

When the executioners had piled up the pyre to an enormous mass, and when from the flame that they had applied it blazed up brightly, Chariclea begged them, as they dragged her towards it, to allow her a brief delay, promising that she would mount the pyre of her own accord. Then, raising her hands to the quarter of the heavens where the sun sent forth his beams, she cried: 'Sun and Earth and Powers that above and beneath our earth are beholders and avengers of wrongdoing in mankind, ye are witnesses to clear me of the charges brought against me and of my willingness to suffer death on account of the intolerable afflictions laid on me by Fortune. Receive me, therefore, with kindly welcome, and be prompt to punish the accursed, the nefarious, the adulterous Arsace, who doth this to me in order to deprive me of my bridegroom.' As soon as she had spoken, all the people cried out at her declaration, and were for deferring her punishment and holding a second trial: some were getting ready, others had even started, to take action. But she forestalled them by mounting the pyre. She took her stand at its very centre, and remained there for a long time unmoved and unaffected, while the fire surged around her without closing in upon her, and did no harm, but retired wherever she stirred towards it. The flames only served to illuminate her and make her conspicuous; and her beauty shone forth in the bright glare of the blaze, so that she seemed like a bride in a nuptial chamber of fire. She began to dart to one side and another of the pyre, wondering at the strange event, while eagerly seeking her death; but all her attempts were in vain, for the fire each time receded, as though quailing before her advance. The executioners, instead of slack-

ening, increased their efforts, urged on by threatening signs from
Arsace. They brought fresh bundles of wood, and piled on reeds
from the river, and did their utmost to foment the blaze. But all
was of no avail; and the citizens became more and more agitated,
conceiving that the girl's deliverance must be wrought by some
divine power. 'She is pure, she is guiltless, poor woman!' they
cried, and going up close they scared away the fuellers from the
pyre. Thyamis led the way and encouraged the people to come
on to the rescue – for he also had come upon the scene, on
learning from the mighty outcry what was going forward. They
were eager enough to pluck Chariclea from the fire but, not
venturing so near it, they urged her to leap out of the blazing
pile, since if she could endure to stay within the flames she
should have no qualms in deciding to quit them. Seeing and
hearing their incitements, and convinced on her own part that it
was a god-sent protection that had preserved her, Chariclea
thought it best not to appear ungrateful to the higher powers by
refusing their benefaction. She leapt forth from the pyre; whereupon the citizens with one voice raised a great shout of mingled
joy and amazement, and extolled the mightiness of the gods,
while Arsace, losing all control of herself, rushed down from the
walls and darted out through a small gate, escorted by a strong
guard and the high Persian officers. She seized Chariclea with
her own hands and, eyeing the people arrogantly, she said: 'You
should be ashamed to attempt the deliverance from punishment
of a pestilent woman, a poisoner, who was caught in the very
act of committing murder, and has confessed to it! By going to
the rescue of a nefarious woman you are thereby revolting
against the laws of Persia, the King himself, the satraps, the
magistrates and the judges. Doubtless the fact that she has not
been consumed by the fire has deluded you into a feeling of pity,
and you ascribe this feat to the gods. Will you not come to your
senses, and reflect that this only the more plainly proves it a case
of poisoning by one who is such an adept in the black arts that
she is able to repel the power of fire? Come, all of you, and
attend, if you please, at the council meeting to be held tomorrow
in public for your satisfaction, when you will witness her
confession, and her conviction on the evidence of the
accomplices whom I am holding in custody.' With these words
she grasped Chariclea tightly by the neck and took her away,
giving orders to the bodyguard to keep back the crowd. Some

of the people were indignant and inclined to resist, but others drew back, as the suspicion of dark practice was getting a hold on them; and there were some also who were deterred by fear of Arsace and the strong force around her. Chariclea was again handed over to Euphrates, and again she was fettered with chains, but with more this time, and was kept in custody for a second trial and a second punishment.

Chariclea is again fettered and committed to prison, where she confers with Theagenes.

One supreme advantage she found now amid her perils, in having the company of Theagenes and giving him a full account of what had been happening to her. Arsace in fact had devised this very thing from a kind of vengeful derision, supposing that the young pair would be more acutely pained by the sight of each other pent up in the same cell and chained, and harassed with punishments. For she knew that the sufferings of the beloved are more distressing to the lover than his own. But to them it was rather a consolation to be so placed, and they considered it an advantage to be enduring the same sort of distresses: if one of them should be punished more lightly than the other, it was felt to be a defeat and a falling short of a lover's duty. They had besides the chance to converse together, and to advise and encourage one another to sustain with a noble and generous spirit the fortunes that befell them and their struggles to preserve their virtue and their loyalty to each other.

(10) And indeed they had much talk to exchange far into the night, as might be expected of a pair who had given up hope of meeting again after that night was passed, and who sought to make the most that they could of each other's company. At length they came to speculate upon the miracle of the burning pyre. Theagenes attributed its cause to benevolence of the gods, who reprobated the injustice of Arsace's slanders and had compassion on a guiltless woman in no way meriting punishment. But Chariclea seemed to be in some doubt. 'The strange manner of my preservation,' she said, 'points of course to some heavenly, some divine beneficence: but our subjection to so many trying misfortunes in close succession, and the manifold and excessive punishments with which we have been tormented, may show that we are pursued by divine displeasure, and are

feeling the weight of Heaven's enmity upon us; unless perchance it was some miraculous act of a deity who meant, while driving us into utter misery, to deliver us from a desperate plight.'

(11) She had hardly ceased uttering these words, and Theagenes was warning her not to speak so rashly, and advising her to observe more reverence and moderation, when she cried out: 'Ye gods, be gracious to us! A strange dream, or perhaps an apparition, has just come to my mind. I saw it last night, and at the time, I know not how, I let it slip from my thoughts: but now it has returned to my memory. My dream was of a poem composed in regular verse, and it was spoken by that divinest of men, Calasiris: either he appeared to me when I had inadvertently fallen asleep, or he came before my eyes in the flesh. The verses, I think, were something of this sort:

> "If thou wear the stone pantarbe, dread not the force of fire,
> For even the unexpected can the Fates easily achieve."

A tremor ran through Theagenes, as through one inspired, and so far as his chains permitted he leapt up and exclaimed: 'Ye gods, be gracious to us! I also, through recollection, am revealed a poet. From the same prophet Calasiris, or else from a god appearing in Calasiris' form, I have received an oracle which seemed to say:

> "To the Ethiopian land shalt thou arrive, in company with a
>   maiden,
> And tomorrow shalt escape from the bonds of Arsace."

I can guess what the oracle portends for me. It seems that "the Ethiopian land" means the subterranean region,* and that I shall dwell there with the maiden Persephone,* and that the release from bonds is the liberation from this terrestrial body. Now, what do you make of your poem, with that self-contradiction in its verses? For the word "pantarbe" signifies "fearing everything", whereas your message bids you have no fear of the fire.' 'My darling Theagenes,' said Chariclea, 'your habitation with misfortunes has inclined you to conceive and imagine everything in its worst possible aspect; for the human mind is apt to be swayed by the course of events. This prophecy appears to me to give a more favourable intimation than you conclude from it: the maiden may well be myself, with whom it is declared that you will set foot on my native land of Ethiopia, after you

have escaped from Arsace and the bonds of Arsace. How that is
to come about is to us neither clear nor easy to take on trust,
but to the gods it is feasible and will be the concern of the beings
who have vouchsafed to us these oracles. The prediction regarding me, indeed, you know to have been already fulfilled by their
intervention: you see me alive at this moment, after being in
utterly desperate straits. I carried upon me then the means of
my own salvation, all unawares; but now I seem to understand
it. For just as always in the former time I was careful to wear
about me the tokens that were exposed with me, I did so
especially when the hour of my judgment, which I expected to
be my last, was approaching. I chose then to sling them secretly
about my loins, so that if I should be saved they should be a
means of providing me with the necessaries of life; while, if
worse should befall, they should serve as my last adornments at
my burial. Now, among these tokens, Theagenes, consisting of
costly necklaces and precious stones of India and Ethiopia, there
is a ring, presented by my father to my mother on their betrothal.
Its bezel is set with a stone called pantarbe, and it bears an
inscription in certain sacred characters which, we may believe,
is instinct with a celestial sanctity and thus, I imagine, confers
on the stone a certain power of repelling fire, and of keeping its
wearers unscathed in conflagrations. This it was, most likely,
that wrought my deliverance, under divine Providence. This
inference and this belief I draw from the admonitions of the
divinely inspired Calasiris, who ofttimes informed me that this
power was stated and explained in the lettering embroidered on
the swathe exposed with me and now wound about my loins.'
'Your surmise is probable, and indeed is true,' said Theagenes;
'it fits so very well with the succour that you received. But from
tomorrow's perils what other kind of pantarbe will deliver you?
For this one does not promise immortality as well, worse luck,
as immunity from burning; while the accursed Arsace, we can
guess, is even now devising some other, and more exquisite,
form of punishment. Would that she might condemn us both to
die together, at the same moment! I should regard that, not as
death, but as a respite from all these troubles.' 'Take heart,' said
Chariclea; 'we have another pantarbe, in that prophecy. Let us
rely upon the gods; then we shall have the greater joy in our
salvation, and amid our sufferings, if they must come, a purer
spirit.'

The messengers from Oroondates arrive at Memphis.

(12) Thus they speculated on their fate, now lamenting and each professing to feel the greater pain and anguish for the other, now making their last requests of one another, and swearing by the gods and their present fortunes to be faithful to their mutual love until death; and so they passed those hours. Bagoas and his troop of fifty horsemen arrived at Memphis while the night was still quite dark and the whole city was fast asleep. They quietly roused the gatekeepers, stated who they were and were recognized; they then proceeded swiftly and noiselessly to the satrap's palace. There Bagoas posted his horsemen all round the palace, so that if he met with any opposition they should be at hand to assist him. He admitted himself by a postern gate known to only a few persons, after forcing open its weakly fastened doors. He gave his name to the porter and ordered him to be silent; he then hastened to find Euphrates, aided by his practical knowledge of the building, and also by a faint glimmer of moonlight. He found the man in his bed and roused him from sleep. In consternation Euphrates cried out: 'Who is there?' The other quieted him, saying: 'It is I, Bagoas; order a light to be brought.' Euphrates summoned a page-boy who was in waiting, and ordered him to light a lamp without awakening the others. The boy came in, set the lamp on its stand and withdrew. 'What is it?' Euphrates asked; 'what message of fresh trouble does your sudden, unexpected appearance bring me?' 'Not a case for much talk,' said Bagoas; 'only take this letter and read it: but before you do so recognize the device on the seal, and be assured that this command comes from Oroondates. Act upon his injunctions, availing yourself of the night time and swiftness as your confederates in avoiding detection. The question whether it would be prudent to deliver first to Arsace the missive addressed to her you must decide for yourself.'

(13) Euphrates received the letters from him, and after reading them both he said: 'Arsace will bewail herself, especially as just now her condition is desperate: a kind of fever, suggesting a divine visitation, seized her yesterday; an extreme heat spread through her and still grips her, allowing scant hope of her survival. I for one would not have handed her this letter even if she had been quite well; for she would rather have died first,

and destroyed us with herself, than have consented to give up
these young people. Now you, let me tell you, have arrived most
opportunely. Take charge of these strangers, fetch them away,
and assist them with all the zeal that you can muster. Have pity
on them without reserve: wretched unfortunates, they have
suffered countless outrages and castigations, by no wish of mine,
but on orders given to me by Arsace. In any case they seem to
be of good family and, as I can tell from my observation of their
behaviour, are perfectly well-conducted persons.' So saying he
led him to the prison. When Bagoas saw the young pair, fettered
and much wasted though they were by the tortures inflicted on
them, he was astonished alike at their stature and their beauty.
They, supposing that this was the end, and that Bagoas had
come with others in the small hours to take them off for their
last breath of life, were for a moment dismayed; then, recovering
themselves, they clearly showed to those present by their cheerful and unstrained looks that they felt, not any anxiety, but an
increase of joy. Indeed, as Euphrates and his men approached
and laid hands on them, and were beginning to release them
from the timbers to which their chains were bolted, Theagenes
exclaimed: 'Well done, accursed Arsace! She thinks to conceal
her nefarious deeds beneath the gloomy shades of night. But the
eye of justice is keen to detect and bring to light even the
closekept secrets of criminals. As for you, carry out your orders;
and whether it be fire or water or the sword that has been
ordained for our execution, indulge us with one and the same
death that we shall suffer together.' Chariclea joined with him
in making the same request. The eunuchs, moved to tears – for
they understood something of what was said – gently led away
the young pair, still in chains.

*Oroondates' emissary Bagoas takes Theagenes and Chariclea
away from Memphis. On their way they learn that Arsace has
hanged herself.*

(14) On their leaving the palace, Euphrates stayed behind.
Then Bagoas and his horsemen relieved the young pair of most
of their chains, leaving on them as much as would serve for
custody but not for punishment. Each was mounted on a horse
and with the troop guarding them in a ring about them they
rode in unremitting haste on their way to Thebes. For the

remainder of the night they travelled without a halt, and on the
following day they nowhere sat down to rest till about the third
hour. The heat of the sun's rays, as it was summer time and in
Egypt, became at length unbearable, and they felt languid from
lack of sleep; in particular they observed that Chariclea was
exhausted by the continuous riding. So they decided to fling
themselves down where they were, for recovery of both their
own and their horses' breath and for the girl's refreshment. Now
the Nile had there an embankment in the form of a headland, at
which the river's flow was broken from its direct course, and
after being diverted into a semicircular detour, turned about to
a course opposite to that taken at its diversion, thus creating in
what it enclosed a kind of earthen gulf on the mainland. This
tract was rich in spacious meadows, well watered throughout as
they were: of its own accord it produced grass in plenty,
affording a generous abundance of fodder for flocks and herds,
while overhead it was amply shaded with Persian trees,* syca-
mores and other leafy growths that flourish by the Nile. There
Bagoas and his troop bivouacked, the trees serving as their tents:
he took some food himself, and offered some to Theagenes and
Chariclea. At first they refused it, but he forced them to take
some; they declared that it was superfluous for those to be fed
who had to die so soon. But he disabused them of this belief,
assuring them that nothing of the sort was to happen; they were
being conducted, he explained, not to their death, but to
Oroondates.

(15) The excessive midday heat was now abating, for the sun,
no longer standing at the zenith, was sending his rays aslant
from the occidental quarter. Bagoas and his men were completing their preparations for proceeding on their journey when a
horseman arrived whose strenuous career, it seemed, had left
him breathless and his horse, which he checked with some
difficulty, streaming with sweat. He went aside with Bagoas,
spoke some words to him and then took his rest. Bagoas stood
for a moment pensive, his mind apparently engrossed by the
news that he had received. 'You strangers,' he said, 'be comforted. Your enemy has paid the penalty: Arsace is dead, having
hanged herself in a strangling noose* as soon as she heard of our
departure with you. By her own choice she has forestalled the
death which she was doomed to die; for she could not have
escaped punishment at the hands of Oroondates and of the

King, and must either have been executed or have spent the rest of her days in the most abject degradation. That is what Euphrates tells me in the message brought by the man who arrived just now; so take heart, keep up your spirits, since you on your part have done no wrong, as I am definitely informed, and you are quit of the woman who has wronged you.' With these words Bagoas sought to conciliate them – though faltering in his use of the Greek tongue and slurring over the words, most of which he mispronounced* – disgusted as he had been by the dissolute and despotic conduct of Arsace in her lifetime, and also because he could thus encourage and console the young pair in the hope, as was true enough, that he would gain great and distinguished credit with Oroondates if he delivered to him safe and sound a youth who put into the shade all the other servants of the satrap and a maiden whose irresistible beauty marked her out to be the satrap's wife in succession to the departed Arsace. Theagenes and Chariclea themselves rejoiced when they heard the news: they acclaimed the might of the gods and of justice, feeling sure that they had no longer any calamity to fear, even should the greatest hardships await them, now that their worst enemy was laid low. So it is that some persons find it pleasant even to perish, if they can see their enemies perish with them. The shades of evening were now well advanced, and with their extension came a rising breeze that brought some coolness to speed wayfarers on their journey. The party made a start, and rode during that evening and all through the ensuing night and the morning of the next day, making haste to reach Thebes in time to find Oroondates there. Nevertheless, they were disappointed; for on their way they were met by a man from the army who reported that the satrap had set out from Thebes, and that he himself had been dispatched to summon with all speed every soldier and man-at-arms, even detachments posted as town garrisons, and to hurry them away to Syene. The whole country, he said, was filled with alarm, and it was to be feared that the city had been captured, the satrap having arrived too late, and the Ethiopian forces having pressed on faster than news of them could travel. Bagoas thereupon turned aside from Thebes and marched towards Syene.

*Theagenes and Chariclea are captured near Syene by a body of
Ethiopian troops.*

(16) As he was drawing near to this place he fell into an
ambush laid by Ethiopians – a body of well-armed youths who
had been sent forward to act as scouts and establish by
investigation whether the route was secure for the main army.
But owing to the night and their ignorance of the locality they
lost their way at a point where they had got as far ahead of their
comrades as was advisable. They crept into a thicket by the river
and kept watch there, holding the thicket as a strong-point
which would be at once a protection for themselves and a trap
for the enemy. When day was just dawning they espied Bagoas
and his horsemen passing by: on discovering that they were but
few in number they allowed them to proceed for a little distance,
and having ascertained that no other troops were following on,
they suddenly emerged with loud cries from the swamp and fell
upon them. Bagoas and his company of horsemen were utterly
scared by the surprise of this outcry. They inferred from the
colour of their assailants that they were Ethiopians, and saw
that their numbers were overwhelming; for they were light-
armed troops, amounting to a thousand, who had been dispatched on scouting duty. Without waiting to observe them
precisely the Persians beat a retreat, moving less hurriedly at
first than they might, that their departure should not have the
appearance of a rout. The Ethiopians followed in pursuit,
sending on in advance all the Troglodytes in their force to the
number of two hundred. The Troglodytes* are a section of the
Ethiopian people leading a nomad life in lands bordering on
those of the Arabs. They excel in swiftness of foot, both by their
nature and by training from childhood: they have never at any
stage been schooled in bearing heavy arms, but by skirmishing
with slings in battle they either strike a sharp blow at their
adversaries or, perceiving them to be in superior strength, evade
them by flight. The enemy at once abandon pursuit of them,
knowing their bird-like fleetness of motion and their skill in
creeping into narrow-mouthed holes and secret clefts in the
rocks. So it was on this occasion: on foot they outdistanced the
horsemen, and they succeeded in wounding some of them by
using their slings; but when counter-attacked they made no
stand, running back helter-skelter to their comrades whom they

had left on the march a long way behind them. The Persians, observing this, and despising the small number of attackers, made bold to counter-attack. They beat off for a little space the men who pressed upon them, and continued their retreat in haste, urging their horses with the spur, giving them the rein, and exerting all the strength and speed of which they were capable. The whole body of them made their escape by keeping close to a bend in the Nile where it formed a kind of promontory and they were screened from the enemy's sight by the projection of the embankment; except that Bagoas was captured after a stumble of his horse had given him a fall and caused an injury to his leg which put him out of action; and Theagenes and Chariclea were also taken, partly because they had not the heart to leave Bagoas in the lurch when he had shown himself to be a man of such kindly disposition towards them as gave them good hopes of him. They had accordingly dismounted to stand by him when they could probably have made their escape. But their chief reason was their willingness to give themselves up; for Theagenes had told Chariclea that his dream was then being realized, and that these Ethiopians were the people whose country they were destined to enter as prisoners taken in battle. It was best therefore to surrender and entrust themselves to an uncertain fortune, rather than to the certain danger that they must face before Oroondates.

(17) Chariclea's understanding went further than this, in her submission to the guidance of her Destiny, and she had high hopes of better things to come: she regarded their assailants as friends rather than foes, but she expressed nothing of her thoughts to Theagenes, merely signifying her assent to his counsel. The Ethiopians, on coming up to them, inferred from Bagoas' looks that he was a eunuch and a non-combatant and, seeing that the young pair were unarmed and in chains, and persons of distinguished beauty and birth, they inquired who they were, conveying their question through one among them who was an Egyptian and also spoke the Persian tongue, and assuming that the young pair would surely comprehend either one or both of these languages. For scouts and spies, dispatched to find out what is being said as well as what is being done, have learnt from expediency to take with them men who can converse in the languages and accents of local inhabitants and the enemy. Theagenes, helped alike by the length of his abode among

Egyptians and the brevity of the question, replied that Bagoas was one of the chief officers of the Persian satrap, but that he and Chariclea, being Greeks by birth, were previously being taken along as prisoners of some Persians but had now, by what seemed a more favourable turn of fortune, passed into the hands of Ethiopians. These latter then decided to spare their lives and carry them off as their prisoners. They regarded this as the first capture made in their hunt, and a grand prize to lay before their king. For they had, first, that man, the most precious possession of the satrap – indeed, at the Persian court the eunuch kind are the eyes and ears of the King, having no children, no family ties, to seduce them from their faithful allegiance, and their only attachment being to the person who has placed his trust in them* – and they also had this young pair, who would be the handsomest gift that they could bring to adorn their king's service and court. So they took their captives away forthwith, mounting them on horses, one because of his wound, and the others since their chains made it impossible for them otherwise to keep up with the rapid pace of the march. This incident was like the prologue and the prelude of a drama.* Strangers, captives in chains, who a little while before had their execution hovering before their eyes, were being not so much carried off as honourably escorted: in the plight of prisoners they were being marched under guard by men who ere long were to be their subjects. This then was their situation.

BOOK 9

Oroondates and his Persian troops are besieged by the Ethiopians in Syene (Assuan), a little below the Lesser Cataracts of the Nile.

(1) Syene by this time was vigorously besieged on every side and was completely enclosed as with a net, by the Ethiopian forces. For Oroondates, having learnt that the Ethiopians would soon be approaching, since after passing the Cataracts they were making straight for Syene, had succeeded in just outstripping them and swiftly entering the city before them. He had the gates closed and the walls fortified with missiles, arms and machines, and waited on the alert for the issue. The King of Ethiopia, Hydaspes, on receiving at some distance the early intelligence from his scouts that the Persians were about to make their entrance into Syene, had gone at once in pursuit of them with the aim of heading them off by bringing them to battle; but he failed to come up with them in time. He proceeded to launch his forces against the city. Ranging his army all round the walls, he laid siege to the place with numbers which at the mere sight of them seemed irresistible, as countless thousands of men, together with their arms and animals, thronged the Syenean plains. Here the troop of scouts met the King and brought their captives before him. He was delighted with the aspect of the young pair, having immediately a kindly feeling for them as his personal belongings, while unaware of the promptings of his prophetic soul. But still more did he rejoice in the omen of prisoners brought to him in chains. 'Praise be to the gods,' he cried, 'for delivering into our hands these enemies in chains as our first spoils of war! These,' he said, 'are our first prisoners, and they must be reserved as firstlings of the war for sacrifice in celebration of our victory, according to the traditional custom of the Ethiopians. They are to be kept in custody for a ritual offering to the gods of our country.' He rewarded the scouts with gifts, and sent them with the prisoners to the baggage train. He then appointed a detachment of men who spoke their language to have the special duty of guarding them, giving order that they were to be treated in all respects with the utmost care, supplied with plenty of good food and kept unsullied by any pollution;

and their sustenance was now to be as that of devoted victims. He further commanded that their chains be replaced by others of gold; for the Ethiopians are accustomed to employ gold for all purposes which with other peoples are served by iron.*

(2) The guards carried out his orders: by releasing the captives from their first chains they kindled in them a hope of freedom; but they brought them no advantage, only fettering them again with links of gold. At this moment Theagenes was moved to laughter and said: 'Ha ha, what a splendid change! See the grand generosity of Fortune towards us! We exchange iron for gold* and, growing rich in captivity, gain value as prisoners.' Chariclea herself smiled, at the same time seeking to alter Theagenes' mood by a heartening reminder of the predictions received from the gods, and by the soothing charm of brighter hopes. Hydaspes then launched an attack on Syene, expecting that the first sound of the battle-cry before the walls would place the city at once in his grasp. But he was in a short time repelled by the defenders, who in action put up a gallant resistance, and in speech assailed him with abusive and exasperating taunts. Angered, therefore, at finding that they had resolved from the first to show a defiant front rather than consent to an immediate surrender, he decided against wearing out his army with the tedium of a siege or trying the effect of siege-engines, which might bring down some of the defenders but would probably allow others of them to escape. He preferred to reduce the place by such a mighty and over-whelming operation as would ensure its complete and summary devastation.

(3) He accordingly went to work on the following plan. He divided the circuit of the walls into sections of sixty feet, to each of which he assigned ten men. He then ordered a trench to be dug which he made as wide and deep in its dimensions as he could. The digging was done by some of his men, while others removed the soil, and others again heaped it high so as to form an embankment, thus opposing another wall to that which was being besieged. Nobody tried to prevent them or to hinder this circumvallation; none ventured to sally out from the city against an army of such immense size, and it was plain to all that arrows shot from the battlements were ineffectual; for Hydaspes had provided for this by so regulating the space between the two walls as to keep his labourers out of range. After completing this work more quickly than words could tell, because of the

vast number of hands hastening it on, he began one of another kind. He had left an open space in the circuit, of fifty feet in breadth, without ditch or dike, and from its two terminal points he led connecting branches of his dike extended to the Nile, and made each ascend gradually from the lower ground to the upper and highest level. One might have compared this work to that of Long Walls:* they continued throughout at an even distance of fifty feet apart, while lengthways they traversed the space between the Nile and Syene. When the two dikes had been led up to the river, he opened a breach in the river-bank and conducted the flow of water into the channel formed by the two branch-dikes. As the water then passed from a superior to an inferior level,* and as it rushed from the enormous breadth of the Nile into a narrow conduit and was pent in by those artificial banks, it produced at the breach a loud, indescribable sort of roar, and along the channel a noise of splashing that was audible even to persons at the farthest point from it. When they heard this sound and began also to observe its cause, the people of Syene became aware of their evil plight, and perceived that the purpose of the circumvallation was to drown them in a flood. They were unable to escape from the city, since they were hemmed in by the dike and the already encroaching water, and at the same time saw the peril of staying where they were. They therefore set about taking such measures for their deliverance as were available to them. First, they caulked the crevices in the timbers of their gates with lamp-wicks and bitumen; next, they strengthened their wall by making its base more secure, some bringing soil, others stones, others wood, and everyone that which chanced to be at hand. No one remained idle; all alike, children, women and old men, bent to the work, for mortal danger is no respecter of sex or age. The more able-bodied and those in their prime for bearing arms were allotted the task of excavating a narrow conduit underground from the city to the dike raised by the enemy.

(4) And here the work was carried out in the following manner. Near to the wall they sank a well to a depth of about five fathoms which had an extension beneath the foundations. Then by torchlight they turned and scooped out a mine running straight across to the dike. The men in their rear, and others again behind those, received the soil from the men in front and carried it out to a part of the city which had long been occupied

by gardens, and there they heaped it into a mound. By making
this conduit they wisely provided an outlet by its vacant course
for any overflow of water that might come upon them. Yet, for
all that, their endeavours were overtaken by disaster. The Nile,
flowing now between the long dikes, rushed forcibly into the
circular space about the town and flooded it all the way round,
thus forming a lagoon between the two lines of walls. Immediately Syene became an island: an inland tract encompassed by
water, with the waves of the Nile surging about it. At first, and
for some part of the day, the wall held out; but the heavy
pressure of the water as it rose higher and higher enabled it to
seep low down through the cracks in the soil, which was black
and loamy and fissured by the summer heats, and so it could
make its way under the foundations of the wall. Then the
groundwork yielded beneath the heavy weight above and, in
parts where it became loose and subsided, the wall began to
sink, and by its tottering clearly indicated its dangerous state.
The battlements were swaying this way and that, and the
defenders were being tossed about by their oscillation.

(5) As evening began to draw in one part of the wall between
two towers collapsed, though not so much as to fall below the
level of the lagoon or to let in the water; but, standing about
five ells higher, it still threatened to become at any moment a
prey to the inundation. This danger caused a confused cry of
lamentation to be sent up throughout the city, loud enough to
be heard by the enemy. Raising their hands to heaven, the people
made great outcry to their last remaining hope – the saviour
gods – and besought Oroondates to send envoys to treat with
Hydaspes. To this he consented, becoming now in his own
despite a bond-slave of Fortune; but, blockaded as he was by
the water, he saw no possible means of sending anyone through
to the enemy. Yet, at the dictate of necessity, he conceived a
plan. He wrote his proposal in a letter which he attached to a
stone and, using a sling to dispatch his parleying, launched his
appeal as a missile over the flood. But in this he had no success,
for the projectile failed to achieve the necessary distance, and
fell futile into the water. Again he wrote a letter in the same
terms and launched it forth, and again he failed; and though all
the archers and slingers vied with one another in efforts to attain
the range, like men striving to hit a mark for their very lives, all
were equally at fault. At last, stretching out their hands towards

the enemy, who were standing upon the dikes to view the spectacle of their distress, the people sought by piteous gestures to express what they could of the purport of their missiles – now reaching out with their palms upturned in supplication, and now bringing their hands round behind their backs, as if chained, to show a willing acceptance of slavery. Hydaspes understood that they were suing for their salvation, and he was prepared to grant it; for an enemy who submits induces good-hearted men to deal humanely. But for the moment he was not able to agree, thinking it well to test with more certainty the temper of his opponents. He had in readiness some river ferry-boats which he had arranged to be floated from the Nile on the flood of his canal and which, after they had drifted within his circumvallation, he was keeping moored there. Of these he selected ten new-built boats, manned them with archers and heavy-armed men and, having instructed them in what they were to say, sent them off to the Persians. They crossed over in battle order, so that if any surprise action were taken by the men on the walls they should be prepared to counter it. The spectacle was indeed a strange one: a vessel making a passage from one wall to another; a sailor voyaging over an inland tract; and a ferry-boat travelling over arable ground. War, ever productive of the new and strange, was then particularly and most unusually producing a marvellous event, in thus engaging marines in a conflict with wall defenders, and arming land troops against lake forces.

For when the men in the city saw the boats, with their crews fully armed, making for the ruined section of the wall, they were panic-stricken, being filled now with abject terror by the perils that beset them; and they imagined those to be hostile who came in fact as their saviours, since everything is suspect and fearful to a man in the grip of imminent danger. So they began to fight at long range, launching missiles and shooting arrows; for even men despairing of their lives regard as a gain each moment that passes in deferment of their deaths. They sent their shafts, not in order to wound, but with the object merely of checking the advance of the boats. The Ethiopians sent off volleys in return: shooting with more effective aim, as not yet understanding the Persians' intentions, they transfixed two or three men, and then some more, so that a few, stung by their sudden and unexpected wounding, hurled themselves headlong from the walls into the water outside. And the fighting might have raged with greater heat between the Persians, who were sparing the oncomers and only trying to stop them in their course, and the Ethiopians, who were angrily defending themselves, had not a man of eminence in Syene, already advanced in years, come among the men on the walls and said: 'You crack-brained people, distracted by your sore straits! These men, whom till now we were so persistently entreating and begging to help us, are we going to repulse them, when beyond all hope they are arriving? If they come to us as friends with a message of peace, they will be our saviours; and if their design is hostile it will be easy enough, even if they effect a landing, to overcome them. And what shall we gain by destroying them when such a vast cloud of others on land and on water encircles our city? No, let us receive them and be fully apprised of their intentions.' Everybody commended his advice, which was approved by the satrap also. They left the ruinous breach, and stationed themselves at each side of it on the wall; then they grounded arms and kept quiet.

(6) When the defenders had evacuated that open space between two towers, and the people signalled by waving white sheets that a landing was permitted, the Ethiopians drew near. From their boats, as though in a public assembly, they spoke thus to their audience of the besieged: 'Persians and Syeneans here present, Hydaspes, King of the Ethiopians in the East and in the West* and now also of you, knows how to wreak havoc on his enemies, but is of his nature disposed to have pity on suppliants, adjudging the one course to a manly spirit, and the other to humane feeling, and assigning the former to the soldier in action, the latter to his personal decision. Holding now your existence in the balance of his absolute will, he grants to you, as declared suppliants, relief from the peril, so evident to all and unquestionable, which war has brought upon you. As to the conditions on which you would be only too glad to escape from your predicament, he lays down none, but leaves the choice of them to you. For he is not tyrannical in victory, but so regulates the lot of men as not to incur divine resentment.' The Syeneans replied that they yielded themselves, their children and their wives to Hydaspes, to be dealt with as he pleased, and handed over their city to him, if it should survive, though at that moment labouring desperately in the storm, unless some timely intervention of the gods, or of Hydaspes, should deliver it.

Oroondates then said that he would renounce the grounds and the prizes of the war, and would surrender the city of Philae and the emerald mines; but for himself he claimed immunity from any compulsion to yield up either himself or his soldiers. If Hydaspes wished to show himself entirely humane, he should allow them, if they refrained from doing any injury or taking any hostile action, to depart to Elephantiné. For he might as well perish at once as accept a seeming survival and then be convicted before the Persian King of the base surrender of his army. Nay, he would fare much worse; for the death now to be suffered by him was likely to be the simple, customary one, whereas that later one would be devised with inventions of extreme cruelty and exquisite forms of torment.

(7) To this proposal Oroondates added a request that two Persians be taken on board the boats with the professed purpose of going to Elephantiné, and he promised that if the people there agreed to submit to servitude, he on his part would hesitate no longer. The envoys received this proposal and returned, taking with them the two Persians, and reported the whole of the parley to Hydaspes. He laughed in scorn, and strongly reprehended the fatuity of Oroondates, a man who discussed terms on a basis of equality when the prospect of his living or dying depended entirely on another and not on himself. 'It would be absurd,' he said, 'to let the folly of one man bring destruction upon so many.' He then gave permission for Oroondates' messengers to proceed to Elephantiné, since he cared not a whit if they should advise its citizens to resist. To one section of his own troops he assigned the task of blocking up the breach in the Nile bank, and to another that of opening a new breach in his dike, so that by the stoppage of the influx of water and by the drainage of the lagoon water through this outlet the ground about Syene might be quickly reclaimed and made dry enough to be passable on foot. Hardly had they started on their appointed tasks when they had to defer their completion to the morrow, because evening, and then night, closed in upon them shortly after the issue of these orders.

(8) The people in the city were not letting slip any practicable means of salvation available to them, never despairing of the possibility of some quite unexpected deliverance. The men who were digging the subterranean tunnel seemed now to be nearing the dike, on calculation of the distance from wall to dike, as it

appeared to the eye and by measurement of the length of their sap with a line. Others were re-erecting the ruined section of the wall, working by lantern light; their building was easily done, since the stones in falling had rolled to the inner side. They considered themselves to be in safety for the time, but not even then did they remain free from alarm. About midnight something happened at that part of the dike where in the evening the Ethiopians had set about cutting their new outlet. Either the soil at that point had been heaped up loosely without being beaten down, so that the under part had become soaked and had given way, or the sappers had also caused that same part to subside into the void that they were creating; or else the new cutting of no great depth, by which the workers had formed a certain depression, had enabled the water, as its level rose during the night, to make its way and overflow, and then, once a passage for it was opened through the breach, insensibly to deepen its course; or again, one might ascribe what happened to divine assistance. Suddenly the dike broke asunder. So great was the resounding rumble which resulted, filling the minds of the hearers with terror, that with no knowledge of what had occurred the Ethiopians and also the Syeneans themselves imagined that the greater part of the walls and of the city had collapsed. The besiegers, who were not in any danger, remained quietly in their bivouacs, waiting to learn the truth of the matter in the morning; while the besieged ran out to man the whole circuit of the walls each perceiving his particular part to be intact, and everyone supposing the blow to have fallen at some other point; until daylight came upon the scene and dispersed the fog of terrors that enveloped them. The breach was then revealed, and the water was seen to have suddenly receded. For already the Ethiopians were blocking up the opening through which their channel was fed, by letting down rafts of planks fastened together and strengthened outside with stout logs and consolidated with earth and brushwood: these were laid in position by many thousands of men, some working on the river bank and some on boats. So the water receded; but yet it was not possible for either of the opposing forces to pass across to meet the other. For the ground was all covered with a deep slime: the surface appeared to have dried, but beneath it was spread a liquid mass of mud which lay in wait to engulf both horse and man in stepping upon it.

(9) They continued thus for the space of two or three days. The Syeneans had opened their gates, and the Ethiopians had laid aside their arms, while both sides indicated their peaceful intentions. It was a truce made without actual parley: neither side was any longer concerned to keep watch on the other; furthermore, the citizens had already given themselves up to merrymaking. For just at that time the Nile festival happened to be held, the greatest one in Egypt: it is celebrated round about the summer solstice,* when the rise in the river begins to appear, and it is observed by the Egyptians more fervently than any other festival. This is because they deify the Nile, and regard him as the greatest of their divinities. They proudly aver that this river acts in emulation of the heavens, since independently of cloud packs and rainfall from the sky it irrigates their tilth, each year regularly watering the soil;* so say the common folk. The things that they reverence as their deities are these: they account the conjunction of the moist and the dry essences to be the principal cause of human existence and life, and they say that the being and manifestation of the other elements are contingent on these, and that whereas the Nile represents moisture their land stands for dryness. So much for what is given out to the public. But to the initiated authority pronounces that the earth is Isis and the Nile Osiris, bestowing these names on material things. Thus the goddess longs for the god in his absence, and rejoices in his union with her; when he disappears she weeps again and detests Typhon as a hostile power.* I conceive that men versed in natural science and theology do not expose to laymen the deeper meanings that lie hidden within these tenets; they merely charm the people into a belief presented in the guise of a myth, but indoctrinate the true initiates more luminously within the sanctuary by the light of the flaming torch of reality.*

(10) Thus far may our account of this matter meet with divine approval; but the deeper secrets of the mysteries must be paid the respect of strict silence,* and we now proceed with the story of the events at Syene. The festival of the Nile, then, had come on, and the inhabitants were engaged in sacrifices and ceremonies, their bodies fatigued by perils facing them on every side, but their souls not unmindful of performing, so far as their situation allowed, their pious duties towards the deity. Oroondates, however, seizing his opportunity at midnight, when the Syeneans

had betaken themselves to a deep slumber consequent upon their feasting, marched his army out of the town. He had previously informed his Persians in secret of the appointed hour and gate at which they were to make their departure: each company commander had instruction to leave horses and beasts of burden where they were, so as to avoid encumbering his movements or causing a disturbance which might lead to their discovery; the men were told to take only their arms with them, and to provide themselves with a beam or a plank of wood.

Oroondates and his Persian troops make their escape in secret from Syene, which is then entirely surrendered to Hydaspes and the Ethiopians.

(11) When they had assembled at the gate to which they had been directed, they flung across the mud the timbers brought along by each company and linked them one to another, the men behind passing them along to those in front, so that over this sort of gangway the whole force was enabled to make a quite easy and rapid crossing. On attaining solid ground Oroondates eluded the Ethiopians who, instead of taking any precautions or troubling to set a watch, were sleeping without any apprehension, and he marched his army at their utmost, breathtaking pace in one long stretch to Elephantiné. He made his way unhindered into the city: the two Persians whom he had sent in advance from Syene were on the look-out each night for his arrival, in accordance with the order given to them; and when the agreed password was spoken they immediately threw the gates wide open. As day began to dawn the Syeneans became aware of their flight. At first each citizen could no longer find in his own house the Persians who were billeted on him; then in groups they conferred together; and finally they caught sight of the gangway. Thus once again they were filled with anguish, feeling themselves liable this second time to a criminal charge more serious than the former – that of treachery in return for the signal humanity with which they had been treated, and of aiding and abetting the flight of the Persians. They therefore resolved to set forth from the city in a body and deliver themselves up to the Ethiopians, attesting with oaths their ignorance of the affair, on the chance of inducing the besiegers to have mercy on them. So they assembled all the people of

every age, and carrying branches betokening supplication, lighting candles and torches, and holding before them sacred
emblems and images of the gods like heralds' wands of peace,
they passed over the gangway, towards the Ethiopians. While
still at some distance they fell on their knees in supplication, and
in this fixed attitude broke, of one accord and with one mournful
voice, into piteous wailing and pleading; and the more to move
compassion they laid on the ground before them their infant
children, and let them stray at random, seeking to soften in
advance the rancour of the Ethiopians by means of this unsus-
pected and blameless portion of their body. The children, in
their fright and their ignorance also of what was going on, were
doubtless scared away by the immense outcry, for they ran off
out of reach of their parents and guardians. They went on in the
direction of the enemy, some crawling, some stumbling in their
steps and whimpering as they went in affecting tones, as though
Fortune were enlisting them for an improvised act of
supplication.

(12) Hydaspes, at the sight of all this, supposed that by it the
people meant to reinforce their original supplication with a view
to a full and unreserved admission of defeat; but he sent to ask
what they wanted, and how it was that they came alone, without
the Persians. They gave him an account of everything: the flight
of the Persians, their own innocence of the scheme and their
ancestral celebration; how, occupied with their pious duties
towards the gods, and then overcome by sleep after their
feasting, they had been unaware of what was doubtless a swift
departure; and even had they observed it they were unarmed
and could have done nothing to stop a body of armed men. On
receiving this intelligence Hydaspes suspected – what was the
case – that some insidious ruse would be employed by Oroondates. He summoned the priests alone, prostrated himself before
the images of the gods which they brought along with them to
ensure due respect, and inquired whether they could inform him
more particularly about the Persians – which way they had
marched, on what support they were relying and whom they
were going to attack. The priests replied that they knew nothing
at all of the matter; but they surmised that the Persians had
marched to Elephantiné, as their main army had been assembled
there, and Oroondates relied especially on his armoured cavalry.

(13) Having told him this they besought him to enter the city

as its master, and to lay aside his resentment against them. But he did not deem it wise to proceed himself into the place for the present: he sent in, however, two phalanxes of armed men, in order to test his suspicion of a trap and, if no such danger should appear, to garrison the city. He then dismissed the Syeneans with gracious promises, and himself drew up his army in order of battle, so that he could either receive an onset of the Persians or else, if they were slow to move, advance against them. The ranks had not yet been fully formed, when scouts rode up with news of the approach of the Persians in battle array. For Oroondates, having arranged for his main army to assemble at Elephantiné, had been himself obliged, on receiving intelligence of the unexpected approach of the Ethiopians, to race to Syene with only a small force. Blockaded there by those earthworks, he had requested, and on giving his parole had been granted, his life by Hydaspes. But he proved to be a man of most untrustworthy character: he arranged to send out two Persians who were to cross the water together with the Ethiopians, pretending that they went to ascertain the inclination of the men in Elephantiné regarding the terms on which they might decide to make their peace with Hydaspes; though in fact the aim was to see if they would rather prepare themselves to do battle as soon as Oroondates might effect his escape. This treacherous plan he proceeded to carry out. Finding that the troops there were fully prepared for action, he led them out forthwith, and advanced without a moment's delay, expecting by his rapid movement to be breaking up the preparations of the enemy.

Oroondates leads an army from Elephantiné to attack Hydaspes at Syene.

(14) And indeed very soon he was visible with his troops in battle array. The brave show of his Persians at once captivated the gaze of all, as their armour, inlaid with silver and gold, flashed across the plain. The sun was just rising and darted his rays upon their front; an indescribable glitter was scattered far and wide as their suits of armour shone resplendent with a lightning all their own. Now, the right wing was formed by the true-born Persians and Medes, with their armoured men in front and the archers close behind, so that, as these wore no full

accoutrements, they should the more safely discharge their arrows from the shelter afforded by the shields of the armoured men. The Egyptian, the Libyan and all the foreign contingents were posted in the left wing; they also had supporting forces attached to them, but on their flanks, where javelin-men and slingers had orders to sally out and harry the enemy sideways with their missiles. Oroondates himself took his position in the centre, mounted in splendour on a scythed chariot and escorted by a phalanx on either side to ensure his safety. In front of him he ranged only the armoured cavalry, which gave him especial confidence in boldly facing the hazards of the battle. For in fact it is this brigade of Persians which is always the most formidable in action; placed in the front line of battle it serves as an unbreakable bulwark.

(15) Their fighting equipment is furnished in this way:* a picked man, chosen for his bodily strength, is capped with a helmet which has been compacted and forged in one piece and skilfully fashioned like a mask into the exact shape of a man's face; this protects him entirely from the top of the head to the neck, except where eye-holes allow him to see through it. His right hand is armed with a pike of greater length than a spear, while his left is at liberty to hold the reins. He has a sabre slung at his side, and his corslet extends, not merely over his breast, but also over all the rest of his body. This corslet is constructed thus: plates of bronze and of iron are forged into a square shape measuring a span each way, and are fitted one to another at the edges on each side, so that the plate above overlaps the one below, and laterally one overlaps the next one to it, all forming a continuous surface; and they are held together by means of hooks and loops under the flaps. Thus is produced a kind of scaly tunic which sits close to the body without causing discomfort, and clings all round each limb with its individual casing and allows unhindered movement to each by its contraction and extension. It has sleeves, and descends from neck to knee, with an opening only for the thighs so far as is required for mounting a horse's back. Such a corslet is proof against any missiles, and is a sure defence against all wounds. The greaves reach from above the flat of the foot to the knee, and are joined on to the corslet. The horse is protected by a similar equipment: round his feet greaves are fastened, and his head is tightly bound all about with frontlets. From his back to his belly hangs on either side a

housing of plaited strips of iron, serving as armour, but at the same time so pliable as not to impede his more rapid paces. The horse being thus equipped and, as it were, encased, the rider bestrides him, not vaulting of himself into the saddle, but lifted up by others because of his weight. When the moment comes to engage in battle, he gives his horse the rein, applies his spurs, and in full career charges the enemy, to all appearance some man made of iron, or a mobile statue wrought with the hammer.* His pike projects with its point thrust far ahead: it is supported by a loop attached to the horse's neck, and has its butt-end suspended by a strap alongside the horse's haunches; so that it does not recede in the dashes of conflict, but lightens the task of the rider's hand, which only directs the blow. He braces himself and, firmly set so as to increase the gravity of the wound, by his mere impetus transfixes anyone who comes in his way, and may often impale two persons at a single stroke.

(16) Such was the cavalry at the service of the satrap, and thus were the Persian forces disposed with which he advanced to make a frontal attack, always keeping the river in his rear; for, his numbers being much inferior to those of the Ethiopians, he relied on the water to protect him against encirclement. Hydaspes on his part marched to meet him. Facing the Persians and Medes on the right wing he ranged the troops from Meroë – heavy-armed fighters, skilled in close, hand-to-hand combat. To the Troglodytes and the dwellers about the cinnamon-bearing country* – light-armed troops, being swift runners and excellent bowmen – he assigned the task of harassing the slingers and javelin-men on the enemy's left. Apprised that the centre of the Persian host vaunted its armoured cavalry, he placed himself and his train of turreted elephants opposite to them, with his heavy-armed Blemmyes and Seres* in front, on whom he had enjoined what they should do at the moment of action.

A great battle between the Persians and the Ethiopians at Syene.

(17) Each side raised its standards; the signal for battle was given by the Persians with trumpets, and by the Ethiopians with tambours and drums: Oroondates, after giving a loud shout, set on his phalanxes at the run; but Hydaspes ordered his troops to advance against them, first at a moderate pace, altering it slightly step by step to make sure that the elephants were not left

unprotected by the front line, and also that the enemy's cavalry should have the force of its charge already reduced by the distance between the two armies. As soon as they came within bowshot, and the Blemmyes observed the armoured cavalry stirring on their horses to the charge, they followed the instructions of Hydaspes. Leaving behind them the Seres as a bulwark to protect the elephants, they dashed out at full speed, far in advance of the ranks, and set about the armoured cavalry. The sight of their action gave the beholders an impression of madness, so few were they to make this sudden attack on so much larger numbers of men completely armed. The Persians then with loosened reins accelerated their pace, accounting the hardihood of these men a godsend, and feeling sure of promptly catching them up on their pikes at the first encounter.

(18) Then the Blemmyes, as they were closing in combat with the enemy and were within an ace of being caught on their pikeheads, suddenly at one signal crouched down and crept under the horses with one knee resting on the ground, and with heads and back so bent as barely to avoid being trampled on. But the surprise of their action came as they inflicted injuries with their swords on the horses by stabbing at their bellies as they passed over. Thus no small number of the horsemen fell, because the animals in their anguish took no heed of the bridle and threw their riders. These, as they lay on the ground like logs, the Blemmyes maimed in the thighs, for the Persian armoured cavalryman is unable to move when he is left in this plight without a helping hand. Those whose horses escaped being wounded in the *mêlée* rode on towards the Seres who, while they were only being approached, retired behind the elephants, as though they found in the live beast the refuge of a ridge or a bastion. There a huge slaughter was done upon the cavalry, destroying almost the whole body of them. For the horses, at the unaccustomed sight of the elephants thus suddenly revealed, and in the terror inspired by their great size, either ran back or were jumbled together in confusion, and quickly threw the ranks of their squadrons into disorder. The turret on each elephant was manned by six archers, two shooting from each of its walls except that towards the tail, which alone was left vacant and inactive. So from these battlements, as though on the walls of a citadel, the archers kept up a continual discharge of well-aimed shafts, so dense that the Persians had the sensation

of a cloud descending upon them,* especially when the Ethiopians made their enemies' eyes their targets and conducted themselves as men not so much fighting a pitched battle as engaged in a trial of marksmanship. So unerring was their aim that those whom they pierced with their shafts rushed about wildly in the throng with the arrows projecting from their eyes like double flutes.* Any who were unable to control their horses in the headlong career of the charge and were perforce carried away into collision with the elephants were, some of them, destroyed thus on the spot, through being tossed and trampled by the elephants, while others were caught by the Seres and the Blemmyes, who sallied out from behind the elephants as from an ambush, and either wounded them with deadly aim or grappled with them and thrust them from their mounts to the ground. Those who escaped made off frustrated, having effected nothing against the elephants; for these beasts go into action with the special protection of iron armour, and besides, they are by nature case-hardened, having a hide in the form of stout scales which extend over the whole surface of their bodies, and are strong enough to break the point of any weapon by their rigid resistance.

(19) As soon as the remnants of the squadron took to flight, the satrap Oroondates, more shamefully than anyone else, abandoned his chariot, and mounting the horse of a Nisaean,* fled from the field. These events were unperceived by the Egyptians and Libyans on the left wing, who were prosecuting the fight with the utmost gallantry, and though suffering heavier losses than they inflicted, were bearing up under their ordeal with stubborn determination. The troops from the cinnamon-bearing country, ranged opposite to them, were pressing fiercely upon them and causing them much embarrassment: those troops, when faced with an advance, retreated and, having the great advantage of their superior speed, aimed their arrows backwards and shot their pursuers even while continuing their flight. When their enemies retired they assailed them either by striking at them on their flanks with slings, or by discharging arrows which, though small in size, were tipped with snake venom and suddenly inflicted an instant death. The men of the cinnamon country use a kind of archery that seems more like a sport than a business. Round their heads they twine a coiled plait in which they fix a circlet of arrows with the feathered ends

enclosing their heads and the points projecting outwards like
rays. Thus each man in battle has them there ready to his hand,
as in a quiver; with an arrogant air and satyr-like prancing he
twists and bends his body, crowned with his arrows, and attacks
his adversaries quite naked, with shafts that do not have to be
pointed with iron.* For the spine of a snake is taken and
whittled to the length of a cubit, and by sharpening the end to a
very fine point a complete arrow, head and all, is produced
which probably thus derived its name from the Greek word for
bone.* For some time the Egyptians maintained their formation,
and by locking their shields together withstood the shafts of the
archers: they are naturally valorous men who make a trifle of
death, not for any material advantage, but rather from an
ambition to excel; yet also perhaps from anticipation of the
punishment meted out for not standing one's ground.

(20) When, however, they learnt that the armoured cavalry,
who were accounted their strongest military arm and hope, had
been annihilated; that the satrap had fled away, and that the
celebrated armed troops of the Medes and Persians, instead of
distinguishing themselves in the battle, had done much less harm
to those from Meroë ranged opposite to them than had been
done to themselves, and were retreating after the rest, they gave
way and in their turn took to headlong flight. Hydaspes, from
the watch-tower in which he rode, beheld the now manifest
victory; and he sent out heralds to his pursuing troops ordering
them to refrain from slaughter and to capture alive any of the
foe whom they could seize and bring them in, and above all
Oroondates. His order was obeyed. The Ethiopians extended
their battalions leftwards, drawing on the ample depth of their
ranks to elongate the front at each end; then, wheeling their
wings, they compressed the Persian army into an arc, so as to
leave the enemy only the single lane to the Nile as an unbarred
way of escape. The greater number of them fell into the river,
being pushed along by the horses, the scythed chariots and the
confused crowding of the whole mass; and they learnt to their
cost how adverse to themselves and imprudent was the apparently shrewd manoeuvre of the satrap, who from his dread at
the outset of their being encircled had in consequence placed
them with their backs to the Nile and had unwittingly obstructed
his own line of retreat. So he also was captured there. Achaemenes, the son of Cybele, had designed to kill Oroondates

offhand in the midst of the tumult, having had intelligence meanwhile of all that had occurred at Memphis, and regretting now the information that he had laid against Arsace, since his means of proving it had perished some time ago; but he failed to deal his man a mortal stroke. However, he was punished on the spot by an Ethiopian who pierced him with an arrow, having recognized the satrap and intending to save his life in accordance with the order given; and he also felt indignant at the criminal attempt of a man who, fleeing before the enemy, should assail his friends and seize on a crisis in their fortunes to pursue what seemed to be a private enmity.

The magnanimous treatment of Oroondates and Syene by the victorious Hydaspes.

(21) So Oroondates was brought by his captor before Hydaspes who, observing that he was at his last gasp and streaming with blood, had its flow checked with a charm applied by his expert practitioners. He was resolved, if he could, to save the satrap's life, and encouraged him with these words: 'Your Excellency, you can count on your safety, so far as the decision rests with me. For it is to one's honour if one conquers one's enemies in prowess while they stand, and in beneficence when they are fallen. But, however, what was your purpose in showing yourself so faithless?' To this the other replied: 'Faithless to you, yet faithful to my master.' Hydaspes then asked him: 'Well, and now that you have been crushed, what punishment do you determine for yourself?' 'That which my King, if he had captured one of your generals,' he said, 'would have inflicted on him for keeping faith with you.' 'Then to be sure,' said Hydaspes, 'he would have commended him and sent him on his way with gifts, if yours is a true king and no tyrant, in order to inspire by his praises of foreigners' actions, ambition for similar actions in his own people. But, my good sir, you say that you are faithful; yet you must admit yourself to be stupid, since you took the field in that foolhardy manner against such immense numbers.' 'It was not stupidity, surely,' he replied, 'to have an eye to the mind of my sovereign, which inclines him to go to greater lengths in punishing any act of cowardice in war than in honouring one of courage. So I resolved to go and face the danger, and either to achieve some great, improbable success – some such miracle as

a crisis often produces in warfare – or else, should I chance to come out of the struggle alive, to have enough scope left me for justifying my action, on the ground of having done all that it was in my power to do.'

(22) After holding this conversation with him Hydaspes commended him and sent him into Syene with an order to the physicians there to tend him with the greatest possible care. The conqueror then entered the city, together with the flower of his army. All the people, of every age, came out to welcome him; they showered on the troops coronals and flowers of the Nile, and glorified Hydaspes with triumphal hymns of praise. When he had ridden inside the walls, borne on his elephant as on a chariot, he immediately attended to the sacred duty of making thank-offerings to the higher powers. He inquired of the priests concerning the origin of the Nile festival, and whether they had anything to show him in the city that was worthy of admiration or observation. They proceeded to show him the cistern that serves to measure the level of the Nile; it resembles that of Memphis, being constructed of polished ashlar and marked with lines incised at intervals of a cubit. The water of the river percolates into it underground and, as its level reaches the lines, indicates plainly to the inhabitants the augmentations and abatements of the Nile; and, according as so many marks are covered or exposed, they calculate the level of high or low water.* They showed him also the indexes of the sundials, which cast no shadow at midday, since in the region of Syene the rays of the sun stand directly overhead at the summer solstice and, by shedding light on the index alike on every side, deprive it of any incidence of shadow; and so the water also at the bottom of the cistern receives a clear illumination for the same reason.* These things held no great surprise of strangeness for Hydaspes, since he knew of similar conditions occurring at Meroë in Ethiopia. They then glorified their festival, highly extolling the Nile, which they entitled Horus, and Life-giver, to whom the whole of Egypt is beholden, the Upper as to its Saviour, and the Lower as to its Father and Creator* through his bringing down a fresh silt year by year, whence he derives the name of Nile;* he also announces the seasons of the year: the summer by his rising, the autumn by his ebbing, and the spring by the flowers growing by his side, and by the crocodiles laying their eggs. The Nile, they hold, is exactly identical with

the year, as is confirmed by his appellation; for the letters of his name, if translated into numerals, will amount to three hundred and sixty-five units, equal to the days in the year.* And they further instanced certain plants, flowers and animals which are peculiar to him, and many other attributes besides. 'But all these proud distinctions,' said Hydaspes, 'belong not to Egypt but to Ethiopia, for in fact this river, or god according to you, and all the river monsters, are sent along here by Ethiopia, and to her you should rightly give your worship, as being to you the mother of the gods.' 'And so indeed we do worship her,' said the priests, 'on many accounts, but especially because she has presented you to us as our saviour and our god.'

(23) Hydaspes advised them to beware of blasphemy in their praises; he then withdrew into his tent and gave the rest of the day to recruiting his strength. He entertained at a banquet the most eminent Ethiopians and the priests of Syene, and granted leave for a like celebration by his troops. The Syeneans supplied the army with numerous herds of oxen, many flocks of sheep, many more of goats, and also droves of pigs,* with abundance of wine, partly as gifts and partly as purchases. On the following day, seated aloft in state, Hydaspes distributed among his forces the beasts of burden, the horses and all the material taken as spoil in the city and in the battle, assigning to each man what was due for his part in the action. When the man who had taken Oroondates prisoner came up: 'Ask what you please,' Hydaspes said to him. 'I have no call to ask for anything,' he replied; 'but if it should agree with your judgment also, I am quite satisfied to keep what I took from Oroondates, and to have saved his life as you commanded.' With that he displayed the sword-belt of the satrap, set with jewels, an article of great value, and of workmanship costing many talents. At this many of the bystanders loudly protested that it was a treasure too fine for an ordinary person, and more suitable for a king. Then Hydaspes smiled and said: 'What could be more kingly than to keep my magnanimity up to the mark of this fellow's cupidity? Besides, the rules of war allow the victor to strip the person of his prisoner; so let him go off with his spoil, which I grant him, and which he could easily have kept in secret, even against my will.'

*Theagenes and Chariclea are reserved by Hydaspes as victims for
a sacrifice of thanksgiving for his victory.*

(24) After him appeared the captors of Theagenes and Chariclea,
who said: 'O King, our spoils are not gold nor jewels; those
things are of no great price in Ethiopia, where the royal palace
has them stored in heaps. But we have brought you a maiden
and a youth, brother and sister of Greek birth, who next after
yourself surpass all the rest of mankind in stature and beauty;
and for this we consider ourselves deserving of your munificent
bounty.' 'It is well,' said Hydaspes, 'that you have recalled them
to my mind. For it was but casually that I had sight of them in
that hour of commotion, when you presented them to me. So let
someone go and fetch them, and let the rest of the prisoners
come here with them.' Immediately they were brought to him,
on word given by a runner, who passed outside the walls to the
baggage train, ordering the guards to take them with all haste
before the King. The young pair asked one of the guards, a half-
Greek, where they were being taken this time; he replied that
King Hydaspes was reviewing the prisoners. 'Ye gods of salvation!' cried the two together, at the mention of Hydaspes' name;
for until that moment they were uncertain whether the King
were he or some other. Then Theagenes said softly to Chariclea:
'Clearly, my dearest, you must tell the King who we are; for
mark you, it is Hydaspes, he who, you have so often told me, is
your father.' 'Darling,' replied Chariclea, 'great affairs require
great prearrangements. A plot, whose beginnings have been laid
out by the deity with many complications, must needs be
brought to its conclusion through detours of some length; and
particularly where a great lapse of time has blurred the story, it
is not clarified to advantage at one sharp stroke, above all, when
the prime mover in the whole scheme affecting us, she on whom
the entire sequence of complication and recognition depends, I
mean Persinna, my mother, is missing. That she too is still living,
by the will of Heaven, is known to us.' 'Then what if they
sacrifice us first,' broke in Theagenes, 'or else make a gift of us
as captives, thus cutting off our return to Ethiopia?' 'Not so;
quite the contrary,' replied Chariclea. 'You know how you have
often heard our guards say that we are being fed as victims for
sacrifice to the gods of Meroë; so there is no fear of our being
presented or previously put to death, when we have been

dedicated to the gods by a vow which it would be criminal for men with a high regard for piety to violate. If, overcome with excess of joy, we should rashly declare the truth about ourselves in the absence of those who could recognize and confirm our story, we might imprudently irritate our hearer and kindle in him a justified anger. He would consider it, very possibly, a piece of insolent mockery, if prisoners consigned to slavery should endeavour by a fictitious and incredible artifice to foist themselves, as in some transformation scene, upon the sovereign as his children.' 'But the tokens of identity,' said Theagenes, 'which I know you carry with you and preserve, will warrant that we are no fiction or fraud.' 'The tokens,' said Chariclea, 'are tokens to those who know them or who exposed them with me; but to those who know them not, or cannot recognize them all, they are mere unmeaning keepsakes or, perchance, necklaces that involve their holders in suspicion of theft and brigandage. And if Hydaspes should chance to recognize them in part, who could be found to persuade him that it was Persinna who provided them, and that it was a mother who gave them to her daughter? An indisputable token, Theagenes, resides in the maternal nature, which causes the parent at the first meeting to experience the tender feeling of affection for her offspring, through the impulse of a secret sympathy. So let us not discount this great token which can establish the credit of all the rest.'

(25) While they were thus talking together they had come near to the king, and Bagoas also had been brought there at the same time. When Hydaspes saw them standing before him he started up for a moment from his throne and said: 'Ye gods, be gracious to me!' and then resumed his seat, in deep thought. The officers in attendance asked what it was that troubled him, and he answered: 'I had in mind a fancy that a daughter like this girl was today born to me, and that of a sudden she had come, like her, to the flower of her age: of this dream I made no account, but just now recalled it, because of the resemblance appearing in her at whom I was looking.' His attendants said that it was a kind of imagery in the mind which often prefigured in definite form the things that were to come. He then had less regard to his vision, and asked the young pair who they were and whence they came. Chariclea was silent; Theagenes then stated that they were brother and sister, and Greeks. 'Well done, Greece!' said the King; 'not only does she bring forth persons of

fine form and character, but she also provides us with well-bred and auspicious victims for the sacrifices of thanksgiving for our victory. But why in that vision did I not have a son also born to me,' he asked the company with a laugh, 'since this young man, the girl's brother, who was to appear now before me, should surely have been foreshadowed, as you tell me, in my dreams?' He then directed his remarks to Chariclea, and speaking in the Greek tongue, which is held in much respect among the Gymnosophists and the kings of Ethiopia, he said: 'And you, girl, why do you remain silent, making no reply to my inquiry?' 'At the altars of the gods,' she said, 'for which we understand that we are reserved as pious offerings, you will learn who I am and who are my parents.' 'And whereabouts are they to be found?' he asked her. 'They are here present,' she replied, 'and will not fail to be present also at my sacrifice.' Hydaspes smiled again and said: 'Of a truth she is dreaming, this dream-born daughter of mine: she imagines that her parents will be sent over from Greece to the midst of Meroë! Well, let these two be taken and tended with the customary care and liberality, so that they do full honour to our sacrifice. But who is this man beside them, looking so like a eunuch?' One of the servants told him: 'He is in truth a eunuch, Bagoas by name, the most precious possession of Oroondates.' 'He shall go along with them,' said the King, 'not to be sacrificed, but as custodian of one of the victims, this girl whose beauty requires that she be guarded with especial precaution, so that she be kept pure for us until the moment of the sacrifice. The eunuch kind have a certain jealousy ingrained in them; for their appointed office is to debar others from that of which they have been deprived.'

(26) When he had thus spoken he turned to his review of the other prisoners as they passed in line before him, and to examining the quality of each. Those whom Fortune designated from infancy to be slaves he bestowed as gifts, while those of gentle birth he set at liberty. He made a choice of ten youths and as many maidens who were distinguished by their blooming age and beauty, and ordered them to be taken along with Theagenes and Chariclea and reserved for a like purpose. When he had dealt with all the requests submitted by the others, he came finally to Oroondates, who on being summoned was brought forward on a litter. 'I have secured,' he said, 'the objects of the campaign, and have placed under my control the primal

grounds of our enmity, namely Philae and the emerald mines. I am not moved by the common passion for exploiting a success to the utmost advantage, or using a victory for an immoderate enlargement of dominion: I rather content myself with the frontiers which nature has set for the division between Egypt and Ethiopia from the beginning – the Cataracts. So, having secured that for which I came out, I shall return with reverence for justice. And you, if you survive, shall hold sway as satrap over those whom you governed originally, and shall send this message to the King of the Persians: "Your brother Hydaspes has conquered by his action, but by his judgment he has ceded to you all your property. He solicits your friendship, if you are pleased to give it, as the finest possession known to mankind; while, if you resume hostilities, he will not decline the challenge. And to the Syeneans I grant release from payment of their prescribed tribute for ten years, and I charge you to do likewise."'

(27) The effect of this speech was to rouse among those present, both townsfolk and soldiers alike, acclamation and applause that were audible far and wide. Oroondates stretched forth his hands and, crossing his left with his right,* bent low in adoration – a form of obeisance not habitually rendered by Persians to any king but their own. Then: 'I aver to all you here present,' he said, 'that I do not consider myself to be infringing the usage of my country if I acknowledge as king the man who presents me with my satrapy, or to be transgressing the law when I adore the most law-abiding of mankind; who, with the power to destroy, has the humanity to let live and, in a position to be my lord and master, allows me to continue in my satrapy. In return for all this I undertake, if I am still living, to establish a profound peace and an everlasting friendship between the Ethiopians and the Persians, and to confirm to the Syeneans the edict regarding them. If anything should happen to me, may the gods reward Hydaspes, and the house and kindred of Hydaspes, for his noble treatment of myself.'

BOOK 10

The victorious King Hydaspes is welcomed to his capital of Meroë in Ethiopia.

(1) So much then for the relation of events at Syene, a city which had suddenly passed out of a dreadful predicament into blissful condition, thanks to the rectitude of a single man. Hydaspes, after sending on in advance the greater part of his army, set out himself for Ethiopia, escorted for a very great distance by an acclaiming multitude of all the people of Syene and all the Persians. At first his route kept close to the banks of the Nile and the region bordering on the river; but when he reached the Cataracts, and had sacrificed to the Nile and the deities of the frontiers, he turned off and pursued a more inland course. Arrived at Philae, he rested his army there for about two days, and again sent forward the majority of his troops, who took the prisoners along with them, while he himself remained to strengthen the walls of that city and post a garrison in it. When he marched away he dispatched two picked cavalrymen with orders to go on ahead and change horses at each village or town, so as to perform with all speed their errand of conveying to the people of Meroë his good news of the victory.

(2) To the sages whom they call Gymnosophists, and who are privy councillors and advisers concerned with the King's business, he wrote as follows: 'To the most reverend Council, King Hydaspes: I send you the good news of my victory over the Persians, making no vain boast of my success, since I would not provoke the fitful caprice of Fortune. But your prophetic gift has evinced its accuracy now, as always, and I hasten to salute it with these lines. I therefore invite and adjure you to come to the accustomed place, that by your presence you may enhance in the eyes of the Ethiopian people the sanctity of the sacrifices of thanksgiving for my victory.' To his wife Persinna he wrote: 'This is to let you know that we have conquered and, what is of more moment to you, we are safe and sound. Make preparations for magnificent processions and sacrifices of thanksgiving for us, and convoke the sages, giving them also the directions that we have sent, and hasten them to the meadows fronting the city*

which are consecrated to the gods of our fathers – Sun, Moon,
and Dionysus.'

(3) On the receipt of these letters Persinna said: 'This must be
the meaning of the dream that I beheld last night. I thought that
I conceived and was at once delivered of a child; it was a
daughter, immediately come to her nubile bloom. The birth
pangs of my dream shadowed forth, it would seem, the ordeals
of the war, and my daughter the victory. Go now and proclaim
the good news throughout the city.' The special messengers
carried out her behest: their heads crowned with lotus of the
Nile, they waved palm branches in their hands as they passed
on horseback through the more important parts of the city,
publishing the victory by the mere guise in which they came.
And Meroë indeed was quickly filled with rejoicing; night and
day each family, street and ward held dances and offered
sacrifices in honour of the gods and decked the temples with
garlands. Their hearts were gladdened not so much by the
victory as by the preservation of Hydaspes, a man who by his
rectitude, combined with his gracious clemency towards his
subjects, had instilled into his people such a love as is felt for a
father.

(4) Persinna first sent to the meadows fronting the city herds
of oxen, horses, sheep, gazelles, griffins and every other kind of
beast, in quantity enough to provide the sacrifice of a hecatomb
of each kind, and to furnish besides a feast for the whole
population. This done, she went to see the Gymnosophists in
the temple of Pan,* where they resided. She handed them the
letter from Hydaspes, and added her own request that they
would comply with the King's appeal to them, and pay herself
also the courtesy of enhancing the festal celebration by their
presence. They bade her wait a little while; they passed into the
sanctuary to pray to the deities according to their practice, and
inquire what they were to do. After a brief interval they
returned; then, while the rest of them kept silence, the president
of the council, Sisimithres, said: 'Persinna, we will come, since
the gods give us permission: but the divine voice foretells that
the sacrifices will be attended with some clamour and disturbance, which, however, will suddenly turn in the end to a good
and pleasing issue. For a limb of your body, or a link in the
monarchy, has been lost; but Destiny intends to restore at that
moment the missing part.' 'Threatened ills of any kind,' said

Persinna, 'will take on a change for the better if you are present; and when I am informed of the approach of Hydaspes I will give you the word.' 'No need to give us word,' said Sisimithres; 'he will arrive tomorrow morning. A letter will give you news of this in a little while.' And so it fell out. As Persinna was returning and was nearing the palace, a horseman delivered to her a letter from the King advising her that he would arrive on the next day. Heralds immediately made announcement of the message, stating that only those of the male sex were allowed to go and meet him: women were prohibited. For in fact as the sacrifice was to be offered up to the purest and brightest of the gods – Sun and Moon – it was against the accepted rule to let the female sex take part, to the end that the victims should be preserved from even an involuntary defilement. The only woman permitted to attend was the priestess of the Moon, who was Persinna: the king officiated for the Sun and the queen for the Moon, according to the rule and custom of the land. Chariclea also, of course, was to be present at the ceremony, not as a spectator, but as an oblation to the Moon. An uncontrollable impulse then took possession of the city: without waiting for the appointed day the people began that evening to cross over the river Astaborras, some by the pontoon bridge, others in ferry-boats made of reeds which were moored in large numbers at many points along the bank, to provide direct crossings for dwellers at too great a distance from the bridge. These boats move at a high speed owing to their light material and load, since they can carry only a burthen of not more than two or three men. They are made of split reeds, each half of a reed forming a skiff.

(5) Meroë, the capital of Ethiopia,* is in the form of a triangular island, round which flow navigable rivers – the Nile, the Astaborras and the Asasobas.* One of these, the Nile, where it touches the apex of the triangle, is parted this way and that; the other two rivers, after flowing along either side of the island, rejoin each other to be one with the Nile, to which they yield up their waters and their names. This city is very large, and hence has the specious appearance of a mainland on an island; for it measures three thousand furlongs in length and a thousand in breadth.* It supports various animals of immense size, especially elephants, and is fertile in trees surpassing any of other lands. For besides palms of enormous height bearing succulent dates

of extraordinary size, the wheat and barley in the ear stand so tall that anyone mounted on a horse or a camel may sometimes be hidden among them, and the seed sown is multiplied in the harvest by as much as three hundred. The species of reeds growing there has already been mentioned.

(6) So all through that night the people crossed over the river at several points, making haste to meet Hydaspes and welcome him with tributes of praise as though he were a god. While they advanced some way farther on, the Gymnosophists met him a little before he reached the meadow-lands, and there they clasped his hands and saluted him with kisses. After them Persinna greeted him within the portico and precincts of the temple: there they prostrated themselves in adoration of the gods, and offered up their vows of thanksgiving for his victory and his safe return. They then came outside the precincts and gave their attention to the public sacrifice. They had seats of state in the tent that had been specially erected on the plain; it was constructed of four newly cut reeds, one of which stood like a column at each corner of the rectangle, and these supports curved inwards at the top to form a vault, being linked together with palm branches so as to provide a roof over the space below. In a second tent near by were displayed on a lofty plinth statues of the national gods and images of the semi-divine Memnon, Perseus and Andromeda, whom the sovereigns of Ethiopia regard as the founders of their line. On a lower level, in order to have the divinities, as it were, above their heads, the Gymnosophists were seated on a secondary dais. Next to them a phalanx of armoured men was ranged in a ring, leaning on their shields, which were held upright and touching one another for the purpose of pressing back the crowd behind them and keeping the middle space free from any interference with the performance of the sacrifices. Hydaspes first made a brief speech to the people in which, after announcing the victory, he told of the advancement thereby secured for the common weal. He then gave the word for the officiating priests to begin the sacrifices. Three lofty altars in all had been erected – two standing close together in a separate position, for the Sun and the Moon, and the third in another part by itself, for Dionysus. On this last all sorts of beasts were slaughtered; and I suppose it is because of this god's appeal to the people at large and his gracious favour towards all men that they propitiate him with oblations of every

kind and variety. To the other altars they led up, for the Sun a team of four white horses – a natural dedication of the swiftest creature to the swiftest god* – and for the Moon an offering of a yoke of oxen, because her nearness to the earth naturally claims for her the consecration of man's fellow-labourers on the land.

The special sacrifice of human victims is demanded by the people.

(7) While these rites were still being performed, a confused, disorderly outcry suddenly arose, such as may come from a huge, promiscuous crowd. 'The traditional ceremonies must be carried out!' was the clamour of the people standing around: 'The customary sacrifice must now be offered for the nation's good; the first-fruits of the war must be presented in oblation to the gods!' Hydaspes understood that they were demanding the human sacrifice which it was their custom to perform, though only on occasions of victory over a foreign enemy, with victims chosen from prisoners that had been taken in the field. He hushed them with a sign of his hand, and indicated by nodding his head that their request would be granted forthwith; and he gave the word for the prisoners already assigned to this purpose to be brought. This was accordingly done, and among them were Theagenes and Chariclea: they had been relieved of their chains and crowned with garlands. They wore a downcast look, as was natural; but Theagenes not so much as the rest, while Chariclea, with a radiant face, was smiling as she kept her gaze fixed so intently on Persinna that she on her part was moved at the sight of her. She heaved a deep sigh and said: 'Husband, what a fine girl you have chosen for the sacrifice! I do not know that I ever saw such beauty. What a noble look in her eyes! What a high spirit in facing her fate! How pitiable, in the fresh bloom of her age! If it were our fortune to have with us yet the one and only child that I bore, our unhappily perished daughter she would be reckoned to be about the same age as this girl. O husband, if only it were somehow possible to exempt her, I should find it a great consolation to have such a girl in my service! And the poor creature may happen to be a Greek, for her face is not that of an Egyptian.' 'She is a Greek,' replied Hydaspes, 'and of parents whom she is just now about to name: she cannot show them to us – how could she? – though she

promised to do so. However, she cannot be delivered from this sacrifice: yet I wish that it were possible, because I too am moved, for some reason, and feel pity for the girl. But, as you know, the law requires that a male be presented and sacrificed to the Sun, and a female to the Moon. This girl is the first female captive brought to me, and she was assigned to this day's sacrifice; to set her aside would be inexcusable in the eyes of the people. One thing alone might rescue her: if she should stand upon the brazier that you know of, and should then be proved to be not untainted by any intimacy with men; for the law ordains that she who is brought as an offering to the goddess shall be pure, as must the victim also that is to be sacrificed to the Sun; though the law has no such concern in the case of a sacrifice to Dionysus. Yet it is a question whether it will be seemly that a girl convicted on the brazier of having had intimacy with some man should be given a place in your household.' 'Let her be convicted,' said Persinna; 'only let her life be saved! Captivity, war, long exile from one's native land – these render such a decision undeserving of blame, especially in her case; for in her beauty she carries about with her the motive of her own undoing, if indeed she has undergone anything of the sort.'

(8) While Persinna was yet speaking, her eyes suffused with tears which she sought to hide from her audience, Hydaspes ordered the brazier to be brought. The attendants thereupon collected from the crowd some children of tender age – the only kind of persons who are able to touch the brazier without taking harm* – and had them carry it out of the temple and set it in the midst of the assembly. The attendants then bade each of the prisoners step upon it. As they took their stand in turn, all immediately had their soles burnt: some could not endure the first touch of it, however brief. It is constructed of a lattice of gold bars, and is endued with the special power of severely burning whoever is impure or has in some way perjured himself; but it allows those who are innocent to take their stand on it without being hurt. Those prisoners they assigned to Dionysus and other gods, except two or three young women who on mounting the braziers were approved as virgins.

The chastity of both Theagenes and Chariclea is proved by the ordeal of the brazier. The Gymnosophists protest against the human sacrifice.

(9) Then Theagenes, when his turn came to go upon the brazier, was shown to be pure. Everybody marvelled, not merely at his stature and beauty, but especially that a man in the fresh bloom of his age should be without experience of the ways of Aphrodite; and he was held in readiness for the sacrifice to the Sun. 'Fine rewards in Ethiopia,' he said softly to Chariclea, 'for those who lead a pure life! Sacrificial slaughter is the prize presented to the chaste! But, dearest one, why do you not declare yourself? For what moment are you still waiting? Till they cut our throats? Speak, I beg you, and disclose the truth about yourself. Perhaps you will save my life also, if you are recognized for what you are, and you then intercede for me. If you fail of that, you will yet for certain escape your own danger: I shall be content, when I have learnt that, to meet my end.' 'The crisis draws near,' she said, 'and Fate now holds our future in the balance.' Without waiting for the order of the officials in charge she produced from a wallet which she carried upon her the sacred tunic of Delphi, bespangled with gold-embroidered rays, and put it on. She loosened her hair and, like one possessed, ran forward and leapt upon the brazier. For a long time she stood there unharmed, flashing forth then the light of her beauty in yet greater brightness; observed by all on every side of that high position, and resembling in her attire rather a statue of a deity than a mortal woman. Amazement, in fact, took hold of everyone at once; they all raised a resounding outcry, confused and inarticulate, but eloquent of the wonder and admiration with which they were filled by the scene, and more particularly by the fact that she could keep unsullied, and manifestly then possessed, such superhuman beauty and the perfect bloom of her youth, enhanced as it was by her modest reserve more than by her charms. Yet it gave pain besides to the populace that she showed herself so suitable for the sacrifice and, god-fearing though they were, they still would have rejoiced to see her deliverance procured by means of some contrivance. Greater grief was felt by Persinna, which moved her to say to Hydaspes: 'Poor unfortunate girl! Priding herself for so long, and now so inopportunely, on her virtue, and gaining death in return for

earning so fair a fame! Ah, what can be done, husband?' 'It is useless,' he replied, 'to pester me thus, and to feel this pity for her who is not to be saved, but because of her extraordinary qualities is reserved for the gods, it would seem, from her earliest days.' He then turned and spoke to the Gymnosophists: 'Most excellent sages,' he said, 'all is now prepared; why do you not begin the rites?' Sisimithres answered him in Greek, so as not to be understood by the crowd: 'Hold your peace: we have incurred up to this moment enough defilement of our sight and hearing. We shall withdraw into the temple,* since such an abomination as human sacrifice is both condemned by ourselves and, we believe, unacceptable to the divine nature. And would that it were possible to have sacrifices of all other live creatures prohibited! Heaven, to our thinking, is well satisfied with offerings only of prayers and perfumes. But you must remain here, for a king is at times obliged to comply with even the senseless impulse of a multitude: perform this sacrifice, impious indeed, but unalterably ordained by the long-standing tradition of Ethiopian custom. You will afterwards have need of purifications; though perhaps that need may not arise; for it seems to me that this sacrifice will not come to pass, to judge by sundry signs divinely given, and especially by the light that shines about these strangers, distinguishing them as aided and protected by some higher power.'

(10) With these words he arose, as did the rest of the council also, and was preparing to withdraw with them, when Chariclea leapt down from the brazier and, running to Sisimithres, threw herself down at his knees, despite every effort of the attendants to restrain her, in their belief that her appeal was for a reprieve from death. 'Excellent sages,' she said, 'stay but a moment: I propose to bring a case for judicial hearing against these sovereign rulers, and you alone, I understand, are the judges of persons in their position. In this trial for my life, be you the arbiters. That I should be slaughtered in sacrifice to the gods is neither possible nor just, as I shall convince you.' They gladly admitted her plea and said to the King: 'Sire, do you hear the challenge and the allegations of the foreign woman?' Hydaspes laughed and said: 'What sort of suit, and how grounded, can there be betwixt me and her? On what kind of pretext or claim of rights does she take her stand?' Sisimithres then told him: 'Her forthcoming statements will suffice to explain all.' 'Why

would not this affair,' he said, 'be thought an insult rather than
a judgment if I, a king, should be put on trial by my prisoner?'
'Justice is not overawed by dignities,' replied Sisimithres; 'he
alone is king in a court of justice who prevails by having the
stronger case.' 'But it is for suits between sovereigns and their
countrymen, not foreigners,' he said, 'that the law appoints you
to be judges.' 'Just decision,' replied Sisimithres, 'is based, for
the truly wise, not on one's personal appearance only, but on
one's conduct as well.' 'It is obvious,' said the King, 'that she
can have nothing serious to say, but after the fashion of those
who stand in peril of their lives she will give us idle tales,
invented to gain time. However, let her speak, since Sisimithres
will have it so.'

*Chariclea claims immunity from sacrifice, as she is no foreigner,
but a daughter of the King himself, and is encouraged by the
presence of the Gymnosophist Sisimithres.*

(11) Chariclea, besides being cheered by the prospect of relief
from her immediate danger, was still more delighted to hear the
name of Sisimithres. For it was he who originally found her
exposed and took her up, and placed her in the keeping of
Charicles, ten years before, when he was sent to the Cataracts
on a mission to Oroondates concerning the emerald mines; at
that time he was merely one of the order of Gymnosophists, but
now he had been appointed president of the council. Chariclea
could not recollect the man's appearance, since she was quite
young, only seven years of age, when she was parted from him;
but she recalled his name, and was especially delighted with the
anticipation of having his advocacy and assistance towards her
recognition. Stretching forth her hands to heaven, she cried in
resounding tones: 'O Sun, founder of the line of my ancestors,
and ye other gods and demigods who are the guiding powers of
our family, I call you as witnesses that I shall say nothing that is
not true. Be my helpers also in the trial that I have now to enter
upon; in it I shall open my plea for the rights that I claim for
myself with these words: Are they foreigners, O king, or people
of the country, whom the law bids you sacrifice?' 'Foreigners,'
he replied. 'Then it is time that you looked about for other
victims,' she said, 'for you will find that I am your country-
woman, a native of this land.'

(12) In his surprise at this statement he called it a falsehood. 'You wonder at the lesser things,' she said; 'the greater are yet to come. Not only am I a native of this land; I am also of royal birth, and nearest in the priority of succession.' Again Hydaspes spurned her words as stuff and nonsense. 'Enough now, father,' she said, 'of vilifying your daughter.' The King then began to treat her words, not merely with contempt, but with resentment, taking them as a piece of insolent jesting. 'Sisimithres and the rest of you,' he said, 'do you see the pass to which my forbearance has brought me? To be sure, the girl is completely brainsick, attempting thus to fend off death by her foolhardy inventions. In her desperation she makes an appearance on the scene, as by a stage device, to declare herself my daughter, when never yet, as you know, have I been blessed with the birth of any child, save only once, when I heard at the same moment of one born and lost to me. So let her be taken away, and let her cease contriving to postpone the sacrifice.' 'No one will take me,' cried Chariclea, 'so long as the judges have not ordered it. And you are a party to this present suit, in no position to act as judge. The slaying of foreigners, O King, may be permitted by the law; but to slay your own children is not allowed to you, father, either by law or by nature. That you are a father the gods this day will declare, deny it though you may. Every cause that comes for judgment, O King, admits these two surest proofs – written affidavits and witnesses' affirmations. I shall produce to you evidence of both these kinds that I am your daughter, by citing as witness, not just a member of the public but the judge himself – and no stronger testimony, I conceive could a pleader have than what is in the knowledge of the judge, while for written evidence I present here a narrative of both my and your fortunes.'

Hydaspes by various signs is at length convinced of Chariclea's identity, but doubts whether she ought not to be sacrificed.

(13) As she spoke these words she drew forth the swathe which was exposed with her and which she wore about her loins, unfolded it and handed it to Persinna. At her first glance the Queen stood dumbfounded and stunned, and for long she kept gazing by turns on the script in the swathe and on the girl. She was seized with a fit of trembling and throbbing, and

sweated profusely, from her gladness at the discovery, but also
from bewilderment at the incredible happening of what was
beyond all hope, and from fear lest Hydaspes should feel
suspicion and mistrust – even, it might be, anger and vengeful-
ness – at these revelations. Hydaspes in consequence, observing
for himself her astonishment and overpowering anguish, said to
her: 'Wife, what means this? What disturbs you so in this
writing that she is showing you?' 'O King,' she replied; 'my lord
and husband, I can speak not a word more; take it and read it;
this swathe will inform you of everything.' She handed it to him,
and relapsed into a sorrowful silence. Hydaspes took it in his
hands, and invited the Gymnosophists to stand by and read it
with him. As he made out the words he was himself filled with
wonder, and was aware besides of the deep amazement of
Sisimithres, whose looks betrayed a multitude of various
thoughts passing through his mind, as he continually turned his
gaze on the swathe and on Chariclea. At length Hydaspes,
having learnt of the exposure and the reason of it, said: 'That a
girl was born to me I know; that she died I was informed at the
time by Persinna herself; I now learn that she was exposed. But
who took her up, saved her life and reared her? Who conveyed
her into Egypt, where she was taken prisoner? And what proof
is there, after all, that this girl here is that same one; that the
exposed child has not perished: and that some person, chancing
upon these tokens of recognition, did not turn his chance
discovery to fraudulent use? Some deity perhaps, to make game
of us, has furnished the girl with these tokens as a sort of mask
and, mocking at our desire for children, would foist upon us a
bastard or suppositious succession, overcasting the truth with
this swathe as with a cloud.'

(14) In answer to his words Sisimithres said: 'The first matters
that you call in question can be cleared up for you. He who
took up the exposed child, who reared her in secret, and who
brought her to Egypt when you sent me there as your envoy is
myself; and that we are forbidden to lie you know from past
experience of us. I recognize this swathe: it is inscribed, as you
see, with the royal lettering of Ethiopia, thus precluding any
question of its production elsewhere; and that the pricking out
is the actual handiwork of Persinna you of all people must
recognize. But there were other tokens exposed with the girl,
which I gave to the man who received her from me, a Greek

and, as was evident, a person of excellent character.' 'Those also are preserved,' said Chariclea, displaying the necklaces as she spoke. The sight of these astounded Persinna still more; and when Hydaspes asked her what they were and whether she had any further explanation to make, her only reply was that she recognized them, but that it would be best to examine them within doors. Again Hydaspes appeared to be much disturbed; then Chariclea told him: 'These should be the tokens of recognition for my mother, but this ring is one particular to you'; and she showed the pantarbe. Hydaspes recognized it as his gift to Persinna at their betrothal. 'My dear lady,' he said, 'this token I recognize as mine; but that you who have the use of it are my child, and have not just happened to acquire it, I still am not sure. For, apart from other reasons, your complexion is of a bright fairness foreign to the Ethiopian colour.' Sisimithres then told him: 'White was she taken up whom I myself then took up; and in particular, the period of years tallies with the present age of this girl: between it and her exposure the time amounts in all to about seventeen years. And to me the very glances of her eyes are convincing; I recognize the whole cast of her features, her miraculous beauty – everything apparent in her now corresponding to what she showed at that time.' 'Your words are excellent, Sisimithres,' said Hydaspes; 'they are more in the style of a most ardent advocate than in that of a judge. But take care that in clearing up one part of the problem you may not be raising up a fresh question: one of such difficulty and gravity that it would be no light matter for my life's partner to clear herself of its import. How could we two Ethiopians have begotten such an unlikely child as a white girl?' Sisimithres looked askance at him, with a smile that had a touch of irony, and said: 'I wonder what has come over you, that you belie your own character by reproaching me now with an advocacy in which I can see nothing base. For I define a genuine judge as the advocate of justice. Why should I not appear as your advocate rather than the girl's? With the gods' aid I prove to you your fatherhood, and this your daughter, whom I saved for you in her swaddling clothes, I cannot desert, now that she is being restored to you in the bloom of her age. Well, hold what opinion you please of us, we take no account of that; for we do not live for complaisance to others, but are content with teaching ourselves to strive after absolute goodness and virtue. However, the solution of the difficulty presented by the girl's colour lies in the message of the swathe. Persinna here acknowledges that she contracted certain shapes or impressions of likeness from looking upon the figure of Andromeda during her union with you. If you still required some further assurance, the original is there before us. Look carefully, and see if Andromeda is not unmistakably manifest in the girl as in the picture.'

(15) The servants were ordered to take down the picture, and they brought it and set it up beside Chariclea. The result was a great burst of applause and clamour from the onlookers, as they explained to one another such fragments as they could gather of what was being said and done, and were struck with an amazement mingled with high delight at the exactness of the resemblance; so true it was that Hydaspes himself could no longer be in doubt, but stood for a long time lost in both joy and wonder. 'One matter still remains,' said Sisimithres; 'the question of the monarchy, of the legitimate succession to the throne and, above all, of the truth itself. Bare your arm, girl: it was discoloured with a black device above the elbow. There is nothing unseemly in laying bare the evidence of your parentage and lineage.' At once Chariclea bared her left arm, and on it was what seemed like a ring of ebony smirching the ivory of its skin.*

(16) Persinna now could no longer contain herself. She started up on a sudden from her throne, and running to the girl embraced her, clung about her weeping and, in the wild transport of her joy, uttered a loud moaning like that of a lowing heifer; for an excess of pleasure will at times produce even wailing, and she came near collapsing with Chariclea on to the ground. Hydaspes was moved with pity at the sight of his wife lamenting, and his mood was swayed to compassion; yet he kept his eyes fixed, as though they were of horn or iron,* upon the scene before him, and stood still, fighting down the travailanguish of his tears: and while his soul tossed on the surges of paternal affection and manly spirit, his judgment was parted in a dissension betwixt these two, being alternately swung over to one and the other as by an ocean swell. He finally gave in to all-conquering Nature: not only was he convinced of his fatherhood but he also proved himself to have all a father's feelings. Persinna now had sunk to the ground with her daughter, and was holding her in a close embrace. In the sight of everyone he raised her up,

took Chariclea in his arms and poured forth on her a flood of tears as a libation solemnizing his paternity. Nevertheless he was not to be deflected from the full discharge of his immediate duties. For a moment he paused, and observed how the people were stirred by the same emotions, and were weeping with mingled joy and pity at the dramatic turn that Fortune had given to events; how they sent up a mighty cry to the heavens* without hearkening to the heralds' calls for silence, or indicating clearly what they meant with all this uproar. He then, with a wave of his outstretched hand, subdued to a calm the stormy tumult of the people. 'You who are here present,' he said, 'you see and hear how the gods beyond all expectation have declared me to be a father, and how this girl is by many proofs discovered to be my daughter. But so extreme is my affection for you and for my native land that, making light of the succession of my line and the appellation of father, although I was like to obtain all this through her, I am intent for your sake on performing the sacrifice to the gods. For, while I see you weeping and yielding to an impulse of human emotion in your pity for the untimely fate of this girl, and also for the frustration of my hopes for the succession, it is nevertheless necessary, though it be against your will, that I obey our country's law and set the claims of our fatherland above any personal advantage. Whether it is in truth the pleasure of the gods that she should be given to me and at the same time taken away – a blow which I suffered once before at her birth, and which I suffer now on her discovery – this I cannot tell; but I leave it to your consideration. Nor do I know whether those gods, having banished her from her native land to the uttermost ends of the earth, and having miraculously restored her to my arms in the plight of a captive, will welcome an offering of the girl this time as a sacrifice upon their altar. When I saw her as an enemy I did not slay her, and when she became my prisoner I did not maltreat her. Yet now that she is found to be my daughter I will not put off her sacrifice, believing it to be your will also that this oblation shall be made; nor will I give way to a feeling that might perhaps be pardoned in another father, and flinch or resort to entreating your indulgence for an unholy breach of the law in this present case, because of your attaching more weight to nature and the feelings that spring therefrom, and pretending that there is some other way in which the deity may be duly served. Just as you have openly shown your sympathy with me, and the grievous pain that you suffer from my affliction as though it were your own, so in like measure it behoves me to set your interests above mine, and to take little account of my loss of an heir, and as little of the lamenting of my unhappy Persinna here, who finds herself at once a mother for the first time and childless. Cease therefore, if you please, your vain weeping and commiseration of us, and let us proceed to the sacrifice.

'To you, my daughter – for it is now for the first, and the last, time that I address you by that longed-for name – let me say this: in vain are you lovely, in vain have you discovered your parents. A hard fate has made your own country more baneful to you than a foreign land; you have come safely through your sojourn on an alien soil, only to meet destruction on entering your native land. Do not perturb my heart with wailing,* but now more than ever display that gallant, that royal spirit which is yours. Follow now the father that begot you; who has not been able to attire you in your bridal garments, nor has led you to the nuptial chamber and bed, but adorns you for sacrifice, lights torches not of the marriage rite but of an altar offering, and presents this peerless flower of beauty as a sacrificial victim. And O ye gods, forgive of your grace those words – it may be impious words – that I have spoken, overborne by the pain of having called one my child only to become that child's slayer!

Hydaspes bows to the people's demand that Chariclea's life be spared.

(17) As he ended this speech he took hold of Chariclea, making as if to lead her to the altar and the pyre upon it; but smouldering in his heart was the stronger fire of his grief, and he prayed that the words which he had speciously addressed to the public assembly might be of none effect. The great throng of Ethiopians had been deeply disturbed by his speech; they would not suffer even the least effort to remove Chariclea, and suddenly cried out in loud protest: 'Save the girl! Save the blood-royal! Save her whom the gods have saved! We are grateful: for us the law has been sufficiently observed; we have acknowledged you to be our king; acknowledge yourself to be a father. May the gods look leniently upon the seeming breach of the law: we shall more truly break it if we set ourselves against their

purposes. Let no one destroy her whose life they have preserved! Father of our people, be now a father in your home!' And uttering a multitude of other such cries they ended by making an active demonstration also against his intention, standing in his way, and in fact withstanding him, and demanding that the deity be propitiated by offering up the other victims. Hydaspes not only willingly but gladly accepted defeat, submitting of his own accord to this wished-for compulsion. When he saw that the masses were continuing overlong to revel in repeated clamouring, and were somewhat insolently sportive in their chanting of his praises, he allowed them to take their fill of delight and waited for them to settle down in time of themselves to calmness.

(18) He then moved close to Chariclea and said: 'My darling, that you are my daughter has been revealed by the tokens of recognition and testified by the sage Sisimithres and, above all, declared by the gods' benevolence. But who may this man be who has been captured with you and has been reserved as a thanksgiving oblation to the gods for our victory, and is now stationed at the altars in readiness for the sacred rite? How came you to call him your brother, when you were first brought to me at Syene? Surely he will not be discovered to be our son, since you are the one and only child conceived by Persinna.' At this Chariclea blushed, hung her head and answered: 'I lied in calling him my brother; necessity framed the fiction. Who he really is he can tell better than I, for he is a man, and will not be ashamed to explain the truth more boldly than is fitting for a woman like me.' Hydaspes, unable to understand the meaning of her words, then said: 'Forgive me, little daughter, for having made you blush by facing you with a question about a young man which was distasteful to your maiden modesty. But go now and rest yourself in the tent with your mother: you will not only fill her heart with gladness, for she labours now more with yearning for the enjoyment of your company than with pain when she was bearing you; but you will also soothe her with the relation of your adventures. It will be for me now to attend to the sacrifice, after selecting the other female victim who is to be slain together with the young man as an offering in your place, if by our best endeavours we can find a worthy substitute.'

(19) Chariclea almost gave utterance to a cry of woe, so sorely was she distressed by this mention of the slaughter of Theagenes: yet with a great effort she turned to what was expedient, and

forced herself to hold out against the maddening power of her passion for the sake of her most practical course. Quietly she crept on in pursuit of her purpose and said: 'Sire, perhaps it became no longer necessary for you to seek another girl when once the people had on my account foregone the offering of a female victim. If, however, some should contentiously insist on taking a pair of victims, one from each sex, for a due perform-ance of the sacrifice, you must hasten to find, not only a girl, but another youth also; or, failing that, to lead, not another girl, but me after all to the slaughter.' 'Do not speak so,' he said; and when he asked her reason for saying this she answered: 'Because this young man is destined by Heaven to live with me while I live, and die with me when I die.'

(20) At these words Hydaspes, having not yet grasped the truth of the matter, said: 'I commend your humane heart, daughter, your goodness in pitying and seeking to save a Greek stranger of your own age, who has shared your captivity and has acquired familiarity with you through the events of your exile; but there is no possibility of delivering him from the sacrifice. For, besides the impiety of an outright rejection of the traditional thank-offering for victory, the people themselves would not tolerate it, after they have been hardly induced, by the gods' grace, to make the concession in your favour.' To this Chariclea rejoined: 'O King – for it seems that I may not call you father – if by the gods' grace my body has been saved alive, it would be expected of the same grace that my soul should be saved likewise, since the gods know that in allotting my destiny they decreed that soul to be truly mine own. But if this consequence should be found unacceptable to the Fates, and it will be necessary to enhance the sacred ritual with the slaughter of this foreign youth, grant me this one boon at least: command that I myself, with my own hand, shall perform the sacrifice, and that having received the sword as a precious keepsake I shall be celebrated and admired throughout Ethiopia for my manly resolution.'

(21) Deeply disturbed by her words, Hydaspes said: 'But I do not understand this reversal of your purpose. A moment ago you were trying to shield this stranger; and now you request that you may slay him with your own hand, as though he were an enemy. No, I can see in such an action nothing noble or glorious redounding to you or any girl of your age; and even if

it were to your honour, it is quite impossible. Only to persons consecrated to the Sun and the Moon has the performance of this service been assigned by ancient tradition, and then not to any of these at random, but only to such as cohabit with wife or husband. Thus your virginity debars your request, put forward I know not with what intent.' 'But there is no impediment on that score,' said Chariclea, leaning over to Persinna and speaking aside in her ear; 'for I myself have one, mother, who has the right to such a name, if you should both give your consent.' 'We shall consent,' said Persinna with a smile, 'and with the gods' blessing we shall bestow on you one whom we may select as worthy both of you and of ourselves.' Then Chariclea said, in a louder tone: 'No need to select one who is mine already.'

(22) She was about to speak more openly – for she was compelled by the pressing emergency to be bold, and by the peril of Theagenes with which she was faced, to ignore her maidenly modesty – when Hydaspes, no longer able to restrain himself, said: 'Ye gods, how you seem to mingle evil with good! The unhoped for happiness that you have vouchsafed to me you partly withhold; you present me with a daughter beyond all expectation, but one out of her mind! How can she not be demented, when she gives vent to such inconsequent statements? She named one a brother who was not; when asked about him, who this stranger was, she said she did not know. Next, she sought to save the life of this unknown man as if he were a friend; and when she learnt that her request could not be granted, she begged that she might sacrifice him herself, as though he were her worst enemy. She was told that this was not lawful, since that kind of sacrifice has been solemnly committed to one woman alone, and that a wedded one; whereupon she declares that she has a husband, without going on to tell who he is. How indeed could she, when she has none, nor ever has had one, as was proved in the ordeal of the brazier? Unless it be that in her case alone an untruth is told us by that trial, ever found truthful by the Ethiopians, as to the purity of persons subjected to it, and it allows her to come off unburnt from treading upon it, and favours her with a spurious virginity. And to her alone it is given to count the same persons in one instant her friends and her enemies, and to invent brothers and sisters who do not exist! Go then, wife, into the tent, and soothe her into a sober mood. Either some god on a visit to our sacred rite has smitten her

with frenzy, or an excess of joy over unhoped for felicity has driven her out of her wits. I go now to order someone to search for and find the female victim whom it is our duty to sacrifice to the gods instead of her; and, until that has been arranged, I shall proceed with interviewing the embassies from various nations and receiving the gifts that they have brought me in honour of my victory.' With these words he took his seat in state on an eminence near the tent, and commanded that the ambassadors should approach and present whatever gifts they might be bringing with them. The announcer, Hermonias,* then asked whether he wished them to be introduced all at once, or by turns, taking each nation separately, one envoy at a time.

Hydaspes, bewildered by the apparently insane behaviour of Chariclea, gives audience to a number of ambassadors. Theagenes skilfully recaptures a runaway bull.

(23) He replied that they should come in order, individually, so that each should be treated with the distinction due to him. The announcer went on to say: 'Then the first to come will be your brother's son, Meroebus; he has just arrived, and is waiting outside the encampment to have himself announced.' 'So, you utterly stupid fool,'* exclaimed Hydaspes, 'you did not immediately inform me? This is no ambassador who has come, but a king, as you are well aware. He is the son of my brother lately deceased; it was I who established him on his father's throne, and I now treat him as my son.' 'So I understood,' said Hermonias; 'but I understood also the prime importance of catching the right moment – a point of particular concern to considerate announcers. Forgive me, therefore, if while you were conversing with the princess I took care not to interrupt your sweetest pleasures.' 'Well, now at any rate let him come to me,' said the King; and the man charged with the errand ran off and returned with his charge the next moment. Meroebus appeared, a comely figure of a youth just passing out of his adolescent years at the age of seventeen. In stature he overtopped almost everybody present and, when he entered with a splendid troop of armed bodyguards preceding him, the Ethiopian soldiery standing around showed their admiration and respect by drawing aside to clear the way for his advance.

(24) Hydaspes on his part could not remain seated on his

throne, but went to meet his visitor, enfolded him in his arms
with a paternal warmth of affection, and seated him by his side;
then, giving him his right hand, he said: 'You have come just in
time, my son, to join in the festival of victory and the sacrificial
celebration of a marriage. For the gods and demigods of our
fathers, the founders of our line, have produced for us a
daughter and for you, as it seems, a bride. But you shall be given
a fuller account later on. If you have any request to make of me
for the people of your kingdom, pray state it to me.' Meroebus,
when he heard the word 'bride', was filled with feelings at once
of such pleasure and of such delicacy that even his black
complexion could not conceal his blushes, as when a sparkle has
run over some soot. He was silent for some moments and then
said: 'The other ambassadors, father, who have come will
compliment you with gifts of choice offerings brought by each
from his country to crown your illustrious victory; but I,
thinking it right that the noble and valiant spirit that you have
evinced in war should be suitably matched with a present of
similar character, bring here for you a man who is as invincible
a combatant in fields of battle and in bloodshed as he is
irresistible when he wrestles and boxes in the dust of the arena.'
And with that he intimated with a nod that this person should
come forward.

(25) The man then advanced into their midst and prostrated
himself before Hydaspes. His frame was of such a size, so much
on the scale of the men of old time, that as he bent to kiss the
King's knee he appeared almost to rival in height the persons
seated on the upper stage. Without even waiting to be bidden,
he undressed and stood there naked, challenging anyone who
might wish to meet him in combat, either armed or weaponless.
When no one came forward after repeated summons from the
King by mouth of a herald, Hydaspes said to the man: 'You
shall receive at my hands the victor's prize in due proportion.'
So saying he ordered an elephant of many years and huge size
to be brought before him. When the creature had arrived the
man received it gladly, while the people gave way to a sudden
outburst of laughter, in their delight at the witty comment of
the King, and with a sense of the consolation that they derived
from this mockery of the man's arrogant behaviour for their
own apparent intimidation. After him were introduced the
ambassadors of the Seres, who brought materials of thread spun

and woven from the cobwebs of their country,* made up in the forms of one robe of purple dye and another of purest white.

(26) When the King had received these gifts, and had granted their request for the release of some men who had been condemned and imprisoned a long time before, the envoys from Arabia Felix advanced with sweet-smelling leaves of cassia, cinnamon and other aromatic plants with which Arabia abounds;* there was a good hundredweight of each sort, and they filled the whole place with a delicious fragrance. These were followed by the envoys from the Troglodytes, bringing gold from ant-hills* and a pair of griffins* in double harness of gold chains. Next came the embassy of the Blemmyes, carrying bows and arrows pointed with python's bone, which they had interlaced so as to form a crown. 'These,' they said, 'O King, are the gifts that we present to you; they do not compare in costliness with those of the other missions; but along the riverside, as you have witnessed, they have shown their worth in war against the Persians. 'Indeed they are more precious,' said Hydaspes, 'than complimentary gifts of many talents' value; for it is owing to them that all the others are brought to me today.' With that he invited them to inform him of any request that they would like to make. They asked for a reduction of their tribute, and he granted them a complete exemption for a period of ten years.

(27) Nearly all of the several embassies had been received, and the King had presented to each of them in return gifts which were equal to and, in most cases, more valuable than those brought by them, when the envoys of the Auxomites* appeared. They were in the position, not of tributaries, but of friends and allies under a treaty with the King, and they showed their gratification at his success by offering gifts like the others; but among these in particular was a strangely shaped animal, of a wonderful kind. Its stature equalled that of a camel in height while its hide was coloured and marked with vivid spots like that of a leopard. Its hindquarters and parts about its flanks were low-built, like those of a lion; but its shoulder-parts, front legs and breast rose up to a height out of all proportion to its other parts. Its neck was slender, and protruded a great way from the main bulk of its body after the fashion of a swan's throat. Its head, shaped like that of a camel, was nearly twice the size of that of a Libyan ostrich; and it rolled its eyes, the

rims of which seemed to be pigmented, with a grim expression. Its uncouth, swaying gait differed from the motion of any other land or water animal: its legs did not step forward alternately, one after another, but the two right legs moved together as one, and then the left legs together took their turn as a distinct pair, each side of the body thus being heaved up by their action. With this lumbering motion, and a gentle disposition, it could be led by its keeper using a slender cord twined about its head, and was kept on its path by his will as surely as if he employed an unbreakable chain. The appearance of this animal astounded the whole multitude, and its form then suggested its name: impressed by its more striking features, the people called it offhand a 'camelopard'.* Nevertheless, it filled the whole assembly with trepidation.

(28) Now this is what happened next. At the altar of the Moon stood a pair of bulls, and at that of the Sun a team of four white horses, duly held ready for the sacrifice. The appearance of that alien, unfamiliar, unheard-of monster caused a great commotion among the victims, as though they beheld some spectre. They were filled with terror and broke the halters by which the attendants held them. One of the bulls – which alone, it seems, had caught sight of the wild beast – and two of the horses sped away in headlong flight. Unable to force their way out of the ring of soldiers, who with a wall of close-locked shields formed a circular barrier of heavy-armed men, they dashed about in distraction, careering and wheeling about the middle space, and upsetting everything that came in their way. whether lifeless object or living creature. Mingled cries of two kinds arose as this was happening – some of fright from people towards whom the animals were rushing, and some of pleasure from those who, as the animals dashed at others, were stirred to amusement and laughter by seeing these people knocked down and trampled on. At this noise Persinna and Chariclea themselves were unable to remain quiet in their tent; drawing the curtains a little aside they obtained a view of what was occurring. At that moment Theagenes, either impelled by the manly spirit that was born in him, or acting on the instigation of some god, observed that the guards posted round him had been dispersed by the impact of the tumult. Suddenly he stood upright: until then he had been crouching on one knee by the altar, and was expecting instant slaughter. He snatched up a

piece of cleft wood that lay upon the altar, seized hold of one of the horses that had not bolted, vaulted on to its back, grasped the hair on its neck and used its mane as a bridle. Stirring on his mount with his heel, and continually urging it on with the piece of wood in place of a whip, he rode after a runaway bull. At first the onlookers supposed this action to show that Theagenes was taking to flight, and each man shouted to his neighbour that the youth must not be allowed to force his way out of the fence of armed soldiers. But as he proceeded in his exploit they had to change their opinion, and to understand that it was no case of cowardice or evasion of the sacrifice. For he speedily caught up with the bull and for a little drove it along from behind, prodding the beast and thus inciting it to run more swiftly. Whichever way it dashed he pursued it closely as it turned about, cautiously eluding it when it swung round to attack him.

(29) When he had brought it to be accustomed to the sight of himself and his procedure, he began to ride alongside it, flank grazing flank, and horse and bull mingling their breath and their sweat together. He regulated his pace so evenly with the bull's that people at a distance could fancy that the heads of the two animals grew upon a single body; and they sang the praises of Theagenes, glorifying him for this novel manner of driving a pair composed of horse and bull. This then was the effect that he produced upon the multitude. But Chariclea at this sight was seized with trembling and palpitation. She was at a loss to know the purpose of his exploit and, fearing that he might come by a fall, was feeling the pangs of the wounds that he might receive as though they were those of her own slaughters; so that Persinna, observing her trouble, asked: 'My child, tell me what is the matter. You seem to be taking the stranger's peril upon yourself. I for my part am affected also, and feel pity for his youth. I pray indeed that he may escape this danger and be preserved for the sacrifice, so that our service to the gods may not be left entirely unperformed and abandoned.' Chariclea replied to this: 'How ridiculous, to pray that he may not die, in order that he may die! But, mother, if it be possible for you, save the man's life, as a favour to me.' Persinna, surmising not the true reason but an ordinary amorous one, said: 'It is not possible to save his life; however, if you have some attachment to this man which gives you such an anxious concern, do not hesitate hereafter to unbosom yourself to me, as your mother.

Even if you have acted on some youthful impulse, even if your conduct has been unbecoming to a maiden, a mother's nature knows how to come to her daughter's aid, and feminine sympathy is able to draw a veil over a woman's lapse.' Upon this Chariclea wept for a great while, and then said: 'This additional misfortune I have to bear, that when I speak to understanding persons I am not understood, and in telling my particular misadventures I am thought to be withholding the tale. From now onward I am compelled to deliver my own indictment, stark and undisguised.'

(30) After making this statement she was intending to reveal the truth, when she was again distracted by an outcry, resounding far and wide, which arose from the multitude. For when Theagenes incited his horse to put forth its utmost speed so as slightly to outpace the bull and bring its breast level with the animal's head, he let the horse run on free while he leapt off it and threw himself on to the bull's neck. He then laid his face down between its horns and, encircling them with his arms as with a coronal, locked his fingers together on the bull's forehead. The rest of his body was slung over the beast's right shoulder, and thus suspended from it he was borne along, only slightly tossed by the bounding of the bull. But when he felt it beginning to gasp beneath its burden and its muscles to relax their extreme tension, at the moment when it came round to the point where Hydaspes sat in state, he swung himself over to the front, thrust his feet against its legs, and so by knocking repeatedly against its hoofs he artfully hampered its progress. Finding itself impeded in its onward course, and overborne by the young man's strength, it gave way at the knees and suddenly lurched headlong; then tumbling on to its shoulders it rolled over on its back, and for a long time lay stretched out, upside-down, with its horns stuck fast in the ground and so implanted there that its head became immovable. Its legs stirred in futile prancing, and beat the empty air in the wild anguish of its defeat.* Leaning upon it, Theagenes made use of his left arm alone for his support, while he raised his right hand heavenward and waved it again and again. On Hydaspes and the whole assembly he cast joyous looks, with a smile that seemed to be inviting them to share his gladness; while the bellowing of the bull served him as a trumpet to proclaim his victory. In response then came the resounding outcry of the people, conveying no articulate words

of definite praise, but from wide-open mouths expressing their admiration as from a single throat, and wafting it in a prolonged and uniform tone to heaven. At the King's command servants ran up: some of them raised up Theagenes and brought him to Hydaspes, while others threw a noosed cord over the horns of the bull and drew it along, sadly crestfallen. They then tethered both it and the horse, which they had caught, once more to the altar.

As Hydaspes was about to speak to Theagenes and be concerned with him, the people, who had been delighted with the youth, having felt kindly towards him since his first appearance, and were now moreover astonished at his bodily strength, but above all were stung with jealousy against the Ethiopian athlete brought by Meroebus, all cried out with one accord: 'Let him be matched with Meroebus' man! Let him who received the elephant contend with him who subdued the bull!' Thus they continued calling out. Their prolonged insistence induced Hydaspes to give his assent, and the Ethiopian was brought into the assembly. He came glancing about with a disdainful, swaggering air; his paces were long and trailing, and he swung up each forearm in turn to meet his other outstretched elbow.

Theagenes wrestles with a gigantic Ethiopian and defeats him.

(31) When the man had drawn near to the royal circle Hydaspes looked towards Theagenes and said in Greek: 'Stranger, you must contend with him; the people demand it.' 'Their will be done,' replied Theagenes, 'but what kind of contest is it to be?' 'Wrestling,' said Hydaspes. To which the youth rejoined: 'Why not a combat with swords and in armour, that by some great stroke given or received I may thrill Chariclea, her who has hitherto maintained a steady silence about me, nay, has utterly dismissed me, it would seem, from her thoughts?' 'For what purpose', said Hydaspes, 'you drag in the name of Chariclea may be known to yourself; but it is in wrestling and not in duelling with swords that you have to contend: for the sight of bloodshed before the moment of the sacrifice is against the law.' Theagenes then, perceiving that Hydaspes feared that he might be killed before the sacrifice, said: 'You do right to reserve me for the gods, who will not be unmindful of us.' With these words he took up some dust and

scattered it over his shoulders and arms, which were still moist with sweat from his bull hunt; he shook off what did not adhere, stretched out his hands before him, took his stand on firmly planted feet, bent his knees, curved his shoulders and back, slightly inclined his neck, braced in his whole frame and stood chafing to be at grips in the wrestling. The Ethiopian eyed him with a sneering smile, and nodded ironically as if he made light of his opponent. Suddenly he ran forward and heaved his arm like a crowbar on to the neck of Theagenes: the noise of the blow was audible afar, and again he swaggered and laughed complacently to himself. Theagenes, as a man trained from early years in the exercises of the gymnasiums, and thoroughly versed in Hermes' art of athletic contests, decided to give way at first, and having tested the power of his adversary, not to fling himself upon this monstrous bulk of a man exasperated to the point of savagery, but to rely on his own practised skill to outwit his mere boorish strength. Immediately then, while somewhat shaken by the blow, he pretended to be in greater distress than he was, and offered the other side of his neck, fully exposed, to meet another stroke. As the Ethiopian launched a second blow Theagenes at once gave way under its force, and feigned to be on the point of falling prostrate on his face.

(32) The Ethiopian, deeming him beaten, was now full of confidence, and made a third onslaught, this time without any caution. Again he raised his outstretched arm, and was about to swing it down, when Theagenes suddenly crouched and darted in beneath him, thus avoiding the downward stroke. With his right forearm he thrust up his opponent's left arm, and staggered him as he was at the same time partly pulled to the ground by the downward sweep of his own hand, which struck only empty air. Theagenes then came up beneath his armpits and got a firm hold around him from behind. Straining hard he just engirdled the man's bulky middle with his hands, upset his footing by hard and repeated hammering with his heel at the joints and bones of the other's ankles, and so forced him to crouch down on one knee. He then, bestriding him with feet apart, thrust his legs into the region of the Ethiopian's groin, dislodged the wrists on which he was relying to uphold his chest, brought the man's forearms round to meet on his brows, drew them over to his back and shoulders, and so compelled him to sprawl with his belly on the ground.* Thereupon the multitude sent forth one

great shout, even more resounding than the former, and the King himself could not forbear to spring up from his throne. 'O hard necessity!' he said; 'what a man it is that under our law is appointed to be sacrificed!' At once he called the young man to him and said: 'A crown is reserved by custom for you at the altar; but take your crown now for this victory, glorious indeed, yet fruitless to you and fleeting. Since it is not possible for me to deliver you – would that I might! – from your appointed fate, I will grant you at least what boons lie in my power. If you have in mind anything that could give you pleasure while life is still yours, pray request it.' With these words he placed on Theagenes' head a golden crown set with jewels, and as he did so was observed to shed some tears. 'Well then,' said Theagenes, 'I will make you my request; and I call on you to grant it, as you promised. If it is beyond the bounds of possibility for me to escape the sacrifice, command that it be performed by your newly discovered daughter.'

(33) Startled by these words, as he recalled to mind the similar request of Chariclea, Hydaspes did not think fit, however, in the hurry of the moment, to trace out their exact meaning. 'They were possible things, stranger,' he said, 'that I both invited you to ask and agreed to give you. She who slaughters the victim must be a married woman, not a maiden so the law declares.' 'But she herself too has a husband,' replied Theagenes. 'This is the talk of an idle babbler,' said Hydaspes; 'of one, in truth, at the point of death. This girl has been proved by the brazier to be a stranger to marriage or intercourse with any man; unless perchance Meroebus be this husband that you mention – I know not on what authority. I have named him, not yet as her husband, but only as her betrothed.' 'Add now that he will never be hers in marriage,' said Theagenes, 'if I have any insight into the mind of Chariclea; and it will be only right to believe me, as a victim moved to prophecy.' At this Meroebus said to him: 'Good sir, it is not in their life, but after their slaughter and dissection that victims intimate to the diviners the signs revealed by their entrails. Thus you were correct, father, in saying that the stranger is speaking wildly at the point of death. Now, if you please, give order that this man be led to the altars, and yourself, when you have settled any business that awaits your attention, proceed to the sacrifice.' So Theagenes was conducted to the appointed place. Chariclea, who had felt a little relief at

the moment of his victory and had built high hopes upon it, at the sight of him being led away relapsed into lamentation. Persinna did all that she could to console her, saying: 'The young man may well be saved, if you will consent to recount to me the yet untold parts of your story, and make everything quite clear.' Then Chariclea, under stress of the occasion, which she saw admitted of no delay, prepared to relate the more important passages in her story.

(34) Hydaspes next inquired of the announcer whether any ambassadors were still waiting to be received. 'Those only from Syene, Sire,' replied Hermonias. 'They bring a letter and friendly gifts from Oroondates, and have just arrived but a moment ago.' 'Let them also come here,' said Hydaspes: they then appeared and handed to him the letter. He opened it and read its contents, as follows: 'To the humane and prosperous King of the Ethiopians, Hydaspes, from Oroondates, satrap of the Great King. Seeing that, conquering me in battle, you have conquered me even more in judgment, and have freely conceded to me my satrapy entire, I should not be surprised if you were to grant me now a small request. A girl who was being brought to me from Memphis has become involved in the warfare: taken prisoner, she was sent on your order to Ethiopia, as I learnt from those who were with her at the time and escaped from that danger. I ask that she be released to me and bestowed on me as a gift, since I have myself some affection for the child, and particularly wish to deliver her safe and sound to her father, who has wandered far and wide over the earth and, while searching for his daughter, was caught up in the fighting at the garrison town of Elephantiné. As I was afterwards reviewing the survivors I saw him, and he demanded to be sent off to your gracious presence. You have the man there with the other envoys: his behaviour suffices to declare his noble birth, and his mere appearance inspires respect. Gladden him, Sire, by returning him to me as a father now not in name only but also in actual fact.' The King, after reading the letter, asked: 'Who among this company is the man searching for his daughter?' They pointed out an old man, to whom he said: 'Stranger, I am prepared to do all this, as Oroondates requests; but I have had only ten young female prisoners brought to me. One so far has been identified as being other than your daughter: inspect the rest and if, in observing them, you can find her, take her.' The old man

prostrated himself and kissed the King's feet. The girls were then fetched; he inspected them and failed to find her whom he sought. Dejected again, he said: 'O King, none of these is she.' 'My mind is wholly yours,' said Hydaspes; 'you must blame Fortune if you do not find her whom you are seeking. That no other girl was brought here, or is in the camp, you can satisfy yourself by looking all around.'

Charicles appears and denounces Theagenes as the abductor of his daughter.

(35) The old man smote his brow and shed tears; then, after raising his head and scanning the throng round about him, he ran off suddenly like one in a frenzy, and on reaching the altars he rolled up the border of his coarse cloak – for that was what he wore – into a loop, flung it about Theagenes' neck* and haled him along, calling out in resonant tones: 'I have got you, ah, my enemy! I have got you, ah, you pernicious villain!' The guards strove to oppose and detach him, but he held on fast and, as though grown into one person with the youth, succeeded in bringing him into the presence of Hydaspes and the council. 'O King,' he said, 'this is the man who has abducted my daughter, who has made my house childless and desolate, and snatched her, my life and soul, from the sanctuary of the altars of Pythian Apollo; and now I find him seated, as one undefiled, by the altars of the gods!' All present were profoundly shocked by this proceeding, and all were astonished, some by what they could gather from his words, and the rest by the sight of his action.

(36) When Hydaspes bade him explain his meaning more clearly, the old man, who was in fact Charicles, concealed the real truth of Chariclea's kinship,* apprehending that he might possibly provoke the enmity of her true parents if she should have previously disappeared during her flight into the interior. He therefore curtailed his account to what could do no harm and said: 'I had a daughter, O King, and only by beholding her could you be convinced of the justice of my description of what she was in mind and in body. She was a virgin and a ministrant of Artemis at Delphi. This fine fellow, a native of Thessaly, had come to Delphi, my city, at the head of a sacred mission for the performance of some national solemnity. Unobserved he

abducted this girl from the very sanctuary, the sanctuary of Apollo. Thus he should in justice be deemed to have committed a sacrilege that affects you also; for he has profaned your national god, Apollo, who is the same as the Sun, and his temple. He had an accomplice in this abominable act, a certain false prophet of Memphis. I went in chase of him through Thessaly, and requested the people of Oeta, his fellow-citizens, to deliver him up, but nowhere could I find him; though they were ready enough to hand him over, even to be slain, wherever he might be found, as an accursed villain. I then guessed that the chief haunt of the fugitives was Memphis, to which city Calasiris belonged. I arrived there, and discovered that Calasiris, as he deserved, had died. From his son Thyamis I received full information about my daughter and, among other things, that she had been dispatched to Oroondates at Syene. I failed to find Oroondates at Syene; for I went on there, and was caught by the warfare at Elephantiné. So I have come here now, and I appeal to you in the terms set forth in that letter. You hold the robber; take up now the search for my daughter; and in doing a kindness to me, a long-suffering man, give yourself the satisfaction of showing your regard for the satrap who intercedes for us.'

(37) He said no more, only adding to his words a mournful lamentation. Hydaspes then asked Theagenes: 'What can you answer to that?' He replied: 'His accusations are all true. I have offended against him by robbery, rapine, violence and injustice; but to you I am a benefactor.' 'Then restore,' said Hydaspes, 'her who belongs to another. Since you are already dedicated to the gods, you shall suffer a slaughter glorified by the sacrifice, and not one of just retribution for wrongdoing.' 'But it is not the wrongdoer,' said Theagenes, 'but the holder of the wrongful spoil who should rightly restore it. You are yourself the holder of it: restore it, unless this man himself should acknowledge that Chariclea is your daughter.' The suspense was now more than anyone could bear; all at the same moment felt confounded. Sisimithres had restrained himself for some time: while he had all along been acquainted with what was being spoken and done, he was still waiting for the revelation from on high to come full circle. But now he ran to Charicles and enfolded him in his arms, saying: 'She is saved, you see, she whom since the day when you took her into your care from me you regarded as

your daughter; but she is in truth the daughter, as has been discovered, of parents that you know.'

The evidence of Chariclea and Sisimithres convinces Hydaspes of the divinely ordained betrothal of Theagenes and Chariclea.

(38) Upon this Chariclea ran out of the tent and, casting aside all the reserve belonging to her sex and age, rushed in a kind of bacchic frenzy to Charicles and fell down at his knees, saying: 'Father, whom I reverence no less than my true parents, punish me as you will; I am a guilty wretch who struck down my father! Even though deeds in the past might be ascribed to the design or ordinance of the gods, pay no heed to that.' Persinna, where she stood apart, embraced Hydaspes, saying: 'It is all as she states, husband; do not doubt it. This Greek youth, be assured, is affianced to our dear daughter, for she has just now, though with some reluctance, told me all.' The people on their part exulted with shouts of congratulation; persons of every age and condition rejoiced in unison over the turn of events. Most of what was being said they could not comprehend; but they conjectured the facts from what had previously transpired concerning Chariclea; or it might be that they were led to surmise the truth by the influence of some divine power that had designed the whole of this dramatic scene, and by whose means extreme contraries were now composed into a harmony. Joy and grief were intertwined, tears were mingled with laughter, and the most baleful proceedings were converted into festivity. Laughing while they wept, rejoicing as they lamented, finding those whom they were not seeking, and losing those whom they thought to have found – in fine, they saw the expected slayings transformed into holy sacraments.

(39) Hydaspes then inquired of Sisimithres: 'What is to be done, my wise friend? To deny the gods their sacrifice is impious; to slaughter those whom they have bestowed on us is unholy: we must devise what course we are to take.' Sisimithres replied, not in Greek, but in Ethiopian, so as to be understood by everyone: 'O King, excess of joy, it would seem, beclouds the minds of even the most sagacious of men. Thus you should long ere now have concluded that the gods do not welcome this sacrifice that is being prepared for them. At this moment, as the most blessed Chariclea stood by the very altar, they have

manifested her to be your daughter, and have sent up here from the depths of Greece her foster-father, as though dropped from the sky; and again, they struck the horses and the bulls held ready at the altars with that alarm and disorder, by which they meant to intimate that what is regarded as the crowning ritual was to be interrupted. And now, to consummate their beneficence and, as it were, bring the drama to a joyous climax,* they have produced this foreign youth here as the betrothed of the maiden. Come, let us recognize the divine miracle that has been wrought, and become collaborators in the gods' design. Let us proceed to the holier oblations, and exclude human sacrifice for all future time.'

Theagenes and Chariclea are married and invested with the insignia of the priesthood, and proceed amid popular acclamation to the celebration of their marriage in Meroë.

(40) When Sisimithres had delivered this speech in loud, clear tones that were audible to all, Hydaspes, himself now also speaking in the language of the country, and laying hold of Chariclea and Theagenes, said: 'And therefore to all present I say that, since these events have been thus brought about by the direction of the gods, it would be criminal to run counter to their will. Calling as witnesses, then, the very powers who have thus ordained, and you who are evidently disposed to comply with their behests, I declare this couple to be duly joined in matrimony, and I sanction their union under the ordinance for the begetting of children. And, if you think fit, let this decision be confirmed by sacrifice, and so let us proceed with the sacred rites.'

(41) His speech was greeted with a chorus of approval from the army, and with hand-clapping in loud applause, as though the marriage were already being celebrated. Hydaspes then moved up to the altars, and before beginning the sacrifice he said: 'O Sun, our Lord, and O Moon, our Lady, if indeed it has been by your design that Theagenes and Chariclea have been declared man and wife, it follows that they are fitted to render you priestly service.' With these words he removed his mitre and that of Persinna, the insignia of their priesthood, and set his upon Theagenes' head and Persinna's upon that of Chariclea. As soon as this was done Charicles called to mind the oracle at

Delphi, and recognized that the divine prediction of long ago was being fulfilled in actual fact. For it had stated that the young pair, after fleeing from Delphi,

> 'Shall arrive at the swarthy land of the Sun.
> There they shall win and wear about their temples, as the noble prize of virtuous lives,
> A white coronal from darkling brows.'

Thus crowned with the white mitres, they were invested with all the priestly insignia, and themselves performed a propitious sacrifice. Then, with torches lit and tuneful fluting and piping they were all escorted to the city – Theagenes with Hydaspes on a horse-drawn chariot, Sisimithres and Charicles on another, and Chariclea and Persinna on a car drawn by white bulls. And so, amid congratulations, plaudits and dances the procession passed on to Meroë, where the city was to be gladdened by the more splendid celebration of the holier marriage rites.

This is the conclusion of the Ethiopian Story of Theagenes and Chariclea, composed by a Phoenician of Emesa, of the line of the descendants of Helios (the Sun), namely Heliodorus, son of Theodosius.

NOTES

Book 1

p. 5 **sudden movement:** an allusion to the *Iliad* 1. 46–7.

p. 5 **deity of that country:** the bow and quiver suggest Artemis, goddess of hunting and chastity, while the pose recalls that of Isis tending the dead Osiris. The divine analogues hint at the girl's purity and devotion.

p. 5 **phantoms of the fallen:** ancient ghosts had black faces.

p. 7 **Herdsmen's Home:** in Greek *Boukolia*. These Herdsmen or *Boukoloi* are attested by classical sources, especially in relation to an uprising against the Romans in 172.

p. 7 **by the hand:** the details are taken from Herodotus 5.16.

p. 9 **the first watch:** the first of three periods taken in turn by Greek sentries during the night.

p. 10 **say in tragedy:** the quotation is from Euripides' *Medea* (1317).

p. 10 **member of the Senate:** the Areopagus Council, composed of all former chief magistrates.

p. 11 **Panathenaean Festival:** celebrated every four years. The centre point was a procession to the Acropolis to take a robe to the cult statue of Athena. This robe was conveyed through the street hoisted on the mast of a wheeled ship.

p. 11 **young Hippolytus:** son of Theseus, was the object of his stepmother Phaedra's infatuation. She killed herself after being rebuffed by him, and left a note accusing him of attempted rape. Theseus in ignorance of the truth cursed his son, and so caused his death.

p. 12 **looked upon as a stepmother:** stepmothers are proverbially hostile to the children of their husband's first marriage.

p. 14 **bespattered with ashes:** to arouse pity.

p. 14 the death-pit: a gully on the western cliff of the Acropolis where offenders against the state were thrown to their death. Stoning was never an official penalty in Athens.

p. 15 as Hesiod says: actually the sentiment comes from Aratus' *Phaenomena* (96ff); Hesiod (*Works and Days* 197ff) says that Shame and Retribution have returned to heaven.

p. 16 to quote the poem: Homer, *Iliad*, 6.202, of the exiled Bellerophon.

p. 18 the Epicureans' monument: Epicurus (d. 270 BC) established his school of philosophy in a garden on the road to the Academy just outside the walls of Athens. The detail is anachronistic.

p. 19 to the heroes: the polemarch ('King of Arms'), the third ranking of the Athenian annual magistrates, made yearly offerings to the tyrannicides Harmodius and Aristogiton, who were buried in the Academy.

p. 22 woman to be silent: almost a proverb; compare Sophocles *Ajax* 293.

p. 23 Ephesian parents: Ephesus, a wealthy city in Asia Minor, was the site of the famous Temple of Artemis (Diana of the Ephesians), one of the Seven Wonders of the World.

p. 23 mission to Delos: Delos was the mythical birthplace of the twins Apollo and Artemis, in whose honour an annual festival was held there.

p. 23 slew and were slain: quoting Homer, *Iliad*, 4.451, 8.65

p. 27 shall be our concern: quoting Homer, *Iliad*, 6.492, Hector's last words to his wife.

p. 29 killing and being killed: alluding to Homer, *Iliad*, 4.451, 8.65.

p. 30 all beloved beings: 'Why should I not, had I the heart to do it/ Like to the Egyptian thief at point of death,/ kill what I love?' (Shakespeare, *Twelfth Night* 5.1.121ff).

Book 2

p. 33 strange bridal torches: on the evening of her wedding day a bride was escorted to her husband's house with a torchlight procession.

p.360 by the infernal shades: until the body was buried the soul could not find peace in the underworld.

p. 38 stage-machine: the *mechane*, a sort of crane used in the tragic theatre to stage the miraculous appearance of a god (*deus ex machina*).

p. 38 Naucratis: a colony of Miletus which was the sole permitted channel of Greek trade in Egypt.

p. 38 their proper position: recalling the story of how Athena threw away her pipes after seeing a reflection of her distorted face.

p. 38 put to the torture: regular practice. Slaves were presumed to be liars unless the truth could be tortured out of them.

p. 39 leaves of the tablet: a writing tablet was made of two pieces of wood coated in wax, and hinged together so that they could be closed to protect what was written in the wax.

p. 41 sanctuary of Pytho might: Pytho is a poetic name for Delphi where Apollo was said to have killed the monstrous serpent Python.

p. 42 clasping the knees: a gesture of formal supplication.

p. 44 perception of the visible world: identical reasoning and interpretation of a dream of losing the right eye are found in Artemidorus' book of dream interpretation (*Onirocritica*, 1.26). The decoding of dreams was a highly developed skill.

p. 44 tripod of your oracle: the Delphic priestess delivered her oracles while seated on a tripod sacred to Apollo.

p. 46 falchions and cauldrons: alluding to, and reversing, Homer's *Odyssey* (17.222), where Odysseus, disguised as a beggar, is described as begging only for scraps, not swords and cauldrons. Cnemon means that, despite their disguise, Chariclea and Theagenes are too beautiful and noble to pass for beggars.

p. 47 wolves or jackals: alluding to Homer, *Iliad*, 16.156ff, 11.474ff.

p. 48 not inappropriate to his character: according to Aelian, there was a variety of viper called *thermouthis* by the Egyptians, whose bite was fatal only to the wicked.

p. 49 summon me from Troy: quoting the words with which Odysseus begins his long retrospective narrative in the *Odyssey* (9.39).

p. 49 in the legend: Midas, king of Phrygia, was given ass's ears by

Apollo after he judged Pan the winner in a musical contest. The ears were known only to the royal barber, who could not contain himself and whispered his secret into a hole in the ground. But the reeds that grew up there whispered the story whenever the wind blew through them; see Ovid, *Metamorphoses*, 11.153ff.

p. 50 **a mother's laments:** inspired by Moschus' poem *Megara* (21ff). The image derives ultimately from Homer, *Iliad*, 2.311ff.

p. 50 **admirably called 'baneful':** quoting Homer, *Odyssey*, 17.287; similar sentiments also at *Iliad*, 19.155ff, 19.216ff, *Odyssey*, 7.215ff.

p. 52 **abode in me:** Dionysus was god of wine, and Cnemon has had a drink. Dionysus was also the patron of the Athenian dramatic festivals, in which capacity he delighted in tales.

p. 52 **the Great King:** i.e. the King of Persia. Egypt became part of the Persian Empire when it was conquered by Cambyses in 525 BC. Like other provinces it was governed by a satrap, or viceroy.

p. 53 **nothing to do with Dionysus:** a proverbial description of irrelevancies. In the word 'trundled' Heliodorus alludes to another device of the tragic stage, the *ekkyklema*, a sort of trolley used to show interior scenes.

p. 53 **Proteus of Pharos:** a sea-god with the power of changing form. In the *Odyssey* (4.383ff), Menelaus can only make him speak the truth by holding on tight through all his transformations.

p. 53 **Calasiris:** according to Herodotus, *calasiris* was an Egyptian word referring to a long robe of fine linen, and also to one class of warriors.

p. 53 **eye of Cronos:** Cronos, the father of Zeus, was identified with the planet Saturn, considered by astrologers to have a malign influence.

p. 53 **Rhodopis;** a famous courtesan, whose story is told by Herodotus (2.134-5). In fact she lived fifty years before the Persian occupation of Egypt.

p. 54 **Great Thebes:** an important and famous city on the Nile.

p. 55 **oversee the ceremonies:** he was a member of the Amphictyonic Council, made up of representatives from different states, and responsible for administering the shrine at Delphi and the Pythian Games which were held there every four years.

p. 56 Lycurgus of Sparta: the semi-mythical law-giver of Sparta, whose greeting by the oracle is recorded by Herodotus (1.65).

p. 56 subterranean mazes: the so-called labyrinths, in fact the burial vaults of the Pharaohs.

p. 56 in the summer season: the peculiar behaviour of the Nile was a source of perpetual fascination to Greek thinkers. The 'monsoons' or Etesian Winds blow from the northwest in summer.

p. 57 high repute in Greece have held: this theory was propounded most notably by Anaxagoras and Democritus.

p. 57 Catadoupa: this strictly denotes the first cataract in the Nile, near Aswan. Heliodorus is the only writer to use it as the name of a town, obviously in error.

p. 57 kindled her funeral pyre: the story of the bride who dies on her wedding day is a common one, and is the subject of a series of epigrams in Book 7 of the Greek Anthology. It was standard to play on the use of torches in both weddings and funerals.

p. 59 Naked Sages: or Gymnosophists. These wise men were usually supposed to live in India. In locating them in Ethiopia, Heliodorus is following the lead of Philostratus' *Life of Apollonius of Tyana.*

p. 61 the emerald mines: these really exist, in the mountains to the east of the Nile on the border between Egypt and Ethiopia.

p. 61 some thriving plant: alluding to Thetis' description of her son Achilles in the *Iliad* (18.437).

p. 62 Egyptian lore and enchantment: the Greeks regarded Egyptians as specialists in magic, of both black and white types.

p. 62 son of Deucalion: the Greeks called themselves *Hellenes*, but in Homer that name is applied to a tribe in southern Thessaly. In identifying themselves with them, the Aenianes are claiming to be the Greekest of the Greeks. Hellen was invented later to explain the name. Deucalion is the Greek mythological version of Noah, sole survivor of a great flood.

p. 62 below Mount Oeta: the explanation depends on untranslatable puns. One opinion derives the name of Hypata from the Greek verb *hypateuein*, to rule; the other from the words *hyp'Oitei*, beneath Oeta.

p. 63 son of Agamemnon: Heliodorus follows the version of Neopto-lemus' death given by Euripides in the *Andromache*. Orestes was in part taking vengeance on Neoptolemus for marrying his fiancée, Hermione, and in part punishing him for mistreating Hermione after their marriage.

p. 63 fictitiously appropriated him: in the *Iliad* Achilles comes from Phthia. This name was applied in classical times to the area around Pharsalus in Thessaly, but the claim here is that in Homer it refers to a different area, which thus has a more legitimate claim on the hero.

p. 63 the Aeacidae: the descendants of Aeacus, Achilles' grandfather. The genealogy of Menesthius is taken from Homer, *Iliad*, 16.173ff.

p. 63 neck was held erect: many of the details of this description are also found in a picture of Achilles by Philostratus (*Heroicus* 19.5). It is possible that both writers had a well-known statue or painting in mind.

p. 64 the Goddess-born: these lines reveal their meaning through untranslatable word-play with the heroes' names. Chariclea's name is a compound of *charis* (grace) and *kleos* (glory). Theagenes is made up of *thea* (goddess) and the ending –*genes* (born from).

Book 3

p. 65 your Attic character: the importance the Athenians attached to their dramatic festivals led to a reputation as a nation of spectators.

p. 65 true sense of the term: etymologically 'hecatomb' derives from *hekaton* (hundred) and *bous* (ox).

p. 65 low in the waist: a Homeric formula; see *Iliad* 9.594,

p. 66 prompting of Zeus: Zeus wanted the sea-nymph Thetis for himself, but was warned that the son she bore would be more powerful than his father. He therefore married her to his favourite mortal, Peleus, whose felicity became proverbial.

p. 66 Lady of Paphos: i.e. for them Thetis takes the place of Aphrod-ite, who had a cult-site at Paphos in Cyprus.

p. 66 Pyrrha: she is introduced to explain Neoptolemus' alternative name, Pyrrhus. His mother is normally said to be Deidamia.

p. 66 earth of the Pythian: i.e. Apollo, god of Delphi.

p. 67 tipped with bronze: recalling Achilles' ash-wood spear in the *Iliad*.

p. 67 with the Centaurs: an appropriately Thessalian theme. The fight occurred when the Centaurs got drunk at the wedding of the Lapith king Pirithous at Larissa.

p. 68 tossed to him apples: the apple was the symbol of Aphrodite, and so signified desire.

p. 68 Homer would have said: a formulaic line which occurs more than twenty times in Homeric poems.

p. 68 ever to repeat it: the description echoes Homer, *Odyssey* 11.613.14, where Odysseus speaks of the baldric worn by the ghost of Heracles.

p. 69 especially Hermes: Hermes was the guide of dead souls, and so could prevent them returning to haunt the dreams of the living.

p. 70 recalling to memory: the idea that Love was a memory of beauty seen by the soul before birth comes from Plato (*Phaedrus* 249 d-e). This whole scene is full of Platonic connotations.

p. 72 works in this way: the following explanation and examples correspond closely – almost word for word in places – to a discussion in Plutarch's *Table Talk* (680c).

p. 72 the subject of animals: despite the claim to privileged sources, this continues with the material found in Plutarch.

p. 73 young men under arms: this dance is named as the *Pyrriche*, so called after Pyrrhus/Neoptolemus.

p. 75 not hard to discern: Homer, *Iliad*, 13.71–2.

p. 75 I have not comprehended: the Homeric poems were often subjected to allegorical reading in late antiquity to draw out concealed (and unintended) philosophy.

p. 76 eyes shone forth: Homer, *Iliad*, 1.200.

p. 76 I *easily* discerned: the wit of the point is rather lost in translation. Calasiris is reading the Homeric lines as if the adverb *rheia* (easily) goes with 'departed' rather than 'discerned'. This is grammatically possible, but unnatural. Further he is suggesting that the adverb *rheia* is etymologically connected with the verb *rhein* (to flow) and thus means 'flowingly'. Neither he nor Heliodorus intends this to be taken seriously.

p. 76 birthplace of the sage: the author of the Homeric epics was a mystery, and many Greek cities fielded competing claims to be Homer's birthplace. The idea that Homer was really an Egyptian was seriously canvassed.

p. 76 he himself tells us: Homer, *Iliad*, 9.383

p. 76 he received his name: untranslatable pun on *ho meros* (the thigh) and *Homeros* (Homer).

Book 4

p. 82 branch of palm: symbol of victory. Usually a wreath of laurel was given as prize in the Pythian Games, but it may be that Heliodorus wants to exploit the multiple meanings of the Greek word *phoinix*: a) 'palm'; b) 'phoenix', the bird of the sun, continually reborn; c) 'Phoenician', in which sense he applies the word to himself in the last sentence of the book.

p. 83 outrunning me in a race: Theagenes' ancestor and analogue, Achilles, is formulaically 'swift of foot' in the *Iliad*.

p. 83 at the River Scamander: Homer, *Iliad*, 21.203ff.

p. 83 Ormenus: literally 'speeding'.

p. 84 as with other things: Homer, *Iliad*, 636–7; 'there is satiety in all things, in sleep, and love-making,/ in the loveliness of singing and the innocent dance.'

p. 85 an old-womanish fashion: a typical folk-spell, apparently still practised. The magician (usually an old woman), draws the evil influence into herself and then yawns to dispel it.

p. 85 like that hero: compare Diomedes' judgement of Achilles in the *Iliad* (9.699).

p. 87 valiant of the Achaeans: she quotes Homer, *Iliad*, 16.21, where Patroclus explains to Achilles the dire results of his absence. Patroclus and Achilles were sometimes regarded as lovers.

p. 87 Akesinus: the name is coined from the verb *akeisthai* 'to heal'.

p. 88 malady is obviously love: this diagnosis of love as the cause of sickness is based on the historical story of the doctor Erasistratus who, in a remarkably similar way, diagnosed the love of the prince Antiochus for his stepmother Stratonice.

p. 89 the Gorgon's head: the head of the Gorgon Medusa, severed by Perseus, was so hideous that anyone who looked at it was turned to stone.

p. 89 writings of the Egyptians: Herodotus (2.36) says that the Egyptians had two scripts, the sacred (i.e. hieroglyphic) and the popular (demotic). The later historian Diodorus (3.3) adds that everyone in Ethiopia could read hieroglyphs. The Meroitic Ethiopians did in fact adapt Egyptian hieroglyphs to their own language.

p. 90 founder of our family, the Sun: according to the Greek historian Bion of Soli, the kings of Ethiopia claimed descent from the Sun.

p. 90 and also Memnon: Andromeda, daughter of king Cepheus of Ethiopia, married Perseus after he rescued her from a sea-monster. Memnon was the son of Eos (the Dawn) and Tithonus, and was king of Ethiopia. This is a relic of a mythical geography which located Ethiopia in far east, close to the rising sun whose heat was the cause of the black skins of its inhabitants.

p. 90 understood the cause: the theory of 'maternal impression' – that a foetus could be formed in the likeness of what the mother saw at the moment of conception, or during pregnancy – was widely accepted by ancient medical writers. Andromeda, although daughter of the Ethiopian king, is usually depicted as white-skinned.

p. 90 should preserve your life: unwanted children (often girls) were commonly exposed, either to die or be adopted by someone else. Objects were left with the child to reward anyone who rescued it, and to prove its identity. The unexpected recognition, by means of tokens and birthmarks, of abandoned children is a common plot format in New Comedy.

p. 91 a stone, pantarbe: an unidentified gemstone, red in colour. Various magical properties were ascribed to it. The name literally means 'all-fear'.

p. 94 adding to it the Ethiopian: Philostratus (*Life of Apollonius of Tyana*, 6.6) tells us that the Ethiopian sages were superior to those of Egypt, but inferior to their Indian counterparts.

p. 97 costliness of my offering: sarcastic. Calasiris is a vegetarian and water-drinker.

p. 97 Carthage in Libya: a trading colony founded by the Phoenicians of Tyre, with whom it retained close ties.

p. 97 the Tyrian Hercules: the Phoenician god Melkart was identified with Hercules.

p. 97 Cape Malea: the southeastern point of the Peloponnese, noted for treacherous winds. The Phoenicians were unable to make progress westwards across the open sea, and had hugged the coast of the Peloponnese, travelling northwards to the opening of the Gulf of Corinth, and thence to Delphi.

p. 99 Parnassus: the mountain above Delphi.

p. 100 the Loves: figures of Eros (Cupid), depicted as little children.

p. 101 even against divinity: Homer, *Iliad*, 17. 103–4, where Menelaus thinks of confronting Apollo, who is assisting his enemy, Hector.

p. 101 bespattered with ashes: Charicles is mourning, as if his daughter were dead.

p. 102 commandant Hegesias: the name is connected with *hegeisthai*, 'to lead'.

p. 102 on future occasions: as far as we know, in reality no priestess of Artemis officiated at the games. Heliodorus' story provides an incidental explanation for the omission.

Book 5

p. 106 woe in the spring time: Tereus, the king of Thrace, raped Philomela, the sister of his wife Procne, and then cut out her tongue. However, Procne discovered the truth and revenged herself on her husband by killing their son Itys. Eventually Procne (or in some versions Philomela) was transformed into a nightingale, which laments eternally for Itys.

p. 107 teeth chattered aloud: this echoes the description of a coward by Idomeneus in the *Iliad* (13.279ff), and the behaviour of the Trojan spy Dolon when cornered by Odysseus and Diomedes (*Iliad* 10.374ff).

p. 109 from a boar hunt: like Odysseus, whose nurse Euryclea recognizes him by such a scar. How he acquired it is narrated in a famous digression (*Odyssey*, 19.392ff).

p. 109 **who was his master:** Apollo, the archer god.

p. 113 **as though in a drama:** Aristotle identified the recognition scene (*anagnorisis*) as one of the most effective elements in a dramatic plot. This type of scene was often used to resolve the complicated plots of New Comedy.

p. 113 **to its full contentment:** alluding to Homer, *Odyssey*, 6.180

p. 114 **inspected the entrails:** the shape and colour of the internal organs of a sacrificial animal allowed a skilled interpreter to read the future.

p. 114 **Spain nor Britain:** neither Ethiopia nor Britain is attested as supplying these stones. The word used for Spain is *Iberia*, which was also applied to a quite different region, roughly corresponding to modern Georgia, where amethysts were in fact mined. Heliodorus has clearly confused the two Iberias.

p. 115 **sobriety in wine parties:** the Greek word *amethysos* literally means 'without drunkenness'.

p. 115 **glorious gifts of the gods:** quoting Homer, *Iliad* 3.65.

p. 116 **in its maiden state:** Nausicles is playing with the two senses of the word *nymphe:* a) a bride-to-be, or virgin; b) a nymph, often the goddess of a spring or river, and hence a poetic way of saying 'water'. Dionysus of course stands for wine.

p. 117 **the cult of Hermes:** Hermes was god of both trade and eloquence. Nausicles' merchant's ritual has thus become an occasion for telling stories under the same god's patronage.

p. 117 **strait of Calydon:** the narrow entrance to the Gulf of Corinth.

p. 1170 **the Crisaean Gulf:** strictly speaking this is the spur of the Gulf of Corinth running up to the port of Delphi. Heliodorus apparently uses it as a synonym for the whole Gulf of Corinth.

p. 118 **Pleiads had begun to set:** the cosmical setting, when the constellation goes beneath the horizon at sunrise. This occurs in Greece around the end of October, roughly coinciding with the onset of winter storms. Thus the setting of the Pleiades conventionally marked the end of navigation for the year.

p. 119 as the saying is: source unknown.

p. 120 as they say: the allusion is to Euripides, *Ion*, 927ff

p. 121 Trachinus: the name is derived from *trachys* 'rough, cruel'.

p. 122 he had been wounded: the description of this figure is stitched together from allusions which would have made his identity obvious to any educated reader. The withering of age refers to the disguise given by Athena (*Odyssey*, 13.398ff); the strong thigh is from *Odyssey*, 18.66ff; the leather helmet from *Iliad*, 10.261ff; the Homeric words for 'sagacious' and 'wily' from *Odyssey*, 13.332 and 1.1; the wound in the leg from *Odyssey* 19.392ff. The wife is Penelope who remained faithful throughout her husband's twenty-year absence.

p. 123 over to Ithaca: Odysseus' homeland, a small island close to Cephallenia.

p. 123 One of our rudders: ancient ships had two steering-oars.

p. 126 life above all else: alluding to Euripides, *Alcestis* 301.

p. 126 limbo betwixt day and night: the phrase is from Aeschylus, *Libation Bearers*. 64.

p. 129 from Sidon and Tyre: recalling Homer, *Iliad*, 6.289ff, which describes the robes which Paris had brought to Troy.

p. 130 Pelorus: his name means 'monstrous'.

p. 131 wage of all my labours: possibly quoted from an unknown tragedy; the Greek words are in poetic metre.

Book 6

p. 137 the merchant of Naucratis: Cnemon knows that this is none other than Nausicles; presumably he is tactfully avoiding causing embarrassment to his host.

p. 138 the Phoenix itself: untranslatable word-play. The word for 'flamingo' is *phoinikopteros* ('crimson-wing'), which suggests *phoinix*. The phoenix was supposed to appear in Egypt once every 500 years.

p. 140 laws of hospitality and friendship: this alludes to the words of Menelaus at *Odyssey*, 15.69ff.

p. 141 O Earth: Ge, the personification of earth, was regarded as a protector of oaths. Cnemon feels almost as if he is breaking a sworn promise.

p. 143 threw it on the bed: Chariclea's action has a double force: hair was often offered to the dead, but hair-offerings also formed part of the marriage rite.

p. 148 clean sweep of the village: a Persian technique described by Herodotus (6.31): soldiers linked arms and moved across the terrain like a net, hunting everyone down.

p. 148 hands of the Persians: Persian punishments were protracted and cruel.

p. 149 a libation of wine: many of these details are taken from the scene in the *Odyssey* (11.24ff) where Odysseus summons the spirits of the dead.

p. 150 ground among corpses: this recalls the distinction made by Calasiris in Book 3.16.

p. 151 utmost borders of the earth: a fragment of verse, from an unknown tragedy.

Book 7

p. 152 his wife Arsace: a typical Persian name, recalling the founder of the Arsacid dynasty.

p. 154 displayed a caduceus: a herald's staff, like that carried by Hermes, the herald of the gods.

p. 156 quaking with fear: this re-enacts the scene from the *Odyssey* (18.75ff) where the suitors force the beggar Irus to fight the disguised Odysseus.

p. 157 sped round the walls: this pursuit is intended to recall that of Hector by Achilles around the walls of Troy (Homer, *Iliad*, 22.199ff). The single combat between brothers is modelled on that between Eteocles and Polynices, sons of Oedipus, over the throne of Thebes.

p. 157 appraising the spectacle below: the crowd is like the panel of judges, who awarded prizes in the annual dramatic festivals at Athens.

p. 161 without giving any order: insomnia is a conventional symptom of love. Heliodorus has in mind particularly Homer's picture of Achilles' sleepless grief for Patroclus (*Iliad*, 24.4ff).

p. 161 my precious child: as Arsace's wet-nurse Cybele retains a special intimacy with her. Her role is modelled on that of Phaedra's nurse in Euripides' *Hippolytus*.

p. 162 golden ornament of down: young men were thought particularly atractive at the time when their first beard was growing.

p. 162 in exchange for bronze: in the *Iliad* (6.234ff) Glaucus exchanges his gold weapons for the bronze of Diomedes, because Zeus 'stole away his wits'. The exchange became proverbial.

p. 164 gladness and felicitation: quoted from Euripides' lost play *Cresphontes*.

p. 165 citizen of Lesbos: the island of Lesbos was associated with exotic sexual practices and promiscuity.

p. 167 your son Achaemenes: another typical name, recalling the founder of the Achaemenid dynasty.

p. 170 do homage to Arsace: Persians prostrated themselves before their rulers, whereas the Greeks reserved this gesture of respect for the gods. Thus prostration came to symbolise for them the subservience of the Persians, paying divine honour to a mortal man. Conversely, refusal to prostrate oneself was, for a Greek, an assertion of freedom and dignity.

p. 172 of Ionian race: i.e. Greeks from the coastal cities of Asia Minor.

p. 174 as the saying is: apparently quoted from an unknown source. The idea that the sun heard and saw everything was commonplace.

p. 178 swaggering of late so haughtily: quoted from Menander's play *The Shorn Woman* (72 Sandbach).

p. 178 as they say: the source of this quotation is unknown.

p. 181 duties of the wine-servers: the art of wine-waiting was highly developed at the Persian court. Compare Xenophon, *The Education of Cyrus*, 1.3.8: 'And, indeed, these royal cup-bearers are neat-handed at their task, mixing the bowl with infinite elegance, and pouring the wine into the beakers without spilling a drop, and when they hand the goblet they poise it deftly between thumb and finger for the banqueter to take.'

p. 181 an artful toast to Theagenes: a normal toast consisted of drinking from a cup and then passing it, with appropriate words, to the other person, who then drank from it also. By leaving wine in her cup Arsace is able to pass the toast on to the wine-waiter.

Book 8

p. 184 Philae lies on the Nile: actually it is an island in the Nile.

p. 184 taken by force of arms: this is largely fiction. The Egyptian exiles are possibly intended to remind the reader of the 'Deserters' mentioned by Herodotus (2.30), who migrated to Ethiopia in the reign of Psammetichus.

p. 186 he summoned Bagoas: this is the archetypal eunuch name borne by several historical Persian eunuchs.

p. 191 our last anchor, as they say: a proverb for a last desperate effort. Greek ships carried several anchors, the last of which would be used only when all else had failed.

p. 198 the subterranean region: both Ethiopia and the Underworld were inhabited by beings with black faces.

p. 198 the maiden Persephone: daughter of Demeter, abducted by Hades to be queen of the dead. Persephone was also known as *Kore* 'Maiden', which is the very word used in the first line of Theagenes' dream-oracle. His interpretation is not without its logic.

p. 202 Persian trees: a tree with succulent fruit like pears. The Egyptians regarded it as holy. This and the sycamore were regarded as characteristic of the Egyptian landscape.

p. 202 in a strangling noose: quoted from Euripides' *Hippolytus* (802), where the chorus breaks the news of Phaedra's suicide to her husband Theseus.

p. 203 most of which he mispronounced: in fact the Greek which Heliodorus puts in Bagoas' mouth is perfectly correct.

p. 204 The Troglodytes: the name was mainly applied to a primitive people living on the coast south of Egypt. Many fantastic stories collected around them. Their fleetness of foot is first mentioned by Herodotus (4.183).

p. 206 placed his trust in them: this is taken from Xenophon's *Edu-*

cation of Cyrus (7.5.60): 'He knew that men with children, or wives, or favourites in whom they delight, must needs love them most: while eunuchs are deprived of all such dear ones . . . the eunuch would be the most faithful of servants.'

p. 206 prologue and prelude of a drama: Heliodorus uses obscure but apparently authentic technical vocabulary. The reference appears to be to some preliminary announcement and parade by the actors. The point lies in the sudden change of status and identity an actor undergoes the moment the play begins.

Book 9

p. 208 served by iron: the wealth of Ethiopia was legendary. Herodotus (3.23) records that prisoners were bound with gold chains.

p. 208 iron for gold: see note on p. 162.

p. 209 that of Long Walls: walls linking a city to the sea. The most famous were those connecting Athens to the port of Piraeus.

p. 209 to an inferior level: the Nile was embanked to control its summer flood, so that the surface of the water was higher than the surrounding country.

p. 212 in the East and in the West: archaic belief placed Ethiopians in the areas of the earth closest to the sun, where it rises and sets; compare Homer, *Odyssey*, 1.22.

p. 215 about the summer solstice: i.e. 21 June. This coincidence of the solstice with the first rise in the level of the Nile was widely remarked.

p. 215 regularly watering the soil: much of this paragraph is taken word for word from a polemical passage in *The Life of Moses* by Philo, a hellenized Alexandrian Jew. It is interesting that Heliodorus knew this author. The comparison of the Nile flood to rain is commonplace.

p. 215 Typhon as a hostile power: Typhon (or Seth) killed and dismembered Osiris, who was reassembled and revived by Isis. In this allegorical interpretation, Typhon is identified with the drought of the desert.

p. 215 flaming torch of reality: the ceremonies and processions of the Isis cult were accompanied with flaming torches.

p. 215 respect of strict silence: the Greeks assimilated the cult of Isis to their own initiation or mystery religions, whose secret truths could only be divulged to initiates. This pose of reverent silence imitates Herodotus' treatment of Egyptian religion. Nothing that Heliodorus says suggests that he had intimate knowledge of the Isis religion, one of Christianity's most significant competitors.

p. 219 furnished in this way: the description that follows is based on the eastern armoured cavalry introduced into the Roman army by Alexander Severus. It has many points of contact with similar descriptions in other writers of the third and fourth centuries.

p. 220 wrought with the hammer: i.e. not cast in a mould as most metal statues, but made by beating metal sheets over wooden shapes. The plates of the riders' mail look like the indentations left by the hammer.

p. 220 the cinnamon-bearing country: the Horn of Africa. The general belief was that cinnamon originated here, although it was actually imported from further east.

p. 220 Blemmyes and Seres: the Blemmyes were nomads ranging to the south of Egypt, who posed an increasing threat to the border in the third and fourth centuries. Like the Troglodytes, they attracted fabulous stories, and were often supposed to have no heads. The Seres are Chinese, another legendarily exotic nation. They were known to the Greeks and Romans mainly as producers of silk. Their presence in the Ethiopian army is due perhaps to the archaic tradition of eastern Ethiopians.

p. 222 descending upon them: alluding to Herodotus' account of the Battle of Thermopylae, where the Persian arrows were so numerous that they hid the sun.

p. 222 like double flutes: the Greek flute, or *aulos*, consisted of two pipes, held at an angle to each other and played simultaneously, one for the melody, the other for a drone bass.

p. 222 of a Nisaean: the horses of the Nisaean plain, to the south of the Caspian sea, were the finest known to the Greeks. The flight of Oroondates from the battlefield is modelled on that of Darius after his defeat by Alexander the Great at Gaugamela.

p. 223 pointed with iron: this description is verbally very close to a passage of Lucian's *On Dancing* (18), with which it probably shares a source. Ethiopian archers of exactly this type are depicted on the frieze of the Arch of Constantine in Rome.

p. 223 Greek word for bone: Heliodorus is trying to draw an etymological connection between the words *oistos* (arrow) and *osteon* (bone). This is apparently his own idea.

p. 225 level of high or low water: devices like this were essential in Egypt, whose agriculture depended entirely on the annual inundation of the river. Heliodorus' description is very close to the geographer Strabo's account of the Nilometer at Elephantine (17.1.48). They probably have a common source.

p. 225 for the same reason: Syene lay almost exactly on the Tropic of Cancer. On the day of the summer solstice – when this section of the novel is set – the sun is directly overhead. The shadowless sundial and illuminated well are well–attested tourist attractions.

p. 225 Father and Creator: Horus was the son of Isis, born after his father Osiris was killed by Seth/Typhon. He is called Saviour of Upper (i.e. southern) Egypt because the Nile provides the only water in that region, and Father and Creator of Lower (i.e. northern) Egypt because it was widely believed that the whole area was the product of the alluvium deposited by the river

p. 225 derives the name of Nile: the point is lost in translation. Heliodorus is arguing that the name *Neilos* (Nile) is a contracted form of *nea ilys* (fresh silt). This idea is quite fanciful, of course, but was not confined to novelists.

p. 226 equal to the days in the year: the letters of the Greek alphabet did double duty as numerals. If the letters of the word *Neilos* are taken as numbers and totalled, the result is indeed 365. If the same is done with Chariclea's name, the figure produced is 777, a mystic number; is this a coincidence?

p. 226 also droves of pigs: the list echoes Homer, *Iliad*, 11. 678–9.

p. 230 left with his right: a symbolic invitation to bind his hands, an authentic gesture of submission.

Book 10

p. 231 meadows fronting the city: this alludes to Herodotus' account of the so-called Table of the Sun, a meadow outside Meroë, where an abundance of sacrificial meats was perpetually replenished.

p. 232 temple of Pan: Heliodorus nowhere else mentions a cult of Pan in Ethiopia, though there was a Greek tradition that he was worshipped there. Although the randy half-goat god seems rather out of place in the purity of Ethiopia, it may be that Heliodorus had in mind the philosophical identification of Pan with *to pan* (the All).

p. 233 **capital of Ethiopia:** Meroë was the historical centre of the powerful Ethiopian kingdom. Its remains are in Sudan, just south of the confluence of the Nile and the Atbara. The area bounded by the Atbara, the Nile and the Blue Nile is known as the Island of Meroë. Many classical writers, however, conceived of it literally as a huge island in the Nile. Heliodorus' description is wildly inaccurate, but very much in line with Greek and Roman belief, especially in its emphasis on the area's remarkable fertility.

p. 233 **and the Asasobas:** these names are authentic enough, but classical writers could not agree on their application.

p. 233 **a thousand in breadth:** these measurements are taken from a source used also by Diodorus and Strabo; these two writers, however, describe the island as 'shield-shaped' rather than triangular.

p. 235 **to the swiftest god:** this alludes to Herodotus on the sun-worshipping Massagetae (1.216).

p. 236 **without taking harm:** because only in pre-adolescent children could sexual purity be taken for granted.

p. 238 **withdraw into the temple:** this is based on an episode in Philostratus' *Life of Apollonius of Tyana*, where Apollonius withdraws from a sacrifice after offering incense.

p. 243 **smirching the ivory of its skin:** recalling Homer, *Iliad* 4.141, where Menelaus' blood-stained leg is likened to stained ivory.

p. 243 **of horn or iron:** alluding to Homer, *Odyssey*, 19.209ff, where the disguised Odysseus suppresses his compassion for his wife as she mourns for her lost husband.

p. 244 **a mighty cry to the heavens:** the phrase is a Homeric formula; see *Iliad*, 8.159, etc.

p. 245 **perturb my heart with wailing:** quoting Achilles' reply, to the appeals of Phoenix at Homer, *Iliad*, 9.612.

p. 249 **Hermonias:** the name is derived from *hermeneuein* 'to interpret'.

p. 249 you utterly stupid fool: this is based on a scene in the *Odyssey* (4.30ff) where Menelaus abuses his steward for not immediately admitting Telemachus.

p. 251 cobwebs of their country; i.e. silk.

p. 251 with which Arabia abounds: Arabia Felix (Fortunate Arabia) corresponds to modern Aden. The inhabitants of this area were the middle-men in the importation of spices from the far east, but most Greeks and Romans believed that the spices were produced in Arabia. It may be that Heliodorus identifies these Arabs with the people from the cinnamon-bearing country, who fought in Hydaspes' army but are otherwise missing from the victory celebrations.

p. 251 gold from ant-hills: gold was supposedly found in the dust ejected from the ant heaps of a kind of giant ant found in India; see Herodotus 3.102. In removing the ants to Ethiopia, Heliodorus is once again following the lead of Philostratus' *Life of Apollonius of Tyana*.

p. 251 a pair of griffins: griffins were originally thought of as the guardians of the gold of the Hyperboreans in the far north. As time passed, however, the gold-guarding griffins were confused with the gold-digging ants, and accordingly relocated.

p. 251 envoys of the Auxomites: the people of Axum, a city in the mountains of Ethiopia. Though insignificant at the dramatic date of the novel, this city was of great importance in Heliodorus' day and had quite eclipsed the older power of Meroë. The special status accorded the Auxomites may reflect these contemporary circumstances.

p. 252 'camelopard': *kamelopardalis* (camel-leopard) was the normal Greek word for 'giraffe'.

p. 254 wild anguish of its defeat: this sport of bull-throwing (*tauro-kathapsia*) was particularly practised in Thessaly, which, of course, is Theagenes' home. It is interesting that biographical tradition links Heliodorus himself with the area. His description is well informed.

p. 256 belly on the ground: this is a textbook wrestling manoeuvre, the *klimakismos* or 'ladder-hold'.

p. 259 about Theagenes' neck: this gesture is an attested form of citizen's arrest. The old man's words also echo a legal formula of arrest.

p. 259 real truth of Chariclea's kinship: how Charicles learned the truth about his adopted daughter's real identity is one of the novel's untied loose ends.

p. 262 to a joyous climax: literally 'like a little torch of a drama', a phrase which has never been satisfactorily explained.

HELIODORUS AND THE CRITICS

The following extracts present a series of snapshots from over a thousand years of criticism. We begin with the three earliest extant discussions of the novel, which are particularly valuable since the Byzantine intellectual culture in which they were produced was in many ways a continuation of late antiquity. The popularity of the *Ethiopian Story* in Byzantium was no doubt due partly to the belief that its author was a Christian.

Photius, *Bibliotheca* cod. 73: (trans. N. G. Wilson, Duckworth 1994, p. 78).

In the ninth century, the patriarch Photius ran a reading circle, whose members contributed summaries of and comments on works they had read. Most of the entry on Heliodorus is taken up by a rather incompetent synopsis, which irons out the chronological complexities of the novel. The commentary is largely confined to Heliodorus' prose style, but contains some judgements which are surprising to a modern reader.

> Read Heliodorus' *Ethiopian Story*. The work is a novel, employing a style suitable for the subject-matter, abundantly simple and pleasant. The narrative is embellished by adventures being experienced or anticipated, also by the unexpected and by incredible salvation from disasters, all expressed in limpid and pure diction. In places, as is natural, the author is unduly prone to use words tending to the figurative; but they are clear and describe events plainly. The periods are of reasonable length or indeed rather short, one might say compressed. The composition and other features suit the narrative.

Michael Psellus, *What is the difference between the novels which deal with Chariclea and Leucippe?* (trans. A. R. Dyck, Vienna 1986).

In the eleventh century, Michael Psellus wrote a comparison between the novels of Heliodorus and Achilles. His preferences lie with Heliodorus, but the defensive tone of his discussion suggests that the novel was coming under criticism on moral grounds. After some comments on style, Psellus homes in on Heliodorus' structural complexities.

At the beginning the reader fancies that most elements are superfluous, but as the narrative progresses, he comes to admire the author's organisation. The beginning of the work itself resembles a coiled snake: the snake conceals its head inside the coils and thrusts the rest of its body forward; so the book makes a beginning of its middle, and the onset of the story, which it has, so to speak, inherited, slips through to end up in the middle . . .

But as for the point which, I know, a great many persons find fault with, namely the fact that the author cannot get Chariclea's speech to sound womanly or feminine, but, contrary to the art, her language has been raised to a more sophistic tone – I myself do not know how to praise this adequately. The author has not introduced a character like ordinary girls, but an initiate and one who comes from Pythian Apollo; hence most of her lamentations contain oracles. She is inspired in the manner of mad prophetesses and is wholly the offspring of the tripod's cauldron. Moreover, the author does not deviate from the probable in the rest of his characterisations. As for the unseemly elements of his plot, which could not be concealed, our author, by the decency of his narration, has made them good in the telling rather than bad in the acting. For instance, he even relieves the old man Calasiris of the blame for pandering, a thing scarcely credible until our author by his varied artistry thrust aside the apparent responsibility. Still more remarkable that in a novel so moist and well irrigated he preserved the firm and, as it were, stubborn quality of chastity; and when he had once drawn Chariclea's soul down to love, he protected it from ordinary lust, and even in defeat she did not divest herself of orderly behaviour.

I notice that the work also attains to great learning: matter drawn from the physical sciences is introduced; there are maxims, theological reflections and even some mention of the moving sphere, nor is the book far removed from the fates that arise from it. Witness the will of Cronos, which Calasiris was eager to escape through certain secret incantations . . . The book takes thought for its reader by relieving him by its variety and by the novelty of its diction, by episodes and various turns of events. It contains maxims as fine as any book I have come upon. To put it in a nutshell, one could find no other work which possesses pleasure blended so beautifully and gracefully with nobility.

The most interesting of these readings comes to us under the name of 'Philip the Philosopher'. The author has been tentatively identified as Philip Philagathus, a native of south Italy and archbishop of Rossano from 1130–54, though it has also been argued that the essay dates from as early as the sixth century. Set in a narrative frame like a Platonic dialogue, the essay *Commentatio in Charicleam* begins by drawing out some moral lessons from the story,[1] and then launches into an elaborate neoplatonic allegory, partly based on wordplay with the characters' names. This was an established way of reading literary texts in late antiquity.

Chariclea is a symbol of the soul and the intellect which directs it. For intellect combined with soul is Glory (*kleos*) and Grace (*charis*). This is not the only reason why her name is compounded, but also because soul is compounded with body, becoming one substance with it. You may see this more clearly if you reckon up the units of her name, which total seven hundred and seventy-seven. Since the number seven is mystic, virgin and revered (*septos*) among numbers, as the Latin language translates it[2], her name has not unreasonably maintained the significance of seven in its hundreds, tens and units, through the seven hundreds signifying the reverend and perfect, through the seven tens adorning the tripartite quality of the soul with the four cardinal virtues (for four tens added to the three make up the seventy). The simple seven expresses the body, to which intellect is conjoined, which possesses five senses through the mediation of the soul, plus the matter and form from which it is made. Chariclea is born of Ethiopians: Man comes from obscurity, as from darkness into the light, and is brought into the earthly life as into Greece. Charicles who brings her up is the practical life, teaching her to slay the passions with her arrows,

[1] This section is translated by N. G. Wilson, *Scholars of Byzantium* (Duckworth 1983) 216–17.

[2] The author affects to see a connection between Latin *septem* (seven) and Greek *septos* (reverend).

and to be a servant of courage and chastity as of Artemis; for Artemis is archeress and virgin. Do not be alarmed if these two have a name in common: for practical virtue is related to the soul itself, and introduces Grace (*charin*) and Glory (*kleos*) to it. But when she leaves the pair of bullocks which convey her and carrying a torch enters the shrine and beholds Theagenes (God-Born), she forgets all else and secretly embraces her beloved wholly in her soul. Understand what the riddle means. When the soul becomes superior to the material dyad, then the intellect of divine knowledge, which comes to us from outside ourselves and leads the soul upwards to sight of its origin (*pros thean tou genous*), is most beautiful in its sight, receiving the torch of desire and implanting in the soul the love of the high knowledge. The soul is filled by it, is possessed by this chaste intoxication, and becomes, so to speak, Love-smitten. It disdains its usual pursuits, neglects the body and focuses its thoughts solely on that which it loves. And being thus drawn upwards by its beloved, it is eager to recapture its first high-birth, and she who once was proud and rejected love, deserts and hurries over to Theagenes, and Artemis does not hinder the abduction but tolerates it, seeing that her acolyte has received a wound of love. The old man Calasiris escorts the bride, directing her in word and deed. He would be the teacher who draws us to the good (*pros ta kala syron*) and leads the soul upwards to the rites of divine knowledge. He will be a good counsellor in what has to be done, bringing the soul unbuffeted over the sea and billows of life. If Trachinus, the savage (*tracheia*) party of passions, attacks her, Calasiris' good counsel will protect her. But he will be the companion of her journey only until she passes the Egypt of ignorance; when she has advanced and escaped the sea and eluded the attacks of bandits, then her teacher will leave her, and the soul luxuriates alone in its beloved's company. Carnal (*sarkike*) pleasure, as Arsace, will attack, with perception, as Cybele, as its procuress which conceives the arrows (*kyousan ta bele*) of attack and shoots darts of argument and lures contemplation towards itself, so as to seduce the thoughts. Then let manly character be further tempered and cast into the furnace of temptation. The pantarbe will preserve her unblemished. Pantarbe is that which fears the all (*to pan tarbousa*), and refers to the fear of God; for God is the all. And if the procuress mixes a poison cup of flattery, she will be destroyed instead, those who scheme will be fatal to themselves, and Cybele who mixed the poison will die, and

Arsace's cure will be removed (*akos arthesetai*) and pain will send mad (*achos ekmanei*) Achaemenes, evil reasoning. He will perish, but the soul will go under escort to its own fatherland and will be tested on the brazier. For the 'fire shall try every man's work of what sort it is'[3] . . .

Theodorus Prodromus (?), *Versus in Charicleam*.

I also include here a poem which is found in a few manuscripts of the *Ethiopian Story*. It may be the work of the Byzantine novelist Theodorus Prodromus (twelfth cent.). In Byzantium the novel was generally known as *Chariclea*.

> I have been hard struck, o maiden Chariclea,
> in my soul, reason, mind and heart.
> I know that you love from true love
> And I am delighted with and astounded
> At your chaste mind, your good counsels,
> Your endurance against an infinity of evils,
> Your steadfast love for Theagenes.
> How blessed you are for maidens who love,
> And yet more blessed for those who are loved in return.
> Even though your earlier life was certainly unhappy,
> Your final marriage was found happy.
> After experiencing the villainy of robbers
> And in sharing countless ordeals
> Measuring out a long time of wandering,
> Finally you were joined, a fine marriage,
> To your thrice-blessed bridegroom Theagenes.
> I love you, maiden, for your chastity,
> I love you, maiden, for your kindness,
> I love you, maiden, for your wisdom,
> For your endurance, your intelligence,
> And your true love for your bridegroom.

Rabelais, *Gargantua and Pantagruel*, 4.63.

By the early sixteenth century, the *Ethiopian Story* was known in western Europe. Not everyone found it a gripping read, as this short extract from Rabelais testifies.

---

[3] Quoting *Corinthians* 1.3.13. At this point the transmitted text breaks off.

Pantagruel was taking a nap, slumbering and nodding on the quarter-deck, by the cuddy, with an Heliodorus in his hand, for still 'twas his custom to sleep better by book than by heart.

Pantagruel was probably reading the translation by Jacques Amyot (*L'Histoire Aethiopique de Heliodorus* [Paris 1547]), whose preface had enormous influence on the development of the novel in France and Spain, developing theories of verisimilitude from the classical criticism of Aristotle and Horace. Amyot remarks particularly on the excellence of Heliodorus' construction.

Its arrangement is singular: for he begins in the middle of his story, like the heroic poets. Which at first causes great amazement to the readers, and engenders in them a passionate desire to learn the beginning. And always he draws them on so well by the ingenious construction of his tale that one is not resolved of what one reads at the beginning of the first book until one has read the end of the fifth. And when one reaches that point, one finds it harder to see the end than one did before reading the beginning. So that one's understanding remains suspended until one comes to the conclusion, which leaves the reader satisfied just as are those who finally come to enjoy a good ardently desired and long awaited.

Alonso López Pinciano, *Philosophía Antigua Poética* (Madrid 1596); cited from the edition by A. Carballo Picazo (Madrid 1953); translations are taken from A. K. Forcione, *Cervantes, Aristotle and the 'Persiles'* (Princeton 1970) 68ff.

At this this period Heliodorus was ranked alongside Homer and Virgil as a classical master of the art of storytelling. By way of example I include here a few extracts from a work of aesthetic theory published in Spain at the end of the century. Heliodorus is a constant presence in this work, written in dialogue form, adduced to illustrate a range of poetic excellences.

Vol.2.38ff. [This passage discusses Aristotle's comments on recognition scenes and argues that Heliodorus fulfils the Aristotelian formula] I have nothing more to say than to verify and illustrate your axiom with Heliodorus' *Ethiopian Story*, which in my opinion is a fine tale; throughout it the poet sowed the seed for the recognition of Chariclea, first with writings, then with gems, and after that with bodily marks; from all of these proceeded the final recognition and the unravelling of a knot so graceful and pleasing that there is none other to rival it. And although in its form the recognition belongs to the category of the least artistic recognitions, which is that of will, nevertheless, the poet was so skilful, and he designed the recognition so artfully, that it equals those of higher categories, because he did not make Chariclea the revealer of herself but rather Sisimithres, who was the man who raised her.

Vol.2.83ff. [In a discussion of the production of accumulation of tension in the plot, Heliodorus is rated higher than Virgil] Then El Pinciano said, 'Heliodorus' history is epic, but, if one examines it carefully, one discovers that it continuously ties the knot of complication and never unravels it until the end. I say this because there is no contradiction between being epic and tying a single knot tighter and tighter throughout the work.' Fadrique said: 'Gift of the sun is Heliodorus, and in this matter of tying and untying knots, he is unsurpassed, and in the other techniques of composition he is excelled by but a few.'

Vol.3.224. As for the *Ethiopian Story*, I must confess that Heliodorus, its author, was a very serious man and an excellent poet, particularly in the art of tying and unravelling; he pleases with his skilfully contrived tale and even with the solid doctrine which he has sown within it. But, if we are seeking epic perfection, it does not seem to me that the *Ethiopian Story* has the necessary grandeur. I am not referring to its language, which, as it is not in metre, is pardoned, but rather to its very subject and plot, because its ordinary characters have a greater role in the action than its lofty characters.

Pierre-Daniel Huet, *Lettre-traité sur l'origine des romans* (first published as preface to Mme. de Lafayette's *Zaïde* (Paris 1669). Cited from the Édition du tricentenaire (Paris 1971), pp. 77–8.

One of the first serious works of scholarship on the Greek novel was a short treatise by the Jesuit P.-D. Huet, which enlisted them to provide a classical pedigree for the fiction of his own time. Huet admires Heliodoros for his structure, but also for his moral sense and emotional impact.

Heliodorus surpassed him (Iamblichus) in the arrangement of his subject-matter as in everything else. Before then nothing had been seen better intended or better executed in the art of romance than the adventures of Theagenes and Chariclea. Nothing is more chaste than their loves; in which it is plain that apart from the Christian faith which the author professed, his own virtue gave him this air of propriety which strikes one throughout the work, and in this respect not only Iamblichus but almost all the other ancients whose novels survive to us are much inferior to him ... In his work one notices great fertility and invention: events are frequent, original, realistic, well arranged, and well resolved. The conclusion is admirable: it is natural, it is born of the subject and there is nothing more touching or full of pathos: the horror of the sacrifice in which Theagenes and Chariclea, whose beauty and worth arouse the compassion of everyone, were to be put to the knife is succeeded by the joy of seeing this girl escape danger through the recognition of her parents and finally bring her long sufferings to an end by a happy marriage with her lover, to whom she brings as dowry the crown of Ethiopia ... One might have wished that Heliodorus, who knew so well how to conclude the whole intrigue of his novel without the *machina*, would have dispensed with it in the rest of his work, where he employs it several times unnecessarily. Photius praises the elegance of his style; for myself, I find it too affected, too decorated with rhetorical figures and too poetical. He indulges in descriptions, has pleasure with them and cannot leave them; it seems to me that he imitated those of Philostratus. This was the style of the great minds of his period, which lasted from the Antonines, that is to say from the decadence of good taste, to the downfall of the Empire. Such as he is, he served as model to all the writers of novels who followed him, and one can as truly say that they all drew water from his spring as that all poets drew water from that of Homer.

Louis Racine, *Mémoires sur la vie de Jean Racine* (Paris 1747).

Heliodorus was much admired by the French playwright Racine, who incorporated elements from the *Ethiopian Story* into his tragedy *Bajazet*. In the following extract Racine's son recounts a famous anecdote.

My father had a remarkable memory. By chance he found the Greek novel about the love of Theagenes and Chariclea. Just as he was devouring this book, he was caught by the sacristan, Claude Lancelot, who snatched the book from him and threw it in the fire. He succeeded in obtaining another copy, which however shared the same fate. So he had to buy a third copy, and in order not to have to fear the proscription of that one too, he learned the novel by heart, and took it to the sacristan with the following words: 'Please burn this one too, like the others!'

Blackwood's Edinburgh Magazine, vol. 54, July–December 1843, pp. 109–20 ('Early Greek Romances – the Ethiopics of Heliodorus').

By the 19th century, however, the Greek novels had become something of a curiosity. The following anonymous discussion introduces Heliodorus to readers who may never have heard of him. It is interesting that the author criticizes some of the features which to a modern mind make Heliodorus a more effective writer than his fellows. Interest has moved from structure to character.

[The story] is far from deficient either in incident or in strikingly imagined situations; but the merit of the conceptions is too often marred by the mismanagement of the details, and the unskilful arrangement of the different parts of the narrative. Thus all the circumstances of the early history of Chariclea, and the rise of the mutual affection between her and Theagenes, and of their adventurous flight, are made known through a long episode awkwardly put in the mouth of a third person, who himself knows great part of them only at second-hand, and voluntarily related by him to one with whom his acquaintance is scarcely of an hour's standing. This mode of narration, in which one of the characters is introduced (like the prologue in an old play) to recount the previous adventures of the others, is in itself at all times defective; since it injures the effect of the relation by depriving it of those accessory touches which the author, from his conventionally admitted insight into the feelings and motives of his characters is privileged to supply . . . the characters are of very different degrees of merit. Theagenes is as insipid and uninteresting as one of Walter Scott's well-behaved heroes. The deeds of strength and valour which he is occasionally made to perform, seem rather to arise from the author's remembering that his hero must do something to support the character, than to result naturally from the situations in which he is placed ... The character of Chariclea herself, however, makes ample amends for the defects of that of her lover; and this superiority of the heroine, it may be observed, is almost invariable in the early Greek romances. The masculine firmness and presence of mind which she evinces in situations of peril and difficulty, combined at all times with feminine delicacy, and the warmth and confiding simplicity of her love for Theagenes, attach to her a degree of interest which belongs to none of the other personages; and her spontaneous burst of grateful affection, on recognizing, at Meroe, the voice of her foster-father, Charicles, is expressed with exquisite tenderness.

Erwin Rohde, *Der griechische Roman und seine Vorlaüfer* (Leipzig 1876), 455ff.

Nineteenth century scholarship neglected the novels. But in 1876 Erwin Rohde's magisterial survey was published. This was more concerned with the origins of the form than with the literary merits of the individual novels, which Rohde does not rank highly. The following extract is typical.

In general he drew the individual features of his representation from books, not without a certain care. Personal experience of the country and the life of the people seems never to have come to his assistance in Lower Egypt, let alone in the distant lands on the Ethiopian border to which he takes us. His knowledge comes out of books and he is generous with his learning. He constantly provides himself with occasions for excursuses and erudite digressions on matters of natural history, both real and fantastic, and antiquity – Egyptian, Persian or Greek: wherein he commits a number of curious errors through lack of first-hand knowledge. The real schoolmaster steps to the fore in a number of etymological ingenuities plumbing the depths of tastelessness, with which he occasionally adorns his narrative. Naturally Homer, whom Kalasiris' priestly wisdom reveals to us as an Egyptian, is abused to this end. Incidentally the transformation of the greatest Greek poet into a barbarian is particularly alarming because Heliodorus, as a true sophist and particularly dependent on Apollonius of Tyana, is well able to discourse at length on the superiority of true Hellenism over the whole barbarian world.

George Saintsbury, Introduction to Underdowne's translation as published in the Abbey Classics series (London 1924).

In the first half of this century, the novels continued to be regarded as a curious by-way of classical literature. I cannot resist the following paragraph. The remarks about Chariclea are wildly offbeam.

> Theagenes is much the less interesting of the two, and it is a good sign. For it shews that the Greeks were beginning to be cured of that amazing bad taste of theirs – almost their only instance of it – which made them prefer boys, the most disagreeable animals as a class in creation, to girls, who are, with the sadly transitory and extremely incomplete exception of kittens, by far the nicest. But Theagenes is not at all a bad fellow – almost as natural as Daphnis besides being much braver – though in this respect he has had hard measure from some critics. His 'propriety' is not only morally commendable but not in the least contemptible even from a point of view which does not straitlace itself. And it is only fair to him to say that it, assisted by some characteristics of his lady's on which we shall dwell further presently, puts him in some very trying situations . . . It is true that [Chariclea] is rather a *maitresse-femme* or a 'grey mare' as well as a *femme-personne*: and it is also true that if in the commonest sense of morality as applied to women she is faultless, there is another – less important perhaps in them than in men at all times and in ancient times generally held less important than in modern – where she is very far from free from fault . . . One might almost say of the divine Chariclea that there is generally nothing that she prefers to falsehood. It is true that she never has any worse object in view in the long run than preserving her fidelity to Theagenes and temporising with her other lovers: but if breach of promise of marriage had been a Greek institution and had not been limited to one sex, Chariclea might have had heavy damages to pay. But she is a good girl and a brave, and if not exactly a charming, quite a nice one, being also probably much better fitted for the hair-breadth escapes she has to go through than if she had been of another sort.

Johannes Geffcken, *Der Ausgang der griechish-römischen Heidentums*; cited from the translation *The Last Days of Greco-Roman Paganism*, trans. S. MacCormack (Amsterdam 1978).

The following extract is the most forceful interpretation of the *Ethiopian Story* as a neoplatonic text. The case is certainly overstated, however.

> We have here more than Neo-Pythagoreanism: the tale is a work of Neoplatonist propaganda. Of course, this romance also must end with the marriage of the lovers, but sensual desire is only mentioned so as to be negated – just as in Christian legends. The main personage of the romance, Chariclea, is not only chaste, but altogether opposed to wedlock, so that her lover must willy-nilly remain within the bounds of strict abstinence. This is not the only manifestation of asceticism. The wise Calasiris, who, having once in the past given way to a temptation of the senses, now spends his days in contemplation and who hears and sees nothing, resembles the Neoplatonist ascetics of whom we know so much: and even the gymnosophists, who were also warmly referred to by Porphyry, appear several times. Throughout the romance prayer is frequent, and by no means must the evening prayer be omitted. Not only are the gods constantly invoked, but the particulars of their appearance, the manner of their flight, are known, as they would be by any good Neoplatonist; in other words, the protagonists have a knowledge of theurgy. In such a context it is natural that Egypt should be regarded as the fountain-head of all knowledge, and that regret should be expressed when even there some unbefitting oracle was to be heard. Allegory, another part of Neoplatonist teaching, finds its place in the work of our pious author, and with it there is the demonology, which although not fully developed, is not altogether omitted. The author's philosophical involvement is at times so extreme that a Neoplatonist idiom is used to describe the most elementary mental states.

Wilhelm Capelle, 'Zwei Quellen des Heliodor', *Rheinisches Museum* 96 (1953) 166–80; passage quoted from pp. 166–7.

This extract, which has acquired a certain notoriety, is an extreme example of the dismissive attitude towards the novels adopted by classical scholars of the old school. It is astounding that these words found their way into a German journal eight years after the defeat of National Socialism.

> This Heliodorus is at bottom nothing but a rhetorical sophist without any deeper *ethos*. His whole presentation aims only at

effect in the reader, as the frequent extensive descriptions of mass-processions and mass-spectacles makes clear, for which he demonstrates a great expertise. But there is no inner development of the plot arising from the characters of the 'heroes', and absolutely no unified plot at all, just a string of plots, or rather events, stuck together, which are invariably provoked by the intervention of a quasi *deus ex machina*, that is by a *vis major* which intervenes from outside and causes a complete alteration of the current situation (robbers, attacks, war, poisoning, murder, suicide etc.). There is no real characterisation of the protagonists to be found whatsoever, either direct or indirect. In fact even the persons of the two 'heroes' (Chariclea and Theagenes) remain totally colourless; they are not portrayed as individuals. Thus we gain no inner relationship with them. As a true sophist Heliodorus decks himself out in borrowed plumage, especially from Homer and Euripides. His attempts at profound aphorisms immediately betray themselves to an expert as watered down copies from earlier Greek authors.

Although he makes the divinity (Apollo, i.e. Helios) intervene at every instant, he has no inner relationship to Greek religion, to the Greek gods. Nor to the Greek ethic, either the national ethic, or that of Plato or Aristotle, or even merely to the popular Stoa. We miss any real psychology of the characters, at least with one hitherto unnoticed exception: namely that in a series of passages he betrays a wonderful knowledge of the psychology of two true lovers, of their inner spiritual relationship to one another. Whether he owes such knowledge to personal experience or to older models is difficult to say although the former appears not totally excluded.

But what causes even greater offence to someone coming from classical antiquity is that he achieves his effects, or tries to achieve them, by means of the crassest miracle-tales, that a real Greek would never have believed, let alone produced in all seriousness in a work intended for publication, as for instance a gruesome scene of necromancy where, among bloodcurdling incantations, a man who has already been dead for several days is finally compelled, groaning, to speech. But there is also the repeated 'fire-ordeal' of Chariclea, who enters the blazing flames and remains completely unscathed.

But Heliodorus was by no means a true Greek, but a Hellenised Syrian from Semitic Emesa. This explains much, including his nature as a writer.

Reinhold Merkelbach, *Roman und Mysterium in der Antike* (Berlin and Munich 1962) 191f.

In 1962, Reinhold Merkelbach attempted to read the novels as allegorical cult texts of various mystery or initiation religions of the Roman Empire. The *Ethiopian Story* is related to the cult of the Sun, and many details of the narrative are given hidden meaning. It is striking how closely Merkelbach revives the reading of Philip the Philosopher.

It is not difficult to see that the plan of the whole novel is strictly symbolic. Chariclea is descended from the Sun and Ethiopia is her true homeland. Even so the human soul is by nature divine and comes from the Land of the Sun. But the soul has sunk into Matter: Chariclea is exposed and passed from Sisimithres to Charicles, who takes her with him to Delphi. Thus the maiden is removed an infinite distance from her true homeland; she is in the world and her task is to escape from the world and seek her true homeland.

But if even the God cannot prevent the fall of the soul into corporality, his care keeps constant watch over a Man who strives towards the God. Chariclea is always under the protection of pious priests, Sisimithres, Charicles, Calasiris. The stations of her return to Ethiopia are Delphi, Cephallenia, the mouth of the Nile, Chemmis, Memphis, Syene, Ethiopia. Some stages of the journey are freely chosen by Chariclea, but others seem accidental. But each new station leads straight on to the south, in the direction of the desired goal. What seemed blind chance reveals itself as benign providence; if the initiate of his own accord sets off to seek his homeland, the God helps him. All Men are descendants of Helios, like Chariclea, exposed and turned out into this world. Life is a twisting path along which Man makes his way back to his heavenly father.

Naturally the whole action refers, in by now familiar fashion, not just to the initiate's journey through life, but also to the various initiation ceremonies through which he must pass. As the rituals of initiation also symbolise the initiate's path through life and the conquest of death, this equation of the plot with life on the one hand and with cult on the other is not surprising. Arrival in Ethiopia corresponds, among other things, to the death of the initiate; only after death has he survived the wanderings of life and reached the haven of salvation.

Heliodorus' Ethiopia has nothing to do with the real Ethiopia. It is the part of the earth which is closest to the Sun. Instead of in the south, Heliodorus could have set Chariclea's homeland in the east, where the Sun rises, and this is hinted at by the Persian names of the royal pair Hydaspes and Persinna, and the leader of the gymnosophists, Sisimithres. 'Ethiopia' is thus a cipher for 'Sunland'; the whole narrative of Chariclea's return to her true homeland is to be understood symbolically. 'Greece' signifies the earthly, material world, 'Delphi' a Helios temple.

B. P. Reardon, *Courants littéraires grecs des II et III siècles après J.C.* (Paris 1971) pp. 385–6.

Beginning in the 1970s there has been an accelerating trend towards rehabilitating the novels as literature. One of the main influences in this movement has been Bryan Reardon, who reads the *Ethiopian Story* as a religious, but not allegorical text.

In the *Ethiopian Story* we find, on the one hand a dynamism, and on the other an obvious religious intention, which are new. They both proceed from the linear, not circular structure of this novel, from the fact that Ethiopia is presented to the heroes (and thus to the reader also) as the positive end of their Odyssey, and not as the rather neutral – can we say dead – point represented for the other heroes by their native city. If in the event all Chariclea does is return home, since she is by origin Ethiopian, neither she nor the reader accepts it as a simple case of return. She has, so to speak, never been at home, and the whole journey is as new for her when she is grown-up as it is for her fiancé; besides she is white and headed for a land of blacks. At the same time, it is a journey which from the beginning has a strong sense of being a pilgrimage; not only is Chariclea herself a priestess of Apollo at Delphi and apparently daughter of a priest, not only is it a priest who discovers her at Delphi and makes himself her guide, but also the very Ethiopia towards which she makes her way is a land reputed since Herodotus to be full of religious zeal – and with better reason after Philostratus' *Life of Apollonius*, if it is true (as it seems to be) that Heliodorus is later than the latter. Once the heroes have reached Ethiopia, it is no surprise to find that there too, in succession to the others, a priest takes up their case, and figures importantly in the story. In short, the role of religion in the *Ethiopian Story* is much more important than some believe: the heroes' adventures only end when they become priests themselves and members of a theocracy. Their love represents only half of their shared experience; their love brings them together, to be sure, but it brings them together in the service of the god. So let us stress what Heliodorus himself stresses: that this linear journey is a progression to a higher level. Charicles, the first of the three priests who guide the heroine's life (leaving aside her early years in Ethiopia) is treated with a certain irony by the author; he is by no means equal to his task with his adopted daughter, he does not understand her and does not know what to make of her. Calasiris, much more competent than Charicles, is nevertheless somewhat suspect himself, a little too devious to be admired without reservation. It is only with Sisimithres that the reader finds the ideal sage; thus the heroes have travelled towards the ideal, and in a way Ethiopia represents Utopia.

John J. Winkler, 'The Mendacity of Kalasiris and the Narrative Strategy of Heliodoros' *Aithiopika*', *Yale Classical Studies* 27 (1982) 93–158.

In the 1980s the new critical vocabularies of structuralism, narratology and deconstruction were applied to the Greek novel. Particularly influential was an essay by Jack Winkler, who proposed to read the *Ethiopian Story* as a self-referential text, theoretically concerned with the conventions of writing and understanding fiction. Winkler was centrally interested in the figure of Calasiris, whom he saw as a cipher for the novelist himself.

To summarize the argument so far: the three principles of Heliodorus' narrative technique are (1) the precise, often aporetic, measurement of degrees of incomplete cognition, (2) the insistence that every part of the text have a relevance to the whole, sometimes discovered after the fact; and (3) the suspension of attention by postponement of expected information, which occurs four times in Book 1, each time so arranged as to provoke the reader to a greater awareness of one of the conventions of reading fiction, which are (3a) an intelligible language, (3b) a sequential plot, (3c) familiar motifs, and (3d) identification with the heroes. Of these (3b) receives very elaborate illustration in the long interpolated tale of Cnemon, which has a complex relation of contrast and equivalence with Calasiris' narrative and with the *Ethiopian Story* as a whole.

One answer to the question of what kind of meaning is to be found in the *Ethiopian Story* is – sentential. The three principles of narrative technique which we have isolated as significant in this novel are exactly the categories which guide our comprehension of any complex, periodic sentence. Heliodorus' sentences are often mobiles of intricately articulated and well-balanced cola, such as test and refine our powers of attention ... Simply to read such a sentence is already to employ the mind in making assessments of the relevance, subordination and completeness of each phrase as it contributes to the intelligible unity of the whole. If the narrative structure of the *Ethiopian Story* be compared to a long sentence, Book I is like an introductory clause about whose meaning we must suspend judgment until much more of the sentence is uttered. Heliodorus has given his novel a narrative movement of discovered coherence analogous to that of reading any sentence. The *Ethiopian Story* belongs to that class of literature which does not naively assume the conventions of some genre but pricks us to the highest awareness of literature as self-referential, as an act of language whose limits and whose accomplishments are those of language itself. Heliodorus plays with the fundamental features of language so as to make us aware that literature is (among other things) a textual game, and is like a sentence in that within its structure our foreknowledge of admissible possibilities is being continually refined and particularized. This is the deepest sense in which the narrative technique of Heliodorus is one of incomplete cognition ...

... in Calasiris' narrative to Cnemon Heliodorus gives us a view – I would say, partly a paradigm and partly a parody – of the literary event. The text of, say, a romance is not just a dead letter or inscribed memorial but a semantic performance in which both author and reader have active parts to play. They are contestants in a sort of 'game for two players', and Heliodorus here offers us a model, often ironic, of the correlative crafts of constructing and appreciating a novel. It is not sufficient to call Calasiris' narrative a flashback, as if it were no more than the absent first stages of a plot into whose *medias res* we have been plunged. As Heliodorus presents it this is not just a romance but a romance-in-frame. The subject in the foreground is Calasiris' act of 'romancing' in the presence of Cnemon. Since both persons, speaking from their present (narrating) time, constantly interrupt the smooth course of the account taking place in past (narrated) time, the conversational impression of a thing-like plot, whose events are independent of the listening audience and usually of the narrator too, cannot gel. Our attention is continually being diverted from the story to its teller and hearer, whether by substantial interruptions or by the simple vocative 'Cnemon'. Calasiris' narrative is at least as much about the roles of narrator and audience (that is, by an obvious extrapolation, author and reader) as it is about a particular pair of lovers. And the question of Calasiris' mendacity can only be properly addressed if his role as romancer is understood.

Inasmuch as Calasiris' narrative to Cnemon is about the performance of literature, as well as being the narrative of a love story, it is operating on two levels. There is a temptation for the eagerly curious part of our minds to regard only the plot of Chariclea and Theagenes as of importance, the interchanges between Calasiris and Cnemon being treated as humorous or suspenseful punctuation. But this attitude is exactly that of Cnemon, who is eager to be treated to the full spectacle of what we would nowadays call a wide-screen technicolor romance. The ironic presentation of Cnemon should be a major caution against dealing with Calasiris' narrative as if it were simply a flashback to the long-awaited beginning of this great love story. Rather Calasiris' narrative is essentially double, not to say duplicitous, in being both that long-desired story of Chariclea and a series of readings, responses and interpretations of it by Cnemon. One of the effects of his interventions is to shape the narrative so that it becomes Chariclea's story more than Calasiris would have it be.

One extension of Winkler's approach has been to deny that the element of religion in the *Ethiopian Story* has any purchase on the 'real world': it is part of the novel's apparatus of self-referentiality. The following extract (Shadi Bartsch, *Decoding the Ancient Novel* [Princeton 1989] pp. 139ff.) powerfully connects the role of the divine with Heliodorus' penchant for describing his action in theatrical terms.

Thus the readers, like the novel's characters, are faced with an incomprehensible spectacle at the work's beginning and one whose meaning is clear at the work's end, and from beginning to end their own role as spectators is stressed by an author who takes pains to present his novel as a play taking place before their eyes.

But if we the readers feel ourselves the spectators of a play, then for us the playwright and the stage manager can be none other than Heliodorus himself. After all, we cannot fail to be conscious of the fact that he and no god wrote the novel, and that he, again, planned the dramatic entry of key characters at crucial moments and the felicitous outcome that prevails at the 'play's' finale. His very use of theatrical terms, his dramatic handling of the descriptions of spectacles, and his emphasis on the visible all stamp him as the one creating and resolving his self-made play. Yet on the surface of things, Heliodorus disclaims his role. Effacing himself as much as possible, he constantly suggests that the stage-managing of these spectacles should be attributed to a divine will or impulse; this is his refrain from his first description of a spectacle to his last. His final ecphrasis in particular, that of the festival of the Ethiopians – which is complete with the recognition of Chariclea, several *deus ex machina* episodes, and a happy denouement – exhibits in an especially striking fashion 'Heliodorus's conception of his Romance as a series of theatrical spectacles arranged by a superhuman agency.'

Not only this, but Heliodorus attributes the character's ability (or lack of it) to interpret these spectacles, and especially their ease of understanding at the end of the work, also to the intention of the divine will. We the readers share the characters' condition both at the work's opening and at its end. But for us, it is the author's own recessive style that creates the initial difficulties (since, gods or no gods, if he wrote as an omniscient author we would not, like the characters, be unable to interpret the spectacle correctly), and it is of course the author's information, whether given here or garnered through the course of the novel, that lets us understand what is happening at its end. Yet, in the narrative, the agent fulfilling this same role, bringing the characters to 'surmise the truth', is called a 'divine impulse'.

In short, Heliodorus has designed his work such that an analogy is clearly manifest between author and divine *choregos*; the god's relation to the novel's characters is that of the author-playwright to us, each with the same power to create, resolve, and clarify events presented as theatre to fictional spectators or to actual readers, the former a reflection of the latter just as the *choregos* is of the author. And if it is true of these ecphrases of spectacles that they are 'theatrical scenes intended to make perceptible the existence of divine powers or hidden forces', then it is also through these ecphrases that the author makes manifest his own similar puissance in relation to his readers. Heliodorus is perhaps hinting at the godlike nature of the author's role and of his ultimate command of the readers.

SUGGESTIONS FOR FURTHER READING

The standard Greek text of the Ethiopian Story is the one edited by R. M. Rattenbury and T. W. Lumb in the Budé series (Collections des Universités de France, Paris 1935–43, 3 vols.) A new edition for the Loeb Classical Library is in preparation.

Readers who wish to read the other Greek novels will find excellent modern translations of all the extant novels, as well as the most important fragments and related texts in:

B. P. Reardon ed., *Collected Ancient Greek Novels* (California UP, 1989).

Much of the scholarship concerning Heliodorus has taken the form of articles in learned journals, and has appeared in languages other than English. Interested but non-specialist readers, however, will find much to inform them in the following books:

Graham Anderson, *The Second Sophistic. A Cultural Phenomenon in the Roman Empire* (Routledge, 1993). Useful background on the intellectual climate.

Shadi Bartsch, *Decoding the Ancient Novel. The Reader and the Role of Description in Heliodorus and Achilles Tatius* (Princeton UP, 1989). Detailed discussion of Heliodorus' narrative technique.

Tomas Hägg, *The Novel in Antiquity* (Blackwell, 1983). A first-rate introduction to the ancient novels.

Arthur Heiserman, *The Novel before the Novel. Essays and Discussions about the Beginnings of Prose Fiction in the West* (Chicago UP, 1977). Accessible if idiosyncratic discussion of the novels as literature.

Niklas Holzberg, *The Ancient Novel* (Routledge, 1995). Excellent discussion of all the ancient novels; the best place to begin.

David Konstan, *Sexual Symmetry. Love in the Ancient Novels and Related Genres* (Princeton UP, 1994). Studies the depiction of romantic love in the novels, unique in antiquity.

J. R. Morgan and Richard Stoneman, eds., *Greek Fiction. The Greek*

Novel in Context (Routledge, 1994). Essays covering the whole range of Greek fiction.

Ben Edwin Perry, *The Ancient Romances. A Literary-historical Account of their Origins* (California UP, 1967). Attempts to relate the ancient novels to a social context.

B. P. Reardon, *The Form of Greek Romance* (Princeton UP, 1991). Explores the literary and cultural framework of the Greek novels.

Gerald N. Sandy, *Heliodorus* (Twayne's World Authors, 1982). Wide-ranging treatment of Heliodorus, with an interesting chapter on his influence on later writers.

James Tatum, ed., *The Search for the Ancient Novel* (Johns Hopkins UP, 1994). Collection of papers on various novels, including Heliodorus.

TEXT SUMMARY

Book 1

A puzzling scene at the mouth of the Nile witnessed by brigands. A second group of brigands intervenes and carries off Theagenes and Chariclea. Cnemon tells them how he was the victim of his stepmother's infatuation and the machinations of her slave Thisbe. Thyamis, the robber chief, is prompted by a dream to propose marriage to Chariclea; she feigns consent. When the robber stronghold is attacked, Chariclea is hidden in a cave by Cnemon. Thyamis, facing defeat, kills a woman he takes to be Chariclea, and is then captured by his enemies.

Book 2

Theagenes laments Chariclea's presumed death, but Cnemon reassures him. At the cave mouth they find the body of Thisbe. Theagenes and Chariclea are reunited. Cnemon concludes the story of Thisbe. Thermouthis, Thisbe's lover, comes to the cave. He and Cnemon set off in search of Thyamis. Cnemon loses Thermouthis and meets Calasiris, an Egyptian priest, who identifies himself as Thyamis' father and tells how he fled Egypt and visited Delphi where he met Charicles, who told him how he had been given a beautiful girl-child in Egypt, whom he adopted as his daughter. He asks Calasiris' help in breaking down her opposition to marriage. An enigmatic oracle foreshadows the future of Theagenes and Chariclea.

Book 3
[Calasiris narrating]
The procession at Delphi and the first meeting of Theagenes and Chariclea. They fall in love. Calasiris persuades Charicles that Chariclea is the victim of an Evil Eye. Calasiris is instructed by the gods to take the lovers to Egypt. Theagenes confesses his love to Calasiris.

Book 4
[Calasiris narrating]
Theagenes wins the foot-race at Delphi. Calasiris persuades Charicles to let him see the embroidered band that was given him with Chariclea.

He learns that she is the daughter of the king and queen of Ethiopia, exposed at birth because of her white skin. He tells all to Chariclea, adding that he has been commissioned by her mother to bring her home. An abduction is staged and the lovers elope with Calasiris on a Phoenician ship.

Book 5

In the night Cnemon discovers a woman in Nausicles' house whom he takes for Thisbe. It is Chariclea; her separation from Theagenes and acquisition by Nausicles are explained; Theagenes is in the hands of Mitranes and will be sent to the satrap Oroondates. Nausicles holds a sacrifice, at which Calasiris gives him a beautiful gem. Calasiris continues his story. The lovers and he take lodgings with a deaf fisherman, but Chariclea attracts the attentions of a local pirate, Trachinus. Calasiris is visited by a vision of Odysseus. They attempt to escape, but are captured by Trachinus, then wrecked by a storm at the mouth of the Nile. Trachinus proposes to marry Chariclea, but is opposed by Pelorus and a fight breaks out, producing the scene described in Book 1.

Book 6

Calasiris, Cnemon and Nausicles set out to find Theagenes, but learn he has been seized by Thyamis and his bandits. Cnemon marries Nausicles' daughter, and Calasiris and Chariclea continue their search alone, disguised as beggars. At Bessa they come across a battlefield: Thyamis has defeated Mitranes and is marching on Memphis. They witness a scene of witchcraft.

Book 7

At Memphis there is a duel between Thyamis and his brother Petosiris over the high-priesthood. The satrap's wife Arsace desires Theagenes. The duel is interrupted by the arrival of Chariclea and Calasiris; a theatrical recognition scene. Arsace enlists the help of her nurse Cybele to seduce Theagenes. Calasiris dies, and the lovers are taken into the satrap's palace, where Cybele's son Achaemenes falls in love with Chariclea, and recognizes Theagenes as the satrap's property. Cybele fails to break down Theagenes' virtue; he enters service in the palace and thwarts Achaemenes' hopes. Achaemenes steals away to Oroondates.

Book 8

War between the Persians and the Ethiopians. Oroondates sends Bagoas to bring him Theagenes and Chariclea. Theagenes is thrown in a cell and tortured, but Cybele's attempt to remove Chariclea misfires when she drinks the poisoned cup herself. Chariclea is tried for her murder and sentenced to be burned, but emerges unscathed from the flames. The lovers ponder their dreams and future. Bagoas comes to take them away, and on their way to Oroondates they hear that Arsace is dead. They are captured by Ethiopians.

Book 9
Oroondates is besieged in Syene. The lovers are brought before Hydaspes the Ethiopian king, and set aside for his victory celebrations. Hydaspes breaks the city walls, but Oroondates escapes, and reappears with his army. Hydaspes is victorious in battle; Achaemenes is killed and Oroondates captured, but spared by Hydaspes. Chariclea does not reveal her identity to her father.

Book 10
Hydaspes returns to Meroë, where the people demand human sacrifice. The virginity of Theagenes and Chariclea is proven by the brazier. Chariclea convinces Hydaspes that she is his daughter, but cannot bring herself to explain who Theagenes is. Theagenes performs two heroic exploits, wrestling with a bull and an Ethiopian giant, but still faces sacrifice. An embassy from Oroondates arrives, with Charicles, who is looking for his 'daughter'. The truth is revealed; the sacrifice is ended, and the lovers are betrothed and made priest and priestess.

ACKNOWLEDGEMENTS

The editor and publishers wish to thank the following for permission to use copyright material:

Cambridge University Press for material from John J. Winkler, 'The Mendacity of Kalasiris and the Narrative Strategy of Helidoros' *Aithiopika*', *Yale Classical Studies*, 27 (1982) 93–158;

Gerald Duckworth & Co Ltd for material from N. G. Wilson, *Scholars of Byzantium*, (1983);

Princeton University Press for material from Shadi Bartsch, *Decoding the Ancient Novel*, (1989). © 1989 Princeton University Press;

J. D. Sauerlander's Verlag for Material from Wilhelm Capelle, 'Zwel Quellen des Heliodor', *Rheinisches Museum*, 96 (1953) 166–80;

Every effort has been made to trace the copyright holders but if any have been inadvertently overlooked the publishers will be pleased to make the necessary arrangement at the first opportunity.

ANCIENT CLASSICS
IN EVERYMAN

Legends of Alexander the Great
edited by Richard Stoneman
*The fascinating adventures of
a dominant figure in European,
Jewish and Arabic folklore until
the fifteenth century*
£5.99

**Juvenal's Satires with the
Satires of Persius**
JUVENAL AND PERSIUS
*Unique and acute observations
of contemporary Roman society*
£5.99

The Epicurean Philosophers
edited by John Gaskin
*The surviving works and wise say-
ings of Epicurus, with the account
of his natural science in Lucretius'
On the Nature of the Universe*
£5.99

**History of the
Peloponnesian War**
THUCYDIDES
*The war that brought to an
end a golden age of democracy*
£5.99

The Discourses
EPICTETUS
*The teachings of one of the
greatest Stoic philosophers*
£6.99

The Education of Cyrus
XENOPHON
*An absorbing insight into the
culture and politics of Ancient
Greece*
£6.99

The Oresteia
AESCHYLUS
*New translation and edition
which analyses the plays in
performance*
£5.99

Suppliants and Other Dramas
AESCHYLUS
*New translation of Aeschylus'
first three surviving plays and
the earliest dramas of western
civilisation*
£5.99

The Odyssey
HOMER
*A classic translation of one of
the greatest adventures ever told*
£5.99

The Republic
PLATO
*The most important and
enduring of Plato's works*
£5.99

All books are available from your local bookshop or direct from:
Littlehampton Book Services Cash Sales, 14 Eldon Way, Lineside Estate,
Littlehampton, West Sussex BN17 7HE (*prices are subject to change*)

To order any of the books, please enclose a cheque (in sterling) made payable to
Littlehampton Book Services, or phone your order through with credit card details (Access,
Visa or Mastercard) on 01903 721596 (24 hour answering service) stating card number
and expiry date. (*Please add £1.25 for package and postage to the total of your order.*)

In the USA, for further information and a complete catalogue call 1-800-526-2778

MEDIEVAL LITERATURE
IN EVERYMAN

The Canterbury Tales
GEOFFREY CHAUCER
The complete medieval text with translations
£4.99

The Vision of Piers Plowman
WILLIAM LANGLAND
edited by A. V. C. Schmidt
The only complete edition of the B-Text available
£6.99

Sir Gawain and the Green Knight, Pearl, Cleanness, Patience
edited by J. J. Anderson
Four major English medieval poems in one volume
£5.99

Arthurian Romances
CHRÉTIEN DE TROYES
translated by D. D. R. Owen
Classic tales from the father of Arthurian romance
£5.99

Everyman and Medieval Miracle Plays
edited by A. C. Cawley
A fully representative selection from the major play cycles
£4.99

Anglo-Saxon Poetry
edited by S. A. J. Bradley
An anthology of prose translations covering most of the surviving poetry of early medieval literature
£6.99

Six Middle English Romances
edited by Maldwyn Mills
Tales of heroism and piety
£4.99

Ywain and Gawain, Sir Percyvell of Gales, The Anturs of Arther
edited by Maldwyn Mills
Three Middle English romances portraying the adventures of Gawain
£5.99

The Birth of Romance: An Anthology
translated by Judith Weiss
The first-ever English translation of fascinating Anglo-Norman romances
£4.99

The Piers Plowman Tradition
edited by Helen Barr
Four medieval poems of political and religious dissent – available together for the first time
£5.99

All books are available from your local bookshop or direct from:
Littlehampton Book Services Cash Sales, 14 Eldon Way, Lineside Estate,
Littlehampton, West Sussex BN17 7HE *(prices are subject to change)*

To order any of the books, please enclose a cheque (in sterling) made payable to
Littlehampton Book Services, or phone your order through with credit card details (Access,
Visa or Mastercard) on 01903 721596 (24 hour answering service) stating card number
and expiry date. *(Please add £1.25 for package and postage to the total of your order.)*

In the USA, for further information and a complete catalogue call 1-800-526-2778

PHILOSOPHY AND RELIGIOUS WRITING IN EVERYMAN

Modern Philosophy of Mind
edited by William Lyons
*This unique anthology of classic
readings in philosophy of mind
over the last hundred years
includes the writings of William
James and Ludwig Wittgenstein*
£6.99

Selected Writings
WILLIAM JAMES
*Taking writings from James's most
famous works, this edition is a
comprehensive and unique selection*
£6.99

**The Prince and Other
Political Writings**
NICCOLÒ MACHIAVELLI
*A clinical analysis of the dynamics
of power, set in the context of
Machiavelli's early political writings*
£4.99

Ethics
SPINOZA
*Spinoza's famous discourse on
the power of understanding*
£5.99

The World as Will and Idea
ARTHUR SCHOPENHAUER
*New translation of abridged text,
Schopenhauer's major work and
key text of modern philosophy*
£7.99

**Utilitarianism, On Liberty,
Considerations on
Representative Government**
J. S. MILL
*Three radical works which
transformed political science*
£5.99

**A Discourse on Method,
Meditations, and Principles**
RENÉ DESCARTES
*Takes the theory of mind over
matter into a new dimension*
£5.99

**An Essay Concerning Human
Understanding**
JOHN LOCKE
*A central work in the development
of modern philosophy*
£5.99

Philosophical Writings
FRANCIS HUTCHESON
*Comprehensive selection of
Hutcheson's most influential writings*
£6.99

Women Philosophers
edited by Mary Warnock
*The great subjects of philosophy
handled by women spanning four
centuries, including Simone de
Beauvoir and Iris Murdoch*
£6.99

All books are available from your local bookshop or direct from:
Littlehampton Book Services Cash Sales, 14 Eldon Way, Lineside Estate,
Littlehampton, West Sussex BN17 7HE (*prices are subject to change*)

To order any of the books, please enclose a cheque (in sterling) made payable to
Littlehampton Book Services, or phone your order through with credit card details (Access,
Visa or Mastercard) on 01903 721596 (24 hour answering service) stating card number
and expiry date. (*Please add £1.25 for package and postage to the total of your order.*)

In the USA, for further information and a complete catalogue call 1-800-526-2778

FOREIGN LITERATURE IN TRANSLATION IN EVERYMAN

A Hero of Our Time
MIKHAIL LERMONTOV
*The Byronic adventures of
a Russian army officer*
£5.99

L'Assommoir
ÉMILE ZOLA
*One of the most successful novels
of the nineteenth century and one
of the most scandalous*
£6.99

Poor Folk and The Gambler
FYODOR DOSTOYEVSKY
*These two short works of doomed
passion are among Dostoyevsky's
quintessential best. Combination
unique to Everyman*
£4.99

Yevgeny Onegin
ALEXANDER PUSHKIN
*Pushkin's novel in verse is Russia's
best-loved literary work. It contains some of the loveliest Russian
poetry ever written*
£5.99

The Three-Cornered Hat
ANTONIO PEDRO DE ALARCÓN
*A rollicking farce and one of
the world's greatest masterpieces
of humour. Available only in
Everyman*
£4.99

Notes from Underground and A Confession
FYODOR DOSTOYEVSKY *and*
LEV TOLSTOY
*Russia's greatest novelists ruthlessly
tackle the subject of their mid-life
crises. Combination unique to
Everyman*
£4.99

Selected Stories
ANTON CHEKHOV
edited and revised by Donald
Rayfield
*Masterpieces of compression and
precision. Selection unique to
Everyman*
£7.99

Selected Writings
VOLTAIRE
*A comprehensive edition of
Voltaire's best writings. Selection
unique to Everyman*
£6.99

Fontamara
IGNAZIO SILONE
*'A beautifully composed tragedy.
Fontamara is as fresh now, and as
moving, as it must have been when
first published.'* London Standard.
Available only in Everyman
£4.99

All books are available from your local bookshop or direct from:
Littlehampton Book Services Cash Sales, 14 Eldon Way, Lineside Estate,
Littlehampton, West Sussex BN17 7HE *(prices are subject to change)*

To order any of the books, please enclose a cheque (in sterling) made payable to
Littlehampton Book Services, or phone your order through with credit card details (Access,
Visa or Mastercard) on 01903 721596 (24 hour answering service) stating card number
and expiry date. *(Please add £1.25 for package and postage to the total of your order.)*

In the USA, for further information and a complete catalogue call 1-800-526-2778

WOMEN'S WRITING
IN EVERYMAN

Poems and Prose
CHRISTINA ROSSETTI
A collection of her writings, poetry and prose, published to mark the centenary of her death
£5.99

Women Philosophers
edited by Mary Warnock
The great subjects of philosophy handled by women spanning four centuries, including Simone de Beauvoir and Iris Murdoch
£6.99

Glenarvon
LADY CAROLINE LAMB
A novel which throws light on the greatest scandal of the early nineteenth century – the infatuation of Caroline Lamb with Lord Byron
£6.99

Women Romantic Poets
1780–1830: An Anthology
edited by Jennifer Breen
Hidden talent from the Romantic era rediscovered
£5.99

Memoirs of the Life of Colonel Hutchinson
LUCY HUTCHINSON
One of the earliest pieces of women's biographical writing, of great historic and feminist interest
£6.99

The Secret Self 1: Short Stories by Women
edited by Hermione Lee
'A superb collection' The Guardian
£4.99

The Age of Innocence
EDITH WHARTON
A tale of the conflict between love and tradition by one of America's finest women novelists
£4.99

Frankenstein
MARY SHELLEY
A masterpiece of Gothic terror in its original 1818 version
£3.99

The Life of Charlotte Brontë
ELIZABETH GASKELL
A moving and perceptive tribute by one writer to another
£4.99

Victorian Women Poets
1830–1900
edited by Jennifer Breen
A superb anthology of the era's finest female poets
£5.99

Female Playwrights of the Restoration: Five Comedies
edited by Paddy Lyons
Rediscovered literary treasure in a unique selection
£5.99

All books are available from your local bookshop or direct from:
Littlehampton Book Services Cash Sales, 14 Eldon Way, Lineside Estate,
Littlehampton, West Sussex BN17 7HE *(prices are subject to change)*

To order any of the books, please enclose a cheque (in sterling) made payable to
Littlehampton Book Services, or phone your order through with credit card details (Access,
Visa or Mastercard) on 01903 721596 (24 hour answering service) stating card number
and expiry date. *(Please add £1.25 for package and postage to the total of your order.)*

In the USA, for further information and a complete catalogue call 1-800-526-2778

ESSAYS, CRITICISM AND HISTORY
IN EVERYMAN

Essays and Poems
R. L. STEVENSON
Stevenson's hidden treasures
£4.99

The Rights of Man
THOMAS PAINE
*One of the great masterpieces
of English radicalism*
£4.99

Speeches and Letters
ABRAHAM LINCOLN
*A key document of the American
Civil War*
£5.99

Essays
FRANCIS BACON
*An excellent introduction to
Bacon's incisive wit and moral
outlook*
£4.99

Biographia Literaria
SAMUEL TAYLOR COLERIDGE
*A masterpiece of criticism,
marrying the study of literature
with philosophy*
£4.99

Selected Writings
JOHN RUSKIN
'An excellent selection'
The Guardian
£7.99

**Chesterton on Dickens:
Criticisms and Appreciations**
G. K. CHESTERTON
*A landmark in Dickens criticism,
rarely surpassed*
£4.99

History of His Own Time
BISHOP GILBERT BURNET
*A highly readable contemporary
account of the Glorious Revolution
of 1688*
£7.99

**Memoirs of the Life of Colonel
Hutchinson**
LUCY HUTCHINSON
*Biography by his wife of a man who
signed Charles I's death warrant*
£6.99

**Puritanism and Liberty: Being
the Army Debates (1647-49)
from the Clarke Manuscripts**
edited by A. S. P. Woodhouse
*A fascinating revelation of Puritan
minds in action*
£7.99

**The Embassy to Constantinople
and Other Writings**
LIUDPRAND OF CREMONA
*An insider's view of political
machinations in medieval Europe*
£5.99

All books are available from your local bookshop or direct from:
Littlehampton Book Services Cash Sales, 14 Eldon Way, Lineside Estate,
Littlehampton, West Sussex BN17 7HE *(prices are subject to change)*

To order any of the books, please enclose a cheque (in sterling) made payable to
Littlehampton Book Services, or phone your order through with credit card details (Access,
Visa or Mastercard) on 01903 721596 (24 hour answering service) stating card number
and expiry date. *(Please add £1.25 for package and postage to the total of your order.)*

In the USA, for further information and a complete catalogue call 1-800-526-2778